Martin

HOSPITALITY

Peggy,
Enjoy the story!

♡ Aba

Martin
HOSPITALITY

Martin Generations, Book One

ABIGAYLE CLAIRE

Abigayle Claire

MARTIN HOSPITALITY

Printed in the United States of America

ISBN-13: 978-1539783879

ISBN-10: 1539783871

Cover design by Mandy Cave

Interior formatting credit to Perry Elisabeth Design | perryelisabethdesign.com

All scriptural quotations and paraphrases taken from the NKJV

Dedicated to the memory of my own Martins:
Walter Farris and Margaret Eloise,
whose house was known for hospitality.

TABLE OF CONTENTS

Martin Index

When I realized that a character index would be beneficial for my readers, due to the size of the Martin family, I soon found it difficult to include all characters without giving anything away. So, I decided to narrow the index down to just those characters whose ages and birth order presented the most difficulty: the Martin family.

Stuart - father to the Martin clan and a well-to-do businessman

Joy - mother to the Martin family and a midwife

David - 27, married to Beth, works in real estate

Belinda - 25

January - 23, engaged to Patrick

Josiah - 19, the oldest Martin at home

Anneliese - 17

Ginger - 16, seeing Elias Jefferson

Emmaline - 13

Mariah - 9

Lisabeth - 5

Gail – 3

Chapter 1

The tip of a young woman's shoe caught on a protruding nail. Gemma's hands slapped the concrete, her shins coming down on the lip of the bottom step. The child inside her stomach lurched and she straightened slowly, supporting her protruding stomach. She cursed the flight of rickety stairs before shuffling into the room on her left that adjoined the lobby. Relieved to find the lone dilapidated chair supported her, she glanced around the greasy room. Its peeling, floral wallpaper and flickering lightbulb did not provide a welcoming ambiance.

I don't care what he says. No one deserves a place like this.

A sigh broke free as she ventured a look at her watch. She had thrown herself down a flight of stairs in order to meet him in this useless room off the lobby and he couldn't even be on time.

Huffing met her ears, followed by an outcry of surprise, as someone else took a tumble. No doubt the same nail was the culprit.

Gemma fought back a smile; already her landlord had proved her point.

A moment's pause followed and then the small man entered the room, chasing his glasses back up his nose in an agitated manner.

"Ah, Miss Ebworthy."

Gemma offered a patient smile.

Mr. Winkle struggled with various facial contortions as he appeared to digest his embarrassment. "I have reviewed your file." He held it up. "You are a s-sloppy and insensitive tenant. I ask that you leave."

The young woman blinked. It wasn't his decision as much as his horrible people skills that shocked her. An all-too-familiar weight settled in the pit of her stomach.

"You work s-strange hours, are frequently s-sick, thus disturbing other residents, and are irregular on your payments."

Could he not see she was pregnant? And it was the likes of irregular payments that had forced her to work such strange hours . . . before she'd gotten fired for falling asleep at the express lane register. She bit her tongue to keep her thoughts to herself, something she had become very good at while around her landlord.

"How long do I have, sir?" Her voice sounded helpless, even to her, and she hated herself for it.

"Don't you s-start none of that s-sir business with me!" He shook a finger and backed away as if she had transformed into a rabid animal about to lunge. Politeness always struck him as a conspiracy.

"How long?" she repeated, growing testy.

"Um . . ." He glanced over his piece of paper with fluttering hands. "An hour."

Her heart sank further. There was no possible way she could find new lodgings with notice that short. Oh well, so be it. She stood to go, a great weariness settling upon her. Her hand went to her midriff out of instinct. What on earth would she do now?

"I'm very sorry," Winkle mumbled. His pity must have overcome him. Even his nervous stutter had the grace to disappear for a moment.

Gemma swallowed the replies that came to mind and nodded. "Goodbye."

She shut the door with haste so he could not delay her further.

Gemma trudged back up the stairs and hastily gathered her few belongings. Within minutes, she lugged a moth-eaten backpack out of the building for the last time. She took one last glance at its grim exterior before marching down the sidewalk. The shoddy apartment, under perpetual construction, held little sentimental value, but several hours ago she knew where she'd be sleeping tonight.

Now she only had a backpack that tugged at her shoulders and a child that weighed on her mind.

Coming to the first intersection on the country road, she looked about her. *What are you gonna do now, Miss Ebworthy?* A squat building with a blue sign caught her attention: a postal office. She begged a piece of paper and jotted a quick note that she addressed to Austin, Texas.

Gemma tuned out her surroundings in the heat and her own self-pity. How long did she walk? The first time she looked up, she no longer stood on the excuse for a sidewalk in the dingy part of town, but had reached a bus stop in the middle of nowhere. She smiled at her luck—her swollen ankles had begun throbbing. Perched on the small green bench, she retrieved her jar of savings from the backpack and counted it out: eighty-seven dollars and three cents. Not a penny could afford to be wasted.

How much did a bus ticket even cost? Where did she even want to go? Wichita was nearby, but the cost of living would be out of her present means.

The intense summer heat caused her to fidget and readjust her camisole as she tried to make a decision. Why couldn't this bus stop be covered?

Gemma tucked the jar back into her bag and plunged into the tall cornfield behind her. It would be another half hour before a bus would arrive. The least she could do was find some shade and rest a while. Another wave of exhaustion had turned her feet to lead and her legs to mush.

After keeping a straight path for several minutes, her eyelids had grown heavy and her head throbbed. If only she had thought to bring water; her tongue stuck to the roof of her mouth.

Bravely she tromped for what seemed like the normal length of a cornfield in one direction and then another. She began to doubt her decision—most of the stalks towered over her, obscuring her sense of direction. Her hope of finding a tree to provide *real* shade dwindled.

Finally, she sat right where she was and tucked herself against the row of tall, green stalks. They provided some fingers of shade, at least. Gemma rested her head on the palms of her hands and sighed. She couldn't sleep now, she couldn't . . .

When Gemma's mind fluttered back to consciousness and her eyes opened, the differences in her surroundings startled her. The sun had almost set and crickets had begun to chirp. She had undoubtedly missed the bus. Shrugging her backpack onto her shoulders, she pushed herself to her feet. Fear gripped her heart; she had no inkling which direction she had come from. Her heart raced and her stomach twisted. She had watched too many horror movies to want to stay out in the dark alone. *Nothing carnivorous will be in a field of vegetables. Just pick a path and stick to it.* There was a good chance she could find the road again since the cornfield bordered an intersection.

She gripped her backpack and steeled her nerves. The corn rustled, growing in noise as she increased her speed. Holding her breath helped keep her imagination from going places she forbade.

Minutes passed and she grew more and more afraid. Pitch black consumed everything. She couldn't hear cars; she couldn't see lights. No hope was in sight. She swatted mosquitoes with mounting frustration and wiped the humidity from her brow. *Someone help me!*

As the first tears began to slide down her cheeks, suddenly stalks no longer clawed her arms and face. Gemma stumbled to a stop in the openness that exposed her. The cornfield began again a few feet in front of her, but a sliver of open dirt stretched to her right and left.

"A road!" She exhaled a shaky laugh as she passed a hand over her stomach. At long last, a shred of hope. She slipped her backpack off her shoulders and rested it at her feet, her shoulders thanking her.

An owl hooted, making her start. She hefted her backpack up by its straps, not bothering to swing it onto her back, and followed the road to her left at a brisk pace. She clutched her bulky backpack closer. Her stomach was beginning to cramp. The uneven road made her feet cry louder and she felt lightheaded from exhaustion and hunger.

"Please, please, please." She heard the owl again, this time beside her. "Please be almost there. Please!" Something soft brushed her arm and she stumbled to the side, heart threatening to break free of her chest. *It's just a bird. Keep going!* Her stomach turned to lead at the thought. *Going where?*

However, the owl seemed determined to deter her, for it dived again, its talons sticking in her tangled hair.

She screamed and dropped her backpack to swat at it. Large wings fluttered and raucous cries sounded before it liberated itself and swooped back to its hollow.

Gemma shook and fought to regain even breathing as she watched its large eyes blink in the distance. It had only been trying to frighten her away from its home in the gnarled tree. If she kept going, it would leave her alone.

Terrified and disoriented, she turned back to her path in the heavy moonlight. A childish laugh of glee escaped her as she spied a structure mere yards away. Lifting her backpack off the ground once more, she forced her feet forward a few more paces. She tugged on the wooden door, relieved she possessed the ability to heave it open. Several horses pricked their ears and peered back at her with sleep in their eyes.

5

Gemma cringed as she splashed handfuls of water into her mouth from the nearby trough. It was lukewarm but wet, and her body thanked her. She pushed past the stalls that lined the walls until she came to one piled with straw. She breathed out a sigh and collapsed into the loose pile of prickly hay, her backpack sufficing as a pillow. Sleep could not claim her fast enough.

A young man buried his head in his feather pillow with a groan. Any minute his mother would remind him he had chores before breakfast with a tone that conveyed he shouldn't need reminding. He could already hear pots clanging in the kitchen and smell bacon frying.

He absorbed several more seconds of sacred comfort before forcing his eyelids back open.

Josiah dragged himself out from under the covers and peered out the window. The sun had just begun to tint the morning air pink. He dressed with haste and stumbled down the stairs, trying to shake his grogginess. Tugging on his boots, he stepped out into the dim light. The morning almost felt cool, but still the air hung thick with moisture. He felt he could almost swat it away like he did mosquitoes.

Josiah jaunted to the barn just a short way off to the left and wondered why the door sat slightly ajar. He shrugged it off, stepping inside and inhaling the dank smell of hay, oats, and horses. His scoop plunged into the bag that held their breakfast and he stroked each velvety nose in turn before offering them the oats. They were too hungry to crave attention this time of day.

He passed the stall that held loose hay; oats pattered onto the floor in his surprise. How on earth had *she* gotten there? He quickly surveyed the barn for any signs of vandalism or theft—nothing. Josiah stooped to look at the strange girl and consider what to do.

The girl's long blonde hair was strewn in front of her face, much as his fair-haired sisters appeared when they slept. But what caught his attention was how thin and frail she looked in contrast to her defined stomach. A large cut on her face made his brow crease. She doubtless needed assistance and could use a good breakfast. His brain reasoned through the best way to wake her up without frightening her.

His nine-year-old sister popped her head into the barn. "Josiah, Momma says to—"

Perfect! He held up a finger and motioned for her to be silent.

Josiah knew how hard it was for his little sister to leave a sentence dangling, but he smiled as her curiosity overcame her. Her eyes grew wide as she tiptoed to her brother's side and saw the pale face amidst the hay.

"Mariah, go get Momma," Josiah whispered, shooing her out.

She scampered to obey with a large grin, always delighted to be the bearer of unusual news.

He studied the sleeping stranger again, trying to discern her circumstance. Due to the size of her bag, she didn't own much, but was going somewhere. How in the world had she ended up here, miles from anything?

Mariah's shouts could be heard across the farm and still the girl didn't stir. Only a few moments passed before his mother, the very picture of maternal kindness and just what the girl would need, hurried into the barn.

"Josiah, what in the world?" Mrs. Martin sank to her knees to peer at the girl's face. "The poor dear," she whispered. "And expecting a baby, too. I wonder what kind of trouble she's in?"

"Mom, you won't have her stay, will you?" He could see where this was headed. It was even more vital they not make a hasty decision without Dad back.

"Don't be ridiculous," she muttered. She passed a gentle and experienced hand over the stowaway's knotted hair.

The girl's eyelids fluttered and then her hollow eyes stared bewildered into the faces around her. She scuttled back into the pile of hay and clutched her backpack close. "W-where am I? Please don't call the police!" she said when she had found her voice.

"We won't, dear. You've managed to find your way to our farm."

Her brown eyes whipped to Mrs. Martin's face, distrustful.

"Look, we're not going to hurt you. You just surprised us, that's all." Josiah did his best to sound reassuring and held out his hand.

"I'm sorry I intruded. I'll be going now." She took the offered hand and started for the door.

"Are you sure there's nothing we can do for you?" Mrs. Martin asked.

Josiah watched her stop brushing herself off and study his mother's sympathetic eyes. "Like what?"

"A hot meal and shower, maybe? Just tell us your name and we'll help you."

Resolve replaced the indecision on the wan face. "I can't. Please just don't . . . do anything. I need to go."

Mrs. Martin opened her mouth to protest as the girl scurried outside, but Josiah placed his hand on her arm. "Mom, you can't force charity on someone. This is probably for the best, don't you think?"

"No, I do *not* think." She displaced his hand and followed the waif out of the barn. "Please come in—just for a few minutes. We've got pancakes on. Aren't you hungry?" The soft, brown eyes pleaded with her.

Josiah tried not to smile at his mother's well-played manipulation as the last of the girl's resolve melted away.

"All right. Just for a few minutes."

Josiah strengthened his convictions on the matter. *Wonderful. Let's see how long this one stays.* He considered the girl as she followed them into the house, glancing around her. How could such an innocent and youthful face have gotten into so much trouble? Now that she was awake, her worries made her look older, but her situation made him guess that she was younger than him—right out of high school.

"Do you have a name?" he asked.

Her doe-like eyes met his without wavering. "Gemma."

"Well, Gemma, just for today, everything's going to be all right."

One glance at her and he knew they led vastly different lives. And yet, as he looked into her face, he found a glimmer of trust. He grinned as a small smile alighted her lips. *Maybe this one won't be so bad after all.*

Chapter 2

Upon being led indoors, Gemma stopped short. *Is that bacon?* Several small children played in the spacious room before her and at least one older girl worked in the kitchen past them, where the mouth-watering smell emanated.

These kids can't all be hers! She felt self-conscious and exposed under all their open stares.

Josiah's spirited smile met her bewildered face. He seemed accustomed to handling her response.

Mrs. Martin, however, took no notice. She was already busy giving orders to accommodate their guest.

"Mariah, run a bath." The little girl pulled her eyes away from the newcomer's face and ran to do as she was told. "Ginger, an extra plate at the table, please. We have company. Anneliese, go find her some clothes."

A blonde, willowy girl with a disgruntled expression untied her apron. She hurried through the living room and stopped in front of Gemma, offering no introduction.

"This is my sister, Anneliese. Just follow her upstairs and the girls will take care of you. I'll hold on to this for you." Josiah laid a gentle hand on her backpack. Gemma hesitated, but relinquished it. Nothing in there could betray her.

Gemma tried to match his smile, but still felt very out of place. She was also rather disappointed to be led away from the inviting smell of breakfast.

At the top of the stairs, a spacious playroom looked down to the room below. Another little girl sat playing with a toddler determined to push cars through the space in the banister. Gemma had counted six children so far. Six!

Across from the head of the stairs stood a hallway that Gemma followed to the left. Anneliese entered the first bedroom and soon returned with a pile of folded clothes. She glanced at Gemma's tattered shorts that hit mid-thigh, a mix of envy and dismay dancing on her face.

"I hope you don't mind wearing a skirt." She held up a long denim piece with simple pleats. "Might be a little tight in the midsection, but it's all I've got."

"I'm sure it will be fine for now. Thank you." Gemma dragged her weary feet down the hall and into the bathroom. A small girl no more than ten tested the temperature of the running water. Satisfied, she raised a lever on top of the faucet and the water transferred to the showerhead.

"Hi, I'm Mariah." She looked exactly like her mother, except for her transparent cornflower eyes. "If you need anything else, just holler. Breakfast'll be ready in about ten minutes, but take your time."

Gemma nodded, not daring to ask how someone would hear her in a remote bathroom on the second floor. Mariah shut the door, making the reality of what had just happened sink in a little.

Prepared for the worst, Gemma glanced at her reflection in the mirror. Her golden hair was a knotted, windblown mess with strands of hay sticking out at all angles. Her large eyes appeared hollow instead of young, as she remembered them. While her stomach had grown, the rest of her had only become thinner, and a fine layer of dust had glued itself to her skin. She resolved to make this shower as effective as possible. Heaven only knew when she might get another chance.

For the first while she just stood there, watching the dirt run off in winding rivulets, reveling in the soothing nature of the water. But eventually, Gemma grabbed the sole bath scrunchie and scoured her skin until it turned splotchy from the friction.

With great reluctance, she turned off the water. However, she wanted to make a better impression this time and that meant not being too late for breakfast.

She hastily donned the clean clothes Anneliese had provided her. She had to wear the second shirt unbuttoned, but it wasn't too problematic for a single day. The end result could have been more pleasing, but a little frumpiness never killed anyone.

After towel-drying her long, liberally conditioned hair until it resumed its former curl, she hurried down the stairs, grateful that the large house seemed easy to navigate.

She followed the smell of food through the two-story living room, frustrated that she couldn't move with as much speed as she'd like. Her stomach felt so hollow, but looked so huge, she wondered how long it would take to fill.

As she caught another glance of the multitude, she wondered for a fleeting moment if this woman was in a similar position as her—all these children to care for all by herself. Did she even have a husband?

Don't be ridiculous! Maybe her husband died, or maybe he actually works.

Mrs. Martin looked over her shoulder as Gemma approached. "You look pretty, all freshened up, dear! Everyone else is eating through there." She pointed to her left with a wooden spoon. "I'll be right in with your plate."

Gemma smiled her thanks and slid under the arch of the ceiling into the nearest chair. The table was the longest she had ever seen, but almost all the chairs were full. She counted heads again in the awkward absence of conversation. *Seven!*

"Here you are." Mrs. Martin placed a steaming plate piled with all the promised delicacies and more. Gemma's mouth began to water on the spot.

Several of the others were already eating, so she stabbed a fluffy egg and did the same.

"Lisabeth, what have I told you about eating before prayer?" her mother said. Her voice held reproach, but her eyes did not.

"Yes, ma'am," the smallest little girl mumbled around a mouthful.

Gemma lowered her fork with discretion and swallowed her eggs whole. She caught Josiah trying to stifle a smile and felt blood rush to her face.

Everyone bowed their heads and clasped their hands, so Gemma followed suit. It had been a long time since she had seen someone pray.

Mrs. Martin's kind, clear voice began. "Thank you, Lord, for this beautiful day and for the food You have given us. Please help it nourish our bodies and help us to glorify You in all we do. We thank You for Gemma and ask that You watch over her and keep her safe. Amen."

Gemma ignored the blush on her cheeks from the mention of her name and quietly resumed her eating.

After several seconds, Lisabeth asked in her childish voice, "Are you going to have a baby?"

Gemma looked at the blonde head of curls and earnest blue eyes. "Yes, I am."

"When are you due?" Anneliese asked, setting an example of politeness.

"Um . . . actually, I'm not . . . I'm not sure yet. A month or two, maybe?"

"You should have your baby next Tuesday. That's my birthday," Lisabeth rejoined with an official nod.

"Really?"

"Where's your husband?" Mariah asked. She appeared to be at that difficult age—just old enough to be curious about everything, but not old enough to always understand. She received a sharp jab in the ribs by an older sister. "Ow!"

"Um . . ." Gemma's brain faltered.

Mrs. Martin sent her an apologetic look.

"Don't you know?" Lisabeth asked. Her blue eyes were large with concern.

Of course she knew. She just wasn't sure how to explain it to five- and nine-year-olds. "The baby's daddy is at college," she said.

"But why—"

"That's enough," Mrs. Martin interrupted. "Gemma's here to get some breakfast and hospitality, not to be questioned to death."

Breathing more easily, Gemma swigged her milk that tasted surprisingly different from the inexpensive drugstore variety.

Gemma welcomed the redirection of chore assignments and quickly polished off her food before anyone could ask her another direct question.

"What should I do with my plate?"

"Scrape it in the chicken bucket and set it in the sink," Lisabeth said, making it sound like a recitation of a statute.

Gemma followed the little girl's example and then took Mrs. Martin aside. Nothing had been said about any arrangements for her.

"Excuse me, but . . ." She didn't want to say 'What about me?' That sounded selfish. "Thank you for the meal. What should I do before I go?" she said.

"Oh, of course, dear." Mrs. Martin pushed a graying curl out of her face. "Why don't you help Anneliese with the laundry and then you can just take it easy. The girls will be more than happy to wait on you. I have some errands to run, but I'll be back this afternoon. Have a good day!"

She hurried away before Gemma had a chance to respond.

Gemma stood there, stunned. *What?! I can't stay!* She expected to be given a bus ticket, not a list of chores and permission to rest. She didn't even know these people!

"The laundry room is down the hallway by the stairs." Anneliese pointed across the living room. "Start with the towels?"

Gemma nodded rather like a robot. "But shouldn't I be going?"

"Going? Oh. Well, all of our other guests stayed for a few days, but if you don't . . ."

A few days! A hot meal and shower. That had been it! What in the world was wrong with this family?

". . . ask Mom when she gets home. All right?"

"Uh . . . yeah. Thanks."

Gemma followed her instructions without thought and stood in the laundry room before her mind had cleared. *Whatever. You can figure it out later.* Her eyes swept the room and found only a pile of empty laundry baskets. She opened one of the cabinets and met with a deluge of wadded clothing. While she scrambled to keep it all from hitting the floor, the chute continued to empty.

A scuffing sound turned her attention to the doorway. Gemma peered over the pile in her arms. She did not want to know how long Josiah had been standing there.

"Need some help?"

"I was just . . . Yes, please."

Josiah relieved her of her burden and piled it into a basket. "There's a cabinet for each room. Towels first, right?"

She nodded.

He grabbed an empty basket and held it under the fourth cabinet. Towels cascaded out as he pulled open the cabinet door. "Usually works better when you use one of these." He tapped the plastic frame of the laundry basket.

"Yeah." She smiled back.

He set the basket next to the washing machine. "I'll leave you to it. Oh, and Gemma? Don't let Anneliese ruffle your feathers." He offered another grin that made the corners of his olive eyes crinkle before he vanished through the doorway.

Why would he say something like that? Perhaps Anneliese could be bossy—she did appear to be the oldest girl.

Gemma glanced at all the empty baskets that littered the floor. This was going to be a long day.

After Gemma finished with the laundry, she helped the vivacious Ginger, just younger than her, with lunch. Then Emmaline, a young teenager, gave her a tour of the house. Mariah wanted her to come and see the horses. Lisabeth wanted her to read books and pet her kitty, but Gail, the only other boy besides Josiah, wanted her full attention for coloring. At least she had conquered the accomplishment of learning all their names.

"Where's Mommy?" Gail asked in his high-pitched voice as the afternoon wore on, scrunching up his shoulders.

"Yeah, where is she? She should have been home by now. It's coming on five o'clock." Josiah glanced at his watch.

"Should you text her and make sure everything's all right?" Gemma suggested, laying aside her coloring book. She really just wanted to take a nap. Lisabeth hadn't found it very funny when she dozed off mid-book.

"I can try calling, but we get terrible reception 'round here." Josiah flipped open his phone and held it to his ear. "Straight to voicemail. It's probably nothing."

Once dinner came and went and Mrs. Martin had still not appeared, it became evident it was not "nothing." All the little children had been shooed to bed, yet she had not been heard from.

The older girls folded laundry in strained silence and Josiah feigned reading.

"Ginger! Leave the towels for me if you can't remember how to fold them!" Anneliese burst, yanking one away from her sister.

Josiah clamped his jaw and widened his eyes behind the cover of his book. Gemma enjoyed watching his animated face.

"Do you think you should take the horse and see if you meet her?" Ginger said. "Maybe the car's stranded or something."

Josiah had already decided it was worth a shot when headlights pierced the dusk.

"Finally," Anneliese breathed, rolling her eyes heavenward.

"What in the world?" Ginger said as Mrs. Martin burst through the front door, her arms weighed down with bags.

"I'm so sorry! There was an awful wreck on the way home. It took hours for them to clear it up, but I was able to talk to the lady who caused it. She felt awful, so I shared the Gospel with her. Isn't that amazing? I hope you weren't too worried."

Josiah shook his head in disbelief as his mother passed her bags to him.

She addressed Gemma. "Hello, dear, how was your day? Everything go all right?"

Gemma nodded. It wasn't a complete lie. She had no choice but to stay the night now and that did not excite her. But everything would be resolved in the morning . . . surely. If for some reason this turned out to be some elaborate hoax and police showed up, at least she would be provided for in prison. But something in the woman's kind face told her she was incapable of such deception.

"Good. I wanted to ask you, do you have a doctor you've been seeing? I'm a midwife, you see, and just wondered what you would be willing to share with me." She crossed to the kitchen and began to unload groceries.

"Oh." *What the heck is a midwife?* "Um, no, I don't have a doctor. I only went once at the beginning to confirm I was pregnant. Things have been . . . complicated since then."

"My goodness! Well, if you don't mind, I'll check into that tomorrow. I have a doctor I trust very much that I'm sure will be willing to take a look and make sure everything's all set to go." She stared at a tomato for a moment, as if unsure what to do with it.

Vacant eyes met Gemma's and lit up once her memory returned. "Would you like that?"

"Sure. I'd like to know when I'm due. I mean, I got pregnant before spring break, but other than that . . ."

"So you don't know the gender yet?" Ginger asked, her large eyes sparkling.

"No. I've been assuming a boy all this time since that's what it feels like. Is that stupid?"

"Of course not, dear," Mrs. Martin said. "A mother's instinct is a very strong thing. I wouldn't be surprised a bit if it were a boy!"

"Well, if this is all you ladies are going to discuss, I think I'll head to bed," Josiah said with raised eyebrows.

"I think I will, too, if you don't mind," Gemma said, smiling nonetheless. "Should I sleep on the couch in the playroom?"

Mrs. Martin balanced boxes of uncooked pasta. "My heavens, no! You can have the boys' room."

". . . What about Josiah?" Gemma said. When she glanced at him, he seemed relieved he hadn't been completely forgotten.

"*He* can take the attic and share it with Gail. You can have some of my pajamas." Mrs. Martin said, leading her up the stairs

Gemma shot Josiah an apologetic look, but he was busy trying to save the soupy ice cream.

She didn't comment on the pajamas being a nightgown when it was handed to her. Heaven knew the last time she'd worn one!

"Goodnight, dear. Sleep well."

"Thank you." She collected her backpack and trudged to the end of the hall.

Gemma had to admit, it felt marvelous having a feather mattress all to herself, even if the roomy nightgown insisted on riding up. She massaged away a cramp in her abdomen as she contemplated the character of this family. Even with everything she had told them so far, she had met no scrutiny or even pity; just love and kindness. The differences from her own family were remarkable.

As Gemma drifted to sleep, for the first time in a very long time, her exhaustion ebbed away into peace. Perhaps everything *could* be all right.

Chapter 3

Gemma stirred as sunlight streamed through the plaid curtains and tickled her eyelids. Repressed laughter and childish giggles met her ears. When she opened her eyes, the smiles of the three youngest Martins met her.

"You make funny noises when you sleep," Mariah chortled. "And your hair is very crazy."

"I believe it," Gemma said, stifling a yawn. She sat up and brushed her hair out of her face.

"That's not nice!" Lisabeth said, speaking to her older sister, stressing every word. Then to Gemma, "I think you're pretty."

Gail nodded his head in agreement with vigor.

"Why, thank you. I return the compliment."

"What's comp'ime't?" Gail asked in his singsong voice, his fair brow furrowed.

"It means I think your sister's pretty, too."

"Oh, I almost forgot," Mariah burst. "We were supposed to get you for breakfast."

Lisabeth gave her hand a tug. "Yeah, you're gonna be late!"

She smiled. "I'll be there in a minute."

The brood scurried away in another burst of shrill merriment. Gemma tried to stay on her feet as she crawled out of bed. The door's lock gave her some trouble, but something told her none of the Martins would ever show up at the breakfast table in pajamas. Except perhaps on Christmas. She gave up before long and leaned against the door as she donned Anneliese's clothes again. At least she wouldn't have to wear them for much longer since she had washed her only outfit yesterday.

Gemma hurried down the stairs with as much speed as she dared, keeping one hand under her protruding tummy. It still took an eternity, but she couldn't afford to lose her balance . . . again. Everyone already sat at the table, making conversation.

"When's Daddy gonna be home?" she heard a little girl ask.

So they do have a dad. An inadvertent chill danced down her spine as memories of the male head of her family appeared. *Don't be silly. He'll be nothing like yours.*

"Just in time for your birthday, dear." Mrs. Martin turned her eyes from her young daughter to Gemma and offered her a warm smile. Taking comfort that she wouldn't have to meet Mr. Martin, Gemma lowered herself into her chair, breathing heavily.

Gemma clasped her hands and closed her eyes for prayer. *I remembered!*

Ginger cleared her throat. "Um . . . we already prayed." Her face radiated apology.

Gemma straightened and withdrew her hands as color crept into her cheeks. She wanted to disappear. "Oh. I was just . . . saying my own." She bit the inside of her cheek as penance for her lie. But it wasn't really a lie, was it? She had been very prepared, even if she hadn't really been praying. It was sincerity that counted.

"Sorry," Mrs. Martin said. "We weren't sure how long you would be and we didn't want to rush you."

"Of course." Her mind turned to eating her steaming oatmeal. That was one thing she would miss with certainty tomorrow morning: a hot breakfast. Maybe she could find an apartment with a working oven this time. Or at least a microwave.

"Mrs. Martin," she began.

"Oh, please call me Joy."

Gemma hated being asked to call her seniors by their first name. It made her feel as if she were being robbed of her one method of displaying good manners.

"Joy—would it be possible to drop me off at the bus station today? It's just that I need to find a new residence."

"Bus stop?" Josiah said. "There's not a bus stop for, like, twenty miles around here."

"Ugh. Josiah, don't say 'like'!" Anneliese said, rolling her eyes.

He ignored her. "Seriously, though. Is that where you came from?"

"Yeah. I walked for a long time, but I can promise you it was no twenty miles. It must be shorter than that by way of cornfield."

"Well, I'll make some calls before we just drop you off. My son David is a real estate agent. Maybe we can find you a nice apartment?"

"Wait. You have more kids?" She regretted the incredulity in her voice. "I-I guess I thought Josiah was the oldest."

"I have three before him. But he took on the role of the eldest around here a while ago."

Holy cow, the lady has ten kids! Now seven didn't sound so bad.

"Anyway," Mrs. Martin continued, "I was hoping we could drag you to the doctor and get you a new wardrobe, too."

Gemma put down her spoon. "Really?"

"Only if you want to," Mrs. Martin said.

"No, that sounds . . . amazing. Thank you."

One hour later, Gemma bounced on the seat of an old Ford pickup. The driveway couldn't have felt more like a ridged potato chip.

"Sorry it's so rough," Ginger said, catching Gemma's eye in the rearview mirror. "The dirt roads through here are pretty bad. But we wouldn't have it any other way for authenticity's sake." She braced herself with the steering wheel.

Gemma gave a shaky smile as the rusted frame of the truck ducked into another pothole. *It'll be authentic when this sends me into labor in the middle of nowhere!* She was reminded to count her blessings as they passed a knotted oak tree with a hollow center.

"This is why I have had my last four kiddos at home. I've never wanted to brave the ride while in labor."

Gemma's eyes went wide. "I thought that was . . . Is that safe— having your kids at home? I mean, don't people . . . die?"

"Not unless there is a freak accident and medical assistance isn't near enough. Statistically speaking, it's safer than being in the middle of doctors who want to deliver your baby their way." Mrs. Martin smiled. "Don't worry, I'll let you make your own decision."

Gemma's mind raced and she hadn't even met the doctor yet. She had never thought of having a baby any other way than at a hospital with painkillers. Maybe better options existed. She resolved not to make any decisions until she knew how long she had to plan.

"Well, Miss Ebworthy, by your measurements I'm guessing you're due in about three weeks." A graying man in a white lab coat placed his pen behind his ear.

Three weeks!

"That would make your due date late September. Joy said you wanted an ultrasound? That'll help me know for certain."

"Yes, sir."

"Down the hall on your left. They'll take care of you while I finish up your report."

"Thank you." Gemma headed toward the waiting room first.

"How'd it go?" Mrs. Martin asked. Both her and Ginger's faces shone with curiosity.

"He guessed I am due in three weeks. But I still need a sonogram."

Mrs. Martin set her knitting magazine aside. "That doesn't leave much time. Would you rather do the sonogram alone?"

"Actually, I'd prefer if y'all came. This is all new to me, so I want *someone* to understand what's going on."

Mrs. Martin gave her a reassuring pat. "Of course, dear. We'd be delighted."

Soon Gemma reclined on a padded gray table and a bubbly girl rubbed a room-temperature gel on her bare stomach. It felt like honey, only smoother.

"First time? That's so exciting! So I'm gonna move around your stomach with this thing." The ultrasound technician held up what looked like a joystick. "And a black and white image of your baby will be displayed on that screen. It should be quite clear since you're so far along."

She placed the larger, rounded end on Gemma's stomach and began to slide it around, pressing gently. Sure enough, a black shape resembling a cone appeared with a fuzzy, gray baby pictured inside.

"There's the cutie's head! Do you want to find out the gender? Some people like it to be a surprise."

"Um . . ." Gemma glanced at Mrs. Martin.

"It's up to you."

"I vote you find out," Ginger said. A hint of eagerness tinged her voice.

Gemma smiled. "Let's find out."

Her eyes never left the screen. She drank in the two-tone image of the tiny baby growing inside of her as the sonographer pointed out different things.

"All right, let's see," the technician said as she swiveled what she had called the probe around. "Well, at this stage I can guarantee you that is *not* the umbilical cord. Congratulations! You're having a boy!"

Ginger clapped her hands and Gemma exhaled a laugh. It was incredible. She was going to have a boy—a son. *I knew it!*

"Let's look around a little more. That's his foot. Aw, and there's his little face. Woo, he's gonna have a head of hair!"

The fact that Gemma could watch her baby—*her* baby—moving and thriving, relying on her for life . . . it took her breath away. Never had she felt so close to her child.

Next, a digital line on the screen measured various parts of the baby to predict his age and ensure he grew as he should.

"Everything looks great from here, missy. I'm guessing you're only about thirty-four or thirty-five weeks, so a little more time than we thought before."

"Why the difference?" Gemma asked.

"Amniotic fluid. Some women have more of it than others and so it makes them look bigger, even though the baby can still be small. That's good, though, because neither of you will feel as crowded or uncomfortable."

The technician wiped the excess goop off Gemma's stomach and gave her hand a squeeze. "Congrats, and let me know how it goes!"

The doctor met them in the lobby and handed Gemma a manila file. "Looks like you're good to go, Gemma. I would like to see you once a week until you give birth. We need to do blood work next week. Until then, take it easy and drink lots of water. Joy will know what to do if anything comes up."

So I'll have to stay local.

Ginger gushed the whole way to the store, her dark curls bouncing. "Isn't that exciting? I knew it was a boy! And October 12 is a lovely day to be due on. Oh, I just can't wait!"

Gemma wasn't sure how Ginger could be so enthusiastic and still concentrate on driving.

"Will you be comfortable with my doctor?" Mrs. Martin asked.

"I think so. He seemed very knowledgeable and sincere. I liked him a lot." Gemma grinned from ear to ear as she reviewed several sonogram pictures they had printed for her.

"So, do you have any good boy names?" Ginger prompted.

"Careful, Ginger named the last two almost on her own," Mrs. Martin chuckled. "Names are Ginger's favorite part of a coming baby."

Gemma tried to summon her impression of classmates' names. "I guess I tend to like names that are rare and creative. But nothing they'll be tripping over all their lives. I knew a girl named Ember and a boy named Braelynn and I liked how they stood out from the sea of Haileys and Jordans and such."

"Mm-hm," Ginger said as they pulled up to a resale maternity store. "I hope you're OK with resale! The podunk Kansas towns don't have much to offer."

Nodding, Gemma decided not to admit that she had hardly shopped anywhere else as a teen as she climbed out of the truck.

"All right, dear. I figure you'll need some seasonal tops, some comfortable bottoms, and undergarments. Yes?"

Entering the store, Gemma glanced at the first price tag she met. *This is going to push my budget.* Selective shopping might allow her to keep the total within reason.

For the next two hours the women explored local shops, trying outfits on Gemma for fit and quality. Gemma showed much patience and great restraint. Their first inclinations were not always hers.

"Look at this lovely top. Do you like it?" Mrs. Martin asked.

Gemma bit her tongue. "Um . . . I can try it on. It looks a little . . ."

Ginger saved the day. "Old. It looks old, Mom."

Gemma took a seat on an antique stool and hoped this was their last stop as the Martins continued to rifle through the racks of clothing. The baby wouldn't stop sticking his foot in her ribs and she kept running out of breath. Besides, they had to be approaching her limit and they had yet to find any well-fitting shirts. Still, she needed every bit they had purchased. *I'll need a job soon.*

"Oh my goodness, look at this darling dress!" Ginger cried, swishing it in front of Gemma. "Don't you love it?"

"It's very pretty." Gemma fingered the soft cream fabric. She'd never owned a thing like it before. "It's not maternity, though." *And I just bought a black one.*

"But it would fit you after the baby and it looks so wonderful with your skin. Do get it and I'll alter it if I have to."

Gemma smiled at her tenacity. It was a steal at twelve dollars, but that was twelve dollars she didn't have. "Maybe another time."

Two casual outfits later, she had all the basics. As the cashier rung the last of it up, Gemma's eyebrows shot up. How on earth would she be able to afford this? She would reimburse what she could now and mail the rest to them later. At least now she had full outfits for any weather and occasion.

Mrs. Martin had a different idea. "Don't worry about a thing. We'll cover it since you were very frugal in your decisions."

Gemma's eyes grew wide. "But I can't let you spend all of that on me!"

Mrs. Martin gave a warm smile. "Oh come now, I insist. It is all necessary and for a very good cause. You must let me. I chose stores that would be thankful for the business on purpose and I *adore* buying for other people."

"Well, at least let me cover the flats. Those were frivolous." Her sneakers had survived high school, so they could survive another year.

"If it will make you feel better, you may."

Gemma relaxed into the lumpy seat of the truck, satisfied. It had been a productive day. But she felt as if she'd run a marathon. She fell asleep on the way back and took another nap once they arrived. However, the rest of the day was kind enough to be low-key to make up for it. Engaging her wits in a chess battle against Emmaline required the most exertion. By the end of the game, she wondered if losing had been worth all the effort.

Just as she prepared to head upstairs so she could crawl between the sheets again, the family gathered in the living room. Gemma was impressed that they all had an enforced curfew and decided to join them.

Everyone collected in a loose circle on and among the furniture with books in their laps. Josiah approached Gemma with a leather-bound copy of the same book. "We have an extra. You're just in time for the climax of Joshua." He winked and slid it to her across the coffee table.

She tried not to look confused. Using the index, she turned to page 294: Joshua. *Ugh, why don't the chapters have names?* Nothing but random phrases listed at the top of each page clued her in on what the climax would be.

"All right, who would like to read tonight?" Mrs. Martin asked over the curly head in her lap.

Emmaline volunteered and as her clear, crisp voice unveiled the dramatic story of the conquering of the city Jericho, Gemma felt herself being drawn in. It was like no other book she'd ever read. It was well written, but it had no attachment to the modern rules of grammar. It meant she had to fix her attention on every word.

When it had ended, Gemma asked if she could keep the Bible, until she left.

Mrs. Martin's face lit at the request. "Of course, dear. I'm so glad you liked it."

As Mrs. Martin and the older girls helped shoo the younger ones to bed, Gemma stayed behind to question Josiah. She wanted to know more about this book before she dove in. It had been forever since she'd read a book for the fun of it.

"Josiah?"

His captivating olive eyes flicked to her face. A grin made their corners crinkle.

"About the Bible . . . why is it better than any other book with morals to the story?"

He resituated himself on the couch, ready to engage in a hearty discussion. "Because God wrote it."

Her heart sank a little. *They really believe all that?* She waited for him to admit he was part of a cult and this is what they gathered in the basement by candlelight to read. The kind of book that contained impossible myths and encouraged you to have ten kids by five wives.

"To us the Bible is more than just a collection of fairy tales or stories," Josiah continued. "It's got real principles and instruction for everyday life. You'd better start it and see for yourself." Disappearing into what Gemma thought was the children's library, he popped back into the room and held out a spiral-bound notebook. "I want you to write any questions you have in this. Leave yourself space to write the answers. Most of them will be answered as you continue to read, because the story does have a plot. For some, you may need outside sources."

"Outside sources like you, huh?"

He scratched the back of his head. "Well, even I don't know everything."

Gemma chuckled and bid him goodnight. *Men have such egos.*

When she crawled into bed, she couldn't resist beginning the book. If Josiah was so unashamedly addicted, she had to know where these talks were headed. A full hour ticked by before she closed the well-worn pages. She had made it through Genesis 11 and scrawled her last question: *Do the Martins believe there's something to this, like the Greek myths where the Tower of Babel is supposed to explain all the different languages today?* For the first time since she had come, she was hit with a sudden desire to stay. She still had so much she wanted to learn. They might be different—very different—but their life was so . . . enjoyable.

As the last event of the day she retrieved her abandoned journal that was supposed to be chronicling her life. She wrote a single sentence: *Staying with the Martins—I am beginning to like it here.*

Chapter 4

"You look pretty," Gemma greeted Emmaline as she met her in the hall the next morning. "Are you going somewhere?" In her thinking, why else would one dress up?

"Yeah, it's Sunday."

Gemma gave a blank stare. The neurons did not fire this early.

"You know, church?"

"Oh." Of course she had seen church buildings spotting the roadsides of small towns, but mystery veiled what happened inside. She knew they used the Bible. *It must be like a book club.*

Upon asking, Mrs. Martin said Gemma could stay home if she'd rather, but her curiosity had been piqued. And once curious, an Ebworthy could not be stopped.

As the morning preparations proceeded, Gemma reveled in the fact that she had a new black dress to wear. She smeared her separating foundation on and turned in circles with her liquid eyeliner in hand. There had to be a way to get closer to the mirror! Her stomach stuck out so far, she couldn't get within a foot of the cabinet unless she turned sideways.

Anneliese joined her in the bathroom. "You look pretty." Gemma detected a twinge of envy in her voice as Anneliese took in the hodge-podge of drugstore cosmetics stuffed inside a blue zipper bag. "I came to tell you we need to leave in about ten minutes."

"OK, thanks." Gemma realized Anneliese wore no makeup herself. Maybe that was something the Martins didn't do; some people were weird about that. She placed her liquid eyeliner back in its bag to play it safe.

Anneliese popped her head back in the bathroom. "Oh, and you might want to wear a slip with that dress. Top drawer." She volunteered the first smile Gemma had seen from Anneliese since she arrived. What had gotten into her?

As Gemma dug for the undergarment, her hand bumped something hard. *That's not clothing.* Gemma drew it out and stroked the top of a little box with a lock and *Anneliese* carved in the top in a fancy script. It must be for jewelry. She returned it to its corner, realizing that "top drawer" might mean the row of tiny ones above where she searched. *Voila!* Once again, the waistband didn't sit comfortably when she put it on, but it would have to do.

How long is this church thing gonna take anyways?

Everyone had just piled outside when Mrs. Martin stopped. "Oh dear, I forgot your father has the other car. We're four seats short."

"I'll take my horse," Josiah said, heading for the stable.

"I'll ride, too," Ginger said.

Mrs. Martin smiled. "I don't trust the other horses. Ride behind your brother, please, and the rest of us will make do. Guess your father's picking up more supplies since he took the van."

With Mrs. Martin behind the wheel and Gemma in the front, Anneliese was forced to the back seat with the four youngest. As Gemma predicted, the ride drew many grumbles from Anneliese.

By the time they arrived, twenty minutes late, every dress held creases ironed in place after the jolting ride. Only the boys escaped the disaster in their durable blue jeans, and Gemma in her knit.

The family hurried up the steps of the peeling white church and filed inside. Josiah grabbed what looked like fliers from a table and proceeded through the double wooden doors ahead.

Gemma took in the rows of people as the Martins filed into a pew themselves. The sound of death resonated. Only an occasional creak of a pew or turn of a page could be heard. All sat motionless with their heads bowed.

Who are they trying to connect with? Gemma shuddered at the thought that it could be departed relatives.

As she took her seat, she noticed an older man with flyaway fuzz and wire-rimmed spectacles bobbing his head on the stage. She and the baby jumped when he began speaking with a booming voice. No one else budged. As he said, "Amen," everyone snapped out of the trance and turned their faces to him. *Oh, it was a prayer. Thank goodness!*

Gemma tuned him out and examined the faces around her. No one she knew, of course, but it amazed her how fixated they all were on the man's face. Everyone looked polished up for the event. What made people want to dress up to come sit in an echoing room for a lecture?

The speaker's voice, though pleasant to listen to, seemed to drag on and on. Gemma stopped examining the drafty room with its accenting crossbeams and stained glass windows and glanced over what looked like a program. On the front it said *Havenfeld Bible Church* and below that, *Pastor Gerald Freeman.*

Pastor. She had seen these guys preaching on television before. They were all into making money for God; poor equaled pagan. At least that was her impression from the little she had gathered. Curious, she tuned her ears to the sermon.

Gemma opened her—or rather, Mr. Martin's—Bible to the appropriate passage. So far, it proved to be less wacko than she'd expected.

"Rahab became an instrument of the Lord despite her circumstances," the pastor said.

Gemma skimmed the page to see what circumstances he spoke of. Spy . . . Israelite . . . city . . . prostitute . . . *Prostitute.* Her eyes widened and she glanced at the serious faces around her. *Why the heck is he talking about a prostitute?*

She sat back to judge how crazy this man was. But none of the Martins flinched.

"Rahab, though she had much sin in her past, had turned her heart to the Lord in a wicked land. And because of her willingness to assist the Israelite spies, she was spared in the destruction of Jericho."

Hadn't they read that story last night?

The pastor seemed to be winding down. "She also became part of the Messiah's line. My friends, there is no sin too great, no heart too cold to be turned to the Lord. Who are we to judge those God may claim for His own? May that be in our hearts and minds as we share His Word this week."

Gemma thought it a strange concept. But in another light, it gave her courage. Maybe she wouldn't be an automatic outcast here.

Everyone bowed their heads in unison and the pastor said a closing prayer. Then a younger, more enthusiastic man bounded onto the stage. He asked everyone to stand and the congregation switched books as he called out a number.

Amazing Grace began to play—one Gemma was familiar with! But it omitted the part at the end about chains and floods. Bummer, too, because she liked that part the best.

The worship leader dismissed them. Then came the lingering—people all eager to share the week's news with each other. And there was Gemma, who stood out like a sore thumb to the throng who seemed so familiar with the usual crowd.

The first woman to come up must have been nearly eighty. "Who've we got here?" she croaked, patting Gemma's hand. "Are you a friend of Joy's?"

"Yes." Gemma stole a glance at Josiah, engaged in conversation. She could seriously use his help.

"I'm Lucinda Jane. Is your husband with you?"

Gemma shifted her weight as she tried shooting telepathic pleas to Josiah. "Um, actually . . . I'm not married." She watched for the woman's reaction, certain she had shocked her old-fashioned concept of morality.

The older lady just smiled wider. "You poor dear. I guess that makes you one of Joy's guests, huh?"

Thinking it curious she guessed so readily, Gemma said, "I'm . . . visiting for a while."

"Oh, all right. If you were a Martin, I'd have to make a blanket for you. I've crocheted one for every one of those Martin babies and I don't intend to stop with their kids, neither, till I can't keep up or drop dead. Would you like one anyhow?"

Wait, is she serious? "If it wouldn't be any trouble, I'd love one. But I don't think I'll be here much longer." She shifted her weight to prevent her feet from falling asleep.

"Oh, you'll be here long enough. Don't you worry about that. It's no trouble a'tall. Is it a boy or a girl?"

"Uh, boy."

"Well won't that be nice. I've got lots of boy yarn. Joy's never given me much chance to use it," she chuckled. "I hope you have a nice stay, dear." She squeezed Gemma's sweaty hand in her own cool, wrinkled one before hobbling off to greet others.

Gemma turned to locate her escorts and realized she was the only one still in the Martin pew. Her heart plummeted. Queer looks and whispers flitted her way as people hurried past. *How can the whole confounded family be out of sight?*

"Hello," a soft voice said.

Gemma hid her panic and faced the stranger. A tall, poised young woman with hair that glinted red stood before her. Gemma felt certain she had never seen this girl before, but something familiar struck her about her face with its gently curved lips and flashing eyes.

"I'm Lydia. Nice to meet you."

Gemma shook the extended hand, beginning to get claustrophobic in her pew. "Gemma."

"Have the Martins taken you in?"

"Yes, actually. I hear they do that quite often?" She tucked a stray curl behind her ear to calm her nerves.

"Fairly." Lydia spoke deliberately and smiled with a slow grace that charmed Gemma. "Is this new to you? You look a little out of place."

The last of her nausea slipped away with the girl's frank approach. "Yeah, I have no idea what I'm doing. I think they were surprised I wanted to come, but Josiah . . ." Gemma decided not to tell the whole story. "He made me curious."

"He's good at that. Thinks he's some sort of evangelist or something."

Josiah's voice at her shoulder made Gemma start. "And why not? We're all supposed to be."

Lydia looked past Gemma and met him with a faint smile. "Very true."

Gemma sensed that something more existed between the two of them as Josiah's gaze lingered on Lydia's face a little longer than necessary.

He turned to Gemma. "Are you ready to go?"

"Yes!" Her feet pulsed from standing and her back stung from sitting. Lydia waved as Gemma followed Josiah's path through the mob with sweaty palms and a ducked head. Spotting Ginger, Josiah stood at her side, listening to a young man explain his new job with machinery.

When he paused, Josiah said, "Sorry, Ginge, we gotta go. Elias, meet Gemma."

Elias smiled and shook her hand. "Nice to meet you. See you guys later."

Josiah motioned to Anneliese from a corner where she sulked and grabbed Lisabeth's hand as she passed. "Come on, time to go."

After another bumpy ride home, they shared a full lunch and went to take afternoon naps. Due to her baby's incredible level of activity, Gemma found it hard to rest. Her active mind didn't help, either. Giving up, she read a chapter or two from Mr. Martin's Bible and then retrieved her journal off the nightstand and began to write.

Went to church with the Martins. The pastor seems inclusive of people like me who are different and the Martins don't seem to mind. I still feel out of place, but I want to go again and see what else I can learn about these people. They all seemed so happy and united . . . what I wouldn't give for that. Met Lucinda Jane (yikes, I know) and Lydia. Both seem sweet but almost too innocent. I feel so different! And I think there's something between Lydia and Josiah. She's very genuine, but always seems to be giving meaningful glances and trying to coax a smile. Josiah seemed uncomfortable . . . Have to pee now, so I'm getting up.

When Gemma reappeared after the attempted nap she found Ginger and Josiah in an animated discussion that dissipated as she entered the room. Gemma caught the name Elias. *Or maybe it was Anneliese.* Ginger seemed grateful for the interruption and drew her over to the piano. There they spent the next hour as Ginger explained to her how using a hymnal and reading music worked. It proved a nice distraction from the baby's incessant squirming, but was not Gemma's forte.

"Give her a break, Ginge," Josiah said.

Ginger flushed. "Sorry."

Gemma gave her a smile. "It's OK. It will be good to know next time I go." She didn't realize there might not be a next time until she said it.

But it was too late. Josiah crossed his arms and picked up the thread. "Planning on staying a while, then?"

"I'm not going to impose. But since I'm here, I'm going to pick your brain."

Ginger excused herself as Josiah relaxed his broad frame against the wall. "Shoot."

"How do the Bible, churches, and hymns all go together? I don't get it."

His face lit up and she wondered if she should take back her question. "What do you believe in, Gemma?"

She knew he had avoided her question. *Best just play along.* "I'm an athiest, I guess."

"Do you believe in the big bang theory?"

She was impressed he wanted to talk about it. This had better not get too scientific! "I guess so? I mean it makes sense that life could start small and simple and progress from there. And besides, there's evidence that it's the truth."

"Funny thing is there's evidence for my view, too—the view printed in the Bible." His index finger emphasized his point.

Gemma frowned. "Can't we both be right?"

"There *are* people who think that life was created and then evolution played out. But for my belief to follow through, that's not possible."

Can't I be curious about Christianity without having to make a choice? "You think I'm wrong."

"No more than you think I'm wrong. No one alive today was there at the start, whether it took place six thousand or six gazillion years ago. Regardless, it's a matter of faith. Look at the world like it's a scientific experiment; when the evidence and your conclusion don't hold, you have to find a new theory."

Man, he is good. Gemma could feel herself falling into a trap that he had been weaving with every word.

"Christianity explains why the world is the way it is today. And more than that, it offers a solution—a comforting one full of hope and certainty. No other religion on the face of the earth can offer that."

This made no sense. "All those people were at church today because they believe the God from the Bible is real. And they believe in Him because it makes them feel good?" Heaven knew she had never received any sort of satisfaction from believing evolution, but she would approach this "alternative" intelligently . . . if at all.

"Not exactly. It's—"

"Gee whiz, Josiah," Emmaline said, passing through the room with a cookie in her hand. "Don't overdo it!"

"It's OK," Gemma said, even though her mind spun. "I haven't heard anyone talk about religion the way you do. It's fascinating. I guess that's what Lydia meant about you being an evangelist."

She noted his flush and muttered reply with a strange satisfaction that made her feel a twinge of guilt.

Mariah burst through the front door. "Guys, come quick! Daddy's home."

Chapter 5

Gemma glanced at Josiah, her heart in her throat. His startled look did not reassure her.

Don't be stupid. This is irrational. There's nothing to be afraid of, just go say hi.

Gemma stepped outside and tried to blend into the side of the house. Most of the family had awakened and wandered outside while she and Josiah talked, because Mr. Martin had quite the crowd to greet him. The little girls squeezed him at whatever level they reached and Gail lifted his arms to be held.

Mrs. Martin gave him a long hug. "We didn't expect you so soon, dear. Did everything go all right?"

It had been a business trip, judging by his suit, slacks, and tie. The deep lines in his suntanned face and the gray shadow of hair that rose almost to his temples made him look distinguished. Gemma wondered if every farmer his age could look as strong, worn, and sophisticated at the same time.

"Quite well. We wrapped up early. I got my plan for the apartments approved and the first down payment. Now all that remains is—" He stopped short when he saw Gemma.

Her stomach twisted into knots. She wiped her sweaty palms on the sides of her legs as she tried to read his expression. *Smile!*

"Who is this?" He gave her a curt nod.

"That's Gemma, Daddy." Mariah looked ready to launch into the whole story, but Ginger motioned to her. Bad timing seemed to be Mariah's specialty.

Mr. Martin gave Gemma a quick look-over, doubt flickering in his face despite his smile, and turned to his wife. "We'll talk about this later."

"Of course, dear. But you must be starved . . ." Her voice trailed off as the throng moved indoors.

The moment the door was closed, Gemma let out a pent-up breath and wrapped her arms around her stomach.

Josiah had hung back. "Are you OK?"

"I'll be fine."

"Look, Dad can be a little overbearing. He's never been too fond of Mom taking in strangers. He worries that they'll make bad impressions on us. But he's really OK once you get to know him . . . and he gets to know you."

"Bad impressions," she repeated, her mind in a different place. He was trying to encourage her and she appreciated it. Yet she couldn't shake a nagging fear that Mr. Martin already hated her. She knew she shouldn't stay much longer anyway, but she'd rather not be thrown out . . . again.

"I'm not the first one y'all have taken in."

Josiah shook his head. "We fostered some kids a few years back. They were a mess, but they needed a home for a while. Dad didn't like the ideas they put into our girls' heads. Then Mom offered a hot meal and lodging in exchange for work to a poor man wandering town. He seemed nice and worked hard, but when we got up one morning he had left and taken all the silver, jewelry, and food he could carry. That's when Dad decided we couldn't keep doing things like that. The cost was too great."

"If you knew all that when you found me in the barn, why . . ."

"I will always help people in any way I can. I didn't see anything dangerous in a hot meal and shower." He sighed. "But I was afraid this would happen. I should have tried harder to find you a place, but the truth is we've all loved having you." He put his hand on her shoulder and captured her with his green gaze. "Don't worry, we'll figure something out. I promise."

She forced a small smile. "OK."

Josiah held the front door for her and Gemma hoped to avoid crossing paths with Mr. Martin immediately, but no such luck. Lisabeth was on her in a moment, dragging her to the set table where her father sat. Already, she could feel a more somber air in the house. Neither Ginger nor Mrs. Martin were smiling. Anneliese hadn't yet made an appearance.

"Gemma, is it?" Mr. Martin looked amiable enough. Except for his eyes—they picked apart every fiber of her being.

Her throat went dry as she took a seat. "Yes, sir."

"How long have you been here, Gemma?"

"This is my third day."

"How . . . come?" His questions were harmless enough, but so carefully put. She felt as if she were on trial.

"Because I've been here one more day than two." She bit her cheek as soon as it came out.

Josiah choked and spluttered on his glass of water.

Mrs. Martin brought in the casserole and looked from one tense face to the next, wrinkles gracing her forehead.

Studying her before continuing, Mr. Martin massaged his shoulder. "Have you not been able to find a place to stay?"

"Not yet. Your son David is supposed to be working on that. I haven't gone to a hotel because your wife has been assisting me with medical care." At least, that's what she told herself.

Mr. Martin looked at his wife for confirmation which she gave with a nod.

"Perfectly understandable. I hear Josiah found you in our stable? Would you mind telling me how you got there?"

"I got disoriented in your cornfield. I had been walking for hours, I was terrified, it was dark, and I needed to sleep." She struggled to keep the edge out of her voice. No doubt the thought of her being a thief had crossed his mind.

"All right then. Are we ready to pray?"

Gemma let out a silent sigh of relief. She had kept her head . . . for the most part.

That evening was a trying one. While Gemma managed to avoid any more poignant questions, the air was charged with a high-voltage tension strong enough to kill. She managed to remain as natural and at ease as possible until the Bible reading. When she heard the topic, Gemma knew what was coming; she had read the passage on Sodom and Gomorrah for herself earlier in the afternoon.

Mr. Martin read the passage and proceeded to explain how important it is not to surround oneself with bad influences. "To avoid God's judgment, the ungodly should be avoided. Lot and his family not only had a narrow escape, but they were also greatly influenced by the wicked ways of the people around them."

There was a pause where Gemma tried to disappear.

"But we don't always have a choice," Josiah said.

His father turned patient eyes upon him.

Josiah continued. "Sometimes people of different backgrounds and beliefs come to you. Are we supposed to avoid them? Of course we are not supposed to be 'of the world,' but is it right to completely segregate ourselves from those who need God's light? Don't seek them out, perhaps, but minister to them when they show up at your door. It's our responsibility as Christians."

"Sometimes it's not that simple, son. Sometimes the good cause has to be weighed against the negative effect it could have on one's family." His look said the conversation was over. "Let's pray."

Gemma bowed her head but had a hard time concentrating. She felt like such a bother. Here she was causing a disturbance in the nicest family she'd ever met. She resolved to give up any silly hopes of staying and leave as soon as she could—for their sake.

Ginger took her aside as the group divided for bedtime preparations. "Don't feel too bad. This is usual."

"But—"

"Look, even Josiah was a little nervous about taking you in without Dad here at first. And now he likes you just as much as the rest of us. They've never seen eye to eye on this matter. It's not you, Gemma."

She nodded. "Thanks, Ginger."

Gemma spent much time in the Bible that night. She didn't know who she sided with—Josiah or his father. They both had valid points, but it didn't seem like Mr. Martin was being very fair. Either way, she was determined to get to the heart of this book. Just like Josiah had said, she had to know what it said before she could decide if it was credible.

She had finished reading before she realized she had better give it back to Mr. Martin. She'd hate to be the source of any other disruptions. So, she tiptoed back down the hall and set the Bible at the foot of the door with a note thanking Mr. Martin for letting her borrow it. Although, technically, he hadn't had any say in her use of it.

Whatever. He'll get the point. With that, she felt she had done all she could to make a good impression. Now she would have to wait for a verdict. Or get out before he could pass one.

Monday could have been worse. As it turned out, Mr. Martin was gone most of the day working on his apartment project. Gemma expected the kids to be shuttled away to school, but when she mentioned it, Mariah gave her an astonished look.

"We don't *go* to school. We do it here. Why do you think we have a schoolroom?"

It was Gemma's turn to look surprised. *So it's not just a children's library. Duh.* Of course the Martins wouldn't send their kids to public school; not after that speech last night.

While Mrs. Martin spent the morning assisting her children with math problems and spelling tests, Gemma entertained herself by flipping through baby name books that Ginger gave her. She was not having very good luck. Her list read: Oliver, Graham, Findlay. None of them seemed to flow with "Ebworthy" as well as she would like. And she still had to find a middle name, too! *Naming is* not *my strong suit.*

"So, how's it coming?" Ginger asked at lunch.

"Not great. I like *F* names. Other than that . . ."

"Hm. That's a hard one. I'll let you know if I come up with anything great." She flashed her enthusiastic smile.

Gemma took lunch out to Josiah and Mariah while they worked in the cornfield. As relaxing as sitting all morning had been, she needed a stretch.

As usual, Mariah was full of ideas. "I think you should name the baby Franklin."

"Franklin?" Josiah scoffed around a bite of sandwich. "Where'd you get that one?"

"From my Franklin the Turtle book. And Benjamin Franklin. Do you like it, Gemma?"

She couldn't lie to those blue eyes. "I'll . . . think on it. Let me know if you have any other ideas. You're on the right track."

"Oh." Josiah pulled a letter out of his back pocket. "You *did* have something at the post office. Just like you said, he mailed it to your apartment but no return address. Your landlord had brought it back to the office since you didn't live there anymore, and they gave it to me no questions asked."

Gemma smiled to herself. She'd told him she had been evicted and yet he still mailed it to her apartment . . . Swallowing, she took the greasy envelope in hand. Nearly illegible handwriting sat on the front. "Thanks."

As soon as she had reached the privacy of her room, she tore it open. It read:

Gemma,
Got yor letter. Sory about yor house. I don't have room rite now. Pleaz make other arangemunts.
Love Uncle Wilfred

Well, there went that idea. If he wouldn't take her back, she'd have to be on her own again when she left here. Just as well. She had raised her standards since she'd sent that letter.

The rest of the day wore on. Gemma couldn't believe her luck when Mr. Martin wasn't due to return home until late that night. She had gone almost the whole day without seeing him. *That's really bad. I should be making friends with him.* But he still unnerved her, even if he wasn't trying to. After much contemplation, she had decided not to hold any detail of her past back. She would tell him everything; there would be no grading on a curve. She felt guilty that this family was becoming close to her and they still didn't know the half of it . . .

Gemma's door flew open and banged into the wall early the next morning. She jumped and tried to blink the fog from her brain. *What in the world?*

"Come on, come on!" Lisabeth cried, pulling on her hand. "It's my birthday! Hurry up. You're going to miss it!" She darted out of the room as quickly as she had come.

It was not the typical birthday celebration, but it suited the family. Instead of a birthday cake, there was a pancake cake—a large stack of gigantic pancakes, layered with Cool Whip and topped with berries. Six candles twinkled on the top while everyone sang.

Lisabeth grinned from ear to ear the entire time. At the end, she screwed her eyes shut for a moment and blew all the candles out with a single breath. Applause, cheers, and whistles formed a pandemonium.

"Do you know what I wished for?" She didn't wait for a response. "I wished that Gemma could stay with us forever!"

Gemma was so touched she felt like crying. Instead, she gave the birthday girl a big hug.

"Well, the thing about birthday wishes is they usually don't come true if you say them out loud," Mr. Martin said.

The family grew quiet, eyes on Mr. Martin.

He's going to announce his decision.

"I have decided that Gemma may spend the rest of the week with us if she would like. It will be a sort of trial run where I can get to know her better and decide if it's wise for her to stay any longer. We will try and make other arrangements during the meantime. Is that satisfactory?"

Cheers broke out among the little girls. Gemma was stunned. She couldn't believe he had actually decided to let her stay. Five days was plenty of time. Now all she had to do was tell her life story. *Totally not a huge deal. You can do it.*

After presents had been opened and the others had moved on to their schoolwork and chores, Gemma caught Mr. Martin alone in his study.

Her hands shook and she felt like she could retch. But it had to be done.

"Sir? I really appreciate your generosity in letting me stay. And if it wouldn't be too much bother, I *would* like to stay longer. I had other plans I was looking into and they've fallen through."

He set his blueprints aside. "I told you I would make that call after—"

"Five days, I know. But there are some things I think you ought to hear from me, first, so you can make that decision based on the facts."

Mr. Martin ran his hands over his shaved head. "All right." He rose and emptied a chair full of boxes so she could sit.

There was a knock at the door simultaneous with Josiah's head popping around the doorframe. "Oh, sorry. If you're busy, I can—"

"Can you stay a minute?" Gemma asked. "I think you should hear this, too."

He took her in for a moment and Gemma saw the first similarity between father and son. "Sure." He slipped inside and shut the door.

Gemma took a deep breath to calm her nerves. *This is going to be harder than I thought.*

Chapter 6

Josiah took a seat and the office grew silent.

Gemma swallowed. *Just start talking.*

"My mom left when I was little and my dad . . . he's in prison for life. That's why I lived with my uncle in Texas. But he was always drinking or hung over, and he never liked me. He had no choice but to take care of me until I turned eighteen. I felt lonely and insecure and I got involved with a gang."

She cleared her throat and lowered her eyes.

"Then this guy showed up at my school and took a liking to me. I was blown away because no one had ever paid any special attention to me. I was gullible and needy and he became my new world. I left all of my criminal activities in order to be with him. He was my boyfriend for several months and then I . . . got pregnant. I decided not to tell him or my uncle until I graduated.

"When I finally told both of them, they flew off the handle. My uncle threw me out. He never liked having to support me and he sure didn't want to support a baby, too. Since I was technically a legal adult then, he had an excuse. And my boyfriend . . . he wasn't willing to forfeit college and his future to support us. He demanded that his family never find out and even . . . yeah.

"So when I realized I was on my own, I moved to Kansas. I needed to get away from the criminal implications and I wanted to be as removed from my past as possible. I had been working at a restaurant and trying to keep up with rent for a crummy little apartment when I got evicted. That's when I landed in your stable."

Gemma stole a look at Josiah's face, which creased with thought as he tried to digest the new information. She hadn't dared to look up since she had begun.

"Now you know the whole story." She fidgeted as her past sank in.

"What made the difference?" Josiah said quietly. "I mean, you seem to have your head on pretty straight now."

"I realized that you can't rely on people. Both my uncle and boyfriend were self-centered. And so was I. We all thought we could make each other happy and still get our way, but that wasn't the case. I had to stop focusing on me and focus on the baby. The men in my life weren't willing to do that. So here I am." Gemma looked directly at Mr. Martin, who hadn't said a word. "I would like to stay, not because it's the only option, but because I think it would be the best for the baby. Please keep that in mind, sir. I leave it up to you to decide how much you want to share with the rest of the family."

She rose to go, feeling as if a great burden had been lifted off her shoulders.

Mr. Martin's voice stopped her. "I have one question, young lady. Were you ever in prison for your 'gang activity'?"

Memories of sidewalk transactions, late night meeting points, and small bags of white powder hammered in her mind. "I would have been had they been able to catch me."

Josiah looked amused. His father did not. "I see. And if the police did catch you today, would they still be able to prove your guilt?"

"Not in Kansas. But if I ever went back to Texas—to my hometown—then that would be something to worry about."

He massaged his wrist. "Thank you for your honesty."

Gemma managed a nod and slipped out the door. As soon as it clicked behind her, she let out a deep breath and slid her arms around her stomach. *I did it.*

The next five days Gemma would always view as the most formative days of her life. She threw herself wholeheartedly into being useful. She brought water out to Josiah while he worked, tried to cook with Ginger, curried horses with Emmaline and Mariah, and played games with Lisabeth and Gail. While few of these ventures came easy, it wasn't for lack of effort.

By far the most courageous attempt was Anneliese's hair. She had been complaining that her ends were dead and jagged, but received little sympathy. The thought struck Gemma one day when Anneliese looked at her hair dejectedly once again. *If I do her a favor, maybe I can get on her good side.* So she offered to cut her hair.

Anneliese's eyes grew round as saucers. "Are you sure?"

"Why not?" Gemma said. "I could give you a blunt cut and maybe even some layers."

She still looked dubious. "Have you cut hair before?"

"I gave myself bangs once."

"Just give her a chance, Anneliese," Mrs. Martin said. "If it doesn't work, then I'll pay for you to go to the salon."

Anneliese flashed a rare smile at Gemma. "All right. Give it a shot."

Moments later, Anneliese settled herself on a barstool with a plastic cape fastened around her shoulders. Gemma wetted down the ends of her hair.

"How much do you want off?"

"As little as you can manage."

"OK, wish me luck."

Anneliese held her breath as Gemma made the first few, slow cuts. Snippets of blonde hair continued to sprinkle the bathroom floor as she struggled to get the bottom even.

After several minutes, Anneliese spoke. "What was it like, going to public school, having no parents . . . things like that?"

Gemma met her eyes in the mirror and wondered what prompted this question. "Stressful. I never had a home I wanted to go back to or a reason to get up in the morning. Always more of the same." She fingered a piece of unsevered hair. "I had freedom, sure, but I didn't want it. I wanted someone to love me and show me how to make it to the next day. That's when I met my boyfriend and made an even bigger mess of things. You're very fortunate."

"How can you say that?" She blushed after it came out. "I just wish I had the opportunity to come to my own conclusions on some things, instead of having to always take my parents' word for it."

"They probably don't want to make you find out the hard way. I understand how you feel, though. Know that most restrictions have their purpose. Why do you think y'all have certain rules like that?" Gemma said.

Anneliese shrugged. "It's a part of our faith. God's perfect, so He disapproves of some things, and we're supposed to be like Him."

"Well, there you go then." She took a step back and surveyed her work. "Not bad, if I do say so myself. It's pretty blunt, though. Do you want me to try layers?"

"Um . . ."

"If not—"

"Go for it."

Using Pinterest as her guide, Gemma brought sections of hair up at an angle and cut off the difference between the ends.

"That looks like a lot of hair," Anneliese muttered.

"Don't worry." Gemma patted her plastic-covered shoulder. "It actually looks pretty good."

After spending well over an hour, Gemma handed Anneliese a mirror to see the final product.

She grinned. "Pretty choppy . . . but it's very even and the ends look way better." She turned to look at Gemma. "Thanks."

That went better than I expected. Gemma let out a sigh of relief.

Gemma awoke with anticipation. Sunday morning had arrived. Big fluffy clouds dotted the blue sky and the birds sang. A slight edge to the air promised fall would soon arrive. Today was the day. Would she be permitted to stay? She supposed she would have to wait until after church to find out . . .

Relax. There's nothing more you can do.

She donned the same black dress and skipped the makeup altogether. Her skin had cleared up with her pregnancy, so why bother? With the baby's growth spurt she couldn't get close enough to the mirror, anyway. Today she needed help with her shoes as well.

"There you go," Anneliese said, slipping Gemma's swollen foot into her last shoe.

"Thanks. It's so weird that I can't even see my feet anymore. I feel like an invalid, making people do things for me."

"Nonsense. We're glad to help." She offered a smile before scampering off to braid her hair. It still looked a little choppy after Gemma's layering job.

What gets into her on Sundays?

Gemma found it worth going to church again. Since they had all been able to pile into the van, they arrived on time. Gemma felt more prepared, so she hoped she would get a more accurate impression of what "going to church" was actually like. Ushers handed them programs, which Gemma discovered were called bulletins, and then they had several minutes to do what they pleased until the service commenced.

Gemma spent that time in the bathroom. Her bladder had shrunk recently. The infernal dirt roads hadn't been doing her any favors, either. She had just enough time to slip into the pew before the opening song began. She tried hard to follow the notes and words this time after what Ginger had taught her. Considering she had no musical bone in her body, it could have gone worse. At least the tune repeated for every set of words.

Josiah had given her a good idea on how to focus better on the sermon. Consequently, when the songs finished and the pastor mounted the stage, she pulled out a notebook and pen. But this week a new distraction presented itself—Anneliese, whom Gemma happened to be sitting by. The girl could not sit still. *Good grief, you'd think she was the one with a child kicking her ribs.* She fidgeted incessantly. Turning her head, shifting her weight, craning her neck. *Is there something she's trying to see?* It certainly wasn't the pastor. The best Gemma could tell, someone sitting diagonal to them had caught her attention. By the end of the sermon, she felt worn out from trying not to be bothered by Anneliese's fidgeting. Had she not known better, she would have delivered Anneliese a sharp jab with her elbow.

Finally, the sermon finished and they stood to sing. Her muscles ached from sitting and trying to block Anneliese out. Once dismissed, Gemma determined not to get left talking to an overly curious stranger this time and so shadowed Josiah. She would love to reassess her vibes about him and Lydia anyway.

As if she had requested it out loud, Lydia made a beeline for them. Gemma couldn't help noting she looked stunning. Her strawberry hair looked even more vibrant than the week before.

"Hello. Still here, I see. How much longer will you be staying?"

Well, I can't tell her I'm on trial with the intense father. She offered what she hoped was a convincing smile. "I'm not sure. We're looking into other arrangements."

"I hope you stay. Don't you, Josiah?" A wicked glint accented her gentle eyes.

He cleared his throat. "Um, yeah, of course. She's been great."

Lydia ducked her head as she laughed softly. "I'm glad."

"I see your brother is back from school," Josiah said.

She rolled her eyes. "Yeah. *Finally* decided to pay us a visit."

Gemma looked past them to see Anneliese fixing her rapt gaze on a young man whose face Gemma couldn't see. They appeared to be having a conversation. So that's why Anneliese got so excited about church. She must have known he was about to have some time off.

"Is that your brother there?" Gemma nodded toward the couple.

"Yes, that's Travis. Have you met him yet? Come on, I'll introduce you."

Travis. Travis!

Realization hit Gemma with the force of a meteor. That's why Lydia looked so familiar. She was her baby's aunt.

No, no, no. This isn't happening. This can't *be happening!*

But it was too late. As Gemma's mind raced with the memories that came flooding back, Lydia led her by the hand to meet him.

A tap on the shoulder made him turn. His smile faded as his golden eyes met Gemma's with only a flicker of recognition. He remained composed.

Lydia said something introductory.

"Pleased to meet you . . . Gemma." The familiar use of her first name made her shiver. Once she would have longed to hear him say it. He removed a hand from his pocket and extended it.

But she was frozen. She wanted to scream and warn them, tell Anneliese he wasn't safe. Didn't all these people know he was dangerous? *Shake it. Just shake his hand, you fool!*

She mechanically extended her arm and mumbled something. As soon as his eyes had stopped boring into her, she fled. The ignorant crowds oppressed her. She kept moving until she stood outside, gulping in air.

How can the father of my child be here? This changed everything.

Gemma rubbed her hand on the front of her dress. She could still feel the warm pressure of his grasp. The baby kicked harder, no doubt wondering about all the commotion.

She sat on the step and slid her arms around her belly. "Nothing's going to happen to you," she whispered. She shook and couldn't stop. How convenient that Travis had always insisted she never meet his family. She vaguely remembered seeing his parents pick him up from school a few times, but never often enough for her to be able to recognize them. Now what was she to do?

Several minutes later, Josiah came out and sat next to her.

Only the sound of rustling leaves filled the silence.

"Wanna tell me what happened?"

She shook her head, still fighting back tears.

"There's nothing wrong with being afraid, Gemma." He gave her shoulder a squeeze.

Gemma remained in a daze for the entire ride home and the meal that followed. All the interaction around her blurred. She couldn't get his face out of her mind. He had been so calm. Almost as if he knew she was going to be here.

Mr. Martin cleared his throat at lunch. "Gemma, I have made my decision if you are ready to hear it."

She snapped to attention. Did she even care anymore? Maybe it would be better if she left. Kept running. Maybe she'd never be safe.

Everyone grew silent in anticipation.

"I must admit I was rather taken aback by your energy and attitude this week. You've borne a lot that is new to you. Since I agree it is best for the baby, you may stay."

Squeals of excitement erupted. Her hands went to her face as emotions brimmed over. *I can stay!* This home offered a security and

58

warmth she had never known before. She wouldn't sacrifice that for anything. *This* is what she wanted.

"Thank you," she managed between sobs and laughter. "Thank you so much."

Gemma felt drained after the overwhelming events of the day and went straight to bed after lunch. She managed to scrawl a sparse journal entry before drifting off to sleep: *I'm going to stay.*

Chapter 7

Since it had been decided that Gemma was going to stay, Mariah poured herself into the task of educating her about the ways of the farm. Josiah warned his sister not to overdo it, but she was not to be stopped. Soon Gemma knew how to sneak the small, greenish eggs out from under hens without getting pecked and check them with a flashlight for chicks. Mariah also taught her how to milk the cows, although Gemma found it extremely uncomfortable sitting on a short stool. The differences between turnip tops and weeds she discovered for herself after several unsuccessful guesses. All of her busy days began to catch up with her. Gemma had been more tired than usual of late, napping almost every day and going to bed early. Mrs. Martin assured her that it was quite normal, but her blood work would tell for sure.

When the doctor called with her results, Gemma felt a little alarmed.

"It appears that you are anemic and have a heart murmur as a result. Nothing to worry about, really. It means that the iron content in your blood is low. Because you're pregnant, too, your heart is doing things a little differently than normal. It should resolve itself after birth if your levels come up. Anemia can contribute to great fatigue and weariness, though, so try and eat as many iron-rich food as you can, and take it easy."

"And it won't hurt the baby at all?"

"The worst thing that could happen is he could come a little sooner than planned. I'll prescribe you a supplement and hopefully your levels will come up a little before the birth. Joy will know what to watch for when you're healing up."

"Thank you."

"Anemic?" Mrs. Martin asked once she had hung up.

"How did you know?"

When she smiled, the corners of her eyes crinkled like Josiah's. "Just a guess. We'll have to get some red meats down you."

"Tell Mariah to stop dragging her all over the fields," Josiah said. "That'll do a whole lot more good than steak."

"I don't drag her around! She likes it, don't you, Gemma? And it's not even hot outside anymore."

"Of course I like it, but I should probably scale it back a little. I almost fell asleep during dinner last night."

"What would you do if she started to have the baby in the middle of the cornfield?" Josiah asked, hands on hips.

Um, isn't that rather worst-case scenario?

"I would deliver him," Mariah retorted. "I've seen dozens of cows birth. It can't be that hard."

Gemma hid her smile behind her hand. Josiah laughed outright.

Mrs. Martin frowned. "Gemma is not a cow, Mariah. Go finish your math page, please." She turned to Gemma as her daughter slunk off. "While we're on the subject, are you comfortable having the baby in a hospital with an obstetrician, or would you like to look at other options?"

"Is there any way I could have a female OB?"

"Well, there's two on call at the hospital and they're both men. You can't even guarantee which one you'll get unless you schedule a C-section, because all the staff is on rotation."

"And the doctor said the baby might come early, so that'd still be taking a chance."

"The baby will come when he's ready if you let him. So the real question is where do you want to have him?"

"Somewhere as cozy as possible. Hospitals kind of give me the creeps, but with anemia . . ."

"Anemia is a concern for bleeding, but we will get as much iron in your blood as we can. The only catch with having the baby somewhere else is they usually don't have pain med options. So you'd probably have to have him naturally. It depends on what you're up for."

Gemma cringed. "I don't know. Is there a reason to not do a hospital?"

"Yes, actually. It has been proven that a natural birth is the healthiest way for mother and baby when it is a safe option. There are hormones that are never released with an epidural that aid in the baby's growth and development and bonding with his mother." Mrs. Martin seemed to realize she was getting carried away. "But it's completely up to you, dear."

Gemma could tell that Mrs. Martin felt strongly about birth options and was well informed. An idea occurred to her. "Could you deliver the baby? Is that what a midwife does?"

Mrs. Martin smiled. "Yes. Yes, I could. Unless he came very early, I have everything we'd need for you to have him right here."

"And that's not a little . . . hippie?"

"Not at all. It's just going back to the way things used to be done when life was simpler."

"But there were higher mortality rates back then."

"I'm not against medicine, Gemma. Of course it has helped people tremendously and is sometimes necessary and life-saving. But there comes a point when even medicine oversteps its boundaries and does more harm than good. People forget that because it has become so integrated." She laughed. "Sorry to overload you. If you want to have the baby at a hospital with an epidural, that's fine. And keep in mind that it's only twelve miles away if anything came up."

Gemma did feel a little overwhelmed, but at least she knew her options now. Thank goodness there was someone knowledgeable she could rely on to lay it all out for her.

"Guys, we have to stop calling him 'the baby' and come up with a name," Ginger said. "The ones I have come up with are Fisher, Farris, and Finn."

Gemma tilted her head. "Farris is different."

"It means 'rock of iron' or something like that. I like it with an *a* as the second letter. That's how it's spelled as a last name. Do you like it?"

"Yeah, I do. Farris Ebworthy." She tried it out on her tongue.

"That's unique," Mrs. Martin said.

Gemma gave a happy sigh. "Well, that's settled. I'm going to go see if Mariah approves and check on the kittens."

Mariah gave her stamp of approval heartily. "That's cuter than Franklin." She picked up a gray kitten and placed it in her lap. "These kittens came at just the right time. They'll be the perfect age to give away at the party."

"What party?" Gemma asked, selecting a wriggling calico.

"The fall party for our church. It's going to be at our house this year. That's why I have to help Josiah with the harvest. We're going to need a lot of corn to feed everyone."

"I see."

Mr. Martin entered the barn shaking his arms out. He looked very authentic in his cowboy hat and boots, covered with sweat and dust. And somehow less intimidating. It struck Gemma again how much Josiah favored his father.

"I've put the new bull in the corral. I want you all to stay away from it. He's got a mind of his own and is not to be trifled with until he's tamed. Understand?"

"Yes, sir," both girls replied.

"I think Daisy's about ready to birth." He hesitated a moment. "You're welcome to observe, Gemma, if you have any interest."

Is he being nice to me? She removed the kitten's claws from her leg. "Thanks, but I'll pass."

He gave a curt nod and disappeared.

Gemma wandered out of the barn and into the cornfield. The stalks waved well above her head now and the silks that peeped out of the husks had just begun to brown. She rubbed her tummy as a sharp pain came and went. They'd be getting worse before long.

Josiah was busy examining the ears and securing paper bags over some of them with rubber bands.

"What on earth are you doing?"

"Designating ears for seed. The ones with the bags we'll leave on the stalk a few extra weeks and then hang to dry for a while. The bag keeps bugs and birds off, but still lets the plant breathe."

"Interesting. I never heard of doing that before. When will the corn be ready?"

Josiah swiped at his brow with his wrist, leaving a large smudge of dirt. "When the silks turn dark brown. Another week or two probably. Then the trick is to harvest only what you can eat or freeze while it's fresh, but still get the crop in while it's milky."

"Milky?"

He beckoned her over and peeled back the husk, revealing the kernels. He punctured one with his thumbnail. "See, the liquid's still clear. When it gets creamy, it's ready. Hope you like corn, Gemma, 'cause we're gonna have plenty of it."

When Gemma had tucked herself in bed by seven thirty that evening, her tumultuous mind wouldn't let her rest. She still couldn't believe Travis was in town. She had left the state knowing that he planned to attend college at University of Texas. Evidently he had changed his mind, because here he was—with his whole family, in Kansas. *He didn't follow me, did he?* He had been so poised when they met that it was not out of the question. But why would he do that? He had sworn to have nothing to do with her or their child, which he considered all her fault. The simplest answer was that he had moved away, too—to the exact same place as Gemma. *That has to be the biggest coincidence in history.*

She pulled out the fraying Bible and read the last few chapters of Exodus to keep her mind off him. His gaze had held such terrible power. And Anneliese was falling for it fast. She resolved to discreetly ask Josiah about the Long family as soon as possible.

That proved to be a lot sooner than she thought. The frantic mooing of a cow awakened Gemma and she glanced at the clock: almost eleven. She eased a shooting pain and rolled over. It returned with a vengeance.

Ugh!

Gemma slipped her phone out of her backpack for the first time in weeks. It had two percent battery . . . and five new messages. Her heart stopped. She bypassed them and Googled "Braxton Hicks." Scrolling past all the material that defined the term and gave the symptoms, she came to ways to relieve the pain. Changing positions hadn't worked and she didn't need to go to the bathroom. That left drinking water.

Gemma heaved a sigh as she dug for her charger and then opened her bedroom door as quietly as possible. She stopped short when she saw someone else in the hall—Anneliese. *Why is she dressed . . . and carrying shoes?* Gemma waited until Anneliese had

66

slipped down the stairs and she heard the back door click. She wanted to see what Anneliese was up to, but she couldn't keep up in this state—she could hardly make it down the stairs!

Man, this water had better do the trick!

She had downed a full glass and was attempting a second when someone entered the back door at her right.

Why is everyone up?

This time it was Josiah and a bleary-eyed Mariah. Gemma was glad she had grabbed her worn, pink sweater since she was in her frumpy nightgown.

"Oh my gosh, are you bleeding?" Gemma said in a hushed voice.

Josiah looked from her large, brown eyes to his arms, encrusted with blood and dirt. "I was birthing a calf. Well, *I* wasn't. I was helping the cow."

She laughed as Josiah washed up. She wondered how on earth Anneliese had managed to miss him on her trip out of the house. Gemma had no doubt she had gone to see Travis. Midnight escapades were a specialty of his. The very thought made her sick.

Josiah dried his hands on a towel. "You OK?"

She tore herself away from her thoughts. "Yeah, I'm fine. Farris is just a little active." *Should I tell him?*

"I see. Nice name, by the way."

No, it can wait.

She slid herself onto a barstool. "Josiah, how long have you known the Long family?"

He hesitated. "Basically forever."

"Have they always lived here?" She took another drink of water.

"They were in Texas for a little while. Something to do with a job change, I think. Why?"

She fidgeted, determined not to reveal the true reason for her inquiry. "Oh, I was just wondering how long you'd been sweet on Lydia."

It was his turn to fidget. "Um . . ." He cleared his throat. "I don't think—"

She grinned at his growing discomfort. "Sorry, that was rude. I couldn't help myself. She's a very sweet girl." *Unlike her brother.*

"What made you think we were . . ."

"I know you're not a couple, but I also know that she likes you. A lot."

"She said that?"

Gemma cocked her head and raised her eyebrows. "Did she have to?"

Josiah sighed. "It's just that Dad has always wanted me to . . . consider her, I guess. And why not? She's fantastic—sweet, kind, motherly, gentle, pretty. I think she knows how much my dad likes her. It's gotten worse lately. Sometimes I feel bad that I've never been able to connect with her in the way they expect. I don't know why; she's nearly perfect."

"No one's perfect."

His face lit up. "You caught on to that, did you? How far have you made it?"

She straightened on her barstool. "I finished Exodus."

"Congratulations. Now you can skip to Matthew."

She frowned. "But, I thought you said the whole thing was important. Shouldn't I read it in order?"

"Of course. But the books aren't all in chronological order. And you have the essential bits that you need. I'll give you selections tomorrow and that will lead you to the climax. You should get the whole picture after that. Then everything else won't seem so abstract if you'd like to read the entire thing."

"Will the inconsistencies clear up?"

"Like what?"

"Like why is the world so bad if God is so good?"

"I promise that one will make sense. God didn't want the world to be bad; man made it that way. You read that in Genesis. God didn't create it bad, He let man choose because He didn't want robots. Man could obey Him and everything would be perfect, or he could disobey and things would go wrong. But even when sin did enter the world, God didn't get stuck, Gemma. He's got a solution to the problem man created."

"In Matthew?"

"Yep." Josiah grinned. "You'll just have to keep reading."

The sound of someone outside interrupted them.

Gemma wondered if it was Anneliese, but Mr. Martin walked in, kicking the mud off his boots.

"Josiah, I think something's been getting into the henhouse. I—" He looked up, surprised. "You guys are up rather late."

Gemma took that as her cue. "I'll go back to bed now that the baby's calmed down."

Josiah volunteered to carry Mariah upstairs. She had fallen asleep on a barstool not long after she dragged herself in.

When Gemma reached her room again, she stared at the cell phone lying on the nightstand. *Should I read the messages?* She could delete them and no one would be the wiser, but then Travis might confront her. Of all the things she wanted to avoid in life, that was number one.

As she expected, they were all from him.

"Why are you in town?"

"If you think I will abandon my future to support you, I won't."

"Please go back to Texas."

"If you so much as give a look that betrays me to my family, I'll make you sorry."

"You can't control me, Gem. Don't try."

The distant tone and cool threats gave her chills. *What does he take me for?* She had promised she wouldn't tell a soul. And if he thought she had followed *him* here, he was crazy. It gave her some relief of mind that he wanted nothing to do with her. He sounded just as scared of her as she was of him. And that's the way she intended to keep it.

Chapter 8

The first thing Gemma noticed when she awoke the next morning was how icy her toes felt even under the quilt. It took a great deal of effort to swing her legs out of bed and find the frigid floor.

I don't own a single pair of socks. The one pair she had been wearing when she arrived had gone out with the trash. This was going to be a problem.

She shrugged on her clothes and tiptoed down the hall. There was no answer to her knock on the door. She swung the door to the girls' room open and searched a top drawer for socks. Her hand bumped the jewelry box again. Out of curiosity, she worked the latch. Gemma was surprised when it clicked and let her lift the lid. Anneliese seemed like a very private person to be leaving her possessions unlocked. But the few pieces of jewelry were not what caught her attention. Several letters, pressed neatly in their envelopes and tied with a red ribbon, sat under the main compartment. She had no doubt who they were from.

Gemma felt tingling creep into her stomach and spread all the way to her fingertips. Farris squirmed as if he competed with them for room. She knew she had discovered something private, but she also knew she had to find out how serious Travis was. She had a feeling she wouldn't discover anything by asking Anneliese. So despite her conscience's desperate pleas, she slid the top letter from the bundle and snuck to the bathroom with it.

As soon as she had locked the door, she carefully slid the letter from its envelope and unfolded it. It was dated September 22—four days ago. His flowing script was unmistakable.

My dearest Anneliese,

It was refreshing to see your face after such a long, dull semester. Lydia thinks it is heartless of me to stay away for so long, living so close. And you must think the worst of me for holding off for so long. But I assure you, if I could have broken away sooner, I would have. It's all the haughty professors who think they know everything and who don't care if you have a girl waiting back home; they load you with essays and exams. But enough about all that. I am at least glad that I am back in the state and not shut up in that stuffy Texas high school anymore. College has managed to top that experience. I would like to make my absence up to you by seeing you as often as possible while I'm here. And I'm afraid it won't be long. How about meeting me at the old tree on the hill at midnight on every odd numbered day? If the tree sounds too common and cliché, we can arrange a more romantic rendezvous at the first meeting. I look forward to seeing your smiling face again soon where there is no one to disturb us.
Yours ever,
Travis

Gemma felt very solemn after she had finished . . . as if he were poking her in the eye with every word he wrote. Yet Anneliese remained oblivious.

She knew now that her hopes to avoid him had been selfish and conceited. He had only left her one choice. She would have to confront him. If he made the right choice, then Anneliese could move on without too much injury.

Oh, if only someone had had the forethought to do the same for me!

She was startled out of her musings by a loud snap that echoed across the plains.

Was that a . . . gunshot?

It came again.

She tried to convince herself that Josiah was just getting in some target practice. But the large house stood eerily silent. Gemma hurried out of the bathroom, intending to return the letter and then investigate.

Anneliese was nose to nose with her when she opened the door. Her eyes looked bleary.

"There you are," she said. Her gaze drifted to the envelope clutched in Gemma's hand. "What do you have there?"

Gemma moistened her dry lips. "This? Just a letter." She held up the back of the envelope, praying Anneliese wouldn't recognize it.

Anneliese just shrugged.

Be natural. Be natural!

"What's all the noise?" Gemma said, turning sideways so her baby bump could fit past her.

"Fox in the henhouse or something . . ." her voice trailed off.

The moment Anneliese had shut the bathroom door, Gemma dashed to replace the letter. She would never read another one. She had all the information she needed.

When Gemma made it downstairs, the dining room table was abandoned, bowls of lukewarm oatmeal left to solidify. She stepped out the front door. Everyone from Emmaline and down huddled at the corner of the house watching Ginger aim her rifle.

Gemma arrived in time to see a flash of gray fur zip in front of the barn and under the corral fence. The chickens were in mayhem.

Ginger groaned as she missed again. A vaguely familiar young man put his hand on Ginger's arm.

"Look." Elias—that was his name—pointed toward the corral and everyone fastened their eyes on the young bull it contained.

Gemma cringed as she watched the testy new bull bring an end to the wily fox with several snorting stamps. It didn't stop with the fox's last breath, though. The animal kept braying, hitting the fence with successive kicks.

Ginger forced the gun into Elias's hands and ran hard toward the barn. Gemma noted that she was wearing pants instead of her usual denim skirt. She emerged moments later. "Elias!" She tossed one coil of rope to him and began knotting another. By now the bull had splintered the top rail.

Josiah appeared out of the cornfield and took the scene in with a single sweeping glance. He ran to Gemma and the kids and hurriedly shooed all of them inside.

"What can we do to help?" Gemma asked.

"Pray!" And he was off.

Naturally, the crowd pressed their faces against the windows to watch. *The bull will be loose and charging in moments.*

"What in the blazes is going on down there?" Mr. Martin called from the top of the stairs. He had no doubt been trying to work. Mariah ran up to meet him, gushing the story.

Gemma kept her eyes on the men. Elias dragged Ginger away and demanded she go inside as the bull broke loose. Instead, she stood against the barn and watched helplessly. Elias swung the rope as Josiah kept a wary position, the animal glaring at him and shimmering with sweat. The lasso came down around his brown head and was pulled tight. The bull continued to buck and paw and snort, tossing its head.

Realizing it had been restrained, it calmed down considerably and was nearly tied to a post, when it gave one more charge. One rope snapped, pulling Josiah to the ground. The other yanked out of Elias's hands as the bull plunged into the cornfield.

Elias was after him in a moment.

Mr. Martin's face appeared next to Gemma's. "They've got to get out of that cornfield," he muttered, tugging on his boots.

Several minutes of tense, anxious silence followed. One could hear an occasional bray or see a swish of the corn as everyone waited with bated breath.

A human cry pierced the still and all the children froze. This was no longer an adventure.

The bull appeared, sauntering out of the cornfield with a frayed rope still around its thick neck. It glared at Josiah and pawed the ground.

The front door slammed and the next moment Mariah stood in front of the bull.

"Mariah, get away!" Gemma heard Mr. Martin yell through the glass. She didn't budge. And they couldn't get to her fast enough.

The little girl stood there, hands clenched, staring the bull down. To Gemma's astonishment, its breathing calmed and challenging position relaxed. Slowly, its gaze dropped from hers. Josiah crept up and grabbed its rope as it assumed an attitude of defeat.

Mariah collapsed, her father barely catching hold of her. He scooped her up as if she weighed nothing and carried her inside.

"That was the stupidest thing you've ever done, and I don't know why it worked," Mr. Martin said. "We're getting rid of that beast tomorrow."

Mariah nodded weakly and everyone made her quite the center of attention . . . except Ginger. She had dived into the cornfield the moment the bull had exited without Elias.

Gemma ventured back to the window to get a better look.

Long moments passed. And then the duo emerged, Elias leaning heavily on Ginger. A trail of blood trickled down his side as they moved slowly across the yard.

As soon as Josiah relieved Ginger, she rushed inside to make room for him on the couch for an examination. Mariah's moment of glory had ended.

Mrs. Martin brought a first aid kit that contained everything from salve and ointment to surgical tape and bandages. Elias was a silent martyr. The diagnosis was a nasty scrape, dislocated shoulder, severe bruising, and a concussion.

"Everyone go away," Ginger said. "He needs quiet to get better." She took a seat beside him and distracted him while Mr. Martin set his shoulder.

Gemma was surprised they didn't need a doctor to do that as he cried out in pain.

"You're going to go straight to the doctor to check for internal bleeding, young man," Mrs. Martin said.

Gemma suddenly remembered where she had seen him before—he was the boy that was always talking to Ginger at church. She recalled how he had taken Ginger by the shoulders and demanded she stay out of harm's way . . .

Later that afternoon, once everyone had somewhat recovered from the shock of the morning and moved on to schoolwork, Mrs. Martin took Gemma aside.

"I know this is all new to you, and since you're going to stay, I wondered if you'd like to talk about some good options and the way everything works in more detail."

Gemma's eyes widened. "Oh, yes, please."

"Great. Let's go to my room. I promise I will do my best not to overwhelm you." Mrs. Martin led the way up the stairs and closed her bedroom door behind them. "Have you thought any more about hospital versus a center or home?"

"I really think a hospital would stress me out." She grimaced. "I . . . don't like them." *That sounded really wimpy.*

"Well, that's not good. Let me briefly outline the differences. If you had the baby here or at a center it would be much homier, lower key, but natural. At a hospital there are going to be monitors, doctors, nurses, and the option of medication. So if you're OK not knowing exactly what's happening all the time *and* birthing unmedicated, there is no reason that I can't help you do so here. I know how to turn babies, get them to breathe, stop your bleeding; so there's really nothing I couldn't handle until an ambulance could get here. It comes down to your state of mind: will a hospital with no pain or a house with pain be more conducive to what you can handle?"

Gemma nodded as she turned over the information in her mind. "Pain versus hospital. I have a very high pain tolerance and the only concern is anemia. How long is a typical birth?"

"It really depends for a first baby. First babies rarely come fast. I would say anywhere from eight to forty-eight hours."

Gemma blew out a breath. "So if it was really long, what would you do?"

"Hot bath, herbal remedies, massages, meditation, breathing, a birthing ball. If you can keep yourself relaxed and in a calm state of mind, things will move as quickly as possible. Tension and anxiety slow things down because your body reads that as a signal to keep the baby from being born until you feel safe."

"I think I could do that better here. And you said no medication is better?"

"If it's unnecessary, then yes. More than just the pain is taken away with medication. Here, let me show you the birthing ball." She rolled a large blue ball out of her closet. It came up to Gemma's knee when she stood. "Here, try it. It takes pressure off your muscles."

Gemma lowered herself onto the slick, rubbery ball, hoping she wouldn't kill herself. "Wow, this is nice."

"The other question I had is whether you intend to use formula or—"

"Oh, no!" Gemma said. "I can't afford it."

"Well, that makes it easy then. Although if it becomes the only option for some reason, I would be glad to help you get some formula. But hopefully I can help you avoid that. Let me know if you notice anything that strikes you as unusual, OK? Early labor often gives signs." Mrs. Martin ran her long fingers through her curly hair.

Gemma smiled. She had finally made some decisions for herself! "Thanks."

"My pleasure! I haven't been this involved in a birth in a long time. And I can always give you more information if you think it will help. Oh! The church would like to give you a baby shower on Sunday. Is that all right? It's rather impromptu."

"Oh, I don't know . . . I hate being the center of attention."

"It's to help you prepare. I think it would be very beneficial. They don't last very long."

Gemma sighed. "All right then. Thank you for everything. I'll keep thinking about it all."

When Travis arrived at church the next morning, Anneliese made a beeline for him. Every coherent thought fled Gemma's mind. She kicked herself for daring to hope he might be stuck back at college and wracked her brain for a plan. She discreetly intercepted Anneliese and asked if she would introduce her to . . . she picked a lady out of the crowd.

Anneliese hesitated and then swallowed her pride. "Um, sure."

Gemma had heard the woman was looking for a tutor.

"You're so far along, though," the woman said. "I don't want to wear you out."

Gemma's hopes sank. She probably wouldn't be employed until months after Farris's birth.

"But I'll give you some money at the baby shower, how's that? It's the least I can do."

"That's very considerate, thank you." It felt like charity—like she had been fishing for money—but she could use something . . . anything.

Gemma was relieved as they broke away from the conversation that her real motive hadn't been evident to Anneliese.

It must have been to Travis. After the service had ended, he brushed against her, whispering, "Meet me outside."

Her stomach knotted at his touch. She glanced at her watch. The baby shower that the church was hosting for her began in fifteen minutes. At least it would give her an excuse for getting away from him.

She mustered all of her courage and slipped out the front door. He was nowhere in sight among the cars parked on the grassy lot.

Smart boy.

She found him around the side of the building mercilessly squashing ants with his index finger as they tried to climb the wall of peeling paint. He looked boyish with the wind tousling his dark hair and his face expressionless—much like he looked when she first met him.

But then he straightened and met her eyes, the leering shadows returning.

"Gemma. What do you think you were doing back there?" His voice was cold enough to give her chills.

"I want you to leave her alone."

"I told you not to interfere."

"With what? Your next target? I won't let you ruin her life, too!"

"Is that what you think I did to you? I only ever did what you wanted."

"I didn't know what I wanted! I was naïve. So is she. If I have learned anything over the last year, it's that I will not let others make the same mistake I did." She glanced around before adding in a hushed whisper, "Especially not with the same person!"

He rolled his eyes and went back to mashing ants. There were several tense moments of silence. Travis broke it.

79

"So it's a boy?"

Gemma nodded. It was the first interest he had ever shown in their child. *Not that I want him to be interested.*

"I was impressed you—I didn't think you were going to keep him."

"I wasn't."

"What changed your mind?"

Gemma inhaled and exhaled slowly. "Travis, I really have to go. Will you please stop seeing Anneliese? At least at night?"

He crumbled another insect between his fingers as he faced her. She realized she had just let her knowledge of their trysts slip.

"No. Not unless you provide some incentive."

She made a noise of disgust. "Incentive?"

"We'll talk about it at midnight. Since you seem to know so much about me and Anneliese, you little snoop, then you'll know where to meet me." He propelled himself off the wall and brushed past her.

It's over. It's over, she kept telling herself as she made her way back inside. Now she just had to clear her mind and put on a smile for the baby shower.

"You can do it, dear," Mrs. Martin said at her elbow, as if she had read her thoughts. "It's the best opportunity you'll have for receiving gifts. It will really put you on your feet."

Gemma nodded. She hadn't thought about it like that before. *Do it for the presents!* The thought made her feel even more unworthy of the seat of honor as she was led to the front of the room by the pastor's wife.

"Most of you here know Gemma," Mrs. Freeman, the pastor's wife, began. "Since she is due to have baby Farris any day now, we want to extend our excitement for her by honoring her as a mother-to-be today."

There was light applause as Gemma took her seat in an extremely springy chair. *It's going to be a long day . . .*

While that was true, it was not hard for Gemma to enjoy all the tiny clothes she received since all the other women seemed so wrapped up in the occasion. They oohed and aahed every time she unwrapped a new item. Even though Gemma couldn't have made better selections herself, she did wonder why everything had to be in shades of blue.

Mrs. Freeman lugged the largest gift bag Gemma had ever seen to her chair and she pulled the tufts of tissue paper—blue again—out of the top. The box inside showed a picture of a car seat. She hadn't even thought of needing that!

"Thank you! It's a car seat." She decided not to try and heave the box out of the bag to show everyone.

Just when Gemma thought she could step out of the spotlight long enough to go relieve her bladder, Miss Lucinda, the older woman she had met on her first day, came hobbling up with a blanket draped over her arm. Gemma hadn't the least idea what it was until the little lady unfolded it and spread it over her lap.

The blanket!

She had crocheted different squares of browns and greens and woven a ribbon through the edge.

"You're as good as a Martin to me, sweetheart," she warbled.

Gemma willed herself not to cry as everyone ignored the fact that she was not actually a Martin and offered hearty applause.

When the shower finally ended and the women dispersed, she had received so many generous gifts, they had to pack the trunk to the ceiling and stuff a few under the girls' feet.

"My goodness!" Mrs. Martin said. "Aren't you glad you went through with it, Gemma? Now you're all fixed up!"

"Now we just have to wait for the baby." Ginger grinned as she wrestled with the handle-less door.

"Actually, I was thinking," Mrs. Martin said, as she pulled out of her parking space, "I don't know why I haven't thought of this before, but I could empty out my little sewing room there under the stairs and make it a bedroom for you, Gemma. It must wear on you having to go up and down those stairs all the time. And it will be more private. What do you think?"

Gemma hesitated. "Are you sure you want to go to the trouble?"

"It's no trouble," she stressed. "As long as you wouldn't mind being under the stairs, I think it's a brilliant idea. It would be good to have some furniture you could take with you anyway."

So it was settled; she was to have her own room on the first floor. It was then that Gemma finally had peace about her crazy plan: she would birth Farris at home.

Chapter 9

Gemma clicked the center button on the front of her phone. The screen lit up, displaying the time in dazzling white numbers.

Almost midnight. She was going to give it another ten minutes just to be safe.

Gemma turned back to her Bible, trying to dispel the sinking feeling that gripped the pit of her stomach. She had completed Josiah's variously assigned chapters about Ruth, David, Esther, Isaiah, and Daniel. Now she had moved on to Matthew. She was intrigued that many of the same names appeared in the genealogy that opened the book. Already, she was beginning to see the coherency Josiah had talked about.

Her phone buzzed, pulling her eyes away from the thin pages once again.

"You coming?" the message read.

Gemma heaved a sigh and slid out of bed—an air mattress that had been purchased that afternoon to fit the little room that the family had emptied for her. It was cozy and quaint with a slanted ceiling and fresh wooden walls. Josiah had been the main helper with the transition, but then again, he had the reward of earning his own bed back. She was glad the progress was made so fast; it would make sneaking out that much easier.

She had had the forethought to keep her clothes on, but she had removed her shoes much earlier in the day.

Josiah's boots. Maybe I can reach those over this baby.

She tiptoed out of her room, around the stairs, and into the laundry room. She was relieved that she could reach the rubbery loops and tug them on her feet. Pulling her rose cardigan tight about her, she stepped out into the inky night. It felt like the night she first stumbled upon this place—dark, empty, alone. This time there wasn't even the presence of corn to comfort her; it whispered on the other side of the house. She had brought a flashlight, but she would save that until she had gotten as far away from the house as possible.

Beginning her journey, she headed in the general direction of the only prominent tree she knew of.

Travis had said a tree in his letter, right?

Gemma had only made it a few paces before she gave in and clicked the flashlight on. She couldn't stand the wide open space where black sky met black earth. Even the stars seemed dismal this evening.

She had to stop several times for breath or to stretch a catch in her tight leg and stomach muscles. After several of the longest, most apprehensive minutes of her life, she reached the tree.

Please let this be the right one! Please.

"Are you alone?" a voice whispered.

Gemma swung around and shone her flashlight in his face.

"Will you cut that out?" He swatted it out of her hand irritably and for one dreadful moment Gemma had no idea what he was doing. She couldn't see a thing.

But he had merely stooped over to pick it up again. He did not give it back to her, but instead held it at his shoulder, pointing it down into *her* face.

Gemma's hands shook and she blamed it on the chill. She was determined to keep this meeting brief. "What do you want, Travis?"

"Three hundred dollars."

She blinked under the flashlight's beam. *That isn't what I meant . . .*

"In return for what?" She knew him—let him think he was going to get what he wanted.

"Me leaving Anneliese alone."

"Why?"

"Look, do you want me to stop or not? I need the money, Gemma."

"No. I refuse to pay your way out of debt, or whatever the case might be!"

"Then no deal." He turned to go, but she called him back.

"Travis, please. Won't you accept anything else?"

"No! Three hundred dollars, Gemma. That's merciful, so take it or leave it. I won't change a whit until it's all delivered. Then I swear I'll disappear."

"How do I know—"

"I'm going to enlist, OK, little miss busybody?"

Thank goodness he's leaving!

Gemma wracked her brain for anything else she could use. "How about I swear I will never tell anyone that you're the father?"

He took a step closer, searching her face with his steely eyes. "You wouldn't dare. Besides, you can't ruin my future since I'm just going into the Army. And even if you did tell, it reflects just as badly on you as it does on me." He grinned. "You must want to save face with the Martins; you've always worried about other people's opinions. I can always give your name to the law in Texas, don't forget. I'd hate for that baby of yours to be born in prison. Three hundred dollars, Gemma, if you're going to dictate my life."

He thrust the flashlight back into her hands and left, leaving her to process the conversation all the way back to the house.

Gemma fought spontaneous contractions as she returned from collecting eggs with Gail. Her need to find a way to earn money weighed on her mind. Especially with the upcoming medical expenses.

Just one more thing to owe the Martins for.

She caught a glimpse of Josiah and Elias at work in the cornfields on the other side of the fence. Well, Josiah was working. Elias had one arm in a sling and was more interested in talking to Ginger.

Now there's a match I wouldn't mind.

Mariah came bounding out of the stable in her overalls—the same ones she had nearly been trampled in.

"I've been playing with the new calf! He's real silly," she giggled. "He keeps butting me and sucking on my fingers and then he acts all scared like it was my idea."

"Well, he's not hurt or anything, is he?" Gemma asked. She knew nothing about animals, but the calf's behavior struck even her as strange.

"I don't think so." Mariah shrugged. "Well, he does have a cut on his nose."

"What's this?" Josiah asked, wiping muddy hands on the front of his pants.

"The new calf is very playful, but he keeps getting scared of me and the mamma."

Josiah frowned. "Huh. I'll check it out. Why don't you go get cleaned up for lunch?"

"What're we having?" Mariah asked.

"I don't know, but I'll bet it's something to do with corn."

He was right. They were having the biggest corn casserole Gemma had ever seen. And it tasted even better than it smelled. There was no beating fresh produce.

"Stay and eat with us, Elias. There's plenty." Mr. Martin clapped him on the back and sat him in a chair as he politely protested. "I insist. Ginger helped prepare it."

Elias flushed. "All right. Thank you, sir."

Gemma looked up from her watch and took all of this in with a keen eye. *I didn't know Mr. Martin was the matchmaker type.* But he had chosen Lydia for Josiah, after all.

"Gemma, I hope you're not tiring yourself out! I emptied out the closet today so Josiah could bring your clothes down. You did bring her clothes down, didn't you, Josiah?" Mrs. Martin looked pointedly at her son.

"Um . . ." He smiled innocently over his casserole. "Right after lunch, I promise. Oh, and, Dad, I think you should take a look at the calf. It's acting real strange."

Gemma's phone chimed and she dug it out of her pocket. It was a message from Travis.

"How about the first installment this afternoon?"

Her heart sank. Was he really that greedy? He must be in deep.

"Have you made a friend?" Mrs. Martin asked hopefully.

"Sort of," Gemma said, tearing her eyes away from the screen. "I'm supposed to run an errand later. Do you mind?"

Anneliese was eyeing her suspiciously, but Gemma ignored her.

"Are you sure you feel up to it? You're having contractions, aren't you?"

How in the world . . . ? "Yeah, but—"

"If you think you're up to it, a walk will probably do you some good. Go right ahead." She patted her hand.

After lunch was finished, Gemma slipped away to her room. What she really wanted was a nap, but there were important matters at hand.

"*Same place?*" she sent.

Yes, came the reply.

She removed her savings jar from under the bed and meticulously counted each coin. Just as she expected, one hundred and fifty-seven dollars and three cents. She would take him twenty dollars today, and that was all.

Surely there's a better way.

She tucked the remaining money away and pulled out the Bible again. Her heart nearly stopped when her eyes met a worn twenty dollar bill between the pages.

That wasn't there before . . . was it?

If it was, it was a great coincidence that it had been placed where she was reading. If not, Josiah was the only one who knew she was in Matthew. Maybe he'd given her an impromptu gift. It could be anyone's money since it was an extra Bible.

But who uses money for bookmarks?

She silenced her conscience and decided to take it. If it had been here for weeks, it could go unnoticed for a little while longer.

There was a curt knock on the door that scared her and the baby.

Josiah entered. "Your clothes, madam." He presented her few items with a flourish.

"Oh, thanks." She relieved him of his burden and tossed it in the bottom of the closet. "You wouldn't mind if I borrowed your rain boots, would you? They're the only shoes I can put on myself."

"Sure. Going on a walk?"

"Yes. Farris is getting fidgety and it helps relieve . . . everything."

"If you insist," he chuckled.

Moments later, Gemma embarked. She meandered on an indirect path so as not to cause too much suspicion if anyone were to notice her. The wind bit, but in a comforting sort of way that made her want to linger even more. Especially since she kept experiencing shooting pains.

She pressed the money in her hand. If Josiah had left it for her, he sure hadn't shown any sign. But it wouldn't be like him to make it known.

She leaned against the knobby oak, waiting for the arrival of her blackmailer, timing her contractions on her watch. He appeared from the edge of the tree line in moments. Gemma realized the only reason this location worked was because they were at the bottom of a slight hill; otherwise they could have surely been seen from the house.

"Did you bring the money?"

She handed him her contribution.

"That's it?"

"I wasn't expecting having to fork it over so soon," she said defensively. The ache in her lower back did not help her attitude.

He held it up to the sun. "Did you mark it?"

"What? Of course not!"

"All right, so it's just a tear. Just don't take too long, OK? This is urgent."

"I gathered that when you decided to blackmail me," she said, squinting at him.

"You agreed."

"No I didn't. And if I can find a better way out of this, I will, so don't hang all your financial hopes on me."

Travis folded his arms. "Not going to happen. You're too determined to play it safe."

"I know. And I keep telling myself I should tell the Martins everything, but ... they're too nice, too 'innocent.'"

"Tell me about it," he mumbled, running his hand through his hair. "See ya."

"Yeah." Gemma watched him walk away and noted the sag in his shoulders. It was new. And for the first time in her life she felt a twinkling of pity for the boy that had done her so much wrong.

Because no matter how deep in a hole he buried himself, that's all he really was—a lost little boy. They really weren't that different. She wondered if she should pray for him . . . or if she would even be able to.

Farris kicked and another pain came on, as if to intentionally interrupt his mother's thoughts.

That's right, stop it. You're being silly.

She braced her weary body and gave herself a little push off the old tree. The uphill climb was the hardest part. As she left, she wondered how many years of secret rendezvous that tree had witnessed.

Mariah was frantic upon her return.

"Daddy thinks the calf's sick and so he's called the vet and he's going to come and look at him and if he can't figure out what's wrong I don't know what we'll do!"

"Really?" Gemma's brain was too exhausted to keep up. She felt like she was running on low battery.

Josiah emerged from the stable. "There's definitely something wrong. It won't nurse at all. It seems to be choking, but I've searched its throat multiple times and there's nothing there. He keeps pawing the ground and butting the corner of the stall. I don't know what else we can do."

She noted ruefully that Josiah was barefoot. *Because I'm wearing his boots.*

Gemma had just brought them out to him when the veterinarian arrived. She watched as he gave an examination by thoroughly running his hands all over the resistant animal and checking its vitals with steel instruments. It proved a good distraction from her growing discomfort.

"Try bottle feeding it," he said. "Call me if he gets worse. I'll do some tests back at the office and let you know if I find anything out."

"You don't think it could be mad cow disease, do you?" Josiah asked.

"It's unlikely it would manifest this early, but there's a theory that it can be passed from cow to calf. Keep an eye on the mother for any strange behavior. I'm guessing that scratch on the calf's nose has gotten something strange into the bloodstream." He tapped the sample he had taken and bid them goodbye.

Gemma thought Josiah looked exceptionally drawn when he finally came inside and plopped on the couch.

She let a contraction pass before she drew attention to herself. "Is it that bad?" she asked.

He peered at her out from under the crook of his arm and heaved a sigh. "We'll just have to wait and see."

"Would losing the calf be that great of a loss?"

"Not really. I mean we will still get the milk from the cow. It's just . . . I don't do well with death."

"Of course, I understand."

"I'm afraid you don't." He sat up and patted the space next to him.

Gemma tried to convince her body to relax onto the furniture as she waited for him to explain.

"I've always had this thing about death. I don't know why, but it paralyzes me. You wouldn't think it would be that big a deal because I understand that it's just part of life, but it completely unnerves me. And to think that if I had just done something different I could have prevented it . . . it makes me feel like a criminal." He rested his head in his hands.

You—a criminal? Gemma shifted uncomfortably. "Josiah, it's not your fault."

"I know that. But I still feel like I could have done more when something dies—even if it is just a calf. Pretty stupid fear for a farmer, huh?"

"It's not stupid at all," she reassured him, massaging the side of her stomach. "It just shows what a caring person you are."

"Hey, are you OK?" he asked, noticing how ill at ease she looked.

"Yeah." She glanced at her phone. "Just a contraction. But they *are* picking up."

"Mom says they'll probably subside unless they get to be every five to eight minutes. At least it won't be too much longer and you'll be on the other side of this."

"Oh. Well, they're coming every four minutes, so . . . ."

His eyes widened. "Um, just . . . stay there. I'll go get Mom." He dashed outside and could be heard yelling across the barnyard, "Hey, Gemma's in labor!"

Her mounting nerves outweighed her momentary embarrassment.

Mrs. Martin was inside in a flash and set the older girls to work. "Why don't you slip into something more comfortable, dear, and we'll make sure this isn't a false alarm."

"All right," Gemma said. She still couldn't believe this was happening, even as another shooting pain came on.

Mrs. Martin helped her into a nightgown. "Seems like the contractions are coming pretty fast."

Gemma glanced at her watch and fought for a deep breath. "Every three minutes now."

Mrs. Martin pulled on gloves and examined her; Gemma tried not to think about it. "Good heavens! You're dilated to a four. Don't look so scared, that's a good thing. Are you sure you still want to have him right here at the house, now that you're in the middle of it? It's not too late to go to the hospital."

"No! No, I want to stay right here," Gemma gasped. She was finding it very difficult to get proper breaths in.

"Good girl. That's right, take deep breaths. Just think about the baby. He's coming to meet you!"

Farris Ebworthy, October 2. She exhaled a long breath. *I can do this.*

Chapter 10

"Just keep breathing, Gemma," Mrs. Martin said. "You're doing beautifully."

"How much longer is this going to take?" Gemma moaned.

"He might be here before supper!"

Gemma glanced at the clock next to her air mattress. *That's still two whole hours away!*

"Everything's ready for him, sweetie, so just try and relax. This is the most tedious part; you just have to push through it. Are you up for that?"

Gemma nodded and forced herself to loosen up and breathe. Though she was glad she had chosen to stay, the thought of some medical relief made a hospital much more enticing at this stage.

Ginger slipped in with some towels. "Here, Mom. Josiah wants to know if there's anything he can do. His pacing is about to drive Anneliese over the edge."

"Why don't you send him to the store for some Epsom salts. Do you want anything, Gemma?"

"Some crackers—would be fantastic," she mumbled from behind her hands.

Mrs. Martin rolled her eyes as the door closed again. "Boys."

Gemma let out a shaky laugh as she wiped sweaty strands of hair away from her face.

To calm her and get her mind off the pain, Mrs. Martin massaged her lower back and had her sit on the birthing ball. When Gemma stopped looking at it dubiously and consented to give it a try, she found it very conducive to relieving her strained muscles.

"Would you read me some of the Bible—please?" she asked as it neared five. She began to feel so exhausted, she dozed between the intense contractions. If she could just remember to keep breathing . . .

"Of course." Mrs. Martin seemed delighted to have such a request. "Where would you like me to read from?"

"Can you read . . . Matthew 1."

Mrs. Martin smiled and read the chapter in her soothing voice. Gemma did not envy poor Mary who had to birth her Son in a stable. She could relate; Mary unmarried when she got pregnant, accused of being unfaithful, and unwanted by anyone who could give her shelter. The only person Mary had to support her as she gave birth to God's Son was her husband, and an angel had to reassure him. *I have a whole family.*

As the chapter ended, Gemma's breathing grew much more labored and she tensed more often. The pressure and contractions felt almost surreal.

"My goodness! I think we'd better get you into bed, dear. This is the home stretch!"

Please, God, give me courage and keep my son safe. Just like You did Yours.

Josiah was beside himself. It had been over three years since Gail had been born and he had almost forgotten how traumatizing it was. Every horrid situation possible raced through his mind as he drove the truck into the parking lot of the convenience store. He knew it was silly to fantasize about worst-case scenarios, but what if something *did* go wrong? That baby meant more to Gemma than anything. He couldn't watch her go through something like that.

He walked into the store and quickly grabbed the necessary items.

"Find everything?" the old man at the register asked. He had known Josiah his whole life.

"Yes, sir." Josiah curled and uncurled his fists as he watched the items ring up.

"You look a mite unsettled, son. Anything the matter?"

"No, sir." He hesitated. *Should I tell him?* "Gemma's having her baby."

"Oh." The old man chuckled knowingly. "Well, you'd best get on back. Little tyke'll be here before ya know it."

Josiah stuffed his wallet in his back pocket. "Thank you, sir."

He dashed back to the truck and forced himself not to speed down the road while it was still paved. The driveway crawled for an eternity as he was forced to inch along. Within sight of the tree meant halfway.

The sun was just beginning to set as he pulled in front of the house. All of the children from Emmaline, the thirteen-year-old, and down had been made to stay outside until they were given the word that the baby had been born. As Mrs. Martin had put it, she didn't want Gemma to feel that she was giving birth in Grand Central Station.

Josiah reassured them and slipped inside as they returned to their game of freeze tag. A hushed silence had fallen over the house which felt queer; silence was always out of place in the Martin household. Only the sound of a few clanging pots could be heard in the kitchen where the girls started on dinner.

"I'm back," Josiah whispered, handing the groceries to Ginger. "Does Gemma want the crackers now?"

"Don't you dare go in there!" Anneliese cried, brandishing a wooden spoon. "She's been making awful noises for the last half hour now. Ginge just asked about a bath, but Gemma doesn't want to move. When Mom gives the all clear, we can ask about the crackers."

"*I* wasn't going to take them," he grumbled, kicking the corner of the cabinet with the toe of his shoe.

A scuffling sound came from the bedroom and all heads swiveled to look at it with bated breath. Moments later, the tiny, shrieking cry of a newborn filled the house. They unanimously released breaths and exchanged smiles. It was over. Gemma had done it.

Ten minutes later, Mrs. Martin popped her head out of the door. "He's here." She removed her gloves and wiped her brow. It took several more minutes to get everything squared away and then the children were allowed a peek.

Gemma smiled on as everyone oohed and ahhed over the newcomer. He was remarkably sedate and peered curiously at every face with wide eyes that slowly blinked.

"Why's he so red?" Lisabeth whispered, as she touched his tiny arm. "And he's soft!"

"Because it's hard work getting born!" Mrs. Martin said, with an encouraging smile at Gemma, who looked as if her happiness was the only thing keeping her from falling asleep.

Mariah grinned from ear to ear and could hardly stand still. "He's so cute and tiny! Can I hold him, Mamma?"

"Not tonight. Go have supper; you can say goodnight later." The crowd thinned, leaving Josiah, Anneliese, and Ginger.

"Oh, Gemma, I'm so happy for you," Ginger beamed, gently stroking the tiny head. "He's perfect."

Anneliese chuckled. "He's so alert." She rubbed the tightly curled fingers. "And he looks just like you."

Gemma sustained a weary smile on her face, her tear-filled eyes never leaving the face of her baby. "What do you think, Josiah?" she asked. "Is he up to muster?"

Josiah smiled. "He's beautiful."

Mariah was by far the child most eager to hold baby Farris.

"OK, he should be good now," Gemma said, patting his back. "Why don't you get in bed with me?"

As soon as Mariah had positioned herself on the air mattress and Gemma was about to hand him over, Farris filled his diaper to overflowing.

"Oh no! Quick, grab me a new diaper and wipes."

Mariah scrambled to do as she was told, giggling all the while. "I'm so glad he did that while you were still holding him," she said.

Gemma wiped the disgusted look off her face and tried to empty her lap. "I think I caught it all, so we shouldn't have to wash the sheets. Can you carefully lay Farris at the end of the bed on his diaper mat? I'll change him as soon as *I've* changed."

Mariah picked Farris up, managing not to spread the mess, and kept him secure on the end of the bed. She chuckled. "He must feel better, because he's falling asleep."

Gemma smiled as she stood up while trying to contain the mess in the folds of her nightgown. "I'm just gonna change with you in here, if that's OK. I've got more pajamas around here somewhere."

"Sure, I won't look."

Gemma unbuttoned the nightgown and managed to contain the mess better than she hoped. She'd have to have someone wipe up the floor, but at least she hadn't gotten it in her hair or on the bed yet.

She tugged on a pair of flowy pants, pulled a soft top over her head, and clipped her hair up. "OK, let's clean you up, mister. Mariah, why don't you go get someone to help me and have someone help you run a bath for Farris? He's too messy to just mop up."

Mariah clapped her hands as Gemma took over. "His first bath!" She darted out of the room to fetch the baby tub.

Ginger came to help Gemma undress Farris and put him in a clean diaper. It shocked Gemma how much there was to learn about tending to a new baby.

Mariah peeked her head around the door. "Mama says we can do it in our sink. She's getting it ready."

"OK." Gemma picked up the baby, who had not been fond of the many wipes Ginger had used, and added his onesie to the pile of stained clothes.

Ginger found a hooded towel and set of rags that someone had given her at the shower and took them with her to the kitchen.

Once the water had reached the right temperature and Farris had been laid in the reclining tub, he quieted and stared at all the faces around him with curiosity.

"It appears he likes baths," Mrs. Martin said, rubbing the damp rag over his arms and face.

"That's a relief," Gemma said, resituating herself on her barstool. She was so tired, she could hardly keep her eyes open to beam at her child's first bath. "At this rate, he might need a lot of them."

After he had been dried off, redressed, and tucked back in bed with Gemma, his eyelids began to droop.

"Can I hold him now?" Mariah said.

Gemma didn't really want to share him, especially since he was happy. It made her a little apprehensive and edgy, sharing him with a nine-year-old, but Mariah had been so patient. When it came down to it, she would be the only one who could satisfy Farris's need for peace and nurturing. She nodded and patted the mattress. Mariah climbed in bed with her and placed one arm behind his head and used the other to hold his hand.

"He's so cute," she whispered.

As Farris grew and settled into his way of life, Gemma relaxed even more. She could hand the baby off for a few minutes if it meant she could get in a nap or a hot bath.

"How in the world did you do it?" Josiah asked one breezy day as he cradled the wakeful baby in his arms.

Gemma chuckled. "Do you really want to know?"

He flushed. "No, I mean everything; finishing school, giving up college, leaving home, working a job. What made you keep going?"

"The thought of the baby. My mother was in a similar situation with me—she got pregnant and the father left. She was horrified, and refused to acknowledge the truth until it was too late to abort me. She tried to . . . kill herself twice before I was born and my uncle— her brother—stopped her." She chewed her lip. "I think he probably regretted that once I was born, because my mom dumped me on Uncle Wilfred and went to live her life without the burden of a child. But even though I never knew my mother, she taught me something." Gemma fiddled with the button on the chair's pillow. "Josiah, I never told you this, but I almost aborted Farris. That's what . . . the father wanted. Then I remembered my mom and she's the one who stopped me from doing it. I remembered . . . what she had done to me and how it made me feel, and I determined never to do anything to my child that would make him hate me like I hated my mom." She looked up at him and smiled. "I was going to do better than she did. That's why. I want to break the single mom stereotype . . . somehow."

"But you have."

Gemma gave him a skeptical look.

"I'm serious. You're amazing, Gemma. You have sacrificed so much to help your baby."

"Well, if I had been truly selfless, I wouldn't have had a baby in the first place," she said quietly.

"Everyone makes mistakes. You have to forgive *yourself* if you're ever going to move on."

"I'll get over everything that has happened to me, but . . ." She shrugged a shoulder. "I can't forgive what I did to others."

Josiah nodded. "Gemma . . . don't let it defeat you. Guilt can do that."

Farris whimpered. His large eyes, already beginning to turn brown, flew open and he began to suck on his fist furiously.

"Is it silly that I worry about him more now that he's born?"

"I think that's normal for first-time mothers."

"But it's more than that. While I was pregnant with him, he was safe and no one could get to him. Now that he's here, he's accessible and vulnerable. Now he can be hurt."

"No one's going to hurt him, Gemma. I won't let them."

She could see the questions behind his steady gaze, but she couldn't tell him yet. How could she ever tell him anything without betraying who the father was? She hated keeping her friends in the dark!

"I'll miss you."

Josiah's head swiveled to her. "You're leaving?"

"Well, not yet. Your brother David found us a reasonable first-floor apartment in Wichita with lots of job and childcare opportunities, so we should probably get settled before Christmas. It's only two hours away." She gave him a knowing look. "Don't worry, we'll still be here for your festival." That was a special point of pride with Josiah.

Gemma stood from her chair and carefully rubbed her baby's velvety head.

"It's the strangest thing. Some days I could swear that I just dreamed all of this, but here he is."

"Is it a good dream or a bad dream?"

"Oh, it starts off wonderful, but goes very dark in the middle."

"And the end?"

She laughed. "Even better, I think."

"Good. I hope I play a part in that happy ending."

A thought flitted through her head as she caught his gaze that she quickly squelched. She cleared her throat. "You already have."

It was late and Farris didn't understand his mother's need to sleep. Gemma had already tried everything she could think of to make him settle down: rocking, nursing, singing, walking, bouncing, patting. She had gone back to pacing outside of her room, but none of it worked. He simply would not unwind. Thankfully, he was a fairly quiet baby for being so wakeful. Rarely did he make any cries unless he was truly desperate for attention.

I wonder what Jesus was like as a baby.

She had been reading further in Matthew when Farris had decided to give her grief. Gemma had been rather disappointed that any details on the infancy of this special child were skipped entirely. She wanted to know if the Son of God cried and kept His mother up at night, or if He ever got sick or scared.

"Not wanting to sleep, huh?"

Gemma turned to see Mr. Martin, glass of milk in hand.

"Oh, I'm sorry, did we wake you?"

"No, I was up. I rarely sleep well myself."

In the pause that followed, Gemma thought how much less scary he appeared in flannel pajamas than he did in his suit and tie.

"How's he doing?" he asked.

"Farris? You tell me. You have more experience."

Mr. Martin set down his glass and reached for the baby. Gemma gratefully handed him over. Though he still had the fragile, fuzzy baby feel, even his little weight could tire arms before long.

"The doctor said he has gained a few ounces since birth, so that's good," she said, pulling her sweater closer about her.

"Yes. I hear David found you a little place to stay. A steal, but requires a monthly payment nonetheless. There's a client of mine in the area who could use a secretary. Filing papers, answering the phone, and such. Interested?"

Gemma's face lit up. "That would be perfect! But what should I do with Farris? I hate to send him somewhere every day, but I have to work."

"Bring him with you. They only need you for a few hours each day. You could feed and nap him all in your office. He's a pretty content little fellow most of the time."

"Would they really let me?" she asked breathlessly. It seemed too good to be true.

"Unless they've changed their mind since this afternoon, they should."

"I don't know what to say. It's perfect!"

"They'll pay you ten an hour to start, so just fit in what you can. They said anything'll be better than what they have now."

"How wonderful! Thank you. Not just for this, but for letting me stay and everything. I know I'm not what you expected."

"No, you're not. I am counting on more surprises."

Gemma smiled and Mr. Martin passed the baby back with an experienced hand.

"I don't think you have anything to worry about; the sleep will come. Parents often tire before their children. He's in good hands."

Gemma patted Farris's back rhythmically and felt relief soothe her frayed nerves. *Finally a chance to earn my keep!*

Mr. Martin retrieved his glass of milk and held it up to her like a toast before disappearing up the stairs.

Chapter 11

Farris's wakeful habits the night before must have caught up with him, because when Gemma rolled over at half past eight, he was still asleep from his early morning feeding.

Thank goodness!

Her body decided to play tricks on her and instead of letting her get some much needed rest, she resorted to pulling out her Bible and journal. Not a thing had been recorded since the morning before Farris was born, nearly a month ago. Gemma was sure she would want to make an entry after the Octoberfest, as it had been named, if it turned out as grand as Josiah and Mariah were making it out to be. So she had better get up to date before then.

Gemma paged through the Bible to Psalm 121 when she suddenly remembered the money she had found in the Bible and taken. A feeling of extreme guilt settled over her like an electric blanket. She hadn't earned a cent since she had taken that money, but she would have to make up for it immediately to ease her conscience.

Evidently, no one was in a great hurry to get it back, or it would have been noticed missing by now.

She recalled that one of the Ten Commandments addressed stealing and felt an extra pang.

To make up for it, she slid her jar out from under the bed and counted out twenty dollars. But what could she do? She couldn't very well pile petty cash between the pages of the Bible.

Farris began to squirm and squawk just as a soft knock came at the door. Gemma shoved the money in her pocket and placed the jar back under the bed. A moment later, Mrs. Martin popped her head in and saved Gemma the trouble of rescuing the baby from his pitiful, gasping cries.

"My goodness, he has strong lungs!"

"Yep, he sure knows how to use them, doesn't he? Overall, though, he's a pretty content baby, wouldn't you say?" Gemma took him in her arms and stroked his cheek, taking a seat back on the bed. Already he was beginning to quiet.

"Yes, he seems to have a very sweet temperament. He reminds me of Josiah as a baby. He was one of my easier ones."

He reminds me of Josiah now. She blinked, grateful she hadn't spoken it aloud. *What a stupid thing to think.*

"How are you feeling, Gemma? Starting to get your strength back a little bit?"

"I think so. I still get tired quickly, but I guess that's normal."

"Yes, and your anemia makes that worse. It may not seem like it now, but overall everything went pretty smoothly for you. I know that your circumstances have been rough, but rare is the young woman who can go thirty-five weeks without seeing a doctor and then deliver a healthy baby boy in six hours' time in someone else's home. Thank you for trusting my judgment on all of that. I know it's not as mainstream."

Gemma resituated Farris on her chest, who was evidently more interested in going back to sleep than nursing. "No problem. I am about as ignorant as they come and you obviously have experience on your side. But it probably helped that I didn't leave myself enough time to overthink it."

Mrs. Martin laughed. "True. You were very brave and did exactly what you were supposed to. I promise your little guy is better off for it. You'll need a postpartum visit to the doctor, though. Is next week OK?"

"Actually, is sooner possible? I just want to make sure we're both good to go."

"All right. I'll make sure Stuart—Mr. Martin—is home so we can take the van. I think breakfast is about ready when you are." She looked from Farris's peaceful face to Gemma's exhausted one. "Try and enjoy the cuddles while you can. They won't last as long as you think."

Gemma knew she was right and decided breakfast could wait. She strained to reach her phone balancing on the far edge of the nightstand. Her fingers could just barely graze the phone's side. She couldn't remember checking it recently and she realized she probably had some frantic messages from Travis. Wiggling her fingers, she inched it toward her and illuminated the screen.

One new message—not as bad as she expected.

Gemma reluctantly opened the message and was glad to see that it was dated only a few days ago.

"Anneliese told me you had the baby, so I've let you go awhile. I'll expect the next payment at the festival."

How considerate, she thought. Yet he would still demand money from a person he had once promised to provide for.

She stared at the screen for a moment, trying to decide how to reply.

A quiet knock came at the door and Gemma tossed her phone aside. Anneliese slipped in, presenting a bowl of oatmeal with blueberries on top.

"Mom thought you might want to eat in here."

She set the bowl on the table and took a seat in the rocking chair.

"What, no corn casserole?" Gemma teased.

"No, that's for lunch." Anneliese's brow wore a crease and her eyes looked distant.

"Something on your mind?" Gemma asked, popping a blueberry into her mouth.

"Me? No, just didn't sleep well." She rested her chin on the palm of her hand.

She met him again. Gemma guessed Travis wasn't going to keep his promise until she paid him in full . . . *if* she could.

Gemma tried to think of a gentle way to broach the subject, but decided it was not her place. She was trying to deal with Travis and that was enough for now. Still, she wanted to find some way to reach out to the poor girl before she got in over her head.

"This isn't about a boy, is it?"

Anneliese's pure blue eyes flicked to hers suspiciously, but she offered a smile. "What makes you say that?"

"Oh, nothing. I'm just guessing that's about how I looked when I first met—my last boyfriend."

She sighed. "I'm only seventeen, but I thought Dad might approve since Ginger's only sixteen and has Elias. But I don't think I'm going to tell him."

Gemma didn't want to disagree, but she was glad the conversation had taken a friendly tone. "I think it's normal to have infatuations, and if this is your first then you've done much better than I did. Won't you tell me who he is?"

Anneliese shook her head. "I really don't want anyone else to know about it. They wouldn't understand."

"Fine, but a word of caution. When you don't share your love life with someone, it's more likely that you'll become so focused on the person that you can't see his flaws. Stay smart. You've got plenty of time to figure it all out."

"I think I'm old enough to know what I want."

"You are. Just think about what you're getting into before you act."

She stood and plopped the throw pillow in the chair. "Look, it's not like *I'm* gonna get pregnant or anything because I'm seeing someone, so relax. It's really none of your business, anyway." She left in a huff, but remembered to close the door quietly.

That went well.

Gemma was delighted to learn that Dr. Hastening had time to see her later that afternoon. She let Ginger hold Farris while she got dressed and applied makeup for the first time since his birth. It was astounding to be able to lean over the bathroom counter again when applying her mascara!

"See, your mommy doesn't always have to look so scary," Gemma cooed, returning to the living room, picking Farris up, and playfully kissing his chubby neck.

He chortled and grabbed a fistful of her hair to stick into his mouth.

"Here, this should make the day easier." Mrs. Martin came down the stairs with an oddly shaped piece of fabric with numerous straps dangling from it.

Gemma lowered her baby down into a carrying position and removed her hair from his grasp. "What is it?"

"It's a baby carrier. You fasten it around you like this." She snapped a cord around Gemma's waist. "And then this part comes up here. That way he can snuggle against you, but your arms are free."

"Oh yeah, I think I've seen one of these. I'll definitely try it when we get there."

"Good. And you can keep it. It's only for small babies and I'll be surprised if I have any more of those." She gave a sad sort of smile. "Josiah was trying to figure out your infant car seat. Once that's accomplished, I think we'll be ready to go."

As they stepped outside, Gemma realized the weather had turned balmy again. *It's going to be perfect for the Octoberfest in a few days.*

Josiah was just securing the last strap as they walked up. "That was more confusing than trying to fix a tractor!" He pointed at the offender with a look of disgust. "And I suppose I'll have to be the one to move it around from now on since I'm the only one who's done it."

"Thanks," Gemma said.

His mother patted his arm with little sympathy. "There are worse things in life, son."

Josiah harrumphed and shut the car door after Gemma.

"I'm pretty sure I've never seen Josiah get worked up in the whole time I've been here," Gemma said.

"And he doesn't often," Mrs. Martin said. "But when he does it's over the strangest things. He'll be back to normal like nothing ever happened when we get back. Probably won't even complain next time he has to mess with it."

"Hm." She finished strapping Farris into the car seat, which seemed to swallow him. He wriggled and grunted and fussed the whole way there in protest of this new experience, removing his hat and socks in the process. No amount of finger holding or pacifier sucking would satisfy him.

"Poor little guy," Mrs. Martin said, lifting him out of the car. "Look at those crocodile tears. But don't worry, he may grow into a car baby yet, especially if you're going to be taking him to work each morning."

"I hope so." Gemma had visions of a screaming child all the way to Wichita and as a prelude to every workday. *Surely they won't let me take him to the office if he always comes in screaming.*

Mrs. Martin fastened him into the baby carrier so he could settle down.

They entered the waiting room and Gemma undertook the battle of trying to get his socks back on his kicking feet.

Nearly a half hour later, a nurse came from the hall and called, "Gemma and Farris."

Mrs. Martin nodded encouragement; they had decided on the way over that it would be better for Gemma to do this on her own and relay the results.

Thankfully, they presented no new concerns.

"Everything looks about normal to me, except that you're still a little anemic," Dr. Hastening said. "I'm going to prescribe an iron supplement so your levels can regulate a little bit and you won't be any more tired than you have to be. However, your heart murmur has mostly subsided, so nothing to worry about there."

"And the baby's—"

"Perfectly healthy. All of his vitals look good so I see nothing to worry about. Your biggest upcoming decision will be whether to give him vaccinations or not, but I leave that up to you."

I hadn't even thought about that . . .

"That brings us to our last order of business." He set his clipboard down and settled himself on his stool. "Since you had Farris at home, there was no birth certificate issued. But he has to have one, so I can get that process started for you if you want."

But I can't list the father! "Sure. Um . . . does the father have to be on there?"

He smiled and scratched his gray stubble. "Totally up to you, assuming you're unmarried."

She nodded.

"Well then, if you know who the father is, he can do some paperwork claiming posterity. Or you can peg someone and we'll do a DNA test to be sure. If you don't want child support, shared custody, or the father's last name, then you can skip it altogether. Joy can be the attendant for verification and you should be set to go."

Thank God! No child support . . . Now that she considered it, she would be just as well without. She was perfectly capable of supporting her own child and in no way wanted any permanent ties to Travis; she was certain the feeling was mutual there. "Thank you so much." She stood to go and shook the doctor's hand.

"Sure thing. Here's your prescription," he handed her a piece of paper with illegible writing, "and let me know if you need anything else."

Gemma breathed a sigh of relief as she retraced her steps down the hall. Everything was turning out exceptionally well!

Mrs. Martin laid down her knitting magazine. "Anything to worry about?"

"Nope. He gave me a prescription for iron, but otherwise everything looks good. And he said he'd request a birth certificate for us."

"Wonderful! I just have one stop I want to make, but you can stay in the car if you'd like," Mrs. Martin said as they stepped out into the glaring sun.

Gemma decided that was a good idea as they pulled up in front of the resale shop where she had come not long after arriving at the Martins'. But since Farris still objected to being restrained, she unstrapped and fed him. It was a little difficult to manage in the back seat of a car with lots of distracting noises and only the side of the car seat to offer support for his little head, but it returned him to his cheery self. He was smiling and laughing at his mommy's silly faces when Mrs. Martin returned.

"I'm glad I finally got that errand out of the way. We had lots of outgrown clothes that no one else wanted as hand-me-downs that I needed to drop off. Oh, and I found these." She handed back a paper bag. "I thought they might fit you."

Gemma drew out a pair of cowboy boots. "How pretty! They're in really good condition, too." Her finger traced the embroidered flowers.

"I thought you could use another pair of shoes, but if you don't like them or they don't fit, just give 'em to one of the girls."

"No, I like them a lot. Thank you!"

Gemma put them away and placed Farris, who was beginning to blink very slowly, back in his seat.

"Don't mention it. You deserve a little something. Wait till you show Ginger!"

Mrs. Martin was right. The moment Gemma drew them out of the bag in the privacy of her bedroom, Ginger gasped.

"How cute! Try them on, Gemma."

Gemma laid the nodding baby in his bed and complied. "They fit!"

"You have to wear them for the Octoberfest. They'll go perfectly with—oh, I haven't shown you yet!"

Ginger flew up the stairs and returned with the dress they had both admired on their shopping trip.

"Ginger, you didn't!"

She worked hard to quiet her merry laugh. "Yes, I did. Don't you love it? You'll look so beautiful this weekend!" She hung it for her in the teeny closet that sat under the stairs and they slipped out so Farris could sleep without interruption.

"You really shouldn't have," Gemma said, even though she was quite glad she had.

"Nonsense. I would have bought it for myself if I'd thought it'd fit," Ginger laughed.

"What's this?" Mr. Martin asked, folding his newspaper.

"I bought her a dress and Mom bought her boots for the Octoberfest. You'll be here, won't you, Dad?"

He smiled. "Yes, actually." He turned to his wife. "The apartment complex I have been designing plans for is now underway. Since my plans have passed muster, I will be free to work from home more often."

"That's wonderful, Stuart. Have they paid you yet?"

"Yes. But perhaps if you're that worried about funds, you shouldn't spend quite so freely."

Gemma flushed and Mrs. Martin kept her eyes on her mending.

"She's entitled to some kindness, dear."

"I will reimburse you for the furniture I will be taking with me, all the birth-related expenses, and anything else you specify as soon as I have steadier income."

"Very well," he said. "I understand that you were taken in out of kindness, but that is no reason to take money that isn't yours." He gave her a knowing look as he rubbed his wrist.

A sick feeling settled in the pit of her stomach. *It was his money in the Bible . . . and he knows I took it. No wonder he was so nice last night!* She looked into his hard golden eyes with resolve. She would tell all of the story that she could, but there were some things even he couldn't know. Not if she was going to preserve Travis's fragile trust and the Martins' good opinion.

Mrs. Martin's mending went limp in her lap. She looked dumbfounded from her husband, to Gemma, and back again. "Children, go outside, please. Take Gail with you and stay away from the bull."

Ginger shook her head. "Dad, what are you talking about?"

Anneliese took a seat and looked at Gemma carefully. "I don't think she would do that, Dad. Are you sure?"

"Quite."

Mrs. Martin finished shooing the children outside and asked Emmaline to supervise. She took her seat again, disbelief clouding her eyes.

Josiah's incredulous voice cut through the silence. "You framed her. Didn't you?"

All heads swiveled to find him filling the entrance to the stairs.

Wait, how does he know?

"That's quite the accusation, son," his father said.

"How else would you know?" He launched himself off the bottom step and took his stand next to Gemma. "You don't keep cash around the house and Gemma wouldn't go looking, so you must have planted it. Planted it and waited for it to go missing. You are the only one who has not been able to accept that she might actually be a good person, even after everything you've put her through!"

"Josiah," Gemma said, her voice pleading.

His olive eyes, vibrant with anger, flicked to her face and his tense muscles relaxed some.

Mr. Martin cleared his throat. "My point still stands. Do you deny taking it, Gemma?"

"No, sir. But I am prepared to reimburse you."

He raised his eyebrows. "Promises are all very well, but—"

She removed the money from her pocket that she had so wisely thought to transfer when she got dressed and piled it on the coffee table. A wad of bills and a heap of quarters splayed out on its ashen surface. One coin slid off the edge and tried to regain its balance on the tile before coming to rest against Mr. Martin's shoe.

"That's my down payment. You *can* expect the rest."

Mr. Martin bent over and retrieved the stray coin, examining it as if he doubted its validity. "May I ask what was so urgent that it compelled you to steal?"

She bit the inside of her cheek. "I'm not at liberty to say."

He was clearly not amused. Everyone else looked just as curious, although in a less sinister way.

"I was—repaying a debt." She headed off any impending questions by sharing everything she was free to say. "I was on a much stricter timetable to pay this person than I am to pay you. And I didn't want to ask for the money because I have promised not to talk about it and you've already done so much—" Emotion choked her voice and she fought to hold back her feelings. "I took the money because I was desperate and I'm sorry. It was really quite a Godsend, because, as you know, I have virtually no money." A sob caught in her throat and she widened her eyes to keep the tears from spilling over. "And the person expects—more, so . . . thanks for providing the first installment." She forced a shaky smile and swiped at her nose.

Mr. Martin gave a thoughtful look toward her payment. He leaned forward and collected it in his hand, piece by piece. Then he stood and faced her, holding out his cupped hands. "Make this the second installment." He let it trickle back into her hands.

"Thank you," she said over the catch in her throat.

He nodded and wearily walked up the stairs, all eyes staring blankly after him, trying to take in what they had just witnessed.

Chapter 12

It was the perfect weather for an evening spent out of doors in the company of friends. The air was cool and crisp with a slight breeze rustling the few seven-foot stalks that still stood proud and erect in the fading October sun.

The Martin women had spent the last several days in the kitchen preparing all sorts of delectable goodies. The other women would contribute, too, of course, but the host family was expected to provide the main meal. Ginger's pumpkin chiffon pies were almost as famous as Mrs. Long's nut loaves.

At ten to five people had already begun to arrive. Gemma was rather surprised when they drove cars instead of horse-drawn wagons; it would have suited the occasion. Thankfully, she had just gotten Farris to sleep in the master bedroom, so she was free to enjoy the evening for a few hours and he could rest further from the busy happenings.

The men had lined up several rectangular card tables the church had provided and were becoming more and more irritated as they tried to restrain red-checked tablecloths. From the window, she could see that Ginger had brought things out to help anchor them.

She wondered if the Jeffersons would come tonight. Elias seemed more and more sweet on Ginger every time they were thrown together. Gemma still hadn't gotten the incident with the bull out of her mind, but maybe she was just being suspicious about Ginger and Elias. With any luck, tonight would tell.

Gemma tore herself away to get dressed so she could go down and be helpful. There was no question about what she would wear—the outfit that had been so graciously given just for this occasion. She couldn't resist its subtle charm with its soft fawn hue, accented by off-white buds resembling heads of wheat. They gradually climbed the skirt until the waistband where they drastically cut off, only to peek again on the capped sleeves. She had been viewing the dress as an incentive to lose her post-baby figure. Sure enough, it accented her more attractive and intentional curves nicely. It helped that certain areas had filled out a bit, too. She threw on her old rose sweater to accent her minimal makeup and keep her warm should the evening prove to be chilly.

Gemma clomped down the stairs and made her way through the bustling kitchen.

"Don't you look a picture," Mrs. Martin said, handing her a plate of chicken accompanied with her usual smile.

Gemma smiled back and hurried to help those who were arriving find a spot for their contributions on the quickly filling tables.

As Anneliese came out, Gemma whispered, "Do you think Farris will be all right in the bedroom?"

"I'm sure he'll be fine," she said, looking Gemma over with envy. Even after the baby, Gemma had more of a figure than her. "People will be going in and out all night. I'm sure someone will tell you if they hear him."

Gemma nodded, reassured. There was nothing to stop her from checking on him periodically, anyway. She could do this. Being a mother did not mean she couldn't enjoy herself.

Anneliese walked off and Ginger came bounding up. Elias was not far behind. "Everyone's talking about how pretty you look," she said.

Gemma blushed and fumbled for a response. *Who qualifies as "everyone"?* She made some feeble excuse about needing to secure a seat and headed toward the red barn.

She noticed Mr. Martin at the door. His disapproving look was absent from his face and instead she met with a smile that she took to be an apology. *Maybe he doesn't recognize me.*

"You look lovely. I believe Josiah saved you a seat," Mr. Martin said, gesturing inside.

She was so startled by the flat compliment that she hardly managed a smile. Mind spinning, she moved inside. The barn's wide doors had been thrown open and rectangular hay bales strategically placed so as to look authentic and provide seating.

She skirted her way around the massive pile of corn in the center of the room, large enough to serve as a bonfire.

Josiah caught her eye and waved. She felt silly moving toward him, since it appeared the men and women would sit on opposite sides, but it was unavoidable now that he had caught her attention.

"I saved you a seat next to Lydia Long," he said when she came within earshot. He pointed and Lydia caught his eye with an innocent blush.

Gemma only half succeeded in holding back a smirk.

Josiah looked uncomfortable and busied himself in talking to his friend. His cowboy hat cast a shadow over his handsome face. She remembered the days when she thought only ranching snobs or country bumpkins wore them—and they didn't wear them well. Here was finally someone who did.

She crossed the barn. "Hello, Lydia," she said.

"Hello."

Gemma took a seat on the prickly hay and tried to find a comfortable position. She noticed how well Lydia's green dress accented her strawberry hair. *And I bet she knows it, too.*

"All right, everyone," came Mr. Martin's commanding voice. Almost instantly, a hush fell. "Time to start, so everyone take a seat. Now, here are the rules for those of you who have forgotten. One, you can only shuck one ear at a time. Two, you have to be seated to do so. I'll be watching, so no cheating. There are two prizes. The person who husks the most corn gets our heifer. There are two red ears. The first boy and girl who discover one get to lead the meal and dancing as a couple. And they each get one of Ginger's pies to take home. Everybody got it?"

There was a general nodding of heads and noises of assent.

"All right. On your mark, get set . . ." He paused for effect. "Go!"

There was a whispering of corn as everyone reached to get their first ear. The pile sprawled so wide that at first no one had to leave their hay bale to secure one. But gradually the stack was whittled down and people would hop up and race back to their seat with their prize, tugging the fibrous leaves off as fast as they could manage.

There was very little conversation. Just the typical laughs, apologies, and short interchanges among the clamorous rustle. Eyes were bright and fingers flew.

Gemma was just beginning to wonder if she shouldn't pause and look in on Farris when she yanked the last piece of stringy foliage off a red-kerneled ear. She stopped in surprise and exchanged an astonished glance with Lydia. Several shouts of the discovery went up and she was immediately showered with congratulations and praise from all sides.

Almost simultaneously, a cheer rose up from the boys' side and Travis Long stood the victor.

Gemma's face blanched as she rose to meet him. *Seriously? What are the odds?*

"Do you forfeit?" he said in a triumphant tone that she found overly seductive.

She forced a swallow past her constricted throat. "Yes." A dark look crossed his brow, but she ignored it and scrambled for an excuse. "I can enjoy Ginger's pies anytime."

She offered a weak smile in relief as the youth seemed satisfied. The women were too anxious to become her replacement to care why she was refusing the honor. They grouped behind her and she stood on her bale to toss it behind her as like a bouquet at a wedding.

Another cry went up and Gemma turned to see who the lucky new girl was.

Anneliese blushed as everyone cheered and Travis claimed his partner for the evening. *Oh great! Maybe I should have kept it.*

Gemma slipped away as everyone resumed husking. The fastest person was yet to be announced, although she had heard it rumored that the Jefferson boys held the record.

She passed the long row of tables, almost oblivious to their heavy decoration of desserts, so great was her frustration that she had exchanged an uncomfortable situation for a possibly harmful one.

Feeling defeated, she entered the house. Mrs. Long met her at the door.

"Why hello, Gemma. Anyone found an Indian yet?"

"Yes, actually." She had to force pleasantness into her voice. "Anneliese and Travis."

"How fortuitous," Mrs. Long said, scrunching her shoulders in excitement.

Gemma tried not to cringe and continued upstairs. She would not let the likes of Travis ruin her day.

She opened the door to the master bedroom as quietly as she could. The hinges creaked but there was no sound of stirring. She tiptoed across the room, no easy feat in her boots, and peered down at her infant son. His sweet face while he slept brought a pride to her heart no one could remove. He resembled his father only in his heavy brows and face shape. The complexion and expressions were all hers. *No, not even your dark shock of hair could give away whose child you are.*

Gemma contented herself that he would be soundly unconscious for a little while longer and peered out the window. From an angle, she could see that the corn was almost depleted. She would wait until the October couple led the way before reemerging. She was almost glad Travis had been chosen. It would make him easier to avoid.

Then she felt sick remembering what Mrs. Long had said. She thought back to all the times she had seen Travis and Anneliese together. Poor Anneliese. The more Gemma reflected, the more it struck her that Anneliese looked how she expected *she* did last year— smitten and intrigued by the bold young man, curious as to what might happen if ever they were alone. Well, she had discovered the answer to that question! It was plain to see their mutual infatuation as they led the way to the procession of food, arm in arm, a crown of wheat resting on her flaxen hair. Gemma resolved to do more.

She took one more peek at her sleeping child before mustering up a smile and slipping outside.

All of the steaming chicken and bright buttered corn suited the sunset. And the many assortments of pies, both cold and warm, presented such a tempting variety that it was hard to sample enough.

Gemma washed hers down with a tart glass of lemonade as Anneliese, looking the picture of autumn in her starched red blouse and khaki skirt, led the dancing.

Josiah approached her with a mischievous grin alighting his face. "Dance with me?"

Gemma was rather surprised the Martins danced. "Shouldn't you ask Lydia?" she countered, peering over the top of her glass.

"I will. But I've got to give the other fellows a chance. Come on, just one dance."

"No," she laughed. "Isn't it singles only?"

"You are single."

"But I'm also a mother," she said as a fiddler began. "I think that excludes me."

"Let's see who reacts then, shall we?" He grinned, taking her hand and pulling her gently away from the table.

She set down her glass, reluctant as she was. "I think I hear Farris." It was her final attempt.

"Then I'm sure someone inside hears him, too." He slipped his arm around her waist and they joined in step.

Gemma fastened her eyes to his feet, attempting to mirror his movements. "I have a confession. I'm not very good at dancing." She couldn't have collided with his white dress shirt sooner if she had been trying to prove her point.

He chuckled. "You never did those prom things at your school?"

"Sure I did. But it was more jumping around than structured dancing. Anyone can do that."

He laughed again as the music came to a close.

She managed to sit out several more dances and enjoy watching Ginger and Elias, Josiah and Lydia. But for the fourth one, a young man she vaguely recognized from church asked her.

That's what I get for staying nearby.

She didn't attempt to tell him no, but was thankful she knew the dance.

Gemma took advantage of the ten-minute break that followed to check on Farris again. She never knew whether he would want to eat once more or be down for the night at this hour.

As she reached the top of the stairs, she chided herself for leaving the door ajar. She swung it open more fully and froze in horror, stifling a gasp.

The dark-haired young man turned at the noise and straightened, removing his hand from his child's face. "He's beautiful," he whispered, a longing gaze fastening on Farris's face. He stroked his soft cheek.

Instantly, any pity Gemma had ever felt for Travis vanished. *Don't touch him! You gave him up. Get out!* Gemma's mind raced with things to shout at him. She couldn't begin to describe the panic that had seized her heart. This man was a predator and a coward. She didn't want him anywhere near her child. Yet she was so terrified she didn't even respond. She just stood there, stunned, her large eyes even larger with fear. Even she couldn't have expected this reaction from herself. Farris had been so much safer in her womb.

"He looks like you, you know. Probably a good thing."

Her pulse quickened as he slowly approached her, just as it always used to do. But this time it was different. She managed a nod.

"I had to see him, Gemma. Just once."

She swept out of the room, trying to control her anger. He followed and clicked the door shut.

"I'm sorry I can't do more for you."

Yeah, right.

His golden eyes looked so downcast that for a moment she almost believed him. *He's become so much more vulnerable.*

"I did love you, you know."

Her eyes flashed and her chin quivered. The words came in a terse whisper now. "If you had loved me, we wouldn't be in this mess in the first place! How is it loving to ensnare a woman only to abandon her?"

His temper flared. "I didn't ensnare you! You came as willingly as any girl ever could."

"Blindly," she said, her voice softer. "No, you didn't love me. And it's only because I know now that God loves me that I can forgive myself. It's only because of Him that I can even begin to forgive you!" Gemma thought a moment about what she had just said and found that she believed it.

She glanced up at Travis and was caught off guard at the open emotions displayed on his face. He didn't look angry or triumphant. Instead he looked sad and surprised, as if she had just slapped him. He swallowed several times, not meeting her eyes.

"Please, Travis. All I ask is that you not do it again. Leave this between you and me. God can forgive you, too, if you will just give Him a chance. Then we can all move on with our lives."

His jaw clenched and he looked her right in the eyes, fury poisoning his voice. "I don't want your advice and I don't need your God's forgiveness," he spat. He brought himself up to his full height. "Now if you'll excuse me, I owe Anneliese another dance." He turned on his heel and sauntered down the stairs, carefree as ever.

Chapter 13

Gemma pushed past the disappointment clouding her brain so she could focus on what she might have done better. *I've only made things worse.*

She looked over the banister and saw no one. *Thank goodness!* They were all too busy enjoying themselves outside, unaware that the answer to many of the questions they wanted to ask had just been revealed upstairs. She tried to think of an excuse not to go back down when Farris's frantic cry provided a perfect one.

Gemma locked the door for good measure and hurried to scoop up her baby and hold him close. She nudged Mrs. Martin's plush sewing stool up against the side of the bed for support. Farris got more and more frantic.

"All right, all right, baby. Hold on."

She sat down on the stool and realized she hadn't thought through the logistics of trying to nurse in her dress. *Right, it buttons down the front.*

As Farris ate, Gemma thought again about how lost Travis was. Not that she was much better. *But I* know *I* need help. Her head sank back into the small amount of cushion the side of the mattress provided. *What do I think I'm doing, anyway? I don't even know how to be a good mother, let alone a good Christian.* Her mind retraced the themes of the Bible and how they all fused in one Man's life. It was quite the story. Is that all it was: a good story? She knew enough to understand that it was for her to decide. No one, not even Josiah, could decide for her.

"Prove You're real," she whispered. "Keep us safe."

Farris stirred at the sound of his mother's voice.

She smiled down into his attentive face. "Sorry, did Mommy disturb you?"

His hand curled around her finger and she brought it to her lips.

"Do you want to venture outside for a few minutes? Lots of people want to meet you." If she put him in the baby carrier, then he would stay warm and calm and people could look at him without having to hold him. *Perfect.* She wasn't quite ready to share him with anyone but the Martins.

Gemma watched her feet as she held Farris with one hand and the railing with the other. She was not going to take any chances on falling down the stairs. She slipped into their bedroom to grab the carrier and a hat to keep his ears warm. The dilemma of fastening the baby to herself one-handed stared her in the face when Josiah rapped on the door.

"Sounded like you could use an extra hand."

She met his hunter green eyes and wondered how long he had been in the house. But he showed no signs of betrayal.

"Yes, please."

She started to hand him the carrier and then decided it would be better if she strapped it around her own waist. He read her change of decision and took the baby instead, cradling him and blowing a loud raspberry on his full stomach.

"Careful, he just—"

126

A tiny hiccup interrupted her as Farris spread his supper on the front of his and Josiah's outfits.

Gemma tried to strangle a laugh and exhaled it through her nose as Josiah's face registered disgust.

"Sorry, I should have told you."

"Well, better me than you." He caught her humored expression and broke into a grin. "It'll be fine."

"I'll go get a rag." She hurried into the kitchen and dampened what looked like a well-worn one. Josiah met her in the living room and watched her rub the curdled residue out of Farris's onesie.

"Here, let's trade."

He gave her the baby and she handed him the rag.

Gemma tucked Farris's left ear into the fine knit hat. "There you go, little buddy." She glanced at Josiah, who vigorously wore the creamy smear into a large, transparent spot on his shirt.

"I'm really sorry," she said again.

"Gemma, it's fine." He leaned into the hall and tossed the rag into the laundry room. "It happens sometimes."

"You're gonna smell. Do you have another shirt?"

"Yeah, be right back."

Gemma changed Farris into a clean onesie and tucked him into the limp carrier. She met Josiah again outside the door, sporting a more typical plaid.

"Better?" Josiah asked.

"Yes! Sorry about that."

"Is Farris gonna go out for a bit?"

"Yeah, I think so. We'll see how he does."

He held the door for her. "Let me know if you need a break."

"Sure, if I can tear you from the dance floor."

He gave a sheepish grin and dashed off to join his buddies in the growing twilight.

Mrs. Long was on Gemma in a moment. "Oh, this must be your little baby. Isn't he precious?" She stroked his cheek as his head bobbed to get a better look at the stranger's face. "What's his name?"

"Farris."

"That's adorable! How old is he now?"

"Three weeks yesterday."

"How sweet!" As Mrs. Long went into a long story about Travis and Lydia as babies, Gemma wondered how the woman's reaction would differ if she knew Farris was her grandson; if she'd see similarities between him and his father, comparing the two in their childhood development. ". . . most stubborn child ever," she was saying. "But Lydia has always been my easy one."

Oh dear, I may have a lot in store. Gemma realized that she was probably not the most congenial child either. Contradiction had been rare, except from teachers at school. And that had never gone over well.

"It's exciting to watch young people grow up, isn't it?" Mrs. Long said.

Gemma knew she thought of Josiah and Lydia, Travis and Anneliese. It wasn't what she'd call "exciting." As much as she liked to tease Josiah, there was something about him and Lydia that did not sit right with her. *It's just because I know her brother so well . . . too well.*

Other women began to crowd around, anxious to see the baby and curious about Gemma's plans for the future. The more she was pressed to explain, the more she realized how much she lacked. No car, few furnishings, little money. It was going to be a long, hard road. But thanks to the Martins, she at least had a start.

"Thank you all very much for the baby shower. It really helped get me on my feet."

"Of course. Just let us know if you need anything else," the pastor's wife said.

Where to start . . . But she didn't want to owe debts to anyone else.

Gemma excused herself from the affectionate throng and roamed the yard of adults, mingling in the light of candles and jack-o-lanterns that many children still attempted to carve. Most of the youth seemed to have disappeared.

A voice materialized at her shoulder. "The boys are getting hay bales on the trailer for a ride." Mr. Martin's solemn eyes found hers, but the shadow of a smile clung to his mouth. "You should join them."

"Oh, that's all right. I'll just go and watch for a while."

He nodded and she could feel his eyes on her as she joined the other young people.

Elias—arm fully recovered—and Josiah stood in the loft at the far side of the high roof, throwing square bales down onto the ready trailer. The heap of corn had been stripped and distributed, only a stringy layer of trampled husks still littering the floor. Others busied themselves loading from the ground or arranging the bales on the trailer bed. Mariah passed out kittens like a diplomat.

Ginger approached her. "Are you going to go with us, Gemma?"

"I don't think so. I should take Farris back in."

"I could keep him for you. I've been on dozens of hay rides."

"No, I'll keep the baby," Emmaline said. "He likes me better. And besides, Elias will be disappointed if you don't go, Ginge. Please, Gemma?"

"How long is the ride going to last?" she asked.

"Just come!" Ginger said. "You'll love it. Em knows how to take care of babies."

Emmaline nodded her reassurance.

Gemma sighed. "Fine. I'll go get him settled and be right back."

"We'll wait for you," Ginger called.

Gemma led Emmaline inside and showed her where Farris's blanket and rattle were. She had him smiling and cooing before Gemma had even stepped outside.

Mrs. Martin tried to persuade her to take a piece of pie as she headed back toward the barn.

"I'm really fine," she insisted. "Maybe later. I have to catch the hay ride." *Everyone is being exceptionally nice to me tonight.*

Josiah sat in the cab of the truck and began to back the trailer out of the barn. Everybody cheered, and as soon as he cleared the giant red doors and shifted gears, they all began to pile on and claim their seats. Travis and Anneliese went first, being the honorary couple. Elias helped Ginger while his brother, Isaiah, gave Gemma a hand.

"So did the Jeffersons win the speed contest again this year?" Gemma asked.

Isaiah nodded as he took a seat next to her. "He beat me by two!" He shook his fist at his brother with a good-natured grin.

Gemma noted that he had the same light, dancing eyes and jovial smile that Elias did, only Isaiah looked more mischievous and less mature than his older brother.

The trailer gave a start as Josiah pulled away and Elias leaned back with a grin. "Yes, I remain reigning champion for a second year. You're losing your luck, little brother. I'm the fastest man around."

Isaiah scoffed. "Well, you're sure taking your time with poor Ginger here. You'd better hurry up before she decides to marry someone else."

Gemma gauged Ginger's reaction, a downward smile, with a trained eye. *Knowing who you're going to marry at sixteen doesn't sound very slow to me.*

Elias looked at Ginger, conflicted. "I'd move quicker, but . . . Josiah told me you'd have to be eighteen before I talked to your father."

Ginger's head snapped up in the gathering darkness, sending her deep chestnut curls swinging. "What does he know? You can talk to Dad whenever you like. He'll never give his permission if you don't ask."

"Then you don't have to be eighteen?"

"Elias, you'll just have to get the nerve to ask him yourself if you want to find out."

He settled into his hay bale as they bumped along. "Maybe I will."

"How old are *you*, Gemma?" Isaiah said.

"Almost nineteen."

"And no one's on your horizon?"

Someone was. "Not everyone gets married before twenty, you know."

She stole a glance down to where Travis and Anneliese sat engaged in avid conversation with several other young people. *How much longer until he enlists?*

Early the next morning as Josiah went down for breakfast, his father stopped him outside the master bedroom.

"May I have a quick word with you?"

Josiah picked through all the possible topics. "Sure."

Mr. Martin led him through the bedroom into his study, the same place where they had witnessed Gemma's confession.

"You put that calf in isolation, like I asked, didn't you?"

"Yes, sir."

"And no one's been going to see it?"

"Only me, to bottle feed it, sir."

"Good. The vet finally called back with the test results and I'm afraid it's not mad cow disease. Has the calf's behavior gotten any stranger?"

Josiah shrugged. "Maybe a little. He's still skittish and indecisive and runs into things a lot. What did the vet think it was?"

"Rabies. But he can't be sure until he runs a post-mortem test."

Josiah's eyes widened. "Rabies?! You mean we've had a rabid calf that Mariah has played with and I have been bottle feeding?" His fist came down on the desk. "Oh, I should have seen this coming!"

"What do you mean, son?"

"That stupid fox that kept killing the chickens—no fox in his right mind would run straight up to a yearling bull. I bet he gave the calf that scratch on his nose and that's how he got the rabies."

"Did we eat the dead chickens?"

"No, they were too far gone when we found them."

"But we have been milking the mother cow."

"Yes, but she's shown no signs of being crazy, so I think we should be OK there."

"It's your calf so I want you to make the call. Decide whether you want the vet to euthanize the calf. The vet will need samples of brain tissue to confirm rabies, but regardless of the results, you and Mariah will need a checkup—maybe a basic saliva test. I'll ask your mother about it."

Josiah met his father's eyes and swallowed. "Yes, sir." He turned to go.

"There's something else, but it will have to wait. Come back when you're free."

He nodded and slipped out the door, his father accompanying him to the breakfast table.

Gemma could tell everyone was exhausted after their busy week of preparations and late night of fun. Anneliese looked pained and Lisabeth could hardly hold her head up. Only Mariah didn't display any of the usual signs of fatigue.

"What time do we need to be at the Farmer's Market, Josiah?"

He set his silverware down and hopped up from the table. "Drat, I almost forgot."

Mariah moved to go, too, but her mother called her back. "You are not going anywhere, young lady. I remember you promised me you'd finish your schoolwork. You've put it off all week, so you'll have to forgo the market and do it today."

"But, Mama—"

Mrs. Martin cut her off with a look. "Yes, ma'am?"

Mariah nodded glumly and resumed her meal.

"Gemma, would you like to go with him?"

Mr. Martin's head whipped up as if he objected, but he remained silent.

Gemma pushed the fuzz out of her brain. "I don't want to take Farris anywhere else; he didn't sleep well."

"I know, I can tell, dear. But you could leave him here, just for an hour or two. All you'd have to do is sit in a chair and look pretty so people buy the produce."

It sounded wonderful. *But I can't leave Farris!* He wasn't even a month old and had never been without her before. What if something happened to her and Farris had to live without his mom . . . just like she had. *Don't be ridiculous.*

"I'm sure it'd be nice, but I can't just leave him with you when you have so much to do."

"It will be over his naptime and he's been sleeping at least two hours. Of course, if you'd rather stay and rest with him, it's up to you."

Gemma *was* going stir-crazy. Last night had been a good distraction, but she had been craving a real outing, even if it was just a run to a grocery store. It sounded perfect, if she could only relax.

"I'll talk to Josiah."

She enlisted Gail's services to play with Farris on the floor; he enjoyed having someone to boss around, as every three-year-old does. She hoped talking to Josiah would make her decision easier.

Pitiful mooing could be heard as she approached the truck and trailer that were parked in front of the house. Someone was securing the calf in the trailer and shaking Josiah's hand. Gemma watched as the man climbed into the cab of the truck and started slowly down the driveway.

Josiah jumped at the crunch of Gemma's footsteps. The terse emotion displayed on his handsome face disarmed her.

"What's wrong?"

"The vet is afraid he has rabies. The fox—I should have known."

Gemma stood there awkwardly, feeling like she was at a funeral and didn't know how to comfort the mourner. She knew the calf would have to be put down.

"There's nothing you could have done to make him better."

Josiah glanced at the trailer disappearing down the driveway. "No. But I could have helped him sooner. I could have helped all of us. There's a good chance I contracted it in all of the slobbery bottle feedings. I was so hung up on the idea that he was born with a condition, since he contracted it so young, that I've put everyone at risk."

She swallowed, blocking out worst-case-scenario thoughts. "What can they do if you've contracted it?"

"A vaccine, I think. We've never got the vaccine as a kid, but they say if you get one or some globulin thing soon after contracting rabies, it can build up a defense in your body. Mariah and I are going tomorrow morning. Any other treatment is more radical."

Mounting fear clawed at her stomach. "Well, you haven't started running into things or getting aggressive, so maybe you're in the clear."

He managed a smile. "Maybe. Sorry, did you need something?"

"Oh, yeah. Your mom suggested I go to the Farmer's Market with you and leave the baby so I can have a break. I just wasn't sure what you thought."

"I'd love to have you. I'm a little off my game this morning, anyway."

She nodded. "Then count me in. I'm really sorry about the calf."

He didn't look up. "Thanks."

Later that afternoon, Josiah and Gemma were on their way to the Farmer's Market. Emmaline had been given permission to join them since she was thirteen and had completed her schoolwork in record time. Gemma still felt anxious about leaving Farris, but Josiah had promised to be as efficient as possible.

"So I kind of know what Farmer's Markets are, but I've never been."

"It's like a community produce sale," Josiah said. "We've done a few while you've been here."

Emmaline spoke up. "We are contributing radishes, turnips, kale, Swiss chard, and corn, of course. We've also got jellies Mom and Ginge made."

"Wow. How popular is something like this?"

Josiah sighed a low whistle as he pulled into a dirt parking lot. "In a farming community? Pretty darn. What you don't grow yourselves, other farmers grow for you. There's not much we get from stores."

"I'll have to stock up before I leave. I hate grocery shopping." Gemma slipped out of the car and surveyed the open air metal building.

"When are you leaving?" Emmaline asked.

"Beginning of December. This complex will charge me a whole month's rent even if I moved in on New Year's Eve, so I want to get settled as soon as possible. Farris just needs to be a little older before making such a big change, I think." She smiled. "I've still got over a month with you."

"Then you'll still be here for Thanksgiving!" Emmaline handed Gemma a large crate of turnips.

"Hey, don't make her carry stuff!" Josiah took it from her and doubled his load before hefting it off to a table just inside the building. People already bustled around, setting out their own products.

Gemma followed him in. "How can I help?"

"Look in that second crate for signs. They should have all the prices we need. Just start . . ." he waved his hands, "setting things out."

Gemma did her best and by the time customers began trickling in, everything had a place and a price.

"Hey, good job," Emmaline said, setting the last bushel of corn under the table. "This looks nice. Here, you want a chair?"

The three of them lined up behind the table. Gemma enticed customers, Josiah answered questions, and Emmaline handled funds. One hour passed and already they had sold most of the garden's produce.

"I hope we sell more corn," Emmaline said. "I'm sick of eating it."

"We could freeze it," Josiah said.

"We've already filled the freezer out in the barn. Maybe you shouldn't plant so much next year."

"This was a good harvest. We'll have plenty in case next year's crop doesn't turn out as well." He snatched the money bag from his sister. "Here. Everybody take twenty dollars and buy yourself something."

"I don't need anything," Gemma said, holding the bill out. Emmaline had already darted off to spend hers.

"Then keep it as payment for your help."

Oh my gosh, I never paid Travis again!

"If you're sure."

"I'm sure." He took a seat next to her. "So how is reading Matthew coming?"

She sighed. "It's coming. I think I'm near the end. It just seems . . . I would have believed if I had seen it. But if Jesus would do all those miracles for the people *then*, why does He make it harder today?"

"If you remember, Jesus did miracles for those who believed in Him. All of those who doubted Him and demanded signs, He would often refuse. Sometimes you have to make the leap before you see its potential. Does that make sense?"

"Yeah. I want to believe it. I'm just not sure I see it yet." She smiled. "I realized the other night that I am beginning to forgive everyone involved in making my life miserable. I don't know how I could do that if I didn't believe that God loved them and forgave them."

"But you haven't managed to apply that to your own life yet."

She shook her head.

Josiah reached over and squeezed her hand. "I still have a hard time forgiving myself sometimes, even just this morning. You'll get there. The story's not over yet."

Emmaline came back, her arms full of her purchases.

Josiah dropped Gemma's hand and stood to relieve his sister. "Wow. That's a lot for only twenty dollars."

"I made bargains. I got chocolate mint," she held up a tiny plant, "jalapenos so we can make poppers, and I swapped three jars of jelly for some apple chicken sausage."

"Not bad, sis." He tossed the sausage in the ice chest and set the other items on top. He glanced at his watch. "We'll give it another half hour and then call it quits for today."

Gemma gave him a grateful smile and resolved to enjoy her last few minutes of freedom.

True to his word, half an hour later, they bumped along the road, an endless strip of pavement through barren fields. Josiah applied the brake and turned into a general store. Its fluorescent lights competed with the dwindling sunlight to illuminate the parking lot. Josiah ran inside to grab more oats and left the girls in the car.

Gemma scanned her phone for any messages conveying the state of her son and found nothing negative. She breathed a sigh of relief and replied to Mrs. Martin, *"Be home soon."*

Home. It wouldn't be her home for much longer. The thought both saddened and invigorated her.

Another truck pulled up beside them, but Gemma paid it no mind until the driver, trying to heft three bags of ice, caught her eye.

Travis! She glanced at Emmaline in the rearview mirror and found her absorbed in a book. There appeared to be no passengers with Travis, and from what she could tell, Josiah wasn't checking out yet.

Just do it.

"I'll be right back," she said.

Emmaline mumbled her response, lifting Gemma's hopes that she wasn't paying attention.

She stepped down out of the car and fumbled for the twenty dollars in her pocket. She mustered confidence as she approached Travis and extended the money.

He gave her a blank look for a moment before accepting it and stuffing it in his back pocket. His eyes darted around the near-empty parking lot. "Better scram before you give yourself away."

She turned to the car, but his voice made her stop.

"Gemma? Thank you."

She offered a nervous smile over her shoulder and climbed back into the car just as Josiah came out of the store. She saw him take note of her closing the car door and give a curt nod to Travis.

Great.

But Josiah didn't make anything of it when he rejoined them and drove the rest of the way home.

The moment they walked in the door, the girls scattered: Emmaline went to give Mariah a report on the doings of the day and Gemma went to reassure her disgruntled baby who had just woken up. Josiah put the remaining corn in the barn and then went to scout out the source of smoke he had seen wafting over the house's roof.

He walked down the hill, past the large oak, and through the pygmy forest into the clearing. The brush pile was dwindling under the heat of the flames.

"You OK, Dad?" Josiah asked.

His father noted his arrival, quit massaging his arm, and turned back to the fire. "Yeah, fine." They fell silent for a long moment. "Josiah, there's something else I need to talk to you about and I want you to be perfectly honest with me."

Josiah's questioning eyes met his father's. "Yes, sir?"

"It has been brought to my attention that your behavior may warrant some correction."

His mind drew a blank.

"I know you, like your mother, are a very kind and considerate person, almost to the point of a fault. That is not my strong suit, so please tell me if people are imagining things when they ask me if there is anything between you and Gemma."

Josiah readjusted his stance and scoffed. "Can I ask what people are making these assumptions?"

"No. Once it came to my attention, I could see what they meant. You need to be more careful."

"I'm not trying to pick a fight, but can I ask exactly how I should do that?"

"You have a tendency to get overly attached to things. You always have. Watch your interactions with Gemma more closely and see if you couldn't take a step back."

Josiah could see his point. "I'll do better. But she's a guest, Dad, and a lost one. She told me today that she feels the Bible might be credible. Why? Because I have done *everything* to encourage and uplift her. I'm sorry if that's coming off as romantic, but she needs our help! If you want me to do less for her, then it's about time you quit treating her like an outcast and gave me a hand."

Mr. Martin absorbed the accusation and moved past it. "Then you don't love her?"

He floundered for a moment. "Not . . . like that!"

"Then all I'm asking is that you consider how you might improve."

"Because I *have* to marry Lydia and you don't want anyone to get the wrong idea." He felt a twinge of guilt after it escaped his lips.

"Josiah, please! This is not about her. This is about keeping your carelessness, however accidental, from hurting Gemma. If you care about her at all, you will re-examine your demeanor. Can you do that?"

Josiah relaxed his defensive posture and reflected on his relationship with her. Even he could see that she might have gotten the wrong idea somewhere. He'd better make sure his motives were all as innocent as he remembered. "Yes, sir."

Chapter 14

Josiah opened the door to his father's office. His heart jumped to his throat when he saw lines of pain creasing his father's face.

"Dad? Dad, are you all right?"

Mr. Martin held up a hand and leaned back in his chair, eyes closed. "I'll be fine."

"What's wrong?"

"Joint pain," he said between clenched teeth. "Think I was a little ambitious clearing all that brush yesterday."

Josiah frowned. "Well, can I do anything?"

Mr. Martin removed his hand from his eyes. "'Fraid not. I took medicine this morning and already used the ointment the doctor gave me."

"Doctor?" Alarm tinged Josiah's voice. His dad never saw a doctor unless he felt truly helpless.

"He thinks it's osteoarthritis. Deterioration of cartilage which causes joint pain. Thankfully it's only my wrists and shoulders for now."

No wonder he's been somewhat out of sorts. "Sorry, I . . . I didn't know."

"It's all right; I'd only told your mother. You worry too much, just like me." Mr. Martin patted his son's arm. "Did you need something?"

Josiah looked carefully at his father's face. When had he gotten so old? "No. No, I can figure it out. I'll let you rest, Dad."

Mr. Martin forced a smile. "Thanks. Don't mention anything to the girls; I'll be down to read to them in a little bit."

Josiah nodded, closing the door behind him. Why hadn't he found out sooner?

Weeks passed. Farris began to settle into his new way of life and Gemma began to look to the future. Since the temperatures had finally bottomed out, she often sat in her lone bedroom chair, making lists for moving, packing, spending, saving, repaying. Gemma soon realized how little she owned. While that would make moving all the easier, it left a great many holes in the necessities of life. When she had brought the list to Mr. Martin, he had dispelled many of her fears by showing pictures of the apartment David Martin found.

"The kitchen's fully equipped with everything you might need. There are built-ins in the closet, so you won't need dressers. You've got a playpen, mattress, and chair, so sounds like all you need is a table and some linens to get you started."

"And a car."

He grimaced. "There is that. Maybe you could get a ride with someone?"

Gemma nodded. "I'll figure it out. How much is this going to cost?"

"Seven hundred a month." He closed his laptop and leaned back in his chair. "It's really just a two-story, u-shaped building with a handful of apartments. Not the highest quality, but David assured me it was a safe neighborhood."

"It sounds perfect." Low-income housing would not be a new experience for her. With her new job, she had already tabulated that she should be making about 1,600 dollars a month. She grabbed a calculator off the desk's polished surface and subtracted 700 for rent, 200 for groceries, 100 for her and Farris's additional expenses, 100 for her various debts, and another 200 for miscellaneous, that left her with 300 dollars to put aside each month.

She lifted her pen from the pad of paper and smiled. *Not bad at all.*

"Happy?"

"It will be so nice to start life over again. I can't thank you enough for this opportunity."

She slipped back downstairs and showed Emmaline her findings. She was quite the deal hunter and enjoyed perusing websites with resale items Gemma might need on the one computer available for the children's use.

"Sweet! There are lots of things near Wichita, so just tell me when you want something and I'll find it for you."

"Thank you, I will."

Gemma was going to go and see what happened next in Matthew's account of the Gospel, but amazing smells coming from the kitchen lured her away.

"Look I made!" Gail said, waving a beater coated in orange. "Pie! Taste, p'ease?"

Gemma held her hair out of the way and complied. "So yummy, Gail."

"Now you can't stick it back in, silly," Ginger said, snatching the bowl brimming with pie filling.

"Yes, I tan. It's good."

"Nobody wants your cooties in the pie. Wait until we do the whipped cream and then you can have another beater. We'll need lots with everyone coming for Thanksgiving."

"What else are you planning to make?" Gemma asked.

"For dessert, just chocolate and pumpkin pies. Belinda's bringing the pecan and January's a pro at the pineapple chess."

"Wow. I've never had pineapple pies before."

"Oh man, you're missing out. Jan's are the best! Then we just have to make all the usual dishes. The girls are going to bring the casseroles."

"That's a lot of food!"

Ginger shrugged as she popped the pies into one of the ovens. "We're a lot of people. But it usually lasts us a few days. And we'll do one of the pies for Josiah's birthday."

Anneliese rifled through the recipe organizer. "Hey, Ginge, what about these for breakfast?" She slid a recipe entitled "Monkey Bread" across the island.

"Oh, sure. That's an easy one. I'll just make some extra dough when we do the rolls."

"Man, I wish I could cook like you guys," Gemma said.

"Don't look at me," said Anneliese. "Ginger's the natural. I don't know what we'll do when Elias whisks her off."

Gemma smiled as Ginger shot her sister a reproachful look and snatched up another ingredient-stained card.

"Did Elias ever ask your dad that night?"

"Actually, he did. I was impressed."

Anneliese rolled her eyes. "And?"

"And Dad said to check back when I'm eighteen, of course. But Elias argued his case really well . . . without it sounding like an argument, I mean. He's already got a good job and a decent savings and some land he could build on. That's a lot more than most and that's what he told Dad. Then they kicked me out."

Josiah entered the kitchen, quirking his eyebrows at Ginger.

"I guess we'll get to finally meet January's fiancé on Wednesday," Anneliese said, drumming her fingers on the counter. "He sounds really nice."

"He sounds stuffy," Ginger said.

"Well, he can't be as stuffy as David," Josiah said, scooping Gail off his stool and taking a seat on it.

"Can you cook, too, Josiah?" Gemma said.

"Um . . . I do eggs and macaroni."

"He's actually pretty good," Ginger said. "He just doesn't get in here enough."

"I want macawoni," Gail said, while trying to make Josiah lick the beater.

Ginger laughed. "No, you don't; you're going to get whipped cream, remember?"

Josiah cringed as pumpkin pie smeared all over his cheek. He took a lick and tossed the beater in the sink behind him. "Thanks, bud."

"Do you have any idea how many people have licked that?" Anneliese said.

Josiah shrugged. "We're all family."

Gemma rinsed a rag and wrung it out for him, but Gail quickly turned cleanup into a game of tag, slinging water all over the kitchen.

"Do I need to sleep somewhere else with all your siblings coming in?" Gemma asked.

"No, I'll go to the attic with Gail," Josiah said, chucking the rag at his brother.

Gemma thought back to the last time Josiah had been forced to relocate there. "I forgot about the attic."

"Yeah, we have some sleeper sofas. But it's actually our extra bedroom."

"What? I didn't know that. Will you show me?"

"All right." Josiah narrowly dodged the flying rag and made a dash for the stairs before he could get pegged again. "Think you can climb a ladder?"

Gemma crossed her arms and raised her eyebrows.

Josiah put his arms up in surrender. "OK, OK. I've just never had a baby before."

She followed him through the playroom and down the hall. He stopped underneath a chiseled square in the ceiling and gave its string a hearty tug. The ladder unfolded and he motioned for her to go first.

"Hey, this is pretty cute," she said, scaling the rungs and pulling herself up onto the attic floor.

The roof was at a steep slant with skylights along it that illuminated all the dust streaming around the room. There was a bed and forgotten play nook, sectioned off with a curtain tacked to the ceiling ahead and treacherous stacks of cardboard boxes behind.

Josiah swung himself into the room. "Pretty cool, huh?" He lay on his stomach and tucked the ladder back up, sliding a plank under it so it wouldn't give. "I broke my arm once when I fell onto this ladder and it opened up, so now we secure it. But look, this is the best part."

He crossed to a skylight, slid the tight, oily latch, and swung it outward. He hefted himself onto the metal roof. Gemma watched him sidle along the slanted edge until he reached a flat part at the corner. "You can see some great sunsets from here in the evenings."

"So that's where you and Elias got off to during the Octoberfest."

He shrugged, but his expression divulged the secret. "You gonna come?"

"No way! I just had a baby, remember? Maybe another time if I'm feeling adventurous."

Josiah crawled back and jumped in. "All right. Roof gets a little slippery with all the leaves in the winter, anyway."

"And hot in the summer?"

"A little, but it's not bad if you've got blue jeans and socks." He re-latched the skylight.

"How many broken arms happened due to falling off the roof?"

"Only one, but it was David." Josiah kicked the plank so it slid under the ladder and off the opening.

"David doesn't count?"

He turned and faced her so he could climb down. "Not really. He broke a toe just by walking once, so he's not exactly what you'd call sturdy."

"Speaking of sturdy," Gemma said, taking her turn down the ladder, "are the doctors satisfied with the results of your and Mariah's rabies vaccine?"

"Yeah, he called just a little bit ago and said we should be in the clear. I kind of doubted we had anything, because even though we were around the calf, it's not like he bit us. So it wouldn't be in our bloodstream."

She breathed a silent prayer of thanks. "Guess you would have gotten isolated to the attic if you'd contracted it, huh?"

"That's not funny," Josiah said as he folded up the ladder, but his smile betrayed him.

"Well, I heard there was a case in Texas a few years ago where the girl had never been vaccinated or anything and she survived. But she completely went off the grid, so no one has been able to study how the disease affected her."

"It was the government," Josiah said. "They probably snatched her and are doing their own testing."

"I didn't take you for such a Mulder."

He gave her a blank look.

"It's a . . . TV show. You know what, never mind." Gemma started down the stairs. "When's your birthday?"

"Tomorrow."

She turned and looked up at him. "Why didn't you tell me? I could have gotten you something."

He shrugged.

"How old are you turning? Twenty?"

"Yep."

"So I guess you decided not to do college, huh?"

"Yeah, that was more up David's alley. He didn't have to have it for real estate but he got a degree in business anyway. Me, I'd wrestle a pig any day to avoid a classroom. I've got about three dozen cows on the Jeffersons' land. Elias has talked about us paying for the back fifty acres and splitting it. We could share some of the responsibilities, stay local—"

"Settle down," Gemma coaxed with a wicked grin.

"Eventually. I wouldn't mind living close to him and Ginge, building a house, that sort of thing."

"What does Lydia think?"

Josiah raised one eyebrow. "I haven't asked her."

"She likes you, you know."

Josiah shoved his hands in his pockets. "I know, I just . . . I know."

"Most girls won't wait forever. She's really quite perfect for you, if you don't mind my saying."

"I know she is. But sometimes I wonder if there's more than one 'right' person out there. Lydia—she almost seems too perfect. Not just for me, but in general."

"Maybe it's just because everyone assumes you'll end up together."

"Maybe. I wish . . . I just hope too many people don't pin their hopes on it."

"Happy birthday!"

Many voices shouted it all throughout the house from very early hours. The pancake cake was served promptly at seven amidst singing to Josiah, whose slice was stuffed so full of candles it hardly held together. Still, he managed to blow them all out in one breath.

Mrs. Martin clapped her hands to get her boisterous children's attention. "Presents can come later after we've gotten some work squared away. We've got a lot to do before everybody gets here tomorrow, so eat quickly and then I'll give you a chore."

Gemma tried to volunteer several times throughout the morning, but no one would let her do anything that required the least bit of exertion. Vacuuming and any detail cleaning that required her getting on the floor were out of the question. Anneliese was in charge of getting all of the food stored and keeping the little kids on task, so she gladly handed the laundry over to Gemma when Farris went down for his morning nap.

Once Gemma had folded several baskets and gotten another load in, she went upstairs to take a bath before it had to be cleaned, too. She felt a little achy and sore and thought a soak would do her good. She still had part of an herbal blend Mrs. Martin had made for a post-baby detox that she should probably finish off, anyway. It looked like loose-leaf tea, but apparently it was good to soak in as well as drink.

As she lay there trying to keep her long hair out of the layer of what looked like dead grass floating on top of the water, Gemma thought about everything that had happened to her in the last year. It was insane, really. Last Thanksgiving she had still been in school, working at McDonald's on the side, and living with her uncle in his low-income housing. He wasn't worth paying minimum wage, so it was up to her to bring in money so they could eat. What didn't go there had gone to his gambling and drinking. At that time, she couldn't see any end to it. She expected that would be her life until he died. Now here she was soaking in a tub in a big house with a baby, two states away from her uncle's crummy life. Sometimes she felt guilty that she wasn't there to help him like she used to. *Or at least I tried.* She decided she would write him again once she got settled in Wichita and see where that led.

She shivered and willed the water to warm back up. *I've probably been in here long enough.* Farris would be up soon and she'd feel bad if she weren't out yet to tend to him. Besides, she still had to wash her hair.

That evening, after a supper filled with Josiah's favorite dishes, of which there were many, they all braved the chilly temperatures for a bonfire. The Jeffersons came over and helped light it up while Mrs. Martin got the s'mores ready. The fire was so huge, three-foot skewers had to be used to roast the marshmallows.

"Is Farris warm enough?" Mrs. Martin asked, handing Gemma another blanket for the sleeping baby.

"I think I'll take him in and lay him down; his nose is getting all red. I didn't dare take him away from everybody while he was still awake. He loves being outside in the middle of all the action." She planted a kiss on the baby's soft head just below his snug hat and struggled to rise from her lawn chair.

"You're not going in, are you?" Isaiah said with disappointment in his voice. "We're going to play capture the flag in the field."

"Yeah, and do a hay slide," Lisabeth pouted. "Don't make Josiah sad on his birthday."

"Leave her alone, Lis," Josiah said. "Gemma can do what she wants."

"I guess I can come back out for a few minutes." She didn't want to leave the baby alone in the house, but they were just outside, so it couldn't hurt anything for a little while.

Gemma got Farris down for the night and slipped out of the bedroom without disturbing him. She turned to find Mrs. Martin in her favorite chair, knitting in her lap.

"It was getting too cold for me," she said. "Why don't you go out and enjoy yourself? I'll finish looking over Farris's birth certificate for you."

"You don't have to—"

She brushed a peppered curl out of her face. "Gemma, you're still young. Take advantage of it! Besides, I don't get a quiet house to myself very often."

She nodded her thanks and did as she was told.

Everyone was in the middle of choosing teams for capture the flag. Apparently, there was some dispute as to whom the other team captain should be. Josiah had been guaranteed a spot since it was his birthday.

"Why don't you just do boys against girls?" Gemma said.

"But there's more of you," Elias said.

Gemma held up her hands. "Oh, I'm not playing."

"Yes, you are," Isaiah said, marching her next to Anneliese. "Besides, the odds will make our victory that much greater." He offered an egomaniacal grin.

Gemma looked around to try and glean what information she could from her surroundings as Josiah recapped the rules. *This is going to be really hard in the dark.*

". . . are the flags." He held up two milk buckets. "You've got three minutes to hide it. And each team can have one flashlight." He tossed one to Ginger, who promptly tested it for battery. "Go!"

Everyone scattered. The boys bolted for the tree line and the girls claimed the front yard as their territory.

"I know just where to hide it," Mariah whispered. "There's a thick clump of cornstalks back in the field. We'd just have to stay away so they don't crinkle."

"I'll guard it," Gemma said. "I don't feel like running, anyway."

Ginger nodded and handed her the bucket. "Good luck. Just yell if you need me."

Mariah crouched and ducked and darted until they had reached her prized spot. Then, as soon as she had pointed it out to Gemma, she was off to try and infiltrate enemy lines.

Gemma sat next to the bucket and wiggled it into the dirt a little, laying a few pieces of the corn parchment on the top so maybe it would be less evident. She pulled her cardigan closer about her as she listened to the screams and scrambles coming from other parts of the yard and smiled. She shook her hands out and wished for the warmth of her baby.

An owl hooted nearby. She tensed and remembered the last time she had encountered him. It hooted again, nearer. *I'll brain it with the bucket if it tries anything funny again.*

She stared up at the dancing stars in the still sky and tried to identify the few constellations she knew while she waited. Just as she was beginning to wonder if the girls had won and they had forgotten about her, she heard footsteps. She waited to catch a glimpse of the person and then suddenly he stood directly in front of her.

She jumped and scrambled to her feet just as he dove for the bucket. She kicked it before he could grab it and then caught it and sat on it before he could recover.

"Oh, come on." The voice was Isaiah's. "Just give it to me."

"No."

"You look cold. I'll trade you my jacket for the flag." He unzipped the camo outerwear and held it out to her. "Please?"

He's desperate, which means we're winning.

More footsteps could be heard and Isaiah turned toward them. Gemma took the opportunity and yanked the jacket from his hand. She shrugged it on and smiled at his face from her increasingly uncomfortable perch.

Josiah appeared and took in the scene. "Go and reinforce Elias. I've got it."

Isaiah was only too happy to find more easily conquered ground.

"I think he has a crush on you," he said as his friend disappeared.

Gemma nodded.

"Aren't you puppy guarding?"

"Probably, but you're not going to shove me off."

A cry of victory rose up from the girls.

Josiah sighed and helped her to her feet. "Well, you got off easy this time. Walk you back."

Chapter 15

Gemma wiped away the tears in her eyes and closed her Bible. She stifled a sniff so she wouldn't wake Farris for his morning feeding. *I feel like such a horrible person . . . I am a horrible person.* Then she felt bad for bullying herself. Clearly, that was not what the takeaway of Matthew was supposed to be. But had the Son of God really lived on earth to experience what people do and, remaining pure, sacrifice Himself for the sins of the world? It made sense, but why? Why would He do it? There was no glory in it, especially not at the time. He didn't want to go through it, so He wasn't proving anything. The thought entered her head unbidden: *He was proving He loved me.*

Another tear slid down her cheek and she buried it in her pillow. She could see that it was God's plan from the beginning. Everything in the Old Testament led up to Jesus's coming. The purpose of it all was to give everyone another chance if they would take it. A second chance is what she had always wanted—it was what she had been working toward ever since she found out she was pregnant. And here, completely unasked for, was the biggest second chance of all.

Good grief, I'm such a wreck. I thought evolution made sense three months ago. But Josiah was right. There was nothing worth having in evolution. There was everything in the salvation of Christianity. It took her biggest struggle in life—her faults—and cured it.

Farris began to work himself up into a cry, rubbing his head against his mattress. He tried to lift his head and looked toward the bed expectantly.

"Are you looking for me, smart boy?"

His face spread into a drooly grin at the sound of her voice.

She slid off the edge of her bed and scooped him up, filling the chubby curve of his neck with kisses. "There are going to be some new people for you to meet today. Are you going to be a sweet baby?"

He cooed his response.

"Good."

They ate another quick breakfast so the last-minute preparations could be completed in plenty of time. David and his wife, Beth, were expected around noon and the girls not until later.

Before everyone could disperse, Gemma cornered Josiah. "Hey, can I talk to you for a minute?"

He turned on his heel to face her. "Sure."

"I finished Matthew."

Understanding grew in Josiah's olive eyes and he nodded his head. "So now you know the basic story."

"Yeah. It did have an impact on me, but I still have questions and such." She shifted Farris to her other shoulder. "So I was wondering if we could talk about it some . . . before I leave and life gets crazier."

"Of course."

Mr. Martin squeezed between them to rewarm his coffee and the spiciness of menthol met Gemma's nostrils. "You really think you're getting a hold on Christianity?"

"I think it's getting a bigger hold on me, sir."

He added a spoonful of sugar and stirred. "What set you looking?"

"I think it's pretty obvious I need help. I thought this was just going to be Josiah's solution, but I was open because I had nothing to go on. Any preconceived notions I had are starting to disappear the more I learn."

"Well, I must say you've been a trooper if you haven't been intimidated yet." He took a long drink of coffee, keeping eye contact.

"Life as I've lived it so far is more intimidating to me right now. Especially with a baby. I'm going to have to do things differently just to survive."

He nodded. "Children will do that to ya, that's for sure. I'd better get back to work. I've got a few things to wrap up before the holiday. Construction stops for no man!"

After he excused himself, Josiah shook his head.

Gemma chuckled. "He's not *that* bad."

"I kept thinking how he's all but burned you at the stake, but then he told me he's got some sort of degenerative cartilage joint pain thing. Doesn't excuse his patronizing behavior, of course, but explains it at least. Poor Dad. Still, I cannot think of a single person in the world who would have come into a situation like this and not have drowned yet."

Gemma frowned. "That sounds painful. I'll admit I've spluttered a few times, but it hasn't been too bad. Just look at everything you've given me. You forget what life I'm coming from."

"I just think he doesn't give you enough credit." He smiled. "But then again, he's never given *humanity* enough credit."

"Well." Gemma's tone was final. "Maybe you give me too much." She grinned and excused herself to change a diaper.

She glanced around her cluttered bedroom as she fished for a new diaper. *Maybe I should clean up a little just in case I need to hand over the room after all.* She placed Farris in the middle of the bed and made a quick job of gathering the dirty laundry and stuffing the pile in the narrower end of the slanted closet. Little feet scampered up and down the stairs above to get ready in time.

Farris called from the mattress, fists waving, and she gladly joined him. His hysterics cut short like nothing had ever been the matter.

"Oh no, are you going to be a Mommy fusser? Does Mommy make you happy?" She rested him on her propped legs. "That's OK; Mommy likes to make you happy."

His dark, round eyes struggled to capture all the features of her face as if he wanted to remember this moment just as much as she did.

"We'd better go see what we can do to help, mister. And then it will be time for your nap."

He gurgled his agreement.

"Ginger." Gemma called the first person she saw. "Are you sure no one needs my room?"

"Don't be silly, Gemma! David and Beth are getting the boys' room and Jan's boyfriend, Patrick, can share the attic. Jan and Belinda can have the sleeper in here or the schoolroom."

"If you're sure. Do they . . . do they know I'm here?"

Ginger shrugged. "I guess so. I mean, David found you the apartment, right? And I'm sure Mom's mentioned it to Jan and Belinda." She stared at the toy in her hand absentmindedly. "Right, upstairs."

Gemma sighed to herself. *I hope I can stay out of the way.*

As if she had read her mind, Anneliese stopped bossing the children around and turned to Gemma. "Hey, don't let anyone ignore you. Seriously. Remember you're just as much a part of this family as they are."

My goodness, what happened to her?

"They're here! They're here!" Mariah cried, flying out the front door.

"It's a little early," Anneliese said, glancing at her watch. "I hope it's January, for your sake."

"Besides, we want to grill Patrick before everyone gets here," Josiah said.

"Don't you dare." A tall, trim brunette with a Starbucks in one hand and a suitcase in the other stood in the doorway. Her close-cropped hair and skinny jeans didn't quite fit Gemma's impression for the Martin style, but her smile was unmistakably her mother's.

Gemma approached gradually, letting family get in all of their hugs first.

"All right! Let me through the door. Where do I put my stuff? Oh, hello, baby!" January tossed her purse in a chair and curled Farris's fingers around her own.

A man in a sweater vest surrounded with curious children shuffled through the door.

"Come in and get out of the cold!" Mrs. Martin closed the door. "You must be Patrick."

"You'll be in the attic with us," Josiah said.

"Oh heavens!" January rolled her eyes. "Good luck, hon."

Mrs. Martin frowned. "Surely we have—"

"I've got it under control, ladies." Josiah winked.

Mrs. Martin submitted to his judgment with a shake of her head. "As long as you'll be comfortable, dear."

Patrick nodded and was followed upstairs by the pack of interested youngsters.

"Oh my gosh, your ring is stunning!" Anneliese said, snatching her sister's hand.

"Isn't it divine? And I even let him pick it out!"

Gemma smiled as January showed off the glistening diamond that was easily one carat against an etched, slender band creamier than silver. "Wow, congratulations."

"Thanks! Are you spending Thanksgiving with us?"

Gemma nodded, gauging her reaction.

"Awesome. I can't wait to—Dad!" She zipped across the room and gave him a long, enthusiastic hug. "How are you feeling?"

He smiled and patted his daughter's back. "Where's this young man of yours?"

January stepped back, oblivious to the fact that he'd ignored her question. "You're not mad, are you? That you haven't met him and we're engaged?"

"Not if your judgment is still as good as it was. But I reserve the right to break the engagement if need be."

She studied the twinkle in his eye. "Ri-ight." She turned back to everyone else. "How long have we got before the others get here?"

"Until after lunch at least," Mrs. Martin said.

"Sweet! I hope you don't mind that we're early. I just couldn't wait to see you all!"

The next few hours were filled with chatter as January recounted the last few months of her life in extreme detail and tried to glean the important details about everyone else's.

"So, Gemma, how long have you been here?" January asked around a bite of pie. She decided not long into the conversation that she wouldn't be able to wait for dessert.

"Um . . . I guess a little over two months. I came in the beginning of September."

"Wow, that's like a new record. Very cool." She poked at another bite of pineapple. "Wait, so did you have your baby here?"

"Yep."

"Like in the house here, or just . . ."

"In the house, actually."

January widened her eyes. "Man, you must be brave. But he's super cute! I told Patrick I want kids, but not right away, you know?"

Gemma nodded. She didn't feel like she was in the position to give parenting advice, mother or not.

January set her Styrofoam plate aside. "OK, who wants to play a game? It's too cold to be outside and I promised Patrick I'd crush him at cards." She cracked her knuckles.

And so the afternoon passed, bathing in the love of reunited family as Gemma tried to stop wishing she could keep it all forever. *Don't be silly. You need to start again.*

The doorbell echoed all through the house, making Gemma jump and sending the children stampeding to the door.

A man that looked startlingly like Mr. Martin hustled inside, laden with bags.

"Anything else?" Josiah asked, shaking his brother's hand.

"Not if Belinda got all her things."

Two women were welcomed into the swarm of ecstatic children. One had the physique of an athlete and coloring of an American Indian. *She must be David's wife.* Gemma vaguely remembered someone mentioning her at church before. That made the blonde businesswoman Belinda.

David's wife swished her silky black hair and removed her coat.

"Oh my goodness, when did this happen, Beth?" Mrs. Martin said. Now that some of her bulky clothing had been set aside, it was quite clear she was expecting.

"I wanted to keep it a surprise." Beth offered a smile as warm as her complexion.

Gemma watched it all from her vantage point at the dining room table, where they had been playing cards. Josiah played bellboy and whisked everything to its proper place while the women began unloading the ice chest.

"If it's called an ice chest, where's all the ice?" Mariah asked, handing a pie to her mother.

"We didn't need it today since it's so cold outside," Belinda said. She glanced up and saw Gemma in the doorway. "Who are you?" It wasn't said unkindly, but the surprise was present in her emerald eyes all the same.

Anneliese's look reminded Gemma of what she had said and she offered a smile. "I'm Gemma. I've been staying with the Martins."

"Oh. That's nice."

"January's engaged, Beth's pregnant. What's up with you, sis?" Josiah flung his arm around her shoulder.

Belinda withstood it only for a moment before shrugging it off. "Oh, you know, just the same old thing. Which means nothing of importance."

"Oh, come on, you must have done something out of the ordinary since I saw you last."

"None of your business." She tossed her caramel hair.

Josiah squinted at Gail with a look that said they'd wheedle it out of her and whispered something in his ear. Belinda glared at them.

"That's enough, you two. Let's keep the hostilities to a minimum this week, shall we?" Their mother gave them both a warning look and the evening proceeded in peace.

The following day was packed with all the usual festivities. There was Ginger's delicious monkey bread for breakfast and a relaxed morning where everyone stayed in pajamas and drank numerous cups of coffee. Cider percolated on the back of the stove and filled the house with a wintry aroma. The cards were brought back out, with everyone joining and dropping games as often as they pleased. Around noon the women secluded themselves in the kitchen, whipping out five kinds of casseroles to go with the expected turkey, stuffing, rolls, and cranberry sauce. Everyone put on their warmest outfit before enjoying the family meal together, although Farris won the prize for the most pairs of socks. Then the multitude of pies were hauled out of the large pantry. All the food was left out and eaten for the remainder of the day.

"Oh my gosh, you guys. It's totally going to snow tonight!" January said, flicking her finger over the screen of her phone.

"Really? Does that mean we can go skating tomorrow? And sledding? And have a snowball fight?" Lisabeth asked.

160

"I'm not sure there'll be *that* much snow. But we'll see. Oh, before I forget, I want to show you these dresses and see what you think. I was hoping to have the wedding in the city since it's not far and then come back here for the reception. Is that OK? I thought it would cut venue cost."

"How many people are we talking?" her father asked.

"Two hundred? But no big supper. Just cake and punch. Here are the dresses. See? They're floor-length and have sleeves, but still look springy. And they have a maternity option, Beth. I just thought the blush would be really pretty with white roses. Yes?"

Mrs. Martin tucked an escaped curl behind her ear and squinted at the phone. "I think they're lovely, dear. Very much your style."

"Then if Mariah and Lisabeth can wear the flower girl dresses from Auntie's wedding, that covers it."

"Do you have a date yet?" Mr. Martin said.

"April on a Saturday. And no one should have to stay here because Patrick's parents are reserving the hotel. They'll host a lovely rehearsal dinner at that fancy restaurant."

"That sounds very nice. Just remember, if you get too expensive this may have to come out of your inheritance. You're not my only daughter."

"Thanks, Dad! I knew you'd approve."

He cracked another smile.

Two in one day? Wow.

"Let's have a little prayer time and then head to bed."

January unfolded the sleeper couch to provide more seating as everyone gathered in the living room.

"Tonight, instead of reading, I want everyone to name something they are thankful for and then I'll pray."

Family, God, and tractors all came up at least once. Gemma was glad that no one was stuck on naming her. David and Belinda still seemed a little leery of her presence, although Farris's cheerfulness had softened them some.

"Let's pray," Mr. Martin said.

Everyone bowed their heads.

"Heavenly Father, we thank You for Your many blessings bestowed upon us this year. We thank You for the addition of Patrick, Beth, and the new life within her this year. And we thank You for Gemma and Farris."

Gemma's head shot up and her eyes flew open. She quickly resumed the proper praying posture and tried to focus on the rest of the prayer.

"We ask that Your mercies and grace would be multiplied toward every one of us as we grow closer to You this year. Amen."

Amen.

Chapter 16

"Snow!"

Gemma started and clicked her phone to life. *Six thirty? Seriously?*

She rolled over and willed the living members of the house to keep it down.

"Come on! Let's get our coats on."

Gemma groaned.

Little feet scampered past her room and the back door slammed shut. Gleeful giggles could be heard outside.

Is it even light enough for them to see what they're doing? Gemma sat up in bed and squinted outside. Everything looked gray, but there was a distinct sheet of white covering the ground. Hard pellets of rain splattered and clung to anything they could.

They shouldn't be out in the sleet.

Gemma reluctantly slid out of bed and pulled a sweatshirt Josiah had lent her over her head. She padded past a sleeping January and down the hallway. She cracked the back door. "Mariah!" Her voice was still thick with sleep. "Mariah, Lisabeth!" She motioned for them to come.

"Do you want to play, too?" Lisabeth asked. Remnants of frost sprinkled her light hair.

"No, not right now. I don't think y'all should be out here before everyone else is awake."

"Why not?" Mariah said.

"Because I don't want you to get hurt or too cold. No one would be able to help you."

"But—"

"Do what she says, Mariah."

Gemma turned to see Mr. Martin standing behind her in the doorway. She scooched aside a little so he could exercise the authority she lacked.

"You can come back out once it's stopped sleeting and people are up."

Mariah's shoulders slumped and she dragged herself inside.

Lisabeth trailed behind her, whining, "I don't want to come inside, Daddy. I don't *want* to!"

Mr. Martin sighed. "You don't even have gloves on, girls. You weren't going to last very long. Let's warm you up a little." He moved to the kitchen and put water on to boil. "Want some hot chocolate?"

Mariah and Lisabeth nodded, grabbing miniature Christmas mugs and taking a seat on the barstools.

Gemma had followed them absentmindedly but was wondering if she shouldn't go back to bed while Farris still slept.

"Do you want some?" Mr. Martin asked, getting a mug down for himself.

Gemma shook her head. "Nah. Thanks, though." She was still trying to get past the picture of Mr. Martin in his pajamas with sleep lines still carved on his face.

Josiah appeared from the kitchen door. His nose and ears were rosy as he tugged his knit hat off his head. "Animals are all fed. The chickens thought they were dying, but other than that, everything seemed fine." His eyes rested on Gemma. "Nice sweatshirt."

Ha. Ha.

A groan came from the living room. Gemma turned to see January brushing her wiry hair out of her face while she stared at her phone screen. "Well, maybe we won't be leaving today after all." She shuffled into the kitchen, stifling a yawn. "There's a massive storm system over most of southern Kansas and northern Oklahoma. We may get iced in."

By mid-day the sleeting had stopped and sealed itself as a glaze over every visible surface. As soon as everyone was dressed for the day, the kids dragged them out to play.

Gemma joined them for a moment, but declined the snowball fight and ice Frisbee. She didn't want to kill herself. Mrs. Martin, Beth, and Belinda remained inside as well.

As Gemma made her way back to the warmth of the kitchen with Farris, she heard Belinda. "Mom, I thought I told you to stop taking in strangers. Some day you're going to get a real creeper."

"I have better judgment than that, dear," came Mrs. Martin's ever-patient voice. "Gemma wouldn't still be here if we didn't trust her."

"I heard she *stole* from you. Mom, you can't let this happen again. It's not safe. And now all the kids are attached to her."

Beth sighed. "That's not fair, Belinda."

Gemma chose the moment to make her entrance before Farris gave her away. She made sure she didn't make eye contact at first, so no one would suspect anything. "So, what's on the agenda today?"

Mrs. Martin shrugged. "Not much. You are all welcome to stay for church tomorrow if you'd like to play it safer."

Belinda frowned and opened her mouth, but January's sudden arrival interrupted her. "Guess—who's here?" She doubled over, holding her stomach so as to catch her breath while everyone waited. "Elias came—all the way."

"Elias? Elias Jefferson?" Belinda said.

January nodded. "He took Dad into the barn a couple minutes ago. Anneliese said he intends to court Ginger."

Belinda's jaw dropped. "What? Why the rush?"

Mrs. Martin smiled. "I give it three minutes."

On the dot, Elias and Ginger were heralded into the kitchen by their host of admirers. Ginger looked more flushed than usual and her face beamed.

"Well, young lady?" her mother said.

"Elias asked if he could court me." She glanced up at him, slipping her hand into his. "And I said yes."

Cheers and squeals erupted from the children.

Belinda blinked as she tried to wipe the sour look off her face. Gemma wondered if romantic relationships were a sensitive topic with Belinda.

Isaiah appeared at Gemma's shoulder. "Hey!"

Gemma turned, stepping away from the group in the kitchen, and smiled. "Hey. How did you guys make it over here?"

"We took a sled. Elias has been pacing for days and he said he couldn't stand it any longer this morning. So I came with him to make sure he didn't get carried away." His clear eyes twinkled. "I told you."

"I know you did, and I never doubted you. Of course they'll get married young; they've known each other a long time." She sighed. "I haven't known anyone a long time, so I'm not going to get married before twenty."

"I am determined to prove you wrong on that point."

"Well, you have a little over a year to marry me off then. But I'm leaving Tuesday, so that may make it harder for you."

His face fell. "Why?"

I have to go over this with everyone?

"Because."

"You just want to prove to yourself that you can. Is that it?"

"What?"

His face was serious, concerned. "You have to know you can support yourself."

"No, I—I have to stop relying on everyone. I *need* to support myself."

"You'll be back."

Gemma frowned and changed Farris to her other shoulder. "No I won't! Isaiah, don't you see, I can't keep feeding off of them. It's not fair. To them or to me."

He shrugged. "Whatever. But I don't think you're ready. It's a lot, and you should ease yourself—"

"I don't have *time* to ease myself in! The plan's been in place for weeks; you're not going to change my mind."

Isaiah looked so worried, it scared her. She wanted to say, *Why do you care, anyway?* but she held her tongue. It was none of his business.

He sighed and let the topic go, his face clearing. "Can I hold the baby?"

"Sure." Gemma handed him the burp cloth first to try and prevent an accident. "He should be getting tired. I'm going to go pack a little."

The road was so thoroughly caked with ice that not only did everyone stay another night, but they debated whether it was safe to venture to church. Mr. Martin, being a devoted churchgoer, determined that not even weather could keep them away as long as he could deem it safe. After nearly skidding into the fence while trying to make it down the driveway, he decided that they would have to forgo it after all.

Gemma was disappointed. She had been hoping to assess Travis's status and catch another sermon before she left. There was no telling when she would collide with either again.

While Beth was getting her baby time, Gemma stole away to her bedroom and pulled out her phone. She hadn't initiated a text to him in over a month. But she had to know that he was going to keep his word before she left.

She selected her contact: Travis, and pondered what to say. *"Leaving Tuesday. Are we good?"*

His reply warranted no wait. *"At Camp Pendleton now."*

She exhaled and held the phone close for a moment before responding with a thanks. She couldn't help wondering why he was still using his phone so freely if he were really in boot camp, but she had no choice other than to trust him.

Or tell Josiah.

She squashed the thought; she couldn't do something like that. As much as she trusted him, it wasn't her secret to tell. Besides, there had been no red flags of late, and Anneliese seemed to be doing better. At least Travis wasn't demanding the rest of the money.

In looking around the room, Gemma was glad to see that she had little left to do before Tuesday. All of the clothes were clean and folded in a neat pile, awaiting a suitcase she had been promised. Her backpack held any personal items, including her makeup and phone charger. That just left the playpen, chair, and air mattress to disassemble and the sheets to pack.

She blew out a breath. It was getting so close. The change would be both refreshing and scary. She'd gotten accustomed to the bustle of a full house and the chatter of children. Having a place to herself again might be a little disconcerting. *But it will be worth it.*

Gemma slipped out of her room and reclaimed her baby.

"He's the most precious thing, Gemma," Beth said, swishing her raven hair over her shoulder. "I hope my baby's as sweet."

"I'm sure he will be. Besides, every mommy loves her own baby."

"I know, I just worry sometimes. But I'm sure God knows what He's doing, and that's what gives me hope. We'll have to have play dates when I have my little one." She rested one hand on her belly and tickled Farris's cheek with the other, eliciting a smile and a squirm.

Gemma didn't think that sounded very likely, but she kept her mouth shut.

"Well, I suppose we'd better hit the road," David said. "The ice appears to have thawed and I'm sure they've scraped the roads by now. It was nice to meet you, Gemma. I hope the apartment works out."

She shook his hand. "Me, too." She hadn't even considered the possibility of it or her job falling through. *Maybe I will be back here pretty soon.* Her mind switched voices. *Don't think like that.*

January and Patrick took the hint and got ready to go, too. It took a solid hour of chiseling sheets of ice off windshields and windows before anyone could depart. No matter what tools were applied, the ice remained firmly glued to the glass until it looked like the men were going to hammer right through the window in an effort to separate the two.

"Sweet! That gives me time to do my makeup," January said. She was just emerging from the bathroom when Patrick came in, sweaty and frozen, to announce that the caravan could commence.

Hugs were spread around in equal amounts and all the children huddled at the window to watch the cars drive away.

"I don't like it when people leave," Lisabeth said.

"Gemma's leaving," Mariah said. Turning to Gemma she said, "Aren't you?"

She nodded and patted Lisabeth's curly head. "In a few days."

"But we get to keep Farris, right?" Lisabeth's eyes were wide and worried.

"I'm afraid he has to come with me. But maybe I'll come and see you."

"For my birthday?"

Gemma smiled. "Sure."

Lisabeth seemed consoled and turned back to the bleary window.

Seeing how sad the children were going to be with her leaving, Gemma made sure she spent extra time with them. She colored, read, and worked puzzles; she played with little plastic animals in their battle against the tractors. Not that this was the first time she engaged the children, but she wanted to be sure they would forgive her for leaving.

When it came to her last full day, she found that they had caught on and weren't going to give her up for anything.

"But you have to work on your letters," Anneliese said. She waved the paper in front of Lisabeth.

"I don't want to. I want to play with Gemma."

"You can't!"

Lisabeth crossed her arms and set her chin on them. "Then I want her to help me."

Anneliese sighed. "Fine, ask her. But if the answer's no, you still have to do them."

Gemma agreed to help with that and many other things in the midst of her last-minute packing. The more she placed in the back of the truck, the more she realized how much Mrs. Martin was sending with her. Bath towels, silverware, shampoo—anything she had that could cut down on the cost of Gemma's living on her own.

At first, Gemma tried to protest. "You know I have lived by myself once before."

"I know, dear. But we want it to be better than that. That's the whole point."

After that, she didn't argue. She knew she could use every item she was being sent with.

Gemma went to bed thoroughly exhausted, but wide awake. While Farris zipped through his most solid hours of sleep, she lay there with her mind too active to shut down. Just as her thoughts were quieting, Farris woke up, eager for his first nighttime feeding.

That accomplished, it was his turn to be restless. Patting, rocking, singing—none of it helped. She was determined to sleep some, because their first night in a new place would most likely be wakeful as well. So she resorted to walking with him outside her room again.

Moments after she emerged, she heard the back door click. She froze and her frazzled mind raced to think who else might be up. She tiptoed to the door, still soothing Farris, and peered out. She could just barely spy a retreating figure.

Oh no, not again! He said he was in California!

That settled it. Anneliese wouldn't listen to reason and she had given Travis a chance. Regardless of the fact that she would sink in the Martins' opinion and anger Travis, her silence was too dangerous. She would have to tell someone.

Tuesday morning dawned long before Gemma was ready. She slugged her feet over the edge of the mattress when her phone buzzed her alarm. With any luck, she could shower before the baby woke.

Once she had selected her long-sleeved shirt and jeans and retreated to the bathroom upstairs, she faced herself in the mirror. Her skin had a healthy glow, despite the extreme cold, and her hair now reached her waist. Any darkness around her eyes had completely vanished. Her post-baby figure looked like she had actually eaten instead of given birth. It was amazing the difference from the first time she stood in this room.

She heard a scuffle outside the door. *Don't get sentimental, just take a shower.*

Once she had finally conditioned the ends of her hair and applied some mascara, she gathered her pajamas and placed them in the suitcase. She tugged the zipper around its track and set it outside her door. Now she just had to find some socks and she was set.

Gemma gave the room one more glance as she tugged them on, just to make sure she had gotten everything. Not that there had been much to get. Only the beds, the baby, and his quilt remained.

She scooped him out of the playpen, breathing in his warm, baby smell, and joined the others for one last breakfast. Anneliese was present, she noted, but looked rather dreary.

If Mrs. Martin's taking me, then I guess I'll have to tell her. She sighed. She didn't want to tell anyone, but what choice did she have? It was for Anneliese's own good. Shuddering to think how *she* would have reacted if someone had tried to break up her and Travis, she strengthened her resolve. No amount of personal discomfort on her part was going to stop her now.

Everyone else appeared rather sullen, even Mr. Martin. *What does he think about me leaving?*

As breakfast came to a quiet conclusion, Lisabeth set down her fork and burst into tears. "I don't want Gemma to go-o."

All eyes turned to Gemma, conveying the same sentiment.

Gemma swallowed and avoided Josiah's gaze. "I'll see you again."

"But my birthday's a long way awa-ay." Lisabeth's voice was even higher than usual with her melancholy onslaught.

Gemma crossed to the other side of the table and gave her a one-armed hug. "I love you. And you have to be a good girl while I'm gone, OK?"

Lisabeth nodded, giving Farris a trembling kiss on the forehead.

No one's emotions were completely in check for the next half hour before Gemma left.

They all lined up, outside this time, to say goodbye. Gemma strapped Farris in his car seat and then gave them all hugs, one at a time. She gave Lisabeth and Anneliese a little extra, just for encouragement.

"Now I'll be keeping in touch with Emmaline so she can find me some things for my house. So I want to hear about everything y'all are doing, OK?"

The younger ones nodded while the older ones smiled.

She came to Mr. Martin, who offered his hand. She took it and offered her most heartwarming smile.

"You've become a big part of this family, Gemma. Don't hesitate if there's anything we can do."

The tears pricked her eyes and she gave a quick nod.

Josiah was next and she had no idea whether she should hug him or shake his hand. She wanted to do both.

"Don't worry, I'm coming with you," he said.

"Really?" She wondered for one horrible second if he was preying on her emotions.

"Yeah, I'm the heavy lifter."

"Oh, great."

She turned and hoisted herself into the car next to her sleeping baby. Mrs. Martin started the engine and all the children began to wave.

Gemma waved back out of the dusty back window until their faces blended together on the horizon.

Chapter 17

The two-hour drive to Wichita passed quickly and with little mishap. Josiah had been the navigator.

"You'll need the next exit," he said.

"No, it's not until after the bridge, right?"

"Mom, it's this exit right here. You'll have to be in the right lane. Mom!"

"Oh, that one?" She craned her neck to see it. "Well, there it goes. Never mind, we'll take the next one, dear."

Josiah threw up his hands. "Mom, why am I even navigating if you aren't going to listen?"

"Oh, stop. I thought it was after the bridge is all."

"I'm the one with the map!"

"All right, smarty," Mrs. Martin said. "Find us a road to a bathroom; I'm about to die and Farris needs a diaper change."

Josiah unfolded the map again, muttering something about his license.

Once everyone had stretched, they completed the last leg of the journey.

As they neared the apartments, they skirted the edge of the city and drove down a quiet residential street. At the end stood the complex just as Mr. Martin had described—a two-story U. It was dingy red brick with concrete stairs leading to the second story. A narrow sidewalk separated the building from the parking lot, a strip of nicely landscaped grass cutting through the middle.

Gemma took it all in. This is what she would wake up and come home to every day. *I can get used to it.* It certainly beat Winkle's old place, especially if the inside looked anything like the pictures.

"What number are you?" Josiah asked.

"Twenty," Gemma said, unsnapping Farris's car seat from its base.

"Nice, you'll be on the end. That way you're not completely boxed in by neighbors. Leaves more room for windows."

Gemma glanced at her phone. "The landlord should be here any minute to give us the tour."

An SUV pulled in as she finished speaking. An older Asian woman climbed out and approached them, a quizzical look on her wrinkled face.

Or landlady.

"Are you Gemma?" The slightest trace of an accent tinged her voice. "I'm Jackie. Follow me, please."

She waddled up to the door with the tarnished number twenty and unlocked it.

They were led into a perfectly square living room, complete with speckled carpet the texture of yarn. A kitchenette nestled against the far wall with an empty place on its tile perfect for a table. A hall to the right held two bedrooms of equal size and a bathroom in between.

"Well, there you have it. Think you'll be happy?"

Gemma nodded. "Yes, it looks perfect. Thank you."

The woman bobbed her head. "I've got the contract with me if you fill it in and sign off. Rent is seven hundred and due first week of every month. That work?"

"Yes, ma'am."

"Good. I'll get you paperwork and then you can unpack."

Gemma signed the paperwork, filling out all the necessary information. She hesitated to list Winkle as her last landlord, but, despite the bad reference he was likely to give, she felt the need to be honest.

Mrs. Martin saw her write it in and before Jackie could copy down the number, she said, "Gemma stayed with us most recently and I can assure you she'll be an excellent tenant."

Gemma breathed an internal sigh of relief.

No doubt Jackie had noticed Gemma's attachment to the Martins. "We are all good now. Thank you and enjoy." She left a black business card on the bar as she left from which Gemma gleaned the woman's phone number.

"Want to start unpacking?" Josiah asked, stretching his arms above his head.

"Actually, I would really like food." She relieved Mrs. Martin of her child.

"Pizza?"

"Pizza would be awesome. You think you can find a place?"

"You could give the map another shot," Mrs. Martin chuckled.

"Why don't we just ask the neighbors?" Josiah said. "They look like the pizza sort, judging by their cars. And then maybe we can get delivery."

"Touché," Gemma said.

"Wait, you have to come with me. You're their new neighbor."

Gemma groaned. "Fine. But I'm only trying one and then you're on your own."

"Yes!" Josiah pumped his fist in victory. "Take the baby, he'll help."

Gemma rolled her eyes. "Be right back."

The troop marched to door nineteen, Josiah giving it a confident knock. A middle-aged man of small stature answered the door, music blaring in the background.

"Look, tell Jackie I paid my rent. And I don't have any dog, either!"

"Actually, we were wondering if you could direct us to the nearest pizza place, delivery preferable," Josiah said.

The man blinked.

"We're new," was all Josiah offered for explanation.

"Domino's." The man disappeared for a moment and returned with a number. He looked Gemma over. "Are you two a couple?"

"No," Josiah said.

At the same time Gemma said, "Yes." She gave Josiah a look. "It's complicated." She shifted Farris to draw attention to the fact that she had a child and did her best not to melt under the man's quizzical stare. The man's brow furrowed, but he didn't really seem to care. He closed the door and Gemma reentered her apartment wondering why in the world they hadn't just Googled "Wichita pizza."

Mrs. Martin appeared to be in the bathroom, so Josiah went ahead and asked, "Why did you lie to him?"

"Because he's a creep and I don't want a neighbor hitting on me."

"You don't know he's a creep."

"Excuse me, but did you see what he had on his TV? He is most definitely a creep."

Josiah shrugged. "All right, so we're a couple to the creeps. Good to know. I'm going to order pizza." He dug for his phone in the pocket of his jeans.

Gemma released her frustration in one exhale and sat against the wall. *At least we know the walls are soundproof.* She propped Farris up against her knees and made a funny face. "You've been such a good boy! What do you think of the new place, huh? You like it? Let's go check out your room again."

She pushed herself to her feet again, noting the burning in her calves. *Man, I need to exercise. A desk job is not going to do me many favors.*

Mrs. Martin came out of the bathroom and joined Gemma in the bedroom. "Nothing looks like it needs very much work, dear. We'll probably want to sanitize those bathroom cabinets before you put anything in there. I want to cover all your bases, so I'll start making a list. Is Josiah handling lunch? Oh, good. It makes me happy to see men do meals."

Gemma smiled and looked around the room. Mrs. Martin was right. As long as the bedroom had a good vacuuming it should be fine. *Vacuum. Maybe the Martins brought theirs.* She blew out a breath. It was going to be an adventure, that was for sure.

The pizza arrived and was devoured. Then Josiah focused on the next task at hand: unpacking. Mrs. Martin had brought a great deal of cleaning supplies with her and put them to use immediately. Farris's bedroom, the one at the back of the apartment, held first priority because he would need to nap soon and Gemma had other uses for her hands.

"I don't know what I'm going to do with him at work. I can't very well bring the playpen with me. And I can't type if I'm holding him."

"Maybe he'll nap in his seat," Mrs. Martin said, patting the baby's back. "That reminds me. Your interview is tomorrow. I thought Josiah could take you and I could keep Farris." She hurried on when a look of concern crossed Gemma's face. "It's just to square some things away before you get started."

"All right. I'll make sure I pump tonight so you can feed him."

Josiah switched on the vacuum in the bedroom, making Farris jump and burst into his high-pitched cry.

"O-oh. You're all right, buddy." Gemma held him closer and kissed his head, but he was not to be consoled. She stepped outside and almost instantly he quieted. "Goodness, you're silly. Are you getting tired, love?"

Farris nestled in and yawned, his tiny features scrunching up. But his large eyes remained open in rebellion until the moment he was placed in the bottom of his playpen with his favorite blanket.

Gemma tiptoed out of the room and left the door open just a crack. She took full advantage of his naptime and conquered the kitchen. A dusting of dirt coated the cabinets, inside and out. Gemma cleaned the lower ones, wetting them down with vinegar and wiping out the grit. Meanwhile, Josiah leisurely wiped at the high cabinets, and Mrs. Martin continued to add to her grocery list.

Once Farris awoke, Gemma's bedroom had been tidied and her air mattress inflated and topped with sheets.

"Now I want a nap."

"You could take one, you know," Josiah said, resting his shoulder against the doorframe.

"No, I can't. But it's all right."

Mrs. Martin approached absentmindedly, pencil in hand. "I think I'm about ready to make a store run, dears. Who wants to come with me?"

Josiah remained mum.

"I can," Gemma said.

"You? Oh no, you don't have to." Mrs. Martin looked around. "I keep forgetting there's so few of us. How about it, son? Then Gemma can really practice settling in."

He propelled himself off the door facing. "All right."

"I'll save anything that requires your decisions until tomorrow, Gemma."

"Just go ahead and get whatever you think will be best. I don't have an opinion."

Mrs. Martin's smile brightened. "All right, if you're sure."

They were gone for nearly two hours, during which time Gemma kept Farris fed and happy and answered any questions Mrs. Martin had via text.

Oh my gosh. My phone bill.

She hadn't thought about in months. When she had left Uncle Wilfred's, he was still paying it. He was supposed to have it transferred to her address at Winkle's place, but never did.

Or if he did it's too late now.

She didn't have the slightest idea how one went about those things. At least she knew her other bills would be covered by Jackie. She would just have to ask the Martins.

When they returned, laden with plastic bags, they had bought more than Gemma could have thought to ask for. Everything from soaps and snacks to a shower curtain and shelf paper was at her disposal. All of it was unpacked and the rest of the day spent convincing the shelf paper to glue itself into cabinets and drawers. The silverware got organized in the divider that had been purchased and the bathroom received a facelift.

When Gemma had eaten cold pizza and felt ready to pass out from exhaustion, Mrs. Martin revealed her frivolous gifts: two throw pillows and a mirror for Gemma's bedroom.

"You shouldn't have," Gemma breathed, even as she fingered the items.

"I thought you'd like them. Maybe you can help me pick some more things out before we leave. It's the little things that make a house a home."

And eat your money.

"Thank you very much." She went to set it all in her room, and did not return.

Gemma woke with a start to the pitch black. Uncertainty gripped her stomach as she struggled to remember where she was.

Then, gradually, everything came filtering back into her memories. What had awakened her? She heard the noise again—a tiny cry.

As she stumbled through the short hall, she heard something stir to her left. It made her stomach tighten until she remembered the Martins had to be sleeping somewhere.

She slipped into Farris's bedroom to feed him and then collapsed back onto her air mattress. She didn't stir again until she heard Mrs. Martin in the kitchen, probably trying to persuade the range to work.

Gemma eased herself off the mattress and was pleased to note she was still in her clothes. That was one less thing to worry about. She was surprised to see Josiah holding Farris, who was just beginning to frown at his stalling.

He held him out. "I think he wants you."

"Aw, thanks for watching him." She lifted the baby to her shoulder. "I didn't hear him wake up."

"Neither did we. I peeked in on him and he was awake, so I got him up."

"Oh." She patted Farris's back and her voice slipped into its baby pitch. "Well, good for you, buddy."

"Eggs are ready," Mrs. Martin said. She set a steaming skillet on the bar, hotpad sandwiched between the two.

"Awesome. I'll be right back." Gemma excused herself, fed the baby, and pumped enough for a feeding while she was gone at her interview, since she'd forgotten to do it the night before.

She set the bottle in the fridge and served herself breakfast. There was no table or chairs so they all stood at the bar, taking turns with the baby.

"What are you going to wear to the interview, dear?" Mrs. Martin asked.

Gemma glanced at her yoga pants. "I could put on my dress."

"Excellent idea. Why don't we conquer wiping out the freezer and vacuuming the baseboards before lunch and then you two can eat and go to your interview."

Josiah ended up doing both the chores because Mrs. Martin left to run more errands and Farris wanted to be held only by his mommy.

Mrs. Martin returned just as Gemma got Farris down for a nap. She went to slip on her dress and comb out her tangled curls. Wanting to make a good first impression, she put on as much makeup as she dared.

She and Josiah snuck out not long after. *Tell him,* her mind pressed, but she shushed it.

"Do you know where we're going?" she asked.

"Yeah, downtown."

She gave him an unamused look as they drove deeper into the heart of the city.

Josiah shuddered. "I hate the city; too many people and not enough space. But look, the Old Cowtown Museum is that way. That sounds nice."

Gemma rolled her eyes as they crossed the river. "I think this is it on the right, so look for a turn." There was a moment of silence. "Thanks for doing this."

"Sure. You know we're only helping you so much because you're more trustworthy than the other people we've helped," he said with a wink.

She chuckled. "Well, thank you. It means a lot that you guys gave me a second chance."

Minutes later, they were walking up to the multi-story structure with alternating stripes of tan building and dark windows.

Gemma ducked her head to get a complete look. "Wow, this is right on the river. That's kind of fun, I guess. Now let's see if we can find the right office."

Gemma, not ashamed to ask for directions, confronted the first person she saw, who directed her to the second floor. They took the elevator and came out in a lobby with two glass doors, black letters painted on them. One led to the Law Office of Walter Franklin.

"Here we are." Josiah held the door open for Gemma and she took it all in, trying to get an accurate first impression.

A woman sat at a desk immediately in front of them with a glass wall behind her, showing the churning, muddy river. She looked shockingly unprofessional with her choppy black pigtails. The office opened up to the left, revealing a network of cubicles from which the incessant typing sounds emanated. Gemma guessed the doors to the right led to the office of the owner. It had windows that would have allowed a view in, but all the blinds had been lowered. The secretary asked her name and they followed the fluorescent lighting and thin, gray carpet several paces to the formal office.

The secretary—her name was Miss James—knocked and let them both in.

"Oh, he's not here," she said, exasperated. "Well, he should be soon. Good luck."

The door closed behind them.

Gemma and Josiah took a seat in the plush, leather chairs. She glanced at the nameplate on the desk. *Walter Franklin. This* is *his office.*

"Is she gone?" A head peeped through a door to their left. "Oh good." The man darted to the chair across from them and rolled it to the desk with the toe of his dress shoe.

"Now, you're here for that job, right?" The edge of his voice and cut of his suit hinted of England.

"Yes, sir."

"Splendid. I've reviewed your application file and I think you'll be excellent. So, I'll come up with a few questions to ask you and then you should be good." He smiled, displaying perfect white teeth. "Let's see. You are comfortable on a computer?"

Gemma nodded.

"And you can get things done in a timely and orderly fashion?" She nodded again and forced her voice to work. "Yes, sir."

"Good. And, um, . . . you don't mind having an office to yourself?"

"That would actually be preferable."

184

"Fantastic! It's just that there are two partners, but the younger isn't around much and we have to have someplace to keep all our filing cabinets. So you're welcome to have that space. Have you ever worked at a law firm before, Gemma?"

"No, sir."

"Well, that's all right. I'll show you your office posthaste and give you a few pointers and then all remains is the drug test and paperwork."

He led the way into the adjoining room, complete with file cabinets, bookshelves, its own desk, and a laptop.

"You'll have to share some of this space with Miss James out there. She's our greeting secretary, but hasn't a lick of organization about her. So we try to get her to just answer the phone and set up appointments. We want you for all the filing and paperwork. Think you can do that?"

"I'll do my best."

"Splendid. You'll have to sign a confidentiality agreement because it's vital that you keep anything you read to yourself."

"Of course."

He led the way back into the office and unlocked a desk drawer, pulling out a stack of papers and grabbing a shiny, reflective pen. "Confidentiality, minimum benefits. Give it a glance and let me know if you have questions."

Gemma took the papers and pen and carefully read the fine print as Josiah amused himself by staring around the room. Having never done anything this official, she asked about a few legal terms, but everything was to her satisfaction in the end. She slid the papers back across the desk, her name signed at the bottom.

"Thank you very much. Everything looks lovely. If you're able to go ahead and take a drug test at the doctor on Hillside, that would be splendid."

"Certainly," Gemma said. Farris would be fine for an extra little while. She'd just have to let Mrs. Martin know.

"Perfection. I'll let you be on your way." He shook her hand.

Excitement blossomed inside of her. Had she actually gotten the job? "When should I start?"

"Oh. Let's see, today's Wednesday. How about Friday for a trial run and if you still feel good about it, you'll be ours from then on?"

"I can do that."

"Good. So long." He shook her hand again and held it out for Josiah, who had remained eerily quiet. "Mister . . . ?"

"Pennyworth," Josiah said.

Gemma refrained from staring at him and exited the office. Miss James stopped her before she made it back to the lobby.

"Gemma. Did he hire you?"

She nodded, fighting a smile. "I still have to take a drug test."

The secretary waved it off. "Congrats, kiddo. Do you live close?"

"Yeah, Franklin Street."

"Sweet! I'm at the Villa Del Mar. Say, I read your file and saw you have a baby with you. Do you need me to pick you up or anything?"

Gemma took a moment to process the offer, but was so grateful this open woman had thought to ask, because she'd already forgotten she wouldn't have a car.

"Actually . . . yeah. If it's not out of your way."

She brushed her off with a flick of her wrist. "Five minutes is all it'll cost me. Friday?"

"Yes, please."

"Count on it, hon. And call me Hollie. Here's my number, because I'm sure the old coot forgot something."

"Thank you so much! Bye."

Josiah held the door again and Gemma waited until they were in the privacy of the elevator to explode.

"Why the heck did you lie about your last name?"

He jumped. "He was a creep."

"What?!"

"You said to be a couple to the creeps."

186

"Pennyworth is *not* my last name."

"It—oh." He took a moment to collect himself. "Well, I don't think he knew that. I doubt he even read your file. And that other secretary lady called him old. He wasn't old!"

The elevator dinged. "What are you talking about? Of course he read the file. And he's not a creep and I don't care how old he is!"

"OK, so he wasn't creepy, but there was definitely something underhanded about him. But I'm glad everything went so smooth. Honest."

"Thanks," she muttered.

She did her best to release her frustration on her way across the parking lot. It took half an hour to get through the drug test process and head back toward the apartment. As she updated Mrs. Martin on their ETA, she contemplated again whether or not she should tell Josiah about Travis since he was still sulking anyway. But he brought it up first.

"Is there anything you want to tell me about Anneliese?"

She stared at the side of his face, placid, as he kept his eyes transfixed on the road. "Why would you ask that?"

"Well, for starters, you were up when she snuck out."

"If you knew, why didn't you say anything?"

"I could ask you the same question. But I just found out."

Gemma settled back in her seat. "What do you think she's up to?"

"Seeing someone? And someone no good by the looks of it. Why else would she sneak out at night?" A crease appeared on his suntanned brow.

"Has she told you anything?"

"Of course not. You?"

"No. What's your other reason for asking?"

"Look, I haven't mentioned anything to Dad yet because I wasn't sure and wanted to get accurate information before I bust her, so I need you to be honest with me. I know you could just be concerned more like me, but I think it's more than that." He stole a glance at her as they pulled up in front of the apartment.

She stared at the number on her door, weighing how much to tell him . . . if anything. The demand shoved its way into her head: *Tell him.*

"It's Travis Long," she blurted.

"Oh." Josiah looked a little relieved until he turned off the car and saw the look on her face. "What? I'll speak to him."

Gemma shook her head, ever so slightly.

He tilted his head back to rest against the window. "What aren't you telling me?"

"I met him in Texas." She dropped her gaze. "He's . . . He's Farris's father. He told me he was at Camp Pendleton now, but I don't think he is."

"Travis is . . ."

Gemma twisted her fingers together, trying to think of what else to say, as Josiah sat in stunned silence.

"You didn't know he lived here. That day at church . . . Is that why you took the money from Dad?"

Gemma nodded.

Understanding dawned in his eyes. "You were protecting Anneliese. Gemma, why didn't you tell me sooner?"

She flinched at the reproach in his voice. "I'm sorry, but it wasn't my secret to tell. I was stupid and scared as always," she spat. "I didn't want everyone to hate me and I thought I could do it by myself but I failed." She heaved a ragged sigh. "Again."

Thoughts still written across his forehead, he squeezed her hand and swung himself out of the car. "Anneliese is in so much trouble."

Chapter 18

"I'm so sorry to cut and run like this, Gemma," Mrs. Martin said, placing her purse on her shoulder. "I hoped to stay longer, but with the younger ones coming down with the stomach flu, Anneliese will want backup. I hope we were helpful and all goes well."

"Thanks for all you've done. I totally understand." Gemma gave her a hug. Then it hit her. *They're leaving . . . for good.* "Thank you."

"Oh of course, it—"

"No, for everything." She stepped back. "I wouldn't have made it without you."

Mrs. Martin's soft, brown eyes went serious. "You're very welcome. See you soon." She gave Gemma another tight squeeze before slipping out the door.

That left Gemma with the "do I hug Josiah" complex yet again, but this time she didn't hesitate. Actually, she kind of clobbered him. But it didn't matter; she couldn't see his face. How else could she say everything she was feeling?

She drew back and didn't make eye contact for a moment. "Thank you so much, Josiah. You've meant a lot to me." She ventured a glance now that her emotions were more controlled.

He offered a small smile. "Anytime. Sorry we didn't get to talk about some of the new Bible concepts."

She shrugged.

He nodded, as if unsure what to say next. "Well, see you 'round."

She stepped outside with him and watched them climb into the truck and drive away. She wondered if she had really overstepped her bounds, but then she remembered . . . he had hugged her back.

A knock sounded on the door. Gemma applied the last dash of baby powder and fastened Farris's diaper. She scooped him up and hurried to open the door; time was everything on her first day of work!

"Hey, Hollie."

"Hey!" The receptionist from the interview stood in the doorway, her hair sitting in a straight cut against her jawline today. "Are you ready to go? First day!"

"Almost." Gemma glanced behind her. "I have to grab his seat. Could you hold him?"

In moments, they were on their way.

"Thanks so much for doing this," Gemma said, clicking her seatbelt.

"Don't mention it, hon. Oh, before we get there, I wanted to ask what you thought of Franklin."

What are the odds my boss has the same name as my street? "He was . . . different. It was the most unique interview I've ever had. I'll get used to it, I guess."

"I hope so. At least you got an office to yourself!"

190

"I know! It will be helpful with Farris, but he's a pretty good kiddo." She reached back and patted his wispy head.

"He's super cute. Hey, and I am totally willing to watch him for you. Or run errands. Whatever you need, I'm here to help!"

"That's very sweet." Gemma tried to imagine this vibrant young woman being responsible for a small human life.

"Here we are," Hollie sang as she whipped into the spacious parking lot. She parked surprisingly straight for how sudden her decision appeared to be.

Gemma unsnapped Farris, still bleary from his interrupted schedule, and walked up to the daunting building with confidence. Hollie clicked ahead of her in her leopard print heels.

Gemma blew out a sigh as they waited on the elevator.

Hollie peered at her. "You nervous?"

"A little. I'm a single mom just short of delinquency with a résumé consisting of fast food." She blinked. *I can't believe I just said all that.*

But Hollie just patted her on the shoulder. "You and me both, kid. That's why I just answer the phone."

Gemma felt encouraged by her newfound friend. If worse came to worst, at least she had an ally. As they passed the other businesses in the lobby and entered the law office, she was surprised to see they were the first ones there. Except for the boss, whose shadow revealed he was smoking what looked like a cigar.

Hollie took her seat. "Good luck, hon."

Gemma nodded and entered her office with as much stealth as she could manage. She set Farris in the corner and opened the laptop on her mahogany desk. It flashed to life and asked for her credentials. She stared. *Credentials?* She chose her profile, which someone had kindly created, and tried to guess what the password might be.

Why would they lock me out of my own computer?

It clicked. They hadn't. She pressed enter and the computer welcomed her into the home screen.

She straightened, proud of her breakthrough.

"Congratulations," a voice boomed from the adjoining doorway.

Gemma jumped and faced a robust, balding man. She was grateful she sat in her leather chair, or else her start would have been more noticeable.

"You just passed my entrance exam, young lady."

Gemma swallowed and squelched her fluttering stomach. "Thank you." *Oh my goodness. I'm so glad!* Her brain raced to understand who this man might be. If this was Walter Franklin . . . who was the man from yesterday?

"I see my nephew, Bradley, hired you. Just as well. I'll have Miss James print a report for you of things to be filed. I have no idea how often we'll need you yet. Bradley will have to make time to train you on the computer soon."

Nephew. How interesting. She wondered if Hollie knew the nephew had conducted her interview.

"Not that he's ever doing anything useful," he muttered, puffing on his cigar some more.

Gemma wished he wouldn't do that with Farris in the room. If it made her brain hazy, there was no telling what it was doing to his. Surely there was a no-smoking policy! But he was the boss. She was grateful when he retreated back into his quarters and shut the adjoining door.

Hollie chose that moment to pop into the room with a legal box full of obscure and slightly crumpled papers.

"File these alphabetically by client. It should say on the letterhead; our client is almost always the plaintiff. Shout if you need any help." She shut the door with a whoosh.

Gemma checked on Farris in the corner, who played happily with his fist. She would have taken it as a good omen if she believed in that sort of thing.

Gemma spent the rest of her morning working on the task before her, and didn't realize until the lunch break sounded and she looked at the remaining pile just how much she had left. Farris was getting fretful over his delayed nap and refused to sleep in his seat, just as she feared.

Hollie made a sad face when Gemma passed her to take Farris out into the network of businesses. She bounced him next to the elevator, hoping his noises weren't penetrating into the other offices. Just as she was beginning to wonder if this was a horrible idea, Farris shuddered slightly and gave in. Hopefully neither Mr. Franklin nor his nephew Mr. Bradley would want to fire her at the end of the day.

Gemma breathed more easily and laid him on a pallet on her office floor. She was about to return to her pile when Hollie tiptoed in.

"Finally out? Poor guy. I brought you lunch." She held up a paper sack.

"Oh my goodness, thanks!" Gemma unwrapped it and bit into the meal, not taking the time to let her taste buds register what it was.

"Hey, if you ever have a free weekend, let me know. I'd love to hang out or go shopping or something." Hollie took a sip of her drive-thru soda.

"My weekends are always free. What do you think I do besides take care of Farris and work? Although, I'd like to find a church." Gemma watched Hollie's face, having no idea if she was a religious person.

She didn't even bat an eyelash. "Try First Baptist. It's where my brother and I go. It's got a good pastor and nice nursery. And I attend a Bible study Thursday evening if you want a ride."

"That's good to know." Gemma brushed the hamburger crumbs off her desk into the wastebasket and threw a glance at her son, tucked on his pallet on the floor. "Do you live with your brother?"

Hollie sucked a breath through her teeth and widened her brown eyes. "Yeah, it was supposed to be temporary, but he hasn't gotten a steady job yet. He's OK, though . . . as far as brothers go, I mean." She slurped loudly on her straw before pitching the styrofoam cup in the trash. She hurled herself out of her chair when the phone rang and never returned to finish her hamburger.

Gemma was very proud of herself when, by the end of the day, the mass of papers was nearly depleted. Her only disappointment was that the mystery nephew never showed. She wanted to speak with him again. Or just listen to him talk—either way.

But Hollie was ready to dash before he ever appeared. She chatted about nothing the whole way to Gemma's apartment and finally ended by handing Gemma a piece of paper with her phone number. "Let me know if you want to go to church Sunday. Have a nice weekend!"

Gemma fed Farris again and put him down for the night. She crashed onto her mattress and clicked her phone out of habit. She smiled and brought the phone closer to her face when she saw a text waiting from Josiah.

"How was your day?"

"Success," she typed, even though the day had been a complete blur. *"Your family feeling better?"*

She waited several minutes, only to receive a *"Yes"* in response. He wasn't nearly as chatty over the phone. Then she remembered that his phone was even more of a relic than her own. At least hers had a sliding keypad. She chuckled, picturing him trying to type with his callused fingers on the little numbered buttons, and soon fell asleep.

Gemma was thankful she had agreed to begin work on a Friday, because nothing could be as relaxing as waking up and remembering the weekend had already arrived. She was careful to use her time wisely, knowing she would feel shorted before long.

Once Farris had gotten used to the idea of waking up, she decided to bathe him in the sink using the blue plastic baby tub she had received at her shower. He was in a terrible mood, but she wanted him fresh in case she attended a church tomorrow.

Gemma read the instructions on the side of the box and all the warning stickers before turning the water on. Mrs. Martin had always helped her before. She turned the stiff knob for warm water just a smidge and then added the cold water to compensate. Once the temperature was OK, she undressed Farris and placed him in the lukewarm water. She supported him with one hand and used the other to wipe him clean with a delicate baby washcloth. It took extreme concentration to keep him comfortable and work at the icky rolls of his neck where everything liked to collect. The mild case of cradle cap was going to be next when he began to exert his little lungs to complain.

"Oh, what's the matter? Are you too cold?" She kissed the top of his wet head and reached for a towel. She wrapped him in it as quickly as she could and was very proud of herself for avoiding a mess.

"Come on, buddy. Let's find you a diaper and some clothes. Thank you very much for not wetting on me this time." She fastened his diaper and tried to work the snaps on his onesie with speed, which did not prove easy. "Did you like that?"

His round eyes blinked back at her.

"You did, didn't you? Calmed right down. Mommy will have to remember that in case of an emergency."

The next item on her nonexistent agenda was exploring the surrounding neighborhood. Franklin Street was smack in the middle of a cozy, rural area at the heart of the city. Gemma, having no car, strapped Farris into his harness and took a long walk. She didn't have the courage to knock on any doors and become that annoying neighbor that shows up unannounced, but she did wave and swap hellos with anyone out in their manicured yards.

She made it halfway down the long street, near where she and Hollie usually crossed the river for work, but she still hadn't seen anything new. So she took a parallel street and enjoyed watching the variety of houses drift past. The only trouble was one terrier who barked at her with a great deal of ferocity from his house, but never

actually ventured past the edge of the driveway. All the same, it made
Farris cry something awful and she kept carrying a large stick in mind
for next time. Also, having something to lean on might help ease the
pain that had grown in her abdomen by the time they arrived back at
the apartment. They'd have to check out the Botanical Gardens
another day.

A more local neighbor from the second floor hauled her trash
down the cement stairs as Gemma fumbled to draw the key out of
her jean pocket.

The woman raised a coffee-colored hand in greeting. "You
new?"

Gemma watched her with sporadic glances as she fumbled with
the lock. "Yes. How about you?"

"Not very."

An indistinguishable voice came from up the stairs and the
woman responded with, "Be right there!" She turned to Gemma.
"Better go now. See you 'round!" She jaunted back up the stairs and
the voices faded into their apartment.

Gemma gave the key one last wrench and the doorknob gave
way. *Success!* She slipped into the room that was already beginning to
feel like home and gave it a scrutinizing glance. She was in desperate
need of something to sit on. Just a chair might do since she grew
tired of having to stand to eat all the time. She'd have to get
something before long. Maybe she'd call Hollie later and see about
going shopping.

Going shopping? She laughed at herself. She didn't have any money
to spend yet. Besides, dining furniture was expensive. Best put
Emmaline on the scent.

Gemma decided to call Hollie anyway, but instead of asking
about a shopping trip, she asked for a ride to church on Sunday.

She agreed without a second's hesitation. "Sure! We can skip
Sunday school for Farris's sake. See you at ten thirty Sunday
morning!"

Gemma smiled at her vivacity even over the phone. "Thank you so much. See you then."

She fed Farris again and put him down for his morning nap. The happy effects of his bath had worn off and the exhaustion from the walk had set in. Gemma felt the same and indulged in a hot shower once she felt certain he was going to stay asleep.

The hot beads of water felt so relaxing, she had to fight to keep her eyes open. Even standing couldn't keep her awake. When she snapped back to consciousness, having inhaled water, she decided she'd better be done and the endless battle of untangling her waist-length hair ensued. She glowered at the knotted, dripping locks contemptuously in the mirror. *I wonder if I have any scissors?* She dressed herself and scoured the corner piled with packing material for some, but no luck. It would have to wait. She forced it into a braid, but banded it off halfway, her arms growing tired.

Gemma drank in the silence of her little home and sank against the steady resistance of her air mattress. Her eyelids promptly became leaden and she surrendered to sleep in no time.

When Gemma woke up, she found herself fumbling to respond to the knock on the front door before her brain had awakened. She blinked rapidly and stifled a yawn before she unbolted the door and pried it open.

Jackie stood at the door, letter in hand. "Hi. Didn't think you find your mailbox, so I bring it to you."

"Oh, thanks." Gemma quit trying to disguise her foggy state since Jackie either hadn't noticed or didn't care.

"You're welcome. All is well?"

Gemma nodded, prodding her brain to catch up as she leaned into the end of the door. "Very nice. My first month's rent is in the deposit box." *Courtesy of the Martins . . .*

Jackie gave a short nod and seemed content. "OK. Bye now!" She waddled down the sidewalk under the awning of the building and Gemma shut the door on her retreating figure.

She felt like returning to bed, but knew she'd better not in case she slept through Farris's crying. She looked down at the envelope she held. Her address was scrawled on the front very neatly, but the return address took up most of the top left quarter and had been written in crayon.

Gemma smiled at the sender: "Martin kids."

She slid to the floor, back resting against the once-white door. She tugged her finger along the fold of the envelope and pulled out the construction papers within. There were five pieces, a coloring page from Gail with three brilliant strokes of green crayon, a flower rendering from Lisabeth, and two drawings from Mariah of her life on the farm. She chuckled at the stick figure girl with the large circle drawn over her stomach and guessed that was supposed to be her. Her own proportions aside, the horses weren't half bad. The other sheet was a nice note from Mrs. Martin inscribed on a piece of notebook paper.

Gemma,

I hope you've settled in some and are enjoying a place to yourself. I wanted to let you know that we contacted your uncle and he was very happy to help us switch the phone bill over to your address. If you need anything else, don't hesitate to call and we'll see what we can do. If you ever need to talk, I'm here. I'm sure everyone would love to know what's going on with you and Farris from time to time. And please feel free to surprise us with a visit whenever you need a break from your new routine.

We're praying for you, dear, and hope all is well.

Joy

Gemma folded the note and placed it back inside the envelope. The pictures she taped to the top of her bathroom mirror with box tape left over from the move. The mirror was so wide, they all fit in side by side, the one dull overhead light illuminating them.

There. They must have sent that right as they got back to get it to me so soon. It was crazy to think that she had still been part of the Martin clan less than a week ago. Already it seemed like a part of her past. But one she would always look back on with good memories.

Chapter 19

Hollie was on the doorstep looking less eccentric than usual at ten thirty sharp.

"Hey, lovelies! Are we ready?"

"Yes, ma'am. Lead the way."

Hollie marched to the car and swung herself into it. Her brother sat in the passenger seat.

He stood and Gemma noted the siblings shared short noses. That was not something she had ever suffered from. "Do you want to sit here?" he asked, his voice rough.

"No, go ahead. I can sit in the back with the baby."

He sank back into the overstuffed leather seat without another word, dark hair hiding his face.

The base to Farris's car seat was still secured in the middle seat from Friday. Since Hollie had begged to be her ride for everything, Gemma had consented to leave it for convenience's sake. She didn't know of anyone else who would be carting her all over the city.

"How far is it to the church?" Gemma asked, as Hollie backed out of the narrow parking lot with little grace and much speed.

"Not far," her brother murmured.

"Just a street or two past work," Hollie said. "Geez, I never even introduced you two. Gemma, this is my brother, Jacob. Jake, Gemma. The baby's Farris."

Gemma was impressed she had remembered her baby's name. *She* probably wouldn't have.

Jake held up a finger in greeting, the rest of his hand gripping the armrest. It was a wonder he ever got in the car with his sister. *Why doesn't he drive?* Then it occurred to her that Hollie probably wouldn't let him. She seemed rather territorial like that; she took over without anyone realizing it and once they did, she was too far gone to be stopped.

They breezed down Franklin Street, the many trees casting speckled shadows as they whizzed past. A right, then a left, and follow the river until the bridge. The office was just over the crossing on the right, but they sailed past it today. They took another turn at the gas station and passed several other prestigious-looking churches before they arrived at the doors of First Baptist. It was a rather plain and disappointing rectangle after all the architectural splendor of its neighbors, but it was still much grander than the Martins' church, Havenfeld. The parking lot alone could have swallowed it twice with room to spare.

Gemma rebuked herself for judging the plain building when they made their way around to the front and she saw the smooth variegated brownstone climbing into a facade that could have rivaled a historic, European home. The entrance they finally utilized was centered under a large flowerlike window.

"There." Hollie came to a stop and looked up. "You just had to see the front. Doesn't it make you want to go to church?" She gave a gleeful scrunch of her shoulders.

Gemma offered her friend a reassuring smile and they entered one of the three doors, each positioned under their own archway. She followed, looking at a conveniently displayed floor map to locate the nursery before the sermon began. Then she made her way back to the auditorium and took her seat with the Jameses. She would keep Farris with her until he got too loud.

"Think he'll be OK through the sermon?" Hollie asked, as the music minister made his way onto the stage.

"I'll probably have to step out, but that's OK," she whispered back.

An amplified guitar began to sound as the leader gave the song title. The words appeared on a large screen high above his head. They were much easier to follow than a hymnal. But the tune, although catchy, was hard to get the hang of since everyone sang on their own time. It didn't sound nearly as unified as it had at the Martins' church and Gemma began to wonder if the song would ever end as she tried to keep Farris happy. Hollie and Jake didn't seem to mind.

The music minister leaned closer to the microphone as he strummed the last chord on his guitar. "You may all be seated."

Gemma took a seat in one of the blue chairs, just barely softer than the burgundy pews from Havenfeld Bible Church.

A Scripture reading, recitation, and special music were all completed before a second congregational hymn. Farris was beginning to get more and more fidgety, but Gemma knew if she could hold out several minutes longer, he would fall asleep.

The pastor climbed the few stairs to the stage covered with musical instruments and cords. He rested his hands on either side of the pulpit and smiled out over the crowd. "Let's pray for wisdom before we examine God's Word today." And with hardly a breath, he delved into his prayer. "Father in Heaven, we thank You for this beautiful morning and for all the people here. We ask that You would bless those who are not here and keep them safe in the week ahead. Thank you for being with us, Father. Give us wisdom and understanding for the passage before us and strength for the days ahead, amen."

He spoke so fast, never pausing where Gemma expected, that she found him a little distracting to listen to. At least while rubbing the back of an infant fighting indigestion and sleep.

The pastor read from 1 Peter 2, a new book to Gemma since she had just begun Acts. But she remembered reading about a Peter and wondered if he was the same.

The pastor cleared his throat and began to read. "'Therefore, laying aside all malice, all deceit, hypocrisy, envy, and all evil speaking, as newborn babes, desire the pure milk of the Word, that you may grow thereby, if indeed you have tasted that the Lord is gracious.'"

Newborn babes. She looked down at Farris, his fair face relaxed and large eyes shut, cheek smushed against her arm. She turned her ears back to the pastor's explanation.

"What this is saying, folks, is that once you have accepted Christ as your Savior, you put all of your sins behind you and move forward. Like a new baby who needs milk, you crave the Word of God so that you can grow, because you have tasted the Lord's blessing, graciousness, by His accepting *you* into His family. And that acceptance is the focus of this chapter."

Gemma thought about what that meant for her. She certainly hadn't been reading from her Bible as consistently, and she couldn't say she craved it. But without time to study what came next, her days felt somehow emptier.

Farris started in her arms and let out a long cry. Gemma patted his back, but stood to make her way to the nursery. He was going to need more comforting than the still, full sanctuary allowed. All of the toddlers had been dismissed for Children's Church, so the sanctuary remained much quieter than Havenfeld ever had.

She was not the only mother to have retreated to the nursery. Several others occupied rocking chairs and were talking quietly amongst themselves. One little girl played with her hair bow on the floor while a boy lay on his tummy and looked at the object wistfully. Gemma noticed one of the mothers had twins as their smiles came up to meet hers.

"Hi," Gemma said, taking a seat next to the mother with twins.

"Hello. I'm Clair."

Another mother, occupied with her children, waved.

"Is this your first time here?" Clair asked. She traded the tiny girl in her lap for her brother on the floor.

"Yes, I came with Hollie James. I work with her."

"Oh, that's nice. How old is your baby?"

"Nine weeks. How old are yours?"

"The twins are five months and Juliet is eighteen months." The cherub girl looked up from her spot on the floor.

Gemma tried to keep her eyes from bugging and looked to the other mother.

"Mine's a year."

Clair widened her eyes and nodded. "I've never had such a high maintenance child as this one." She placed her youngest daughter on the floor. "Her brother and older sister are very laid back, but she's had a harder time of it than they have. The twins were born two months early, and it looked like she'd been robbed of all the nutrition."

Gemma looked at the roly-poly baby boy chortling in Clair's lap as she soothed Farris on her shoulder. Gemma'd never had other babies to compare Farris to, but, for being so young, he fell right in the middle of the twins. He was round, but not chunky.

After about half an hour, Farris had settled down and the sermon was coming to a close. The other moms began gathering all the snacks and toys that had been distributed and tucked them into diaper bags and strollers. Gemma made her way back to the sanctuary, wanting to catch the end of the sermon.

"The past is in the past," the pastor was saying. "You have to let go of your old sin, surrender it to Him. Once you are secure in His forgiveness, you can move forward into the new person you are. Set a higher expectation for yourself and never let falling back into your old ways be good enough. Do not be afraid to taste, to crave, the

Lord's graciousness and His mercy. That is not who you have to be anymore, thanks to His sacrifice. Let's pray."

Gemma stood at the back, with her head bowed but her eyes open, swaying to keep Farris quiet. Is that what it meant to live the Christian life? Once she had surrendered her sin and accepted the sacrifice, she had to move forward into a new life? *Don't be just a better person. Be more like Him.* That's why Genesis started the way it did. This is what God created His people to be. Josiah was right; knowing the whole story, it all made sense. It all fell together. The individual authors and books didn't matter. It was all God's story of saving His creation.

Josiah heard the back door click from his perch on the couch, book over his face. He sat up and dashed out the door after Anneliese. The sun was just beginning to set on the lazy Sunday. "Hey, wait up, sis."

She turned and frowned. "Josiah, do you have to come with me?"

Stuffing his hands in his pockets, he fell into step beside her. "Yeah, I kinda do. Don't you think it's a little early for a rendezvous?"

Anneliese halted and searched his eyes. "What do you mean? I'm not meeting anyone."

Josiah took a quick glance around. "Look, I don't know most of what you've been up to, but I know enough. You gotta stop this."

Her jaw tightened and she straightened. "I haven't done anything wrong."

"Anneliese, you know Travis is not a good person or you wouldn't be doing this behind all of our backs. You know I have to tell Dad."

"No! You know he wouldn't understand."

"What are any of us supposed to understand about this? This is crazy and you are going to get yourself in over your head."

"You don't have someone, so you don't understand! It's just like you to go telling Dad without knowing anything about it!"

Josiah brought himself up to his full height. "Listen, miss. I'm learning about it now. If you want me to defend you in the *slightest* you had better get your act together and tell me what's going on."

She swallowed. "I just meet him. We talk or go somewhere together."

"Where?"

"The theatre! Good heavens, Josiah, it's not like he's going to hurt me!"

Josiah shook his head. "Sis, I know things you don't. You're gonna have to trust me and end it, OK?" She was already shaking her head, and he took her hands to keep her from fleeing. "Just, please, talk it over with me and Dad. I know you're scared, but you can't keep running off with him." He tried to think of what else to say as she fought back tears.

"It's nothing. Please, Josiah. You don't know what it's like."

"I know more than you think," he said gently. "I have to tell Dad, with or without your permission." A tear slid down her cheek and he nudged her. "Hey, I'll help you out. Everything's going to be OK."

She sniffed and blew a blonde strand of hair out of her face. "You'd do that? I mean, he's Lydia's brother."

He grinned. "Come on. Let's get this over with."

"Just don't let him do anything to Travis, OK?"

"All right."

Josiah convinced Anneliese to return to the house and mount the stairs to their parents' bedroom. He passed through to the office to prep his dad. Heaven knew how he was going to take this.

"Dad, is now an OK time?"

Mr. Martin closed his laptop. "Sure, I need a distraction."

Josiah's stomach turned to lead. "Well, I've got one." Best to just come out and say it. "Anneliese . . . she's been seeing someone."

His brow clenched above his steepled fingers. "Romantically?"

"Please hear me out. It's Travis Long and she's really torn up about it all. I think the secret's been killing her."

"How long has—"

"I don't know, I didn't get much out of her. Dad, I know we trust the Longs, but we can't trust Travis. This has got to completely end and Anneliese is not taking it well."

Mr. Martin took a deep breath. "I take it you're not going to tell me how you found all this out."

"All that matters is that I *have* found out. I'll go get her."

"No, I'll go to her. I don't want this to feel like an interrogation."

He followed Josiah into the bedroom where Anneliese stood biting her thumbnail.

"Dad, I'm . . . I know it was wrong and I'm sorry for sneaking around, but we haven't done anything wrong and I trust him." Her hand continued to hover at her mouth as she took deep breaths.

"How long has this been going on?"

"Couple months."

"If Josiah hadn't found out, what was your plan?"

Her chin quivered and she shrugged.

"Anneliese, honey, part of being sorry is being willing to change."

"It's not fair," she whispered.

"I don't know the full story and I don't know who does, but you're going to have to stop this. No more secrets. I can talk to Travis and explain."

"No, please! I'll end it abruptly. A letter or something."

Mr. Martin examined his daughter's face. "Can you do that?"

Eventually she nodded and Josiah felt relief surge through him. This was going well.

"Anneliese." Mr. Martin reached out a hand for her shoulder, but she stepped back.

"I'm not doing this for you." She fled the bedroom, ignoring her mother's voice in the hallway.

Josiah couldn't tell if it had ended well or not. Perhaps she just needed time. He glanced at his father's conflicted face.

"She takes after me, I'm afraid." There was a reason Josiah had never met his paternal grandparents. Mr. Martin squeezed Josiah's shoulder. "Thanks for noticing, son."

Gemma's alarm went off on her dying phone. She quickly silenced it and returned to her book. A constant ache in her abdomen had woken her long before it was due to chime. But she never complained about a chance to fit more reading into her hectic schedule.

She recalled him handing it to her, telling her she could keep it. A frantic tingle had shot through her, muddling her thoughts and making her wish even more that they—he—could stay. His talks had meant so much to her and she just wished she could think of some way to pound that gratitude into his head. The hug had been going out on a limb, but it still didn't seem like enough.

Farris's cry interrupted her reverie. She removed the idle book from her lap to tend to him.

"Hello, sweet baby! Are you ready to go to work again? No fussing this time so you can stay with me."

Gemma fed and changed him and spent more time filling his diaper bag now that she knew how an ordinary day at work would go. She grabbed a baby bottle, extra blanket, stale pizza, and a water bottle before Hollie knocked. This time she was ready.

"Hey cuties!" She pinched Farris's cheek and helped Gemma transfer all her necessities into the car.

Gemma slid into her seat, noticing how nice it was not to have to climb up into a truck. Once she had buckled, she took note of a jagged crack in the windshield. How had she not noticed all the things before? Hopefully her brain would be in less of a funk today.

She was glad to see Mr. Franklin's nephew as she lugged Farris into the office. She only had a little left to her paper stack and couldn't wait to learn more tailored skills. But she didn't seem able to catch his eye.

She shouldn't have worried, because Hollie steered him into her office with a single glare.

He looked over his shoulder and shuddered. "That woman!" He closed Gemma's door. "Hello. How are you getting on?"

"Well." She offered a smile and unstrapped Farris from his seat.

"Marvelous. Who's this?"

"This is Farris." She held him up.

"How sweet." His chocolate eyes returned to her face. "Look, I don't want to be a bother, but is there anything I can do in here? I don't have the energy to face Miss James."

Gemma tried to imagine him lacking energy for anything. "Could you show me what to do on the computer?"

"Oh." He smacked his forehead with his palm. "Of course. I do apologize!" He bent over the desk and clicked around while Gemma bounced Farris in the chair. "OK. So this is our Case Manager program where most of your work will be done. We also have this for billing and the internet, of course." He proceeded to explain how to navigate on the programs and walked her through basic situations.

"So that was a lot, but you can always give a shout if you need another tutorial."

"Thank you, Mr. . . . ?"

"Oh, my apologies. Bradley, call me Bradley. My last name, but what I respond to."

"Mr. Bradley it is." There was no way she was dropping the formal address this early, especially since she took him to be under thirty and wanted to maintain professionalism. "You know I thought you were your uncle, Mr. Franklin, during our interview."

"About that." He rubbed the back of his neck. "I was trying to come across that way, really. I've just stepped into the business, you see, and I wanted to get to know you since I am your supervisor for software use. I apologize; that wasn't fair to you."

Gemma smiled at his constant use of "apologize" over "sorry." "That's all right. I understand. Thank you for telling me." She resituated Farris in her lap.

"Well, I hope we can start afresh and honest."

"Me, too."

The tension in his shoulders relaxed. "Super. Have a nice day." He clicked the door behind him.

Gemma told Hollie about her conversation with Mr. Bradley over lunch.

"Oh my gosh, I'm so sorry, Gem! I had no idea he was the one who interviewed you!"

"It's OK," Gemma said, glancing at Farris who was sitting in his car seat, staring at his garland of toys with large brown eyes. "I got hired and I'm not sure Mr. Franklin would have liked me that much at first blush."

"Don't be stupid. I loved you from day one and I have excellent judgment. Which means I *hate* most people."

"Sounds great for a secretary," Gemma said around a bite of pizza. "Are you sure you don't like me just because I'm here to ease your burden?"

Hollie scowled. "Of course not! You're awesome." Her eyes flicked to Gemma's lunch. "Do I need to take you to the grocery store?"

"Hm? No, I—" She stopped at Hollie's skeptical face. "Yeah, that would be nice."

"I could take you clothes shopping, too, unless you have another dress."

"That would be helpful, too, unless there's a pajama day coming up."

"Oh, I wish!"

Gemma's head came up as the door swung open. Mr. Franklin's stern eyes panned the room. Hollie swung her heels off the desk and faced her employer.

"Don't you think your lunch break has lasted long enough, ladies?" His presence reeked of stale smoke.

"Yes, sir." Hollie squeezed herself past his bulldog frame.

Gemma brought her hands up to her open laptop, poised on the keyboard, and smiled.

Mr. Franklin backed out of the doorway and closed the door.

Gemma let out a sigh and turned her mind back to locating current addresses for missing defendants. Mr. Franklin was hard to read, due to his lack of expression, unlike Mr. Bradley's spontaneous behavior. Mr. Bradley had seemed much more collected the first day. Maybe he was nervous, too.

By the time the weekend came, Gemma was exhausted, but she also had money in her pocket for the first time in months. Still, she thought a break from the apartment and office would do her good. So she spent her Saturday shopping with Hollie.

Farris was not very excited when Gemma placed him in the back of Hollie's car for the seventh day in a row.

"Aw, poor little guy. This week's been kind of rough on him, hasn't it?" Hollie smiled down at him as she backed out of the parking lot. "You won't have to work every day in the office for very long. I think you're nearly caught up."

"Yeah, it's been different. But we're both adjusting, aren't we, buddy?"

"So, am I your friend enough to know the story behind him?" She gave Gemma a sideways glance.

"Who, Farris?"

"Yeah. I mean he had to come from somewhere."

Gemma shrugged. "There was a guy in high school that I fell for and got in too deep with. Once I knew I was pregnant he left and my uncle that I lived with dumped me."

"High school? Wait, how old are you?"

"Nineteen."

"What?" Hollie frowned at the road in front of her. "That doesn't quite line up," she muttered. "Anyway! You look older, kid. I'm sorry about the way everything went down, though. Did you go to school here?"

"No, I'm from Texas. I moved to Kansas to escape it all. I got evicted in September and landed in this family's barn. They took me in and got me my apartment."

"How cool. Is that who came with you to the interview?"

"Yeah, one of them."

"How old is he?"

Gemma looked at Hollie's stubby profile with suspicion. "Twenty."

"And you lived with him for how long?" She arched a dark eyebrow.

She smiled at the notion. "There were others. Lots of others, actually." *And, oh, how I miss them.*

Chapter 20

As they drove up, Gemma saw a woman taking out her trash—the same one as before. The neighbor woman headed for the mailbox.

Oh yeah! Mail.

"Could you stay in the car with Farris for just a second? I need to grab my mail."

"Sure, hon," Hollie said.

Gemma was glad to see that there was very little waiting for her. She looked over the pieces on her way back to the car. Just a phone bill, not yet overdue, and a letter from Josiah. Her heart skipped a beat. But she would wait to open it until she was in the privacy of her apartment.

"Thanks." She unclicked Farris's car seat and supported it in the crook of her arm as Hollie began to unload their purchases. Due to a bug going through the office, everyone had been advised to work from home. Naturally, Hollie had suggested furnishing Gemma's apartment instead since Hollie being a receptionist from home was just as ridiculous as Gemma doing paperwork.

Farris still snoozed away, so she set down the car seat gingerly, unlocking the apartment.

"Where do you want all this?" Hollie whispered.

"Anywhere." Gemma set Farris's car seat inside his bedroom. "Why don't you help me assemble the dining room table. I was surprised Emmaline couldn't find a small one for sale around here. But she did find a couch, so that should be arriving soon."

"Fun! It's about time you had some places to sit."

Gemma and Hollie spent the next hour screwing the small circular table and its two chairs together. By then Farris had woken up and they could hang the light-filtering curtains Hollie had suggested.

"Two for the bedrooms, one for the living room. Now all you need is a television!" Hollie clapped her hands as they stood back to survey their work on the living room window.

"Haha. Like I have time to watch TV."

Hollie shrugged. "The glare from this window would be something, anyway. Gotta run, Gem, but have a great day."

Gemma waved at her from the covered sidewalk outside her door, Farris on her hip. It still amazed her how fast her friend could come and go. She heard more shouting before she closed the door and went to retrieve her mail from the kitchen counter. Brushing the phone bill aside, she ripped open the letter from Josiah. There was another sealed note inside that she ignored while she read the first message.

Gemma,

This came at the post office for you. Thought you might want to see it. Just let me know what you need me to do.

Josiah

Gemma turned the other envelope over in her hand. It was oily and smelled vaguely familiar. She read the inscription and her heart plummeted. What in the world was he doing, writing her? She sank to the floor and ran her hand over her eyes. She inhaled slowly and turned back to the letter.

Gemma,
Wundered where you are now. Culd use yur help. Let me no.
Uncle Wilfred

Gemma's eyes panned over the letter's content several times, hardly taking it in. She tossed it away from her in disgust. *Help?* What trouble had he gotten himself into now? Last time, she had written him for help and he had turned her down, making some lousy excuse. Why should she help him? She shouldn't. Not really. He was a parasite and not the sort of person she wanted her child growing up around. Not that her uncle had even asked about him.

A pang of guilt pierced her gut and she plopped in one of her new dining chairs. She had no right to think such ungrateful things about her uncle. If she hadn't been given a second chance by the Martins—and God—where would she be?

She sighed and pulled out her phone, speed dialing Josiah.

It rang only once before it clicked. "Hello?"

Happiness flooded her and a smile grew on her face, just hearing his voice again. "Hi, it's Gemma. I got your letter."

"Hey, I was just going to call you about that. What do you want me to do?"

"I'll write him back and see what the problem is, but I'm not going to give him money or let him know where I live. I've made those mistakes before. If his problem is more tangible than that, I might be able to help, but I'm not getting involved if I can help it."

"OK. So, just be on the lookout for a reply?"

"Exactly. Anyway, I just wanted to let you know what I was thinking."

"Thanks. How's your new life?" An unnatural heaviness tinted his voice.

"Pretty good. I'm busy, but my bosses are interesting and I made a new friend."

"Good, I'm glad. Look, I hate to hang up on you, but I'd better go. I'm about to get to an auction, and—"

"It's fine, I'll let you go."

"Thanks, bye." He hung up.

Gemma slowly pulled the phone from her ear and set it next to her. Just hearing his voice again made her feel encouraged. She crawled over to Farris and unstrapped him. He was still trying to decide if he wanted to wake up or not.

"Aw, come on, little buddy. Time to get up. If you don't wake up now you won't sleep tonight and that would make Mommy sad," she said in a singsong voice.

He screwed up his face and howled as she drew him out of his car seat and rested him against her. He stuck his fist in his mouth and rubbed his forehead against her shoulder, sucking furiously.

"How mean of Mommy to wake you up. Are you hungry? OK, OK."

She smiled as he calmed, leaning her head back and closing her eyes. It had been a productive day. If only she could get some more sleep.

Gemma woke up to a quiet apartment, a nice break from the shouting she'd heard last night, so she took the opportunity to conquer the mounting pile of dirty dishes. She had almost finished when the neighborhood dogs began barking.

What now? At least they hadn't been too obnoxious so far. They must wear themselves out during the day, because they had never caused trouble in the evening.

Gemma went back to scrubbing a scummy knife. When they started up again, she jumped, the knife's point drawing blood next to her fingernail. She sucked in air through her teeth, shaking her hand out and cursing the dogs.

She looked out the window again to see a creature attempt to dart under the fence, toward the apartments, only to be pulled back by the ferocious animals.

Poor guy. It was putting up too much of a fight to be a squirrel. She tried to shift her focus back to her knife, but couldn't. She looked out the window again. *Why don't the owners of the dogs save it?* Half the complex had to be awake by now. Farris could sleep through a hurricane after being born in the Martin household.

Gemma banged the knife on the countertop and rushed out the front door. She went around the side of the complex and toward the slanted, wooden fence. Across the few yards of field, wet grass making her ankles itch, she stomped until she came face to face with the fence. She smacked her palm on the surface. "Hey, leave it alone!"

The dogs didn't so much as take a breath.

Painfully aware that Farris was just on the other side of the brick wall, but still in the apartment alone, she threw a glance behind her. *What am I doing anyway?* She stretched out on her stomach and looked under the gap between the crooked panels and the damp grass.

A dog yelped and a ball of orange fur pelted into her.

She screamed and jumped to her feet. The creature stood there, hissing and spitting, its fur on end and matted with mud, blood streaming from its nose and tail.

Gemma took off her jacket and dropped it on the animal. It attacked the offending piece of cloth, but she scooped him up anyway, keeping him at arm's length.

The dogs continued to bark and scratch under the fence as she walked away, delirious with anger that their plaything had escaped.

The kitten fought all the way inside the apartment. She set it in the sink and removed the jacket and still it glared at her, hunched in the corner. Filling a bowl she had just washed, she set it in front of the frazzled cat.

He beheld her with distrust and edged toward the bowl, keeping his clear blue eyes fixed on her. She chuckled as he finally gave in and lapped the bowl dry, even letting her pet him a little, but not without a low growl.

"What am I going to do with you now? I'm pretty sure there's a no-pet policy."

He beheld her with contempt but purred lightly. She took a moment to blot the blood off his face and rub the mud out of the fur on his back with a paper towel.

"One sign of trouble and I'll throw you back over that fence. And you'll have to stay out of the windows until I get some curtains. I won't have you giving me any trouble with Jackie."

He skipped off the counter and leaned his full weight against her feet. He arched his back and curled into a tiny ball of fluff.

"Oh, no you don't." She scooped him up. "You'll have to stay out from underfoot, too." She hastily doused him under the kitchen faucet and applied dish soap, glad to find no signs of fleas. Tugging a small cardboard box out of the pile in the corner of the living room, she set him inside. "You can sleep in there, you weasel."

He meowed up at her and licked his paw. The poor thing looked half his normal size with damp fur.

"Weasel. I think I'm going to call you Weasley. How's that, you ginger kitten?" She gave his head a pat and stood. "I hope you like Farris before he gets mobile." That reminded her . . . she'd better peek on her baby. She only had half an hour before Hollie would appear to take her to work.

Gemma poked her head in and was glad to see that he remained still and breathed evenly. Leaving his door ajar so he might think wakeful thoughts, she donned her old black knit dress. Even though it was maternity, it didn't look too frumpy and hid the rounder parts of her shape with ease. She slipped her feet into her faithful black flats and tied her hair off in a ponytail. Fighting Farris for her hair every time she picked him up irked her.

Gemma stuck her makeup things in the diaper bag so she could mess with it in the car and roused Farris. Her eye caught the pile of orange and her heart grew heavy in her chest. She tiptoed over and peered at the kitten, nestled contentedly against Farris's side. That would never do. She deposited Weasley outside of the playpen and sighed as he sank his claws into the side, pricking them in and out repeatedly. Picking up Farris, she held him close as he struggled to wake up. Something warm met her arm and she withdrew it. *Great. No wonder he was sleeping so well.*

Gemma held him close the best she could with one hand while she positioned a slick mat on her bed with the other. She grabbed a tiny diaper, wipes, and a new outfit and set to work. In no time, Farris was wide awake and wailed as she used wipe after wipe with a determined grimace.

"Almost done, baby. Hold on. I know it's not fun." She pulled the fresh onesie over his head and slid a clean pair of pants on. It was still a little chilly out for bare legs. Using an extra wipe to rub a damp spot out of the front of her dress, she thanked heaven she had chosen to wear black.

The usual knock came at the door just as she finished fastening the last strap on Farris's seat.

"Come in!"

Hollie stepped inside with her usual cheery countenance. "Good morning."

"Hi. I'll be just a minute. Oh, don't let the cat out." Gemma motioned to the orange creature that was stalking his way to the opening as she disappeared into the bathroom. She took care of everything as quickly as she could. Her fatigue had lessened considerably since Farris's birth, but this pain in her abdomen that persisted in annoying her was not to be reckoned with. She grabbed a handful of packing paper and spread it in and around Weasley's box.

"No messes, kitty kitty." Her eyes narrowed at the purring puddle in Hollie's hands. She filled him a bowl of water and hoisted the diaper bag onto her shoulder.

Hollie set Weasley down and went for Farris. "I've got him. Climb on in."

Gemma passed a hand over the shooting pain in her stomach as she took her seat. She glanced at the clock. "Oh, I'm sorry. We're going to be late."

"No worries, hon."

Hollie was right, Gemma shouldn't have worried. Hollie floored it and they were there at three minutes past. Gemma had hardly gotten her makeup done.

Hollie waited for her and she grabbed Farris. "Is that a new dress?"

"New?" She glanced at her friend while she wrestled with the seat. "No, it's maternity."

"Well, it's flattering."

"Thanks. Is it OK for work?"

"Hon, black is always OK." Hollie put on her sunglasses for the ten-yard walk to the building. "Do you need some groceries or anything? We could hang out again this weekend. If you want. It is Friday, after all."

"Groceries would be good." She remembered the carton of milk's filmy appearance as she stepped into the elevator. "And I need to set up a bank account."

Hollie's eyes widened as they reached the second floor. "You're not just leaving all that money around your apartment?"

"They're checks, but of course not. It's in the diaper bag. No one ever thinks to rob a diaper bag."

Hollie chuckled as she held the door into the office.

Gemma looked to her left, amazed at what a difference their three minutes had made. Already employees filled styrofoam cups with coffee and took their place in their cubicles. There had to be at least ten of the office spaces. It was stunning how easy it was to

222

forget how many people she worked with when she had her own little corner all to herself. Rumor had it, it was supposed to be Mr. Bradley's office, but he was hardly ever in and it had been filled with file cabinets Gemma utilized.

"What's this I hear about a robbery?" a rumbling voice came from behind her, interrupting her musings.

Gemma turned and met nut brown eyes. "Oh, nothing. I just said I need a bank account." She heard Mr. Franklin grumbling something about paperwork and she took the hint. But Mr. Bradley interrupted her once again.

"Well, I could do that. I mean, we have a good bank and you're an employee."

Hollie raised an eyebrow. "The company can do that?"

"Of course. I'll do it myself." He returned to Gemma. "If it would save you any trouble, Miss Ebworthy."

"Thank you. I might take you up on that. I'll let you know later?"

He nodded and she offered a hasty smile before stepping into her office. *One less thing to worry about.*

Farris did not make it very long in church this time before Gemma had to take him back to the nursery. He was learning to suck on his third and fourth fingers which helped; Google had told her it was a developmental achievement for self-soothing. Nearly a dozen mothers visited with one another over their children's banter this time, so Gemma introduced herself and then halfheartedly participated in the conversations while she tried to keep Farris happy.

Soon Clair detached herself from the conversation and sat next to Gemma on the floor. "You look nice. Your week go well?"

Gemma smiled. "Yeah, pretty well. How about yours?"

"All right, but the twins are teething again."

223

Gemma grimaced. Thank goodness she hadn't had to deal with that ordeal yet.

"Say," Clair said, taking a drooly block from her son before he could smack his twin with it. "Would you be interested in a play date or something? I'd like to get to know you better and I'm always looking for something to do with these hoodlums."

Gemma's spirits lightened a little. "Sure! The Botanical Gardens are right behind my house. Otherwise, I'm sure there's a park somewhere."

"Let's do the Gardens. When are you free?"

"I work Monday to Friday, but I'm about to catch up on the work and then it won't be so often. I could ask for a day off."

"Brave woman! Tuesdays are the best for me because I never have anything going, so I'll give you my number and you can keep me posted. And it's not a huge deal if it doesn't work out this week. I know Christmas is coming." She handed Gemma a slip of paper and held the pen out of her child's reach.

"Thanks. I'll let you know."

Clair flashed her a smile. "Sweet." She glanced at the clock on the wall. "They should be wrapping up." She restrained the twins in the double stroller and took Juliet's hand. "Time to go, sweetie. Let's find your daddy." She gave Gemma a wave before leaving the nursery.

Gemma spent a few minutes helping some of the other moms straighten up before slipping out into the quickly filling halls. Before she had a chance to locate Hollie and her brother, the face of Mr. Bradley caught her eye.

She flushed when he caught her looking at him, his eyebrows high, and remembered to smile just in time. To her chagrin, he waded through the crowd in her direction.

"Hello, Miss Ebworthy," he said, when close enough.

"Hello, Mr. Bradley." Her brain fought for something else to say.

"Your bank account is in order. I can give you the information tomorrow."

"Oh, thank you. It was nice not having to worry about that."

"Precisely." He looked around. "Would you like to go to lunch with me? Or do you have plans?"

Her mouth went dry and her heart pounded in her ears. Could he not see she had a grumpy baby?

"No. I mean, I came with Hollie. But I don't have plans."

"So, that's a yes?"

"I—" Her mind jumped to the freezer meal awaiting her at home. "Yes. That would be lovely."

"Fantastic. If you want to tell Miss James, I'll bring the car around."

Did he read my mind? "Sure."

Thankfully, Hollie was easy to spot in her hot pink dress and Gemma explained the situation as quickly as she could, ignoring the funny feeling in the pit of her stomach.

Hollie narrowed her eyes, but smiled. "OK. See you tomorrow."

Gemma made do without the base to Farris's car seat and secured it with a seatbelt. She was about to strap herself next to him before she realized that would probably be rude.

She climbed into the front passenger seat and fiddled with the fringe of her navy crepe dress.

"Where would you like to go?" Mr. Bradley asked.

Gemma shrugged. "I've only tried pizza, so I'm game for anything."

"Well, I think I can top that. Why don't we do Café Bel Ami and you can choose between French and Mediterranean?"

Whoa! "That sounds incredible."

"Yeah? All right." There was silence for a moment as he worked his way out of the parking lot maze.

"So how are you enjoying work at the law office?"

"It's been nice. I think I'm getting the hang of it. And it's wonderful to have somewhere I can take the baby."

He nodded and resituated his hands on the steering wheel. Gemma tried not to study his chiseled profile.

Within a couple minutes they had arrived and taken what looked to be the last parking spot.

"They look a little crowded," Gemma said.

"Never fear, madam." He walked in and signaled a waitress with too much eye makeup. She smiled and led them to a remote table.

The waitress set up a sling for the car seat and gave them place settings and menus. "Let me know when you're ready."

Gemma looked the menu over and tried to ignore the prices.

"What sounds good to you?" Mr. Bradley asked.

"I think I'll do the toast baguette sandwich thing." She flushed, realizing how unintelligent that had sounded.

"All right. I'll do their Mediterranean club and we can split if you'd rather. Can I get anything for the baby, or . . .?"

"No, he's on a strict diet."

Mr. Bradley's brow creased and she decided not to try another joke. He set his menu aside and leaned forward, fingers linked.

"Would you like any wine?"

She kept her jaw from dropping, but just barely. "Uh, no. I . . . it's not good for Farris. I'll take a root beer, though." *Does he not know I'm under-aged?*

He raised two fingers and the waitress materialized, pen and pad ready.

Once Gemma had eaten as much toasted baguette with butter and rich, warm meat as she could manage, Mr. Bradley was gracious enough to take her cue. Despite the treat and pleasant conversation, Farris was growing sleepy. She left the boys alone for a quick minute while she ran to the restroom. It had been days since she'd been able to do that without the company of her child. She noted how well a baby complimented Mr. Bradley as she took Farris in her arms and followed him into the parking lot.

"I hope you enjoyed the meal," Mr. Bradley said, securing Farris's seat.

"Yes, it was great. Thank you very much."

"My pleasure." He slid into the driver's seat and coaxed the engine to life.

Gemma felt that she was too quiet on the way home, but she couldn't think of anything to say that he'd be interested to hear.

Then he asked, "What are your plans for Christmas?"

Gemma's mind went blank. Was it really just a few days away? "I haven't really thought about it. But I'll be here. I guess I should do some shopping."

"Well, there will be a party after the half day of work on Christmas Eve. So you can plan on that. You'll have the rest of the week off."

Gemma hadn't figured that into her planning with Clair earlier, but maybe she'd forgotten the holiday, too. "That sounds nice. I guess it'd completely slipped my mind since it doesn't feel very festive."

"We usually do a gift exchange. Nothing big, but it's fun. And I'll be sure to have some sparkling grape juice there so you can enjoy the fizz with the rest of us."

Gemma smiled. He was obviously more of a socialite than she. "That's very considerate."

"Where do you live again?"

"Franklin Street."

"Ah." They arrived momentarily and Gemma thanked him again for the nice meal.

"Why are you so fussy, love?" She bounced Farris with one arm while she dialed Josiah with the other.

"Hey again," he said.

"Hi. Is Emmaline around? I could use an early Christmas present."

"Sure." The phone went silent for a moment and Gemma repositioned the baby.

"Hi, Gemma!" Emmaline's voice came. "Do you want me to find something for you?"

Gemma smiled at her down-to-business attitude. "Yes, please. I realized just today that Christmas is coming right up. So if you could look for a stroller, a scratching post, and a nightstand, that would complete my Christmas list."

"Sure! I'll see if Mom will give me some computer time this afternoon."

"Thanks. And if you have any ideas of something your family would like, that would be awesome."

Emmaline laughed. "You don't have to get us anything!"

"But I want to, silly. I have to do a white elephant gift, too. I can find that locally, but I'd love to hear your ideas."

"Just do something versatile," she said. "A scarf or cool mug. Maybe something deco. You get the idea."

"OK." She shifted Farris again and swayed more dramatically to quiet him. "I'm serious about a gift for your family. Keep me posted, OK? Have a good day. Bye."

Gemma set her phone on the counter and lay on her bed with Farris. "What is your problem, mister?" He didn't want to be fed or played with. Even staring at Weasley or sitting outside hadn't soothed him. "Mommy doesn't know what to do with you."

He only cried harder as she set him down next to her.

"Oh, poor baby. You'll be OK." She rubbed her throbbing abdomen as she stroked his little cheek. Surely he would stop crying soon. But he didn't.

For the rest of the evening, Farris was in a sour mood. He didn't seem to be in pain; he was just determined to wail about everything. The more she tried to make him happy, the more he got fed up with her handling.

Gemma was about ready to sit on the floor and cry with him when his shrieks gave way to violent hiccups. Even those subsided as his eyelids grew heavy. Finally, he stopped trying to refocus his brown eyes on her face after every slow and deliberate blink and they stayed closed.

She held her breath and stayed frozen on the edge of her bed until she was certain he couldn't fall into a deeper sleep. Then she laid him in his playpen and flopped into her own bed.

What seemed like minutes later, he was crying again. But it was inky black, so more time must have passed. Gemma stood to tend to him only to be overwhelmed by dizziness. She leaned against the wall for a moment before proceeding. They were both relieved when nursing soothed him enough to drift back into a fitful sleep.

Gemma tried to make it back to her room, but everything spun and her head felt like it was wired to explode. Her stomach tied itself in knots, beyond just the usual pain. She took a detour into the bathroom and soon all of her expensive lunch floated in the toilet. She splashed some cool water on her sweaty face before crawling back into bed.

Chapter 21

Gemma started. Her mind, heavy with sleep, raced to recollect why. It was eerily still.

A knock sounded at the door.

What in the world? She squinted at her alarm clock—9:26.

"Shoot!"

She flew out of bed and drew her curtains back with one hand as she tried to regain her balance with the other. Dazzling light met her eyes; the outside world carried on without her. She flung her bedroom door open and twisted her hair up as she hurried toward the front door.

The knock came again.

Gemma stumbled through the dusk-colored room, wondering if she shouldn't have gotten the light-filtering curtains, when her hip banged something hard, throwing her off balance. A teetering lamp jumped to its death, sending the pieces of its light bulb all over the floor. She hissed in a breath and made a lunge for the door as pain climbed her leg.

Her shock nearly overwhelmed her as she blinked into the glare of day. "Mr. Bradley." Heat flushed her cheeks.

"Yes, hello. Sorry to come unannounced, but Miss James said she couldn't get ahold of you this morning, and I wanted to see if everything was all right."

"Oh." She steadied herself on the doorframe as a wave of nausea assaulted her. "I just overslept."

"Well, that's a relief. Miss James was afraid you and I had a falling out yesterday and I wanted to make sure—good heavens, you're bleeding!"

Gemma followed his glance to her bare feet. When she shifted to get a better look, a tingling pain traveled through the arch of her foot.

"No, don't move. You'll get blood everywhere." Mr. Bradley was already removing his suit coat and helping her to the ground. "Just sit down and tell me where you keep your washcloths."

"Kitchen sink," she breathed as he slipped past her through the doorway. *I'm so glad I did the dishes.*

He returned momentarily and crouched to wipe the excess blood that was starting to drip off her heel.

"Oh dear, we've got glass. I'm dreadfully sorry, but I'm going to have to carry you inside." His brown eyes searched hers for permission. Something told her he wasn't very sorry at all, but she had no choice.

He lifted her without effort and deposited her on the couch. She was becoming more and more grateful for the crazy way things had gone down last night. If she hadn't been too tired to change, she'd be in a frumpy nightgown right now. *And thank goodness I have a couch, or this would be even worse.*

He retrieved his jacket from outside and closed the front door. "Will you tell me your first name, Miss Ebworthy?" He brought a bowl of water and a handful of paper towels and set them on his lap as he took a seat at the end of the couch.

Gemma stroked a yawning Weasley. "Only if you tell me yours." She flushed at how flirtatious it came out and gladly buried her face in Weasley's fur.

Mr. Bradley took her left foot in his hands and looked at it with renewed intensity. "I don't use my first name. Tweezers?"

"Um . . . bathroom cabinet. The blue bag."

Gemma cast a self-conscious glance around the room as he explored more of her house. *Thank heaven I hung the curtains and swept the floor.*

"Why don't you—use your first name, I mean?" she said when he reappeared.

"It's awful." He took his seat again and rolled up the sleeves of his dress shirt.

She smiled. "Now you'll have to tell me."

"Swear you won't leak it at the office?"

She nodded, cradling the cat in her lap.

"Leopold."

She hissed in a breath as he removed the first piece of glass, a fresh rivulet of blood trickling down her foot, but some of the ache subsiding. He was prepared and contained the mess in the bowl.

"That's not bad at all, it just sounds . . ."

"Dreadful?"

"Aristocratic."

"Well, that's kind of you to say." He held up the second piece of blood-stained glass.

Gemma resisted the urge to yank her foot out of his hands as he grabbed at another piece. "How's it coming?"

"You look like a porcupine minus two quills." Mr. Bradley plopped another tiny fragment in the water and she released her held breath. When he repositioned his hands above her ankle, she thanked God she had remembered to shave her legs.

"Thanks for checking on me, or I'd be doing this myself."

233

"You probably wouldn't have broken the lamp if I hadn't woken you up."

"True." She flinched as another piece came loose. Maybe Farris would wake up and spare her the rest of this.

"One more; keep talking." Mr. Bradley bent over her foot again.

Gemma wracked her brain. Verbalizing her thoughts on his deep voice, brown eyes, or stark jawline would be entirely inappropriate.

"How old are you?" was the best she could come up with. She had no doubt that it came from her conscience.

His stormy eyes held hers for a moment and she struggled to swallow. "Twenty-seven. You know you're the first secretary to not be scared of me."

She cringed as the tweezers grated against some of the glass still embedded in her foot.

"I'm under-aged," she blurted.

Mr. Bradley looked up, concentration broken.

Gemma's fears were confirmed at the gravity in his eyes.

"Well, that does put a spin on things." He plucked the last piece of glass. "When I read your file it said you had a college degree and a recommendation letter."

Gemma swallowed. "I swear I didn't lie. Mr. Martin arranged it with your uncle."

"Yes. You were going to get a trial run out of kindness, but . . ."

". . . he was going to hire the other girl." Her spirits sank further. *Josiah was right. I knew it was too good to be true.* The application folders must have gotten mixed up.

Mr. Bradley pressed the paper towels to the bottom of her foot and then applied a butterfly bandage. "Several small cuts, some a mite deep. Keep your foot up for the day."

Gemma swung her good foot off the couch and pressed off the shaggy carpet with her toes in order to sit up.

She cleared her throat. "So, is your unintimidated secretary fired?"

He waited to answer until his silence made her uncomfortable enough to meet his eyes again. "No, you've been too brilliant for that." He gave her hand a squeeze, before returning all the items back to the kitchen counter.

Farris began to cry and Mr. Bradley helped Gemma hop into the bedroom. "Let me prepare you a breakfast before I depart to make things simpler."

Gemma nodded and fed Farris while heavenly smells enticed her from the kitchen.

"If I had a rosemary sprig, I would add it here." Mr. Bradley presented a plate with a picturesque omelet and a fork. "Enjoy your day off and don't leave the couch if you can help it." He lifted Weasley off his suit coat and tugged it on. "See you later, Gemma."

She bit the inside of her cheek as he let himself out. *So he did know my name.*

Gemma reflected on how much more composed Leopold Bradley had been as she finished her breakfast. He must have had to settle into the work at the law firm just like her. Being less high strung made him seem older.

She soon polished off her egg and left the plate on the floor for Weasley to lick. Farris had fallen back to sleep on her shoulder, so she turned lengthways on the couch and did the same. After being up for a little while, she felt ready for more sleep.

Gemma had no idea what time it was when she woke up, and was surprised to hear the mail truck outside. They must have been out for at least two hours. Mail wasn't usually delivered until after noon.

The shooting pains in the arch of her foot had ceased to exist, but a dull ache still swelled with every movement. She was very content to stay on the couch underneath her sweet-smelling baby.

His dimpled fingers were curled around the edge of her shirt and every so often he would suck on his bottom lip. Gemma fingered the thick wisps of hair that were lightening in color. If they grew any further over his ears, she would have to locate some hair-cutting scissors. She'd been considering a haircut for herself, too, since Farris strangled himself in it, Weasley entangled it in his claws, and it always trailed into everything she ate. Hollie would be the person to ask for ideas.

Hollie. Sometime between now and Thursday, Gemma would have to arrange Christmas shopping, finalize gifts with Emmaline, and tell Clair the play date would have to wait a week. And get back to work. All with a busted foot. She blew out a sigh and rubbed Farris's back. Once he woke up, she would have to find her phone and make some calls.

As if Farris had heard his mother's thoughts, he began to whimper. He pushed against her with his pudgy arms and she caught a glimpse of a button pattern on his sweaty pink cheek.

"Do you feel better after your nap? You were pretty restless last night, weren't you? What was bothering my poor little Farris? Huh?" *Noisy upstairs neighbors for one.* But whatever had been in their systems seemed to be mostly gone, thank goodness.

She hoisted herself up to more of a sitting position in order to feed him and tried to remember what she'd done with her phone last night. It was probably still in the diaper bag, which sat on the floor at the other end of the couch. Gemma dangled her good foot off the couch and tried to grab the strap with her toes. After several tries, she tugged it close enough for her hand to reach.

Farris snorted his complaint about all the movement, and her foot joined him in protest.

"Sorry, buddy." She dug the phone out of the bag—it was at the bottom, of course—and dialed Josiah.

"Hey, Gemma."

He saved my number. "Hi. Sorry, I know this is a weird time to call, but I have an unexpected day off."

"Not a problem. What's up?"

Does something have to be up? She hesitated. "Maybe I just want to talk to you." She scrunched her shoulder to hold the phone so she could burp Farris. She hoped he was smiling in the moment of silence that followed. "If you're not too busy."

"Of course not. Go for it."

"Are you sure?"

"Yeah. Seriously, I'm always here."

"All right. I have attended the First Baptist church here a few times and I wondered if you thought it was a good one. I know you haven't been to this exact one, but I . . . I just don't really know what I'm doing. I want to be learning about the right things, I mean. Because if I need to go somewhere different, there's a Methodist and Catholic church on the same street. I didn't know if it mattered."

"They all have different traditions and ideas, but Baptist is pretty close to what my church is. The best thing you can do, though, is to keep reading the Bible for yourself. You don't have to agree with the pastor. He's still a person, just like you, and he can make mistakes."

"Oh, good! I haven't actually heard much of the sermons yet, but the people seem nice. I haven't been reading my Bible as much as I want to, either, but I was so glad my coworker goes to church! I go with her and her brother."

"That's great, Gemma! Her brother isn't that weird guy who hired you, is he?"

She felt a pang of guilt for not having paid more attention to Josiah's intuition and repositioned Farris, who seemed content to stare at the cat, just out of his reach. "No. Speaking of strange people, has Travis vanished yet?"

"Yes, actually. He enlisted as promised and is in California. He could reappear, I suppose, but not until boot camp ends. I've talked to Anneliese about it confidentially and she had no idea it was coming. She's pretty sullen."

Gemma knew what that felt like all too well. "Poor girl. It's for the best, though. Did you tell your dad?"

"Yeah. It sounds awful, but I almost wished I hadn't when it dissipated so easily. He's felt awful of late, so it was just one more thing. I didn't include anything about you, though."

Emotion clutched at her throat. "That's . . . that's really thoughtful. Telling him was the right thing. Just be there for her and discourage the relationship if he shows back up."

"I'll do a lot more than that if he ever shows his face around here again," Josiah said tersely.

Gemma smiled—she didn't doubt it. "Travis wants to be happy just like everybody else. He just can't seem to manage it without hurting other people. I imagine that's what Anneliese wanted, too."

"Yeah, but I don't know how you can stand being that nice to *him*."

Gemma thought about that for a moment. *How* can *I be that nice?* "I'll let you get back to life. Could I talk to Emmaline again for a minute?"

"Sure. It may be a second. I'm out in the field."

"Why does that not surprise me?"

He chuckled. "It's different without you here, you know that?"

"I should hope so. I kind of upended y'all's life."

"You know that's not what I meant." His voice grew serious. "We miss you."

She swallowed the empty feeling settling in her stomach. It might have been called homesickness if the Martins' had actually been her home. "I'll Skype you all on Christmas, OK?"

"Yeah. Have a good week. Here's Emmaline."

Gemma jotted down the gift ideas Emmaline had for her family and the Christmas party. In return, Gemma gave her her work e-mail so she could check out the local items for sale by owner over her lunch break tomorrow.

Then she called Hollie, who agreed to take her to the laundromat on her way home from work. The piles of laundry in both bedrooms were getting ridiculous and she wasn't about to let an entire day off go by without conquering something domestic.

She had just sent a message to Clair suggesting they wait to get together until next week when her bladder began to cramp.

Gemma swung her feet off the couch with precision, like a crane at a construction site. She would have laid Farris on the floor, but she didn't trust Weasley with him yet. So she hobbled into the bathroom with him and rested him on her knees with great difficulty. It wasn't the first time she'd shared the bathroom with him, but her pulsing foot made it all the harder. She had just flushed when her phone lunged out of her jacket pocket. Her eyes widened as it plopped into the toilet and she released a slow sigh.

"Well, no more phone bill."

Chapter 22

Gemma managed to entertain herself and Farris until Hollie arrived that evening.

"Oh, Gemma, you look so pitiful!" she said as she burst through the door. "And I'm *so* sorry about the mix-up with your application. I remember I had to give the files to Mr. Franklin and I must have mixed up some of the latter sheets!" She knelt next to the couch at Gemma's head. "Can you ever forgive me?"

Gemma smiled. "Forgive you? You're the reason I got hired!"

A look of relief brightened Hollie's face. "Oh good. I brought supper," she sang, unloading the plastic sack onto the counter. "Is your foot any better?"

Gemma shrugged. "It'll be fine. Can you still see blood on the carpet?" She dreaded what her landlady would say if she saw the large brown drops against the speckled shag.

"Didn't even notice. Got your laundry ready?"

"It's still in the bedrooms. I have a basket somewhere."

"I'll get it," she said, with a shooing motion as Gemma tried to stand from the couch.

"Could you bring me a pair of shoes, too?"

Hollie popped back into the room momentarily. "Oh, you don't have to come. I can run it for you and be back before supper cools off."

"But—"

"No buts. I'll even take the baby if you'd like. Give you a moment's peace?"

Gemma tried to imagine having a moment's peace with her child strapped in the back seat of a car with Hollie at the wheel. *Not like my going will make him any safer.* "I guess so. Just be quick." She told herself it was the right decision and that maybe he'd nap again as Hollie whisked laundry basket and baby carrier out the door.

Gemma hoisted herself to a standing position and hopped to the bar. She was going to enjoy her peace with food. One hand groped for chopsticks while the other popped the lid off the Styrofoam bowl. Oily steam caressed her face and she didn't give her rice a second thought before digging in.

Both Gemma and Farris called it an early night after Hollie left. She couldn't believe it when she woke up in time to go to work— thanks to the loud upstairs neighbors—and Farris was still asleep. Whatever had bothered him the night before mustn't have been completely out of his system. His diapers were returning to normal as was her appetite, so that gave her hope.

She spent several minutes reading from her Bible and placed two ounces of milk she had pumped on the counter. Weasley sprang to her side as she rattled his food bowl. "There you go, kitty." She turned and managed to swing the refrigerator door open without moving. *What to have for breakfast* . . . She settled on her faithful yogurt to help coat her last two iron tablets. Locating some iron-rich foods like her doctor had suggested was on her mental to-do list.

Gemma tried to make it to the silverware drawer, but found that since she had put a little weight on her foot earlier in the morning, hopping was the only thing that would not further injure it. Getting over having to hop around work might not be such a big deal, if she didn't have to carry a baby simultaneously. And going in a wheelchair was even less of an option.

Hollie completely understood when she arrived and agreed to help with shopping that evening. Last time Gemma had checked, she didn't have quite as much in her bank account as she'd expected, but she would make it work. It was Christmas!

Farris called to her loudly from the floor and she shut the door on Hollie's retreating figure, realizing it was going to be another long day.

She stretched out next to her son and tickled his tummy, producing a half smile. Weasley picked his way between the two of them and tucked himself into a neat little ball. "Look at us," Gemma murmured through her arm. "We're pathetic."

When noon rolled around, Gemma was ready to go insane. She hadn't realized what a great distraction work provided from the daily grind of life. Her apartment was so small and her foot hurt so bad that there was really nothing she could do, even if it needed to be done.

Farris snoozed in the crook of her arm, dreams playing across his face. Somehow, between entertaining and feeding him, she managed to pass the time until Hollie got off work. By that point she would do anything to leave the house.

"Where do you want to go?" her friend asked.

Gemma stopped strapping Farris into his seat to think. "I don't know. Is there a T.J. Maxx anywhere? Man, I haven't been there in forever."

"Yeah, I think there's one across from the airport." Hollie brought it up on her touchscreen phone. "Yep. T.J. Maxx it is then. Here, let me get the baby in the car and then I'll help you. They don't sell crutches, do they?"

"No," Gemma scoffed. "Besides, I still couldn't carry Farris with them."

"True." Hollie held onto Gemma's arm and bore the brunt of the weight as she hopped to the car. "Wow, this is sad, hon. You really need to let this heal up properly. Feet are important." She slipped into the driver's seat.

"I know. But I've taken it easy for two days and I can't take it any longer. Neither can my bank account."

Hollie rubbed her arm sympathetically. "Don't worry. You'll be back to yourself soon. And I tackled some of your filing pile today because old Mr. Franklin was frantic. I didn't want to; I still felt so bad for mucking up your application paperwork that it made me nervous handling anything. But I relented eventually and used your system, so nothing should be out of order."

Gemma smiled. "Thanks, Hollie."

Upon arriving at the store, Hollie was thrilled to find that they had motorized shopping carts. Gemma was appalled when her friend insisted she use one, but her only other option was to ride in a basket. Eventually, she consented. Farris went on the front of Hollie's cart in his seat, and the Christmas shopping commenced.

Once Gemma got over the nostalgia of being in what had been one of her favorite stores as a young teen, she was able to find everything Emmaline had suggested. A gender neutral journal for the white elephant gift, classy mugs for her bosses, earrings for Hollie that she hid in the journal, and a rustic piece of art for the Martins. And all for fifty dollars. She was feeling very satisfied as she whirred her way down the sidewalk. Hollie had doodled a makeshift handicapped tag since she wanted to park close for Gemma's sake. Thankfully, no one of importance had noticed the difference; no ticket awaited them.

Gemma fingered her wrapping paper tube on the drive back. "Isn't this pretty? They carry the best wrapping papers. I used some at a friend's house once."

"Mm-hm." Hollie glanced in her rearview mirror for the umpteenth time.

"Why do you keep doing that? Is something wrong?"

Hollie turned dazed eyes to Gemma's face. "Oh, no. I just keep thinking about something Mr. Bradley said about you today."

"Me?"

Hollie nodded, but didn't offer any further information. "Look, I'm saying this as your friend and your coworker, but please don't get involved with him."

Gemma blinked. "I know you don't like him—"

"It's not just that. I just . . . Will you be careful? I don't want to see you get hurt again."

Gemma nodded, still not sure she knew exactly what Hollie was getting at. "Thanks."

Hollie stayed to help Gemma wrap that Tuesday night and mail the gift to the Martins, so everything was in order by the time Thursday's party rolled around, including the re-sorting of papers that Hollie had misfiled.

Bradley slipped into her office several minutes before the party was due to officially begin.

"I come bearing nonalcoholic drink."

Gemma couldn't resist grinning as he brandished a green glass bottle labeled "Sparkling Grape Juice" and two glasses.

"I swear no one will know the difference," he said, breaking the foil seal. "Not if you keep this tucked away in here, I mean."

"I don't care if they do know," Gemma said. "Women with babies shouldn't be drinking alcohol anyway. They don't have to know I'm still under-aged."

"Does it really matter if you're not driving home tonight?" Bradley asked.

Gemma hesitated, her eyes growing wide. That was exactly the sort of question she might have posed once. She was glad he was still focused on unscrewing the gold lid. "It's against the law, either way. And I can't with the baby even if I wanted to."

"Oh, right. Still, I can't believe you've never had a champagne. Jolly shame." He filled the glasses with the foaming liquid.

"I tried my share of beer once and all of my friends promptly went to jail, so I learned my lesson then."

He looked up, surprised. "Perfectly reasonable. And just the sort of decision I'd expect from someone as smart as you." Bradley held up the glasses and clinked his against hers. "Cheers!" He winked.

The juice caused her tongue to tingle and forced her to swallow quickly. She placed her stemmed glass on the desk. "I have to run to the bathroom. See you in a minute." She scooped up her dozing child before Bradley could offer to watch him for her.

According to plan, Hollie met her in the bathroom and braided her hair up into a golden crown with deft fingers.

"Thanks for doing this," Gemma said, as Hollie inserted the final pins.

"Sure! You look gorgeous. Now hold still while I touch up your makeup."

Gemma did as she was told and waited with closed eyes as her friend brushed colors on her face.

"Eyeshadow for depth . . . blush for height . . . Ugh, you're so pretty!"

Gemma opened her eyes and saw dramatic but tasteful makeup painting her face to look more mature and defined. She chuckled at Farris in the sink's mirror, head bobbing over her hold on his ribcage, warm drool oozing down her hand.

"I don't want to conquer your eyebrows tonight, so take some lipstick and you'll be set." Hollie handed her a black twist tube. "Go have fun, Gemma. Merry Christmas Eve." She gave her a long hug before tripping out of the bathroom in her ridiculous high heels.

Gemma collected her self-confidence and left the bathroom, walking on her heel. It was the only thing she had found that helped ease some of the tension in her foot. She laid Farris down on his pallet, watched him with a smile until he was breathing deeply, and grabbed her presents and juice.

"You look stunning," Bradley said.

Gemma inwardly cringed, but offered a smile. Something about this man did not sit right tonight. "He'll be fine if I leave the door cracked, right?"

"Sure," Bradley said. "Someone will tell you if he wakes up."

That was hardly reassuring.

She crossed the sitting area and passed Hollie's desk, entering the room that opened into the mass of cubicles. Many of the faces were new to her, since she never spent any time in this area of the office, but it looked splendid in Christmas decorations. All the cubicles had Christmas lights climbing the walls and garlands looped from the ceiling. There was a spicy smell to the air and everyone had done their best to look festive despite the unseasonably warm weather. The soft sound of Christmas music in the background completed the atmosphere.

"The gifts for the anonymous exchange go under the tree." Bradley pointed across the room to a fir tree adorned with ribbon and topped with a bow.

Gemma made her way through the maze of cubicles since that path was much emptier than the girth around the office spaces. She added her journal to the mounting pile of presents and set the two for her employers aside. She'd wait to pass them out until later.

Some people attempted to circle up and sing Christmas songs, some took advantage of the mistletoe, and everyone enjoyed the afternoon off among friends. There was much discussion about who would be announced as employee of the year. When they gave the ten minute warning before Mr. Franklin would make the announcement, Gemma excused herself and checked on Farris.

He had begun to fuss quite vigorously and was doing his best to lift his head and look for his mother.

"Hey, buddy. It's all right." Gemma dropped to her knees and picked him up. "I didn't forget about you. Are you hungry?" She bounced him as she closed the office door and settled in her chair to feed him. Her dress buttoned up the front—the one requirement she had kept reminding Hollie about when shopping. Farris had gotten used to eating fast, so she reentered the room with her son strapped to the front of her just as Mr. Franklin announced, "Mr. Alan Jones."

Everyone clapped politely as the man of honor made his way to Mr. Franklin for a handshake and certificate. Gemma headed toward Hollie, trying not to limp too much. "Who is he?" she asked.

Hollie shrugged. "Marketing, I think. Kept our website snazzy and upped viewings or something. He asked me out right before it was announced."

"Did you say yes?"

"I was going to say no, but now that he's employee of the year, I'd hate to ruin his evening. One date isn't that big a deal, anyway." She took another sip of her champagne.

Gemma bit the inside of her cheek to keep from rolling her eyes. Hadn't her friend just given her the opposite advice on an office romance?

Once the white elephant gifts had been passed around and the floor littered with red and green paper, Hollie and Gemma excused themselves. Gemma's foot was killing her and she wanted nothing more than to crawl into bed in her fuzzy socks that she had received. Hollie just wanted to avoid being part of the cleanup crew with people who had had too much to drink.

Gemma deposited her presents on Mr. Franklin's desk. It didn't matter who got what since they were identical and she wasn't in the mood to hand them out. She grabbed her laptop as an afterthought so she could Skype the Martins for Christmas morning tomorrow as promised.

"Well, I hope you had fun, hon," Hollie said as Gemma climbed into the car she had pulled around.

"Yes."

"What are your plans for tomorrow?"

"Nothing much. The last present is arriving this evening. If I get that wrapped, I can help Farris and Weasley unwrap them tomorrow."

Hollie flashed a wicked grin. "You wouldn't want company, would you?"

"You're welcome to come over if you'd like to. And your brother, too."

"Sweet! I'll bring cinnamon rolls and fruit for a brunch, huh? Don't stress about cleaning up. We can help with that once we're there. Have a good evening, love." She planted a kiss on Gemma's cheek before grinding out of the parking lot.

Chapter 23

Christmas morning dawned bright and moderate. Gemma had managed to get all the remaining gifts wrapped once Farris had gone to bed, although she'd had to shut Weasley in her room to do it. As was becoming normal, she was awake a good hour before Farris. She spent a while rereading the Christmas story from her Bible and recognizing for the first time the parallels between the actual account and the traditions held today.

Gemma reluctantly bookmarked her Bible so she could go take a shower and pondered it again as she sat in the tub, the water from the shower trickling down her back. All the to-do because of one baby born in a foreign country centuries ago. Surely there was more to Him than the world wanted to understand, just like the Bible said.

Regaining her sense of time, Gemma turned off the water and towel dried her hair. She would ask Hollie to cut it for her, because the tangles were getting ridiculous.

Gemma spent her last few minutes before Farris was due to wake scarfing down a yogurt and sweeping what she could of the kitchen area while standing in one spot. Once Farris had woken up and been fed, Gemma sat on the couch and interested him in a brightly colored box.

"What is it? You want to tear the paper?" She ripped a corner and placed the strip in Farris's slimy grip.

He promptly shoved it in his mouth, creating a large tear in the paper that made him jump.

"Nice, Farris." Gemma fished the wad out of his mouth and finished opening the present for him. "Look, it's a book for you!" She turned one of the cardboard pages and showed him the different textures on the page. He cooed at it, but was more interested in sticking it in his mouth than touching it.

"We'll save the rest until Auntie Hollie gets here. Now it's Weasley's turn." She scooped up the kitten and placed him in her lap. He quickly caught on to the game when she wiggled the shreds of paper at him and he began to sink his tiny claws into the box.

"Goose. This is why you get a present." She pulled the scratching post out of the box and placed the kitten on the platform. He stretched and flexed his claws happily before settling in for a nap.

She pulled her laptop to her and flipped it open. Its clock said it was almost nine. Surely the Martins would be up and done with most of their morning festivities.

Gemma opened her Skype app and called their computer, nestling Farris next to her.

She didn't have to wait long before Emmaline's face appeared on the screen. "Hey, Gemma!"

There was a clamor and more little faces appeared, grinning and smeared with chocolate. "Hi, Gemma! The baby's so big! We miss you! Merry Christmas!"

Gemma smiled and tested her limit listening to multiple kids at once.

"OK, OK, y'all are done. Go have more candy." Josiah shooed them away as Ginger took a seat at the computer.

"Oh my goodness, Farris is so cute! Is he having a good first Christmas?"

"Yeah, pretty good," Gemma said, trying to keep him from licking the screen.

Ginger laughed and Anneliese's blonde head appeared next to hers. "So tell us, how are you liking your new life?"

"It's good. I'm busy, but the job is good and I've made friends and found a church. Actually, my coworker will be here soon."

"Well, we won't keep you too long, we just wanted to see you all again," Anneliese said.

Gemma was glad to note that she didn't seem to be harboring any remnant of hate for spilling her story.

"Oh, that's OK. How's everything going with Elias?"

Ginger ducked her head and Anneliese rolled her eyes.

"It's going very well," Ginger said. "I'm counting the days until I'm eighteen! And Josiah may be getting a job with Elias's family. I've told you, right, that the Jeffersons work for a big corporate farming industry thing? Anyway, he's watching some land for sale and may start his own crops for the company. Wouldn't that be amazing? Then he can homestead right near me and Elias!"

"Josiah, that's awesome."

He smiled, the corners of his eyes crinkling. "We'll see what happens, but it would be great. It's hard at first, but once the profit is high enough, you can hire laborers and expand."

Gemma could tell how excited he was beneath his stoic surface.

"You should be getting an invitation to Jan's wedding at some point. Please come!"

"I'll certainly try." The prospect of a trip to the Martins' sounded very appealing about now.

Mrs. Martin's head appeared between Ginger's and Anneliese's. "Gemma, look at the both of you! It's so good to see you again. Is everything going all right? You're both healthy and doing OK?"

"Yes, everything's great."

Her relief showed through the screen. "Wonderful. Don't hesitate to call if there's anything we can do to help. And thank you so much for the present! We opened it this morning. You really didn't have to do that."

Gemma beamed and resituated Farris. "I wanted to. Glad you liked it."

"Well, I guess we'd better let you get back to your morning; we're about ready for breakfast here. Come on, everyone. Come tell them goodbye."

Everyone tried to fit their faces—or part of them—into the screen and they all waved and blew kisses and shouted until Farris didn't know what to think. Then the screen went black and something inside Gemma sank. How was it that they had been such a part of her life for such a short time, yet they meant the world to her?

True to her word, Hollie and her brother arrived mid-morning with brunch food. Sometime between last night and this morning she had expanded that to include sausage and eggs in addition to the cinnamon rolls and fruit.

"I also brought stuff for queso and cider if we want any. It's not as cold as I'd hoped, but if we turn the air down in here, we might be able to trick ourselves into feeling festive."

Gemma smiled, remembering the Texas Christmases when long sleeves were completely out of the question. "Sounds great."

Hollie pressed a button on the thermostat. "You seem kind of glum. Is everything OK?"

"Yeah, I'm fine. A little tired, I guess. Thanks for coming."

Hollie smiled and gave her a hug from her perch on the arm of the couch. "You'll cheer up when you see what I got you! Hand me hers, Jake." She waved her hand at her brother. "Actually, I have a lot of stuff for you, but this one's the big, official present."

"Hollie," Gemma said with mock disapproval.

"Open it!" Hollie took it from her brother and set it in Gemma's lap.

Farris made quick work of the tissue paper, making his mother struggle to save the paper bag. At the bottom sat a silver key with a Chevrolet cross imprinted in the black base.

"What? You did not get me a car." Gemma fished the key out and turned it over in her hand, disbelief fogging her brain.

"Surprise!" Hollie burst. "Aw, you look so happy. It's only my old car, but I thought you could use it. Jake and I went in on a new one."

Gemma shook her head. "No way. You guys are the best!"

Hollie flashed another grin and even Jake cracked a smile. "You're very welcome. I even had it vacuumed out and the oil changed. Now here's something else." She signaled her brother again and he pushed the hair out of his eyes before withdrawing a phone from the pocket of his distressed jeans.

"Here," he said, reaching over Weasley to hand it to her. "It's old, but it still works. You'll just have to get it activated with your phone company."

Gemma grinned, taking the smartphone in her hand while keeping Farris from jabbing himself with the key. "Thank you, Jake. But how did you know?"

"Know what?" he said.

"That I'd killed my other one."

Hollie laughed. "I didn't know that! I just thought you might like an update. How perfect! But what happened to your other one?"

"I dropped it in the toilet."

This brought another peal of laughter from Hollie, who stumbled around Gemma and plopped next to her on the couch.

"Oh, Gemma," she said, wiping tears from her eyes. "Why don't you tell me these things? You know we're here to take care of you."

Gemma shrugged and examined the phone. Despite the scuffs, it was still much newer than the one she'd fried: no sliding keypad.

A door slammed outside, making Farris jump. Shouting could be heard and then a car peeled out. Gemma handed the baby to Hollie and limped to the window. She sighed as she recognized the woman she had seen taking out the trash several times slumped on the bottom of the stairs.

"I'll be right back," Gemma said. She didn't bother closing the door behind her and winced as she hurried down the sidewalk.

Gemma paused for a moment when she reached the woman. Purple and yellowing bruises showed even on her coffee-colored skin. She kicked herself for not thinking more of the racket before. "Are you OK?" she asked.

The woman's head whipped up, revealing a tear-stained face. She hastily wiped at her eyes and slid her hands up her arms to hide her bruises. "Yeah, it was just a fight. He'll be back." She stood and sighed. "Thanks anyway." She turned to head back up the stairs, but Gemma couldn't let her.

"It's Christmas and you shouldn't spend it alone. Don't you want to come to my apartment and have some brunch?"

The woman paused and her hollow eyes stared back at Gemma from under mousey brown hair. She glanced at the empty parking space with uncertainty.

"I don't think he'll be back for a while."

The woman nodded slowly. "I'll just go change clothes."

Gemma smiled, realizing she hadn't gotten dressed yet, either. "I'm the last one." She pointed to her apartment. "Come whenever you're ready."

The woman nodded again and offered a slight smile. "I'm Julie, by the way."

"Gemma."

Julie offered a slight smile before ascending the stairs with a great deal more confidence than she'd had several minutes ago.

Gemma ignored the shooting pains in her foot as she made her way back down the sidewalk. She felt very satisfied for having convinced the woman of her good intent.

"What was that all about?" Hollie asked from the doorway.

"I'm afraid that poor woman's boyfriend or husband or whatever abuses her. He just left on one of his tirades so I invited her over."

Hollie's eyes widened in a look of uncertainty that was met by a frown from Gemma. She dropped her expression. "That was very sweet."

Gemma came inside and closed the door. "Let's get her some breakfast. She's skinnier than the last time I saw her."

Julie knocked at the door several minutes later. She had washed her face and changed into a simple knit dress.

"Julie, this is Hollie and Jake," Gemma said, ushering her inside. "And this is my baby, Farris."

Julie's near-black eyes dilated when she saw Farris. "May I hold him, please?"

"Sure." Gemma handed him over with a burp cloth; he had just eaten. "If you're hungry, we have some cider and breakfast foods."

"Thanks." Julie didn't even glance her way. Her eyes were fixed on the baby's face as she took a seat with him on the couch.

Gemma began to wonder if it had been a smart idea to have Julie over. She seemed to be reliving some sort of emotional trauma just by looking at her son. Gemma gave her an encouraging smile and excused herself to her room to see if she had something she could give Julie for Christmas. Something told her the poor woman had yet to receive any gifts. As she rifled through her closet, it struck her that perhaps the man she lived with would disapprove if he knew, so she'd better keep it subtle. Scanning the room, her eyes rested on her white elephant gift—fuzzy socks—that rested on her new nightstand from the Martins. She'd only worn them once and would likely slip and kill herself anyway.

She collected them and wrapped them in a stray piece of tissue paper that had meandered into the hall on her way back to the living room.

Gemma was struck again by the intense longing found in Julie's eyes as she smiled down into Farris's wondering face.

"How old is he?" she asked, not breaking her gaze.

"Twelve weeks today."

"Twelve weeks," she repeated. "He's beautiful. I've never seen such a perfect head." She planted a kiss on his forehead and then stood and handed him to Hollie. "I think I'll take some of that food now."

Gemma nodded, pushing all the questions she had about this woman to the back of her mind, and began piling food on a festive paper plate.

For the rest of the morning they did nothing—talked about life, passed the baby around until he conked out, petted the cat—and it was wonderful. They indulged in Hollie's queso for lunch and had no qualms eating cinnamon rolls again.

"Thanks so much for bringing all the food, Hollie. It's so good!" Gemma said around a bite of sausage.

"My pleasure."

Julie had been sinking out of her high spirits for the last half hour and now bordered on somber.

"Is something the matter, Julie?" Hollie asked in a gentle voice.

Julie looked up, almost as if she didn't comprehend. "What? No, I'm fine. Only this is all so wonderful. It makes me miss my family."

"Where does your family live?" Hollie prompted.

"Alaska. I moved here when I met Bryan." Her smile was sad.

Gemma glanced to her ring finger—empty. "You should visit them," she said.

Julie shook her head. "They didn't approve of Bryan and I haven't talked to them since. It's been several years now."

"And you're happy?" Gemma said.

Julie's chin came up just a little. "I have nothing to complain about."

Gemma smiled again and Julie stood. "Well, I suppose I should be going. Bryan will probably be back soon and I don't want him to think—well, anything. Thank you for a lovely day, Gemma."

Before she had the chance to slink back to her apartment, Gemma placed the tissue paper package in her hand. "This is for you. Please come back whenever you'd like. I work weekdays, but I'm here every evening and weekend."

Julie nodded absentmindedly and fingered the ribbon on the package. "Thank you." And then she was gone.

Jake shook his head in the silence that followed. "That woman's broken."

Hollie and Gemma nodded and sipped their cider contemplatively.

Gemma didn't see Julie for most of Saturday, although she hoped she might come by again. She never saw Bryan, either, so she took that as a good sign. When Julie knocked Saturday evening, however, her face told a different story.

Gemma stifled a gasp as her eyes met the bloodied face of the girl. Her lip was swelling, her eye was truly black, and a cut above her eyebrow was just beginning to dry. Gemma pulled her inside and turned the lock, fear gnawing at her insides. This was worse than she'd thought. She had to get Julie somewhere and fast!

But first she wetted a rag and sat next to her on the couch, wiping at her injuries.

"Do you want to tell me what happened?"

Julie petted the cat in silence.

"Was it Bryan?"

Julie stopped her steady strokes and eventually gave a shadow of a nod. She resumed her petting, much to Weasley's satisfaction.

"Julie, how often does this happen?"

She sighed, low and long. "Not very often. He just had too much to drink. He'll be himself in the morning. Can I stay here for the night?"

Gemma hesitated. She couldn't send her back, but she couldn't handle this situation on her own.

She stood and rinsed out the rag at the sink before answering. "Julie, you don't *ever* have to go back if you don't want to."

Julie shrugged. "He's all I have."

Gemma remembered how many times she'd heard that same line from girls in her high school. They felt that whoever they were living with gave them the love they craved, despite their behavior. The boy was always "just physical" and had moody days like everyone else. No matter how bad it got, they would stay because it was all they had. Here sat a woman in her twenties struggling with the same issue.

Gemma shuddered and hung the rag over the faucet. "I'll take you somewhere for tonight. Somewhere that will help you. Please think about staying there. They can give you something better than anything Bryan has to offer." She sat back on the couch and Googled the shelters in Wichita.

"It's my fault," Julie whispered. She ran one brown hand through her silky hair, just a few shades darker.

Gemma looked up, heart slowing. "What is?"

"For wanting a baby." She blinked rapidly. "Bryan doesn't want one. I shouldn't have brought it up when he was drunk."

Things began to click into place in Gemma's head. That's why she had been so attached to Farris. She was clinging to Bryan as her only hope of having a baby when he was set on denying her just that. *God, please help me help this woman. I don't know what to do!*

260

"I keep thinking if he agrees just once, he'll change his mind once the baby's here." A tear slid down her cheek.

Gemma's heart broke for the woman in front of her and she gave her hand a squeeze. What Gemma had feared for so long was this woman's dream. How selfish of her to ever think of her child as a burden when every child was a blessing and a miracle.

She put her arm around Julie as she dialed the shelter. "Yes, I need to bring a woman in for domestic violence. Yes. Yes, thank you. Bye." She forced her phone into her pocket and looked Julie in the eye. "I'm going to take you to a shelter, OK? Let me get the baby up."

Julie nodded and stood. She was still there when Gemma returned with a groggy baby and keys. She had the forethought to look out the window before venturing outside. There was a light on in Julie's apartment and she couldn't see anyone outside in the growing darkness.

"Come with me." She took Julie's hand and held Farris to her shoulder with the other. She strapped only Farris's top strap and slid into the driver's seat, turning it on almost before she was seated. It made sense to her now why Hollie had given her the car two days ago. *God knew I'd need it for tonight.*

She locked the doors, turned the lights on, and backed out. As she pulled away, her heart stuttered as her rearview mirror reflected a dark figure leaning against the doorway to the stairwell, bottle in hand.

Chapter 24

Gemma couldn't shake the image of the man she'd seen as she left her apartment. As much as sleeping in her own bed appealed, she thought it wiser not to risk facing Julie's boyfriend alone. The staff agreed it would be better to spend the night at the shelter.

When Gemma woke up to the cramped room she shared with Julie and three other women, it was later than usual. The light outside had grown vibrant. She reached for her phone, careful not to disturb Farris, who was tucked in the middle of the claustrophobic bed between her and Julie. It was already after ten a.m.

She tried to figure out how to open the unread text message it displayed and realized it was from Hollie.

"I guess you don't need a ride today, huh?"

Gemma's heart sank. It was Sunday. She hated to miss church, but she didn't want to rush off and leave Julie, either.

Julie rolled over. "What time is it?" she whispered.

Gemma held up her phone.

"I'll be all right," Julie said.

"And you won't go back?"

Julie fixed her eyes on Farris's relaxed face.

"You're not married and he's abusive. There's no reason to go back. Let the people here find you something better."

Julie nodded and Gemma's gut squirmed at the open-ended situation. What if Julie did go back? She'd never forgive herself for leaving her.

"I can stay," Gemma said. "I *will* stay and help you, if you want me to."

Julie shook her head. "Go. You've done more than I could have asked. Everything will be fine. Thank you."

Gemma patted her arm and picked up Farris from the middle of the bed. "You've got my number now and so does the shelter. Stay in touch, OK? I want to know how everything works out."

Julie offered a weary smile before Gemma tiptoed out of the room.

From the lobby, she got in her car and dashed back to her apartment. She had to get out of her crumpled clothes and feed her irritated baby before she could leave for church. It took her twice as long as it should have, but she snuck into the service during the opening song, so she didn't feel too bad.

She slid in next to Hollie and let out a long breath. What a day, already.

"I thought maybe you weren't coming," her friend said.

"I'll tell you later."

As soon as the sermon had ended, Gemma slipped back into the auditorium for the closing songs. Farris dozed in her arms and she wanted to soak up as much worship as she could. She stood against the back wall, swaying with her baby, and read the words off the screen for the first two verses.

Then sings my soul, My Savior God, to Thee,
How great Thou art, How great Thou art.
Then sings my soul, My Savior God, to Thee,
How great Thou art, How great Thou art!

As the chorus was sung a second time, Gemma considered if her soul had ever sung to God. Is that what worship was all about? She remembered people singing in the desert. But, according to this song, you didn't have to sing with your voice in order to worship. She listened to the third verse, hoping for more clarity.

And when I think of God, His Son not sparing;
Sent Him to die, I scarce can take it in;
That on the Cross, my burden gladly bearing,
He bled and died to take away my sin.

That verse didn't make her uncomfortable, but it made her stomach churn. She remembered reading about this before she had left the Martins. She knew in the back of her mind that it was true. Perhaps she even believed it. Then why didn't she feel any different?

When Christ shall come, with shout of acclamation,
And take me home, what joy shall fill my heart.
Then I shall bow, in humble adoration,
And then proclaim: "My God, how great Thou art!"

Gemma sighed as everyone began to filter out of their pews. She wished she could "scarce take it in" and that "joy would fill her heart," but it didn't. It had, the first time she had read the story, but it hadn't lasted. Not like it should have.

"Hey, I told Jake he needs to buy us lunch so you can tell me what's up," Hollie said.

Gemma smiled at Jake. "That would be very nice."

He shrugged and led the way out the door.

"Oh, I forgot to get Clair's number again," Gemma said as they were driving off. She could get her car on their way back home.

"I have a church directory that should have it at home," Hollie said. "Now, what was up this morning?"

"Julie, the girl who spent Christmas with us, came by last night and I decided to call the shelter, because she had obviously been beaten up. I saw her boyfriend, Bryan, as we were leaving, so we slept at the shelter with her. I didn't see Bryan at all when I dashed back home to get ready, and I left Julie at the shelter. Can we bring her some food from lunch?"

"Of course," Hollie said, her voice full of pity. "That poor woman. Lousy men like that make me so mad! Where do you guys want to go for lunch?"

"McDonald's," Jake said.

Hollie whacked him in the arm. "Jerk. How about that Mexican place? Good, that's what I want, too. Are you all right with that, Gemma?" She glanced in the rearview mirror.

She met her dark eyes and smiled. "Yes."

Jake threw his hands up and slumped further into his seat.

"Only if Jake wants to, though," Gemma added.

Hollie gave her brother a sideways glance.

"Fine," he muttered. "But no appetizers."

Thursday brought the long-awaited play date with Clair and her children. Just as originally intended, they met up at the Botanical Gardens behind Gemma's neighborhood. Despite the lack of blooming flowers in the beds, the weather couldn't have been better and the greenhouse gardens still had some nice blooms to offer.

"So, do you see yourself staying in Wichita?" Clair asked.

"I don't know," Gemma said. "That sounds lame, but while I can't see anything that would make me move, it doesn't feel permanent yet."

"But you haven't been here very long." Clair tucked a sippy cup back in the double stroller's cup holder.

"True—not quite a month. I am enjoying it, though."

"What is it that you miss so much about your other life? I can tell that you do, so don't try to hide it," Clair said, tilting her head.

Gemma repositioned Farris on her front. "The people. The honest, hard work of every day. The simplicity."

"Family?"

A slow smile spread over her face. "No. Better than any family I ever had."

Clair moved Juliet out of the path of a bicycle, never stopping the double stroller. "Anyone special among this better-than-family?"

"They're all special," Gemma laughed.

"You know that's not what I meant. I am right in perceiving you're unmarried, aren't I?"

Gemma nodded.

"So?"

"We come from very different backgrounds for anything more than friendship. Even that is a miracle."

"I knew it! You have a lovesick look about you. And I should know, too. My husband was the only bachelor for miles when I met him. Do you know how unattainable that made him? It frustrated me so much! But everything worked out, just like God always knew it would."

"I don't think missing Josiah means I'm in love with him. I was 'in love' once before, and it was very different." She placed a kiss on top of Farris's head.

"I promise not to bring it up again. But if he's ever in town, I want to meet him."

Gemma rolled her eyes as she laughed.

Clair stopped pushing her stroller and sat on the bench of the circular fountain. "Have you thought about children's ministry? You seem very good with small children in the nursery. Maybe pray about it?"

Gemma took a seat next to her. She didn't want to admit praying still didn't feel natural, so she stared at the glinting pennies beneath the water's surface instead. "If I thought it feasible, I'd say yes. I'm not as confident in my abilities with children as you are, though."

"Hm. Well, I mentioned it to my husband and he wasn't at all deterred by you being so new. We have to do a background check for liability reasons and that would eliminate most concerns, I would think."

Gemma squirmed and suddenly felt exposed under the December sun. "I wish I could, Clair. Trust me when I tell you a background check would reveal a past that would not recommend me to be around any child, ever."

The eager light that had been in Clair's deep, kind eyes diminished and she reached for Gemma's hand. "Don't ever say anything like that again. A different past only shows how far you've come."

Gemma lowered her head. *Is that really true?*

Gemma thought of Julie all the way home and wondered what else she could do for her. When she had seen her Monday afternoon, she was still looking at opportunities with the shelter, but seemed more at peace with moving on. Remembering how they met, she was reminded to check her mail again and send in her second month's rent. She'd hate for Jackie to show up at her door for rent only to evict her for having a cat.

A bank statement, advertisement, and letter. It was good to know that Bradley really had gotten everything in order like he said as she reviewed the financial ins and outs of the month. She had no interest whatsoever in a local ribbon cutting, but the letter held her attention. She had no doubt it was from Uncle Wilfred.

Gemma had told herself that if there was some way she could help, she would. But no money or housing could be involved. She couldn't trust him.

Gemma,

Annything wood help. Got a tiket and wife to pay for. I hope you are good. Mayby I can meet the baby sometime. Ant Cindy wood like to meet you to. Thanks, Gemmy.

Love Uncle Wilfred

Gemma shook her head. The poor man. She almost felt sorry for him as she read the letter. She couldn't believe he'd had the gall to use her banned nickname, but it made her smile in hindsight. He'd always meant it well. *Good old Uncle Wilfred.* She wondered what sort of woman had agreed to marry him.

"You don't want to meet your aunt Cindy and uncle Wilfred, do you?"

Farris blinked back at her.

"I didn't think so." She shifted her position and reread the letter.

The ticket—that was a legitimate debt that should be paid. Maybe she could cover it for him directly so that he would have no chance to misuse the money. Goodness knows what he'd use it for if she gave it to *him.*

Gemma sighed. However, after locating the telephone number for her uncle's local police department and agreeing to pay the soliciting ticket, she felt a measure of peace restored. Now she just wanted to sleep off her discomfort. She may have judged her uncle too harshly, but at least she'd been able to do him a little good after all.

Chapter 25

The new year treated Gemma well. Mr. Franklin was very pleased with her progress and told her she could stay on, so Bradley trained her further. Her relationships with Clair, Hollie, and Julie deepened. Farris grew fatter and happier each day, winning the hearts of everyone he met. Weasley hadn't been discovered by the landlady yet and her uncle had not bothered her further. She had begun to feel at home in Wichita.

"How's the office romance coming?" Gemma asked Hollie one spring morning.

She leaned back in her office chair. "The glory of his Employee of the Year award must have worn off, because he broke up with me last night. Can you believe that? The week of Valentine's Day. Why couldn't he have waited until Monday?"

"You seem more miffed than disappointed." Gemma massaged her abdomen.

"I guess we both knew it wasn't going anywhere. I still would have liked some chocolate on Sunday."

"Hollie, I promise to buy you chocolate over the weekend."

She forced a smile. "Thanks, hon. That means a lot after letting me cut your hair."

Gemma grinned. Her friend had done a very nice job of cutting her hair to shoulder length.

"Did I hear the word chocolate?" Bradley asked.

Hollie rolled her eyes and busied herself with papers. "I was just mourning the fact that I no longer have a boyfriend for Valentine's Day."

"I'm not volunteering," Bradley said. "But since we'll all be at church that morning, why don't we do something together? It can be a double date type thing if your brother comes along."

"All right," Hollie said, perking up a little. "How about it, Gemma?"

Gemma shrugged. "Sure. And if Jake doesn't want to go, Farris can be my date."

"Wait a minute, I'm not going with Hollie," Bradley said.

"I can't go with my brother, stupid."

Bradley cringed and they both looked at Gemma for a way out.

"Why don't we all go together and forget the date thing?"

"Thank you, voice of reason," Hollie said, shooting Bradley a glare.

He put his hands up in surrender. "Fine. It was just a hypothesis. See you ladies Sunday." He slung his computer bag onto his shoulder and exited the office.

"Just a hypothesis," Hollie muttered. "That man's never had a hypothesis in his entire life."

Gemma laughed lightly. "Hollie, why are you so intent on hating him?"

"I don't know. Maybe because he's so hateable. The real question is why don't *you* hate him? Everyone else does. You don't still like him, do you?"

"I simply don't hate him and there's nothing wrong with that."

Hollie sighed. "Well, he's bound to be better than that country bumpkin you're still mooning over. It's obvious that Mr. Bradley's liked you since the beginning."

Gemma reshaped a stray paperclip. "I've not been mooning over anyone. I like Bradley, but I'm not completely comfortable with his character yet. There are some things that concern me."

"Picky, picky. Good for you, though. Not all of us can afford to be."

"Oh, Hollie. You'll find someone, but you shouldn't need another person to be happy."

Hollie straightened her papers again and stood with a melodramatic sigh. "I know, I'm just in post-relationship depression. Wake your baby. I think I need chocolate *now*."

Sunday came and Farris slept through the entire sermon for the first time. She enjoyed hearing what the pastor had to say in full for once. Being Valentine's Day, the topic was a higher love that only Jesus had to offer.

Gemma listened with particular focus. She still felt disconnected from the life-changing effect that God's love was supposed to bring and didn't know what to do differently. She read her Bible, came to church, prayed, and—deep down—knew it was all true. Why else would it be such a part of her life? Still, she was missing something that everyone else seemed to have.

The pastor brought his sermon to a close. "You must claim Christ's voluntary, unending, sacrificial love and, in turn, love others. Let's pray."

Gemma bowed her head out of habit, but her mind wondered what he had meant by that. Was that her problem? Had she not claimed that love? Her head hurt from thinking about it and she left a

273

mental note to herself to ask Josiah sometime if she couldn't find it in the Bible for herself.

They sang the final lines to O *the Deep, Deep Love of Jesus* and then the people began trickling out of their pews. Gemma took the side aisle since it was less congested.

Somehow Bradley managed to find her in the crowd. "May I escort you in my car?"

"Sure," she said over the din of people. "Let me get his stuff out of the car." She knelt in the lobby where she had left Farris's car seat and strapped him in, trying to keep him asleep. It would be great if she could feed him in the car right before they went inside the restaurant.

"We can take yours if it'd be easier."

"Yeah, let's do that."

She handed him the car seat at his insistence and led the way through the vast parking lot, swarming with bodies. They had already agreed with Hollie and Jake on a restaurant, so there was no need to wait for them.

"I thought it was a very good sermon today," Gemma said, sliding the diaper bag into the back seat.

"Oh? I guess I wasn't really listening." She gave the back of his head a curious look as he carefully locked the seat into its base.

"I don't get to listen very often, so it stood out to me." She took her seat behind the wheel and coaxed Hollie's old car to life.

"I guess I've gotten tired of hearing the same old thing," Bradley said, closing his car door.

Gemma nodded, but it irked her that he was treating something so complex to her as trivial. But she said nothing more about it. Farris realized he had been duped halfway there and was quite the vehement protester by the time they arrived.

"You go ahead. I'm going to feed him before we go in." She unstrapped Farris, sweaty and red-faced from his fit. "Goodness gracious, mister. You're not forgotten!"

As soon as he was finished eating—it took longer than usual because he was so upset—she stepped inside the bustling building and was shown to their table. Hollie and Jake were already seated on one side of the booth and a highchair sat at the end of the table.

Gemma stuck Farris in the chair and stuffed his blanket around him. He had almost mastered the talent of sitting up, but not quite. And though he had no teeth yet, he loved chewing on anything he could get ahold of. So Gemma promptly moved the poky silverware out of his reach and handed him the spoon.

"Hey, little dude," Hollie said. She stroked Farris's bicep. "You make my arms look good."

Gemma shook her head. "He's definitely not going to starve anytime soon. He's just fat and happy, yes he is." She planted a kiss on Farris's forehead. "Do you want to share something, Hollie? I'm not very hungry."

"Sure."

"I figure we can handle something ourselves, Jake," Bradley said.

Jake cracked his knuckles and nodded, flipping to the page with excessively large burgers.

Hollie and Gemma's sarcastic looks met each other over the tops of their menus. Gemma decided on fish since it was iron-rich and she couldn't stand to have her apartment smell like it.

After they placed their orders, Bradley asked Gemma if she wanted to dance.

"Dance?" She tried to think why one would dance in a restaurant.

"Yes, they have a live band in there." He gestured to the other half of the restaurant.

She rubbed the hem of her dress between her thumb and forefinger. "I don't dance."

He cocked his head. "Please?"

"Bradley, I really don't want to."

"Fine." He nudged Hollie out of the booth and held out his hand.

Much to Gemma's surprise, Hollie accepted with a gracious smile. She couldn't help thinking as they walked off that Hollie suited Bradley more than she did.

Jake must have been thinking along the same lines because he said, "I don't know why she won't let herself like him." He sighed and rested his cheek in the palm of his hand. "Happy Valentine's Day, Gemma."

She smiled. Hollie had such a quirky brother. "You, too, Jake."

During the entire next week, Gemma watched Hollie and Bradley together and continued to wonder if they didn't secretly like each other. It reminded her of Frank Churchill and Jane Fairfax from *Emma*. Did they really hate each other, or was that affection she could see glinting in their eyes?

Hollie's boisterous laughter could be heard all throughout the office and brought grumblings from Mr. Franklin in the adjoining office. Bradley popped his head through Gemma's door as he often did, this time with a large smile still on his face. "I'm going to have an after-hours meeting once the old uncle's outta the way. Don't feel like you have to stay for my sake."

"I wouldn't stay just for you." She regretted saying it as soon as her own words reached her ears. She sounded jealous.

His smile fell. "Well, it's fine, but—"

"No, don't worry about it. I just want to finish up some stuff so I can take tomorrow off." She offered a faint smile over the top of her computer screen.

He seemed relieved and promptly disappeared again. It left Gemma wondering what kind of meeting would require an almost-empty office. What was he up to?

Ten minutes after the last person had gone home for the weekend, Gemma heard a gentleman being welcomed into the office.

The man had a high, wheezy voice that sounded as if he were in the middle of a constant fit of nerves or hay fever.

She was trying her best to wrap up, but still had a few corporations to invoice. Only snippets of the conversation in the next room reached her ears, but she didn't really care. Not until the name Winkle wafted through the closed door.

She sat up straighter. *Winkle?* As in her old landlord? Surely not! But the voice and agitated stuttering sounded identical. Her eyes grew wide and she tiptoed to the door connecting the two offices so she could hear better. What in the world was Bradley doing, dealing with such a louse?

"I understand completely, Mr. Winkle," came Bradley's voice. "I cannot promise you more funds. I tried to set up a bank account so that I could wheedle that for you, but it didn't work out. The current young lady is too perceptive. However, I promise that you will keep my apartments and no one but you and I need know the legal implications. Now, if . . ."

His voice trailed off as Gemma tuned him out. Her stomach churned and her head swam with the weight of what she had just learned. *His apartments?* The dreadful apartments that had almost killed her every day on the way to work—Bradley was somehow involved in allowing them to remain in their dilapidated condition. Her hands grew white from clenching them and she stood defiantly in front of the two men before she knew what she was doing.

"Gemma, what . . .?"

Mr. Winkle had already pinned himself against the far wall and shook a knobby finger at her. "That woman. Where did s-she come from?"

Gemma ignored him and let him continue to cower in the corner.

Bradley looked from one to the other curiously. "Gemma, we're in the middle of a meeting, could you please—"

"I heard. Is it true? Are you responsible for the condition of those horrific apartments?" Her jaw ached with the tension held there to keep it all from flying out of her mouth in hateful words.

Bradley huffed a sigh. "What could you possibly know about them? Now is not the time to grow a conscience for my sake."

"I lived there! I lived there for four miserable months!"

Bradley pressed his index fingers against his lips and leaned back in his uncle's leather chair. "They're still a work in progress."

"What did you take from my bank account?"

"No, I had to . . ."

"What? Bud up to Hollie to dupe her, too? Give me lists of fake invoices to bill? What did you do?"

"I—nothing! I'll make it all right again."

She exhaled all the venom she was trying so hard to contain and slumped into a chair. "Liar. All you've done is lie."

Hurt crossed Bradley's face, but Winkle flew to his shoulder like an evil advisor. "Sh-she's a tricky one. Don't listen to a word she s-says."

"Shut up." Despite how calmly she said it, it still sent Winkle back a pace.

"Gemma, I want you to listen to me. You don't have the whole story," Bradley said, laying his arms across the polished desk. "Those apartments were a failed business venture of mine. I ran out of money for the developer so they quit building. I couldn't afford bankruptcy, so I made them work anyway. Only Winkle and I know the full extent of the cover-up. I am still working to make them up to code and everything will be right and legal by the end of this year."

Gemma shook her head. "There is nothing right and legal about lying your way into making money. No, listen to me. You cannot keep housing people there while they are unfinished. It's not safe!"

His eyes pleaded with her to understand his point of view. "All the tenants choose to live there, yourself included."

"It doesn't matter. You are putting people at risk. You can't finish apartments if they're full of people!" She relaxed back into her chair, exhausted. "Selfish. Selfish and unethical. How *could* you?"

Bradley didn't meet her eyes. "I had to have the money." His voice cracked.

"*My* money. Alone, pregnant, teenage, desperate." Her voice rose in pitch with each word. Farris began to cry in the next room, making Mr. Winkle even more nervous. She stood and brushed the wrinkles out of her dress, blinking back the tears that had formed in her eyes. "You're nothing but a predator. Both of you. Enjoy the rest of your meeting, *gentlemen.*"

She left them in the silence of their guilt, collected her child, and left.

Chapter 26

Gemma didn't breathe a word of what she had learned to anyone over the weekend. She pondered what it all meant and if she needed to tell Mr. Franklin. Violating safety codes and forging documents was serious, but if it didn't affect his work at the law office, did she have to tell anyone?

But it *had* affected Bradley's work, she kept telling herself. He had wanted to take money from her bank account. Despite her deepest convictions that what he had done was wrong, she wanted to believe he really was trying to make it better. If she told his uncle and he made him correct everything, those dreadful apartments might never get finished. People would lose their homes, Mr. Winkle would lose his job, and Bradley would be in debt. She couldn't bring herself to do that to people all because some words on a piece of paper would be incorrect for a little while longer.

Finally, after avoiding Bradley at church and deciding against saying anything to Hollie, she considered calling Josiah on Monday.

Maybe he had been wise to dislike Bradley from the beginning. Everyone had . . . except her.

After she had laid Farris down for a nap, she tucked Weasley next to her on the couch and dialed. She chewed on the inside of her cheek as she waited for Josiah to pick up. Wouldn't this be one more thing that proved she couldn't handle life on her own? *But what choice do I have?*

"Hello?"

A mix of emotions flooded her and she tried to think of what to say. "Hi. It's Gemma."

"Hey. What's up?"

"Well . . . some things fell apart at work and I wondered if I could talk to you about it."

His voice bordered on reproach. "Of course you can! That weirdo didn't fire you, did he?"

Gemma smiled, despite her dismal attitude. He might actually relish what she was going to say. "No, just the opposite. Did I ever tell you about the apartments I lived in?"

"The ones you got evicted from?"

"Yeah. Well, they were crummy and unsafe. My old landlord came to work yesterday and it turns out Bradley owns them." She held her breath as she waited for a response.

"So . . . what does that mean?"

She pulled Weasley's claws out of her thigh. "He's responsible for their safety violations and has been lying to the appraisal district about their condition in order to avoid bankruptcy. I suppose that means he'd have to be tipping off the safety inspector or something."

Josiah blew out a breath. "Wow. You just can't avoid trouble, can you?"

Gemma shook her head, then realized he wasn't actually there with her. "No. My dilemma is, I don't know what to do about it. It's his own personal venture and free of the law firm. It's not safe to leave it the way it is, but if I say something and the paperwork gets corrected, everybody gets hurt." She waited for his solution, but it didn't come. "So what do I do?" Emotion choked her voice.

"Gemma, I'm not going to tell you what to do."

"But I'm stuck." She took a shaky breath. "Please, do you have any ideas? He was trying to take money from bank accounts to get the funding and—"

"From who?"

"Me!"

There was a moment's silence. "OK, I have a thought. Who have you told?"

"Just you."

"Really?"

Gemma wondered in the pause that followed if Josiah expected an answer to that question, but then he continued.

"Anyway, I'm thinking I'll ask Dad to check the building out. He's an architect so he should be able to tell how bad off everything is. If it's not structurally sound, it'll have to be torn down anyway. Just send me the address. Dad might be able to point out the errors in the paperwork, even, if you don't want to be the direct cause of this guy's problems. I would have no qualms, but I'm not as nice as you."

Gemma smiled. "Let me know how it goes and thank your dad for me. And Josiah?"

"Yeah?"

"Thank you."

Josiah finished feeding the animals and stepped through the back door. He scuffed the mud off his boots and passed through the empty living room into the schoolroom. All the smaller children sat at a table with workbooks before them and pencils in hand. Mrs. Martin was breaking up a fight about who could add the fastest.

"Mariah, if you kick her again, you're going to your room."

"I want to go to my room," Lisabeth said with a toss of her golden hair. "Then I wouldn't have to do school."

Josiah smirked. "I just got off the phone with Gemma." Everyone's faces met his, cheered at the mention of her name.

Mrs. Martin tucked a curl behind her ear. "How is she?"

"Fine, I guess, but she had a question. Do you know where Dad is?"

Mrs. Martin rolled her eyes. "Next time let me talk to her. I want to know how she *really* is. He should be in his office." She turned back to the teacher's manual before her.

"Thanks." He jaunted up the stairs and found his father seated at his desk. His phone chimed and he flipped it open to find a message from Gemma with the address. He had everything he needed.

He leaned on the desk and waited for his father to look up. "Gemma called and she needs our help with something."

Mr. Martin raised an eyebrow.

"Come on, Dad. It's not like she's going to ask us for money or anything. She busted a guy at work for lying about the safety of an apartment building where she used to live. She's too nice to expose him, so I told her we'd check it out. It's about fifteen minutes from here if we drive. Are you free?"

"Why not? It sounds more exciting than trying to remodel an office building." He stood and straightened his tie. "Who is this person she found out?"

"Something Bradley. He's a head dude at the office."

"Of course he is. That girl has a knack for trouble." He passed Josiah, who launched himself off the desk, and they headed downstairs.

"Yeah, but I'd say she has a knack for truth, too." He shrugged.

"I suppose that's one way of looking at it," Mr. Martin said. "I'll drive, please."

Josiah went around the car and hopped in.

"Where are you going?" Ginger called from the garden.

"Just a quick errand!" Josiah said before slamming his door.

Even with Josiah's less-than-superior navigation skills, it did not take them long to find the apartment building. It was tucked at the bottom of a grassy hill, almost unseen from any surrounding roads. At first glance, there was nothing conspicuous about it except that there was only a single building where there might have been room for twenty. Otherwise, it looked just like any other low-income, multi-family housing.

"Here we are," Mr. Martin said, bringing the car to a halt and looking around. "They've got a real parking lot and sidewalk, at least."

Josiah got out of the car and looked the building up and down. "It's kind of small. Probably can't hold more than ten families. They can't be making that much money on only a few people."

"Let's find out, shall we. Pay attention; there's no telling what sort of manipulation we'll need to use." Mr. Martin massaged his hands and shook them out.

Josiah grinned. "Yes, sir."

They approached the building—three stories of dingy tan brick—and entered what looked like a lobby.

Josiah struggled to keep a grimace from his face as he took in the bare room. The lighting was dim, the wallpaper distasteful, and the floor nothing but rough concrete. There was a spindly man at a desk to their left, a room that opened to their right, and a staircase ahead. *People actually live here?* But it appeared so. There was a door facing them with a brass number 1 on it.

The man at the desk straightened and brushed his sparse hair across his head with his jittery fingers. "How may I help you?"

"We'd like to see your empty room," Mr. Martin said.

"I don't have an empty room."

Mr. Martin's brow furrowed. "Well, how many do you have?"

"S-seven."

"And they're all full?"

"That's what I s-said."

Mr. Martin straightened. "That's unfortunate. You have the best price in town, I'm told."

The weasel-like man relaxed his defensive posture some. "That's true. Four hundred a month is hard to beat. One of our residents is out at the moment. Perhaps I can show you around anyway, just so you know what's comparable."

"That would be very nice."

Josiah felt victory surge inside him as the little man led the way up the stairs. He noted how his father took his time, trying the steps and rattling the railing. It was all so subtle, the man didn't notice.

Josiah avoided a protruding nail and beat it back into submission with the toe of his boot.

The landing creaked as they turned the corner, but the boards were new and unstained. At the top of the stairs they were met with an L-shaped hallway that held six of the rooms.

"Where's your seventh room?" Mr. Martin asked.

"First floor, for handicapped tenants."

Josiah pointed his thumb at a bathroom stood across the hall from the rooms. "Is this the only bathroom?"

"S-simplified plumbing," the landlord said. He drew a key from his pocket and stuck it in the keyhole of the last door.

It swung open to reveal a small room with very little furniture. The brick wall that constituted the outside also formed the exterior walls of this space. An ajar door to the right showed a bed. Past that, the space the bedroom filled died away into a kitchenette consisting of a small counter with a single cabinet, sink, microwave, and miniature fridge.

"There you have it," said Mr. Winkle. "All the necessities and a nice window overlooking the hillside. If you'd like to leave your contact information, I can notify you when one opens up. They're pretty high demand."

"Uh-huh," Mr. Martin said. He strolled to the window and leaned against it. "Very nice. Thank you." He glanced up at the ceiling fan and smiled. "Thank you very much, but that won't be necessary."

Josiah looked from his father to the ceiling fan in wonder and followed him back down the steep staircase.

"Dad, what—"

He held up a hand and Josiah remained silent until they were back in their car.

"Well? I didn't see anything wrong. It was bare to a creative level, but still four walls and a roof."

"First of all, there are rules about having no insulation and drywall. You did notice the outside walls also happened to be the inside walls?"

"Yeah."

"Second, if that won't get them, where's the third story? They have completely unexplained height."

Josiah raised his eyebrows, unimpressed. "Anything else?"

"Electrical. The fan was hooked up, but any wires not connected were open ended. You get an electrical surge in there and sparks fly. Related to that particular danger is the issue of how many people they house. Those rooms were around four hundred square feet and there was seating for five. That's more than should be allowed to live there."

Josiah pumped his fist. "I knew we'd find something. That place was dreadful, wasn't it?"

Mr. Martin exhaled slowly. "Yes, it was. Now you call Gemma back and tell her we've got them one way or another."

Josiah smiled. "Yes, sir."

Gemma remained silent for the entirety of the work week. She only saw Bradley once and he had escorted her into her office and begged her not to say a thing, using the exact same reasoning Gemma had when trying to convince herself. And she had agreed; Mr. Martin had already proved the apartments' unsafe nature to the county. The solution he had presented was to undertake the project himself, bring the apartments up to where they needed to be, and then resell them to Bradley. Neither the county nor Gemma would have to do a thing and there would be no losses.

When she was first told of the plan, it had seemed almost too nice. The two scheming men deserved to be thrown out and pay the consequences. It was Josiah who had prevailed in the end, suggesting the resale to prevent making Bradley and Mr. Winkle destitute.

Gemma thanked God that she had such steady and selfless friends. They never failed to meet the task whenever she brought herself to ask for help.

Farris began to cry, startling her from her reverie. She finished scrubbing solidified freezer meal off her plate and dried her hands on a towel before tending to him.

Weasley was seated at the bedroom door, looking up at the doorknob, waiting to see his favorite baby when Gemma got there. Contrary to her fears when she had first adopted the creature, he watched out for Farris as if he were his own kitten.

"Go get him." She opened the door and Weasley darted inside, his fluffy tail waving. He hopped into the playpen and rubbed against the crying baby. While Farris had grown, Weasley had grown faster. They were almost the same size now.

"Hi, sweet boy." She lifted him out, set him on her hip, and called Weasley. If she wasn't careful, he'd stay behind and take *his* nap.

Gemma tried not to fidget as she fed Farris, but the dull cramp in her abdomen had come back. Even with her body returning to normal since having a baby, she didn't remember anything quite like this. But since it came and went, she didn't give it much consideration.

Her phone began to vibrate in her back pocket and she twisted to the side so she could fish it out. *Josiah.*

"Hey, what's up?"

"The apartment fraud and our solution was approved today, so Bradley should be finding out pretty soon if he hasn't already. Don't let him catch on to you being mixed up in all this."

"Thank you so much. I promise I'll be careful. Hey, this is random, but you haven't heard anything else from my uncle, have you? It's just been a while and I don't know if no news is good news or not."

"No, nothing new."

"And Travis has been totally silent?" She sat Farris up in her lap and beat on his back while he tried to eat his toes.

"Just like he promised. With any luck we won't hear from either of them for a while yet."

"Good. Thanks again, Josiah. It means a lot."

"You bet. Love you, bye."

"Bye." She held the phone in her hand, call ended, before her brain processed what he had said. She chuckled. Slips of the tongue could get you in a lot of trouble; he was probably mortified.

She moved to the kitchen and swallowed a pill for mounting lightheadedness. Sighing in frustration, she added "iron-rich" food to her sticky note on the fridge. Perhaps this switch from supplements wasn't doing her as much good as she'd hoped.

A commotion outside distracted her and she tucked Farris more securely on her hip. "Come on, little guy. Let's go see what the ruckus is all about."

The moment she left her doorway, she comprehended the scene in full. The flashing lights, tall man in handcuffs, and irate Asian woman told her all she needed to know.

"I cannot believe I not know about this!" Jackie kept saying, pacing back and forth behind the police car. "Why did you not tell me?" She glared at Gemma.

She held up her free hand. "I reported the domestic abuse, and if that didn't get your attention, why would drug dealing?"

The landlady's mouth fell open.

Gemma let her stay that way and moved toward the police car. It was definitely Bryan in the back seat, mostly inebriated.

"Ma'am, can I ask you what you knew of this matter?" a suntanned policeman asked, pad of paper in hand.

"I rescued his girlfriend from abuse and knew he was prone to alcoholism and violence."

The officer scratched down words for a moment. "Did you ever see regular people visiting his apartment?"

She refrained from fidgeting; talking to an officer of the law made her guilt bubble up. "No, sir, but I'm not usually here during the day."

"Very good. Thank you. And your name?"

"Gemma Ebworthy, just like it sounds."

The pen went to the paper again. "Thank you very much. Have a nice day."

I'll have a better shot at that if you don't find my criminal records. But the chances of him spelling her name exactly right, running it in the system, and caring enough to wonder if she was the Gemma with the misdemeanors in Texas were slim . . . she hoped. Her fear of not being around for Farris mounted, but she reassured herself.

She proceeded down the sidewalk, through the crowd of whispering neighbors, and to her mailbox. Gemma drew the key out of her pocket and opened the lockbox. Besides the reminder that rent was due soon, there was a letter.

Gemma's eyes widened when she saw it was from Cindy Ebworthy. *Who? How on earth did she get my address?* She tore open the envelope and quickly scanned the contents. The opening line stunned her:

Your uncle passed away . . .

Chapter 27

Gemma pushed her way back to her apartment in a daze. *Dead?* She reread the letter in its entirety once she was back in the privacy of her home.

Gemma,

Your uncle passed away yesterday. They told me he was knocked down a flight of stairs while drunk and broke his neck. To my surprise, I was not the only one mentioned in his will; he left you the stuff and me the money. Apparently he had a decent savings account, but his debts aren't covered yet. If there's anything you can do to help with funeral expenses, that would be great. I just thought you should know. I would love to meet you and the baby sometime.

Aunt Cindy

Gemma shook her head and tossed the piece of notebook paper aside. She sank onto the couch and kissed the top of Farris's head. Her uncle, simultaneously her plague and provider, and only family, had died. And in his own bizarre way. There was still her aunt Cindy, of course, but she didn't really count since Gemma had never met her.

"He left me everything?" Tears welled up in her eyes unbidden. For all the awful things she'd thought about that man through the years, they'd managed to rely upon each other until the very end. She wouldn't have made it without him.

"Oh, Farris, what are we going to do?" She swiped at her eyes. "We'll have to help Aunt Cindy and go to the funeral. Are you up for that, mister?"

The child gurgled his response.

"Of course you are. You're up for anything Mommy's up for."

Gemma dug a pen out of the diaper bag and jotted down a reply on a spare piece of paper. She'd have to get the details before she could do anything, so she included her phone number. Then she wondered if she'd be fast enough, even then. If the letter was written several days ago, the funeral could be today or tomorrow.

Gemma sighed. She could still help cover expenses if she needed to, but it would be nice to actually have someone attend. The poor man never had any friends except at the bar and it sounded like they were the ones who aided his death. She couldn't imagine a funeral where only the town drunks and bums showed up. Perhaps it was a better idea to skip it anyway.

She realized how stupid that sounded as she folded the piece of paper. *You'd think I'd be done running from things in my past by now.* But no. The longer she lived, the more she feared it would be a lifelong struggle. Why couldn't the past just die?

Gemma got a call Monday morning from Aunt Cindy. The funeral was Wednesday at two. Would she be able to make it? It was very important to her aunt, since she and Farris were the only other relatives.

"I'll try my best," Gemma assured the woman, who sounded desperate enough to be holding the phone with both hands. "Thank you for calling."

"Uh-huh, sure thing, Gemma. Bye-bye."

Gemma sighed. She had no idea what that woman was thinking, marrying her uncle, but she must feel even worse now that he had died only a few months later. She still sounded rattled, even though her letter had been composed.

Gemma could afford a plane ticket from her savings and perhaps even enjoy the mini vacation if only she could get time off.

When she arrived at the office Monday morning, she went straight into Mr. Franklin's office.

Bradley was sitting on the edge of his uncle's desk, but Gemma refused to make eye contact with him and instead focused on her boss, puffing away on a cigar. "Sir, may I have some time off? I have a funeral to attend."

Bradley shifted, presumably out of concern, but she still ignored him.

"How much time, Gemma?"

"Tuesday and Wednesday, this week."

Mr. Franklin rubbed his chin. "Short notice, but I don't see why not. Sorry for your loss. I was just discussing with Leo what we should train you in next. You're one of the best secretaries I've ever had, even if you were hired on a clerical error." The man waved his cigar to emphasize his statement and Gemma wondered for the umpteenth time if he was breaking some kind of rule, smoking indoors.

Bradley had turned very red and Gemma wasn't sure if it was because his uncle had acknowledged they were talking about her or because of the use of his despised first name. But she didn't care.

"Thank you, sir." Gemma dismissed herself, but much to her chagrin, Bradley followed her out.

"Why didn't you tell me someone had died? You know I could have given you time off."

Gemma refrained from clenching her jaw as she set Farris down and opened her laptop. Relying on him had gotten her into trouble thus far.

"I didn't know last time I saw you," she said, eyes stubbornly fixed on her computer screen.

"Gemma—" His hand went to her arm, but she jerked it away.

"Don't touch me," she said in a terse whisper, glancing past him to where Hollie sat, alert at her desk. She fixed her narrowed eyes on his apologetic—pathetic—ones. "You're the third man in my life to betray me, and I can count on one hand the number I've known well." She showed him her palm. "Don't keep pretending that you're my friend."

"But I am your friend!"

Her gaze was scathing. "Friends do not lie. Or steal. Or cheat."

Bradley's jaw went taut and he glanced over his shoulder. "It got shut down, you know. Does that make you happy? Someone started snooping around and it's all done for." His voice cracked and he looked at his shoes. "*I'm* done for."

Gemma let him kick her desk for a moment. Then she said, "I'm sorry."

His eyes met hers again, questioning.

"I really am," she said, nodding. "But I don't know what you expected. Could you really have enjoyed a false victory?"

He shrugged, defeat written on every line of his body, and left the room, closing the door.

Gemma let out an involuntary sigh. Why were good, honest, genuine people so hard to come by? Didn't people see what happened—what always happened? No one could live like that without getting burned over time. Heaven knew she had.

She turned her head and lost herself in the face of her sleeping baby. Her voice came out in a subconscious whisper. "But I could have gotten burned so much worse."

The trip to Austin, Texas, was a whirlwind. Gemma felt sick all day at the prospect of taking Farris, little as he still was, on a plane ride. The sanity of her fellow passengers did not concern her as much as the health and wellbeing of her child. What if he picked up an illness during the flight? It was going to be an exhausting trip on every front already; she didn't need a bug to boot.

When Gemma arrived mid-day Tuesday, she was struck with the changes that had taken place. Austin was always, always growing. But despite that, it never lost the charm of being the unashamed capital of a state. It would forever hold captive a tiny corner of her heart, even if it didn't quite feel like home anymore.

She took in the sights during the taxi ride on the way to her hotel, her shortened hair falling in her face. She spotted old hangouts and her route to her first job. There were one or two places that she figured still had fuzzy video footage of her from several years ago. A mental note formed in her head; she would make it up to them somehow, without announcing herself the thief, before she left town. As long as she didn't get stuck in jail, she and Farris would pull through.

Poor Farris, though he had remained content on the trip, was exhausted by the time they reached the hotel room. Being on best behavior for hours at a time would drain anyone. Gemma hadn't traveled with his playpen, since it was so large even disassembled, so he slept in the roomy bed with her. Despite his spells of fidgeting and whimpering, she enjoyed having him next to her where she could soothe him at a moment's notice and not have to drag her weary body across her apartment.

Having his mother close at hand seemed to soothe him, too, for he slept through the night for the first time since she had entered her third trimester. She could hardly believe it when she woke up and he was still splayed beside her. While he had been somewhat restless, he had never demanded to be fed. In fact, this was so out of the ordinary for him that the first thing she did was check to make sure he was still breathing.

Of course, the moment after she got up to go to the bathroom, he woke up. She came flying back out to tend to him before he had a chance to make his way off the bed. She was not confident that her pillow barrier would hold against his growing strength, even though she had yet to see him roll over.

Gemma spent the morning enjoying having nothing to do and sustained herself with an iron-rich breakfast bar. When they ventured out of the hotel for lunch, she took a detour by way of the shops that had stood out to her the night before. The first one, a deplorable gas station, made her cringe now. But she still felt she owed it her five dollars' worth of stolen soda and so left that amount on the counter when the cashier wasn't watching. She was very pleased with herself for getting away with it; she hadn't lost her touch.

The second store presented a little more difficulty as it now possessed an armed guard, no doubt due to the sort of activity Gemma and her friends used to provide. In the end, her only solution was to buy motion sickness medicine and give a very generous donation to the children's hospital fund.

Gemma knew there were more places she must have plagued and harmed, but she couldn't call to mind another and that encouraged her. Maybe it was possible to forget part of her past after all.

Gemma took Farris back to the hotel room before the funeral so he would have a chance to nap and she could freshen up. She unpacked her navy dress and shook the wrinkles out of it. It took her twice as long as it should have because Farris sleeping on the high bed all by himself made her nervous. But he remained in the center where she had put him, nevertheless.

The weather proved perfect for a funeral that was going to take place all outside, and Gemma was grateful for that. Two dozen chairs sat stark and empty under a pavilion at the graveside when she arrived. The spindly woman, dressed all in black and kneeling in front of the simple casket, Gemma assumed was her aunt. She climbed out of the taxi, Farris's seat on her arm, and asked the driver to be back in an hour.

As Gemma approached, the woman stood. Her gray eyes were remarkably young, but her makeup-plastered face was lined with hardship. She held out her arms. "You must be Gemma."

Gemma rested Farris's seat on the green carpet that had been laid and embraced the woman. "I'm very sorry," she said.

"That's all right, I know you are." She drew back and took her seat again, staring straight ahead. "You know how he was."

Gemma smiled distantly, looking at the shiny surface of the closed casket, topped with a bouquet. "O-oh yes."

The pastor stood, Bible in hand, and pronounced his few words over the body. One of Uncle Wilfred's friends had some nice things to say, although Gemma couldn't attest to the truth of all of them.

"Would you like us to sing something?" the pastor asked her aunt.

Aunt Cindy nodded, but the pastor seemed to be uncertain as to what would be appropriate. He was young, and Gemma guessed this was his first funeral to perform for a stranger.

So Gemma started to sing. "Amazing grace, how sweet the sound." By the time she had forced the first few shaky notes out, the pastor caught on and joined her. Faint mumbling came from the men behind her and Aunt Cindy just closed her eyes and rocked back and forth.

Once the pastor thanked and dismissed them, Gemma took an envelope out of the diaper bag. "Here. I know it isn't much, but hopefully it will help. The service was everything he could have wanted it to be."

Aunt Cindy wiped her eyes and smoothed frizzy caramel strands of hair away from her face. "Thank you. Do you want to come back to the house? Or do you need to go?"

"I've got four hours before my plane leaves, but I still have to pack up at the hotel. Why don't you come there with me and we can talk a little?"

Aunt Cindy nodded and gave Farris a smile. "Sure."

The shaken woman sat silently the entire way to the hotel. She gazed out the window, chin on palm, watching the tree-lined sidewalks go by. Gemma spent her time wondering what on earth someone so nice as this lady had seen in her uncle. He had been kind, but devoutly selfish and always intoxicated. She was astonished every time she glanced at this aunt of hers, who couldn't have been more than ten years her senior, and saw such deep sadness in her youthful eyes. What story could they be hiding?

As Gemma stood in the elevator, trying to block out the musty, electrical smell, she thought of how to ask Aunt Cindy politely about what had happened. Not just about her uncle's death, but everything.

The words were forming on her lips when the elevator jerked a little and came to a stop. Gemma waited for it to open, but it didn't. She ignored the sense of panic climbing up her throat and pressed the "Open Door" button.

Nothing happened.

She exchanged glances with her aunt and set the baby down. Gemma examined the panel of buttons. "What do I do?"

"Push a number—any of them. It may just need a command."

"Two" was still illuminated since it had been her original choice. So she punched "3" and then "4." Still, nothing happened.

"Well, there's an emergency button for a reason." Aunt Cindy pushed the speaker button and put her mouth to the circular pattern of dots. "Hello? Our elevator is stuck between floors one and two." She straightened and waited.

"I'm sorry?" a voice came.

"We're stuck in the elevator between floors one and two," she repeated.

Gemma sank down the wall and swiped at the sweat that gathered on her forehead and the back of her neck. "Hang on just a minute, little guy." She let Farris's fist curl around her index finger and he sucked on it contentedly.

"He said we should be out within the half hour," Aunt Cindy said. She joined Gemma on the floor and rested her chin on her knees. "I do hope you don't miss your plane."

Chapter 28

Within a matter of minutes, they could hear voices outside the elevator. "Ma'am? We're gonna work on getting the doors open, all right?"

"Thank you!" Cindy shouted.

Farris was growing frantic, so Gemma decided to feed him anyway. Her aunt would have to be OK with that, given the circumstances.

Despite her attempt at indifference, Gemma was glad when her aunt smiled. "He's a really pretty baby."

"Thank you." She sat in silence for a moment, but then decided to ask the unavoidable question on her mind. "How did you and Uncle Wilfred . . . he just never seemed like the romantic type. Did it work out OK?"

Cindy sat, leaning against the side of the elevator while the men worked to open the doors from the top. "Yes, it was going well. We met a couple times on accident: at a bar, on the street. My friends couldn't believe I actually enjoyed talking to him, as I'm sure you can imagine. But he was very kind and really had no idea what he was doing." She laughed. "I had no intention of the relationship becoming romantic, but we started to see each other more and when he proposed one night I accepted. He still had bad habits, but he was really trying for me, Gemma. I wish you could have seen him like that. It must be hard for you to imagine."

Gemma raised her eyebrows. Associating anything romantic with her uncle did seem odd and almost repulsive, but Cindy's eyes had shone as she told the story. "Yeah, nothing ever convinced him there was a reason to be a better person while I lived with him. You must have been very special to him, Cindy."

Her face clouded and she rested her chin on her knees. "He said so. Then one night he went to the bar and didn't come back. I didn't know what had happened until the next morning."

Gemma sat Farris up and burped him. "That must have been so awful."

There was a groaning noise and the women glanced to the top of the elevator doors as they eased open several inches.

"Hey in there," a man's voice came. "Doing all right?"

"Yes, thank you," Cindy called back.

His face appeared in the gap. While he must have been lying on the floor, he was still at the very top of the elevator. "The elevator needs to raise several feet before we'll have space to pull you through, so we'll work on that next."

It was another half hour before the crew had succeeded and helped the three passengers out of the elevator. Gemma did not miss her plane but neither did she have a minute to spare. She hugged her newfound aunt goodbye and hailed a cab.

Gemma was still running all the details of Cindy's story through her head when she landed at the Wichita airport. She collected her things in the bright, fluorescent lighting of the plane only to enter the nippy, sunset air to wait for Hollie. There was no point in waiting for her luggage by herself, since she couldn't possibly carry it with Farris asleep on her shoulder.

Within moments, Hollie whipped her new car into a parallel park alongside the sidewalk.

She hopped out and gave her a hug. "Where's your luggage?"

"I haven't gotten it yet. Just let me get Farris in the car, and—"

"I got it!" Hollie raced off toward the main entrance and returned several minutes later with the suitcase. She tossed the bag in her trunk and swung herself into the driver's seat. "Are you coming to work tomorrow, or do you have another day off?"

"No, I need to work tomorrow."

"Oh, good! Mr. Bradley's been in a terrible mood lately and you always seem to cheer him up."

Gemma slid down her seat a little. "Hm. He must not have gotten his aristocratic way."

Hollie cut her eyes to her friend. "That's a little judgmental coming from you."

Gemma shrugged. "I think he's a little spoiled is all."

"Oh, don't apologize to me. I couldn't agree with you more."

Gemma couldn't help but feel a little relieved. Maybe her friend had distanced herself from Bradley again while she was gone. "How did Weasley do?" He had stayed with Hollie while she was gone.

"He did well. He's a cat, so as long as he had food and a window, he was happy. I think Jake liked having him around, though. They were bachelor buddies."

While Bradley did not appear to have said anything about his situation to anyone else at work, he grew increasingly agitated as the week passed. If she really dug into her emotional reservoir, Gemma could feel sorry for him, but she was still thankful that the situation rested in more honest hands.

When she received an invitation to January Martin and Patrick Rose's wedding, set for April 8, she was reminded to call Josiah again and ensure their Bradley scheme was going as planned.

"Everything's going just as we hoped, in case you're wondering," he said when he answered.

Gemma smiled at his perceptiveness. "That's exactly why I was calling. He's very distressed at work, but I don't think he's told anyone else. He mentioned it to me. Does he know he can buy it back yet?"

"Yes, but I doubt he'll have the funds."

"That bad?" Gemma said, repositioning the phone on her ear.

"He's bankrupt, so I don't know what he'll decide to do. Dad's been able to rehouse the tenants, though, and get a start on renovations."

"Wow! Thank him again for me. It's going to be worth it in the end, I think."

"For sure."

There was a moment of silence as Gemma tried to think of something to talk about just so she didn't have to hang up.

"I got January's wedding invitation. It was sweet of her to invite me."

"Oh, yeah. Are you going to come? She's having the reception here at the house."

"I don't know. I'd like to, but I hadn't really considered it. I just got back a few days ago from my trip to Texas."

"Didn't get apprehended, I take it?"

"Ha. Ha. I told you, I made a pretty clean escape."

"What *did* you do, anyway?"

Gemma sighed. "Petty theft, vandalism, that sort of thing. I was a public menace. While it was all bad, the worst thing I ever did was sell drugs."

Josiah blew out a breath. "Wow, that's . . . scary."

Gemma chuckled. "It was. I never took any, though. I wasn't as brave as all that. I did it for the money."

"Well, if Bradley does find you out and sacks you, don't go back to selling drugs, OK? We'll work something else out."

She could detect the glint of humor in his voice and it made her feel whole inside, even if he was teasing her about such a dire prospect. "Promise."

"Oh, before I forget, Mom was thinking about visiting you."

"Really?" She felt her spirits lift considerably at the possibility of a visit from Mrs. Martin.

"Yeah. David's wife, Beth, is getting induced not far from where you live next week. First grandchild and all that. All the kids will be on spring break, so she thought she'd stop in. We don't know who all will be able to come yet, but she'll probably want to talk to you about it at some point."

Gemma remembered when she was in that decision-making stage for Farris's arrival. She was certain David and Beth had formed their plans much sooner than she had. "Sure. That would be awesome."

"Yeah? Great. I'll let you go; I have a business meeting to see about this commercial farming idea. Wish me luck!"

"Good luck. Talk to you later."

"OK, bye."

Gemma felt a twinge of disappointment when he didn't repeat his mistake from last time and was surprised at herself. It confirmed in her mind that his slip of the tongue *had* been a mistake. And she would have to be all right with that.

Gemma filled the first weeks of March with improvements around the apartment. Even though Mrs. Martin had assured her not to worry about doing anything extra when the whole family had decided to make a vacation out of it, leaving the Jeffersons in charge of the farm for a few days, Gemma felt more pressure to make sure everything was in good order. Even fitting the entire family into the house for a visit would be difficult. Mrs. Martin guaranteed they could spend the night at a hotel. They would have two days to devote entirely to her before Beth was due to deliver her baby, half an hour away.

Gemma also continued to plug in more at her church. Since she had made it quite clear to Clair that it would be impossible for her to teach, she had instead worked toward getting Gemma helpful side jobs with the children—ones that did not require a background check. Her friend had said she couldn't bear to see talent go to waste and remembered how disappointed Gemma had been that she couldn't help.

Farris had grown into a chubby, gurgling, brown-eyed baby always strapped to the front of his mother. As long as he was by her side, he was content to chew on anything at hand. Now that he brandished his first tooth on his bottom gum, he was drooling and chewing even more than before.

Living life more fully than ever came with Gemma feeling extremely fatigued and lightheaded of late. The spontaneous pain in her abdomen had returned yet again, and Gemma was beginning to record it on her wall calendar so she could find a pattern, if there was one. This had caused her to be less productive at work and she had actually fallen asleep on her computer when Hollie came to get her for lunch break.

"Are you sure you're OK, Gemma? You're making me nervous." Hollie felt her forehead and checked her pupil dilation.

"I'm fine. I've been more determined to eat red meats and fish and such for iron, so I've felt a bit better. It's this confounded pain. It was in my thighs and back this morning."

"Go home and rest. You've got the day off tomorrow, so don't do anything. I can come and check on you."

"Don't bother. The Martins are coming to visit tomorrow. I vacuumed this morning, so I just have to wash the dishes and then I'll go to bed."

Hollie gave her a sideways look.

"I promise! At least I'll try. I think Farris is cutting another tooth." She heaved herself out of her chair and picked up the fussing baby, who was sucking on his thumb around the steady stream of drool escaping his rashy mouth.

"Poor buddy," Hollie cooed, patting his head and wiping his face with his clammy bib. "It's no fun cutting teeth."

Gemma sighed. "I think he takes it pretty well. He's not too fussy, he just doesn't sleep or relax. I can tell he's uncomfortable and it makes me sad." She kissed the top of his dark head.

Hollie rubbed Gemma's arm. "Why don't you take the rest of the day off. I can wrap up your filing."

Gemma started to protest, but she was feeling nauseous again and wanted to be well before the Martins came. Sinking into bed an hour later with a restless Farris by her side was the best decision she had made all week.

Gemma was disheartened and weary when she got very little sleep that Friday night. Farris had needed Tylenol in the middle of the night because his gums were swollen and hurting. Gemma took ibuprofen with a spoonful of beans (supposedly iron-rich) just for good measure before going back to bed with a cup of water; she was so thirsty and continued to feel flutters in her head, stomach, legs—everywhere. If only she could get some sleep.

After she got Farris back to sleep at six a.m., she rested on the couch with Weasley. She woke up to a phone call several hours later from Josiah.

"Hello?" She massaged her temple and tried to mask the weariness in her voice.

"Hey, we're headed your way, so we'll be there in around two hours."

Gemma pulled her phone away from her ear and looked at the time. "OK. I don't have a lunch plan; I guess we'll just order something. Y'all like pizza, right? I guess I'll do that then."

"OK. Rest up and we'll see you soon."

"All right, bye."

She tossed her phone onto the speckled carpet and laid back down, tucking Weasley against her. She wasn't going to miss the opportunity to sleep some more—not while Farris was quiet.

When she woke up at eleven thirty, she felt much better. The shooting pains she'd been having had dissipated and her headache was gone. She drank another glass of water and took some more ibuprofen to be safe. She felt more human than she had for several days.

She fed Farris and gave him a bath to get the drool out of the folds of his neck and arms before he'd be held by company.

"You'd better be on your best behavior, little man. People are coming to see you."

He splashed soap bubbles in her eye as a response.

She chuckled as she pressed on the burning eye and watched him with the other. "Ow! Not funny, Farris. Let's get you dried off before we make a mess."

She lifted him out of his baby tub that she had wedged in the kitchen sink. He had nearly outgrown it. As soon as he could sit up with a little more confidence, she could use the normal bathtub. She wrapped him in a towel and took him to the couch where she had laid out his outfit for the day—one the Martins had sent a few weeks back and almost the only thing that fit him now.

Several minutes later, the Martins arrived in full force. Gemma had just slipped into fresh clothes and was still brushing her hair when they knocked. She tossed her brush back into a bathroom drawer and went to get the door. A hoard of smiling faces met her when she flung the door open. The entire family hardly fit under the covered sidewalk.

"Hi! It's so good to see all of you. Come inside!" Gemma stood back and exchanged hugs and hellos as they all filed inside. "Sorry, there's not much seating, but feel free to spread out into Farris's bedroom." She pointed toward the hallway. "The pizza I ordered should be here any minute."

All the kids swapped smiles as they found a place to sit.

"That sounds great," Mrs. Martin said. "Look at you, you look so wonderful. And Farris has gotten so big!" She rubbed his back. "May I hold him?"

"Sure," Gemma said, glad to get him off her hip. "He's teething, so he may not be as friendly as usual."

Farris surveyed his full house, taking in each face by turn with wide eyes.

"He's so cute and little!" Lisabeth said, stroking his foot since it was on her level.

"If you think he's little, wait until you get to meet your new niece or nephew," Gemma said.

"Oh, she's going to be a niece," Mariah said. "They're naming her Joyanna."

"Awesome. Y'all must be so excited."

Everyone nodded vigorously.

"Well, I'm afraid I don't have much to do here, but there's an empty lot behind the apartments if y'all want to go play out there. Just don't go too close to the fence; the dogs are mean."

Mariah and Gail jumped to their feet immediately and were escorted outside with Emmaline. Lisabeth was busy petting Weasley. "She's a pretty kitty," she said, stroking his fluffy back.

"His name is Weasley," Gemma said, scratching his chin. "He's a good boy."

"I thought there was a no-pet policy," Josiah said, gesturing to the cat.

Gemma looked up from her crouched stance on the floor and gave him a smile. "Well, as far as my landlady is concerned, I have no pet."

He smiled back at her. "I see."

"Is everything with the Bradley project going all right?" Gemma directed her question to Mr. Martin, who stood against the bar. She could smell menthol; was it part of his treatment?

"Yes, it's coming along nicely. The fixes are a little complicated, which is probably why they hadn't corrected any of the cheap mistakes they chose to make. It won't take but another month and people will be able to move back in."

"Thank you so much for taking it on," she said, straightening. "I know it can't be of great profit to you, but it was very important to me that we not dump all those people. You're kind to do something so adventurous."

"Not a problem, Gemma. I'm glad I could help and that you asked me. It was about time that I had something out of the ordinary to stretch my abilities."

Gemma returned his smile and handed Farris a toy so he would remain happy in Mrs. Martin's lap. "How has life been for you girls?"

Anneliese shrugged. "Good."

"Excellent," Ginger said. "It's been a lot of fun."

"With Elias?" Gemma arched an eyebrow.

Ginger flushed. "Maybe."

Gemma shifted in discomfort as the conversation continued around her. The shooting pain had returned next to her right hip, where it always was, and worse than before. She resisted the urge to rub the pained spot.

She crossed to the kitchen, listening halfheartedly to the discussion on whether Josiah had remembered to give Elias complete instructions.

"He knows what he's doing," Josiah said, crossing his arms.

Gemma got some more ibuprofen and Mrs. Martin crossed to her with Farris since he was getting fussier.

"You OK?"

"Yeah, I just have this weird pain that keeps coming back. But I'm not lightheaded like I was earlier." She took Farris from Mrs.

Martin. "I'm going to go feed him. The pizza should be here anytime."

"All right. Let me know if you need anything. I don't want you to be put out by us being here." Her brown eyes were sincere.

"I'll be fine once this kicks in," Gemma assured her. "I think it's just part of everything returning to normal."

Mrs. Martin patted her back. "Oh, the joys of being a woman."

Gemma slipped into her bedroom and stuffed a pillow on her lap, under Farris, so she could feed him with some support. She tried to remain still while he nursed, but the pain was only getting stronger, making it hard for her to concentrate.

By the time he had finished eating, it was so severe she couldn't catch her breath. She lowered her shirt and forced her way into the living room again. Everything was pitching as if she were on a ship and it all came back to the pulsing, fiery pain. She registered the pizza boxes on the counter.

"Could you take him?" Gemma mumbled, holding Farris out with shaking hands. Ginger and Josiah crossed the room together. Or at least she thought they did; she was seeing double.

No sooner had her child left her arms than the pain spiraled. She let out a small cry as she tried to remain on her feet. She felt Josiah's hand on her arm as she battled for consciousness. The edges of her vision fizzled as her eyes struggled to focus on Josiah's face. Everything slipped away.

Chapter 29

Josiah's insides lurched as he scrambled to break Gemma' fall. He didn't exactly catch her, but kept her from hitting anything and lowered her to the ground.

"Oh my goodness!" Mrs. Martin leaped from the couch and knelt beside her.

Josiah's gut wrenched and he watched his mother check for a pulse.

"It's faint."

"What's wrong with her? What do I do?"

"I don't know yet," Mrs. Martin said, checking her eyes and forehead. "She told me she was in pain, but I don't know where . . ." Her voice trailed off.

Ginger bounced the baby and rifled through Gemma's medicine cabinet. "She's not on medication for anything."

Mrs. Martin nodded. "Sit her up so she gets better circulation. Hurry!"

Josiah did as he was told. Her body was getting warmer, but held no resistance. "Come on, Gemma," he murmured.

Mrs. Martin shook her—gently—but nothing changed. Gemma's face was pale and painless.

Josiah couldn't look away. There was nothing to do. What could he do? "Her stomach," he said. It surprised him how far away his own words seemed; they took effort, as if the air were made of honey. "Her hand went to her stomach before she blacked out." His words came out faster and seemed to trip over themselves.

Mrs. Martin passed a hand over her stomach, gently. "She's swelling here. It's probably her appendix. We need to get her to a hospital fast. Anneliese, call 911!"

Anneliese snatched Josiah's phone and flew out the front door, describing their location. Mr. Martin followed her, leaving the door open.

Josiah swallowed and his brain raced for a solution. How dangerous could appendicitis be? He glanced up at Ginger, still bouncing the baby, and found a gravity in her expression that scared him.

Mr. Martin reentered the apartment, somber, wide-eyed children at his side. "Get her outside now."

Josiah stood and lifted her limp body, careful not to bump her head or legs on the doorframe.

Gathering sirens could be heard in the distance and he prayed they were for her. There was a hospital just a few miles away, but how long would it take to get here?

"Is she going to be OK?" one of his sisters asked.

Anneliese shooed them all inside. "She'll be fine. Look, the pizza came. Everybody sit on the kitchen floor and eat."

"Get anything you might need for the baby, Ginge, and get in the car. We'll follow the ambulance to the hospital," Mr. Martin said, turning the key as he spoke. "Anneliese, stay with the children. Keep the phone."

The muscles in Josiah's arms burned from supporting the extra weight—the dead weight—of Gemma's body. He stood rigid for several minutes before hurrying toward the ambulance as it pulled into the narrow lot. Paramedics streamed out with a rolling stretcher and took her from him.

He let go and stood there, watching, as they tied her arms down and placed an oxygen mask over her face.

What do I do?

Neighbors had gathered on the sidewalk, hands over mouths.

"Josiah, get in the car!" his father shouted.

He started and rushed to climb in, adrenaline jolting him to action despite his numbed mind. One thought stood out among the clutter of hazy memories from the last few minutes: *I can't lose her.*

When Gemma began to stir, her head was a swamp of confusion. But one thing she noticed immediately—there was no pain. She forced her heavy eyelids to flutter open and take in the IV in her arm and the beeping machine to her right. *I'm in the hospital.* Her spirits sank. She must have grossly misjudged her condition and now it was going to cost her—physically and financially.

A red-haired nurse entered the room just then. Her face lit up when she saw Gemma. "I'm so glad you're awake. You've got some friends who would like to see you."

Gemma forced a small smile. The poor Martins; she'd probably given them quite the scare. Not to mention ruined their vacation.

"What happened to me?" Gemma asked, her throat dry and voice hoarse.

"You had an ovarian cyst rupture. We had to run some scans, and since you're a bleeder with your anemia, we performed laparoscopic surgery. You should be in good shape now, but we're keeping an eye on your abdominal cavity, since that's where all the fluid empties. It's a good thing we caught it when we did or it could have been much worse."

Gemma blinked and tried to take it all in. "So there's no lasting effects?"

"No, ma'am. It's a standard complication and while yours was rather complex, they found no signs of cancer. As long as you heal up all right and don't have a propensity to this sort of thing, you don't have anything to worry about."

"Thank you."

The nurse smiled, tucking her vibrant hair behind her ears. "You want me to bring your friends in?"

Gemma nodded. "Yes, please."

Mr. and Mrs. Martin, Ginger, Josiah, and Farris all trickled into the room, each wearing an expression of concern that made Gemma's heart warm.

"Don't look so worried, I'm fine."

"That's what you said earlier." Mrs. Martin smiled and planted a kiss on Gemma's forehead. "I'm glad you're safe. We were worried it was appendicitis and that can be so dangerous." She sighed. "I feel responsible for not taking better care of you. Had I kept up a little better—"

"It's not your fault," Gemma said. "I was too dismissive."

"We didn't think the doctors were taking it seriously enough, but when you started bleeding, they took you straight in for surgery," Ginger said.

Gemma winced. "Oh, dear. I'm sorry for all the trouble I've caused."

Farris whimpered and leaned toward Gemma.

"Can I hold him?"

The nurse nodded. "Just keep him on your left side and don't move around too much."

Ginger placed Farris next to her and he quieted, grinning at the faces around him.

Gemma kissed the top of his head and rubbed his squishy arm. "Did you miss Mommy?" She looked up at Mrs. Martin. "Did you find the milk in the freezer?"

"Yeah, we're good."

Gemma smiled sadly. She had relied on only herself again, and now she couldn't even be the mom Farris needed. "Thanks for watching out for him. Where are the others?"

"With Anneliese at your apartment," Mr. Martin said. "She found your phone and was able to call a Hollie James and tell her of your situation. She'll be here soon."

"Awesome. She always cheers me up." But her voice sounded dejected, despite her attempt at enthusiasm.

"We'll let you rest," Mrs. Martin said, kissing her again. "Let us know if you need anything. The nurse said you might be released as early as tomorrow."

The red-headed nurse nodded. "If all goes well."

"Beth's hospital is close, so we'll have someone stay with you for as long as you need."

Tears welled up in Gemma's eyes. She wasn't sure if they were from gratitude, hopelessness, or exhaustion. "Thank you." She kissed Farris again before letting Ginger take him. "Be a good baby."

Gemma glanced at Josiah, who hadn't said a word, as the others began to leave. "Can you stay for a minute?"

He glanced at the nurse, who shrugged, and followed the others out of the room.

He turned his eyes to her as the door clicked shut and she was surprised to see how stormy they were. He took a seat on the stool by her bed and waited for her to broach whatever topic of conversation she had in mind.

"I want you to promise me something," she said, holding his gaze.

He waited.

"Promise me that if anything ever happens to me, you'll look after Farris."

Josiah shook his head. "Gemma, that's—"

"I know it's not likely. But I could have died if y'all hadn't been there."

His jaw tightened. "You don't think I know that? I am *very* aware of the fact you almost died."

Gemma's breath caught in her throat and she took Josiah's callused hand in hers. "Promise me you will take care of my son if anything happens."

He relaxed and rubbed his thumb across the top of her hand. "It goes unsaid."

She exhaled a shaky sigh. "Thank you."

Josiah stood and smoothed her hair with his hands, planting a firm kiss on the top of her head. Gemma gaped at his back as he slipped out the door, all the churning emotions of the day threatening to swell into a hurricane.

Gemma thought she was going to go crazy during the next twenty-four hours. The steady stream of morphine into her arm and the continual beep of the machine next to her grated on her frayed nerves. While she was in minimal pain, she grew weary of lying in bed.

The Martins did everything they could to keep her comfortable. Ginger let her hold Farris and Mrs. Martin kept up with the doctors to ensure that all was going as it should. Josiah read to her while Mr. Martin made trips back and forth from the apartment to get things Gemma needed and check on his other children. Hollie came for a brief visit and was horrified that she hadn't thought to take Gemma to the doctor sooner.

After a restless night, the doctor who had performed the surgery came to check on her. "How did you sleep?" He took a seat on the stool and balanced his clipboard on his knee.

"Not great."

"Are you in any pain?"

"Not really, but I'm a little uncomfortable."

He smiled. "Well, the nurse was able to lower your morphine dosage and I think I should be able to cut it altogether and put you on standard painkillers before long. We took some blood work while you were out and it showed you're also dehydrated. Your body was under stress at the time, so that's not unusual. I'd like to take another sample and if it shows similar results, we may need to get you on another IV. Your hemoglobin concentration was also low, which means you're anemic. Was that the case before?"

Gemma nodded as a nurse she hadn't seen before unwrapped a syringe and lifted up the sleeve of her hospital gown. She hadn't even noticed the cotton ball taped to her arm from the last puncture.

"I thought so," the doctor said. "Good news is there is no infection shown. We'll need to perform an ultrasound later to make sure the bleeding into your abdomen has stopped."

The nurse poked the needle into her arm and Gemma winced. She watched as the nurse labeled the syringe and left it for the doctor.

"How long had you been experiencing pain and weakness before you passed out?"

"About a week."

"Has this happened before?"

"Never before I had the baby. But I remember first noticing the pain in December. It didn't come back until February. I blamed it on not eating enough foods with iron and then my body returning to normal after the pregnancy."

The doctor smiled and nodded. "I understand. I'm sorry it got as far as it did, but I noticed nothing during the surgery to give me concern for the future. Unless it's genetic, you should be spared any repeat episodes."

"I hope so," Gemma said. "What if it *does* come back?"

"You would need hormones to balance you out again or birth control. But I'm guessing everything will be regulated soon." He gave her a reassuring pat on the arm and took her vial of blood with him.

She would just have to wait for the results. Gemma never thought she had been impatient, but this hospital stay was putting her to the test. If someone came and told her to just wait and see one more time she was going to scream.

A knock came at the door and Josiah's head popped in the room; she tried to squash her blossoming feelings of frustration and offer him a smile.

"I brought your Bible," he said. "Has the doctor seen you yet?"

"Yep."

"What'd he say?" He took a seat next to her bed.

"He's doing another blood test and ultrasound to see where I'm at."

"I guess we'll just have to—"

"Don't say it!"

He paused, the word still formed on his lips. He shut his mouth and grinned. "Sorry."

Gemma sighed and pinched the bridge of her nose. "It's all right. I don't know why I'm so testy. Guess I'm just sick of laying around. Thanks for bringing the Bible." She took it from him and set it beside her.

"It'd probably do you good to read it, Gemma. When you give all your problems to God, it becomes much easier to wait."

She scowled at him playfully for daring to utter that word in her presence. "I know. I still seem to be missing some connection, though."

Josiah rested his chin on his hands and studied her face. "What do you mean?"

"Knowing what it says isn't enough, I guess, because I know what it says now and I *do* believe it's true. But nothing's different."

"Think about it like this," Josiah said, gesturing with his hands. "You know you have a lot of money in your bank account. Because you know that—believe it—you're a step ahead of everyone else who has no idea they have money, too. But your knowledge can't do anything for you until you decide to get it out of your account."

"That's when it makes a difference," Gemma said.

Josiah nodded, triumphant. "For you and other people. Not a bad analogy if I do say so myself. I'll have to remember that one."

Gemma couldn't resist smiling at his gleeful satisfaction. "It was a good one. Thank you."

"Sure."

"How's Farris doing?"

"Fine. He's been very content with Ginger this morning."

"She's so good with kids," Gemma mused. "I hope Elias knows that."

"I think Elias knows everything there is to know about Ginger by now. They spend a crazy amount of time together!"

Gemma cocked an eyebrow. "Have you been spending any more time with Lydia?"

Josiah shrugged. "Yes, actually, but I think it's a bad idea. She's so sweet, she really is. But the more time I spend with her, the more attached she gets and—"

"That freaks you out," Gemma said. She couldn't help but feel a twinge of relief; perhaps he would marry someone much more unlikely. Stupid as it felt, she had to acknowledge the jealousy and hope that peppered her relief.

"Not exactly," he said. "I just don't want her to be too hurt if I have to tell her it's not going to work out."

"Josiah, if you're not feeling any better about it, you should probably tell her that *now* instead of playing along and hoping for the best. Ending a relationship is always difficult for everyone involved, but dragging it on isn't always a good thing."

He ran his hands through his ash brown hair. "I know."

"But your knowledge can't do anything for you until you decide to get out of the relationship."

He narrowed his eyes at her with a mischievous grin. "I'm going to have to remember that, too."

Gemma's test results showed that the internal bleeding had stopped, but she needed to be drinking more water and get more oxygen into her blood before her body could sustain normality. Mrs. Martin promptly went out and bought liver, since it was notorious for being iron-rich. The doctor went ahead and gave her an injection of iron to help stabilize her as well. Her body hadn't built it back up and the diet she was on hadn't been sufficient. Now she would probably have to take supplements as well.

The doctor told her he thought she could be released the next morning as long as she continued to improve and promised to take it easy.

Gemma was not looking forward to another night in the middle of downtown. Even on the second floor, the lights and noise of the city permeated her room. One would think she would have gotten used to it, but her apartment was buried just far enough in the suburbs to shelter her from the perpetual commotion.

However, Gemma began to read some of her Bible just as Josiah had suggested and found it did help calm her. After flipping through the Psalms and underlining some of the verses that stood out to her, she set the book aside and began to pray. It was the first time she had *really* prayed in weeks.

"When Farris was born, I asked You to keep us safe—keep him safe—and You have. I asked You to prove You exist by watching over us. I want to ask for Your forgiveness for relying too much on myself. I've listened to what You have to say but refused to apply it to my own life. Lord, I accept the sacrifice You made and give my troubles to You."

An overwhelming peace flooded her and within moments she was asleep.

Chapter 30

Gemma was discharged the next morning just as her doctor hoped. He encouraged her to schedule regular visits so he could monitor her progress and catch anything like another cyst before it got out of hand. Despite the financial strain it added, even as a pay plan, Gemma now realized how important it was to take care of herself and agreed to the appointments. At least she had her own car now.

None of the Martins left her side until she was safely back home with Farris. Things were slow going with Beth, so they made sure Gemma was comfortable and relaxed before continuing on to the hospital where the first grandchild was due to enter the world. Mrs. Martin promised her they'd keep in touch and check on her again before going back home.

Despite all the unexpected theatrics and the extra morning she got the Martins for, she was sorry to see them go so soon. She would never be able to explain to anyone how much they meant to her. She supposed it was how everyone felt about their family, but she wouldn't know. So instead she told the newest Member of her family, because He could understand her feelings as she talked through them, just trying to get them straight in her own mind. Having Someone she could tell anything to was truly freeing and did much to preserve her emotional state with fellow people.

In the interim before the Martins' return, Julie stayed with Gemma so everything could go smoother. Hollie would have volunteered if she thought the office could afford to have both her and Gemma out at the same time. But no one wanted to see what that would do to Bradley's worsening mood.

Gemma was glad Julie could spare a few days. Now that her ex-boyfriend wasn't living in the same apartment complex, Julie seemed more at ease. She had a part-time job on the other side of Wichita, but had managed to obtain a few days off. And Gemma felt like it would be a good opportunity to pour out some extra love on her friend, even as Julie was there to serve *her*.

By the time the Martins stopped in on her again over the weekend, Gemma was almost back to her normal self and had survived her first day on her own since the surgery.

"And you're sure everything's all right?" Mrs. Martin kept asking.

"Yes," Gemma kept answering. "I'll be wonderful."

"Let me know if anything comes up. I'm always here for you." She patted Gemma's arm.

"I'll try to do a better job of keeping in touch. I decided to attend January and Patrick's wedding on the ninth as long as nothing comes up. Farris did well on his trip to Texas, so I think he can handle a two-hour drive. I have my own car now, so that makes it much easier."

All the kids squealed and hugged each other. This announcement even drew a smile from Anneliese and a nod from Mr. Martin.

"Of course, you'll have to stay with us," Mrs. Martin said. "You can have your old room back. I don't know who all is going to be spending the night yet, but we'll make it work."

"Even if we have to go to the attic again," Josiah said, clapping a hand on Gail's shoulder.

Gail nodded. "Farris can has my bed."

Gemma grinned. "That's very sweet! But I'm not sure he's big and brave enough, like you. Maybe once he's a little older."

A lopsided smile lit his face. "Next time."

All too soon, the hours they spent together came to a close. Gemma found herself hugging each of them goodbye as they all piled in the van. She put her hand on Josiah's arm before he had a chance to slip by her.

"I didn't get to talk to you very much about this new job of yours. You'll have to remember to tell me about it when I come in April. Deal?"

He shrugged. "If you're interested. Don't be, just for my sake."

Gemma arched an eyebrow. "Of course I'm interested! I can see it makes you very happy and I'm glad."

His countenance brightened a little. "I can show you the land and the old house, too."

Gemma smiled her consent as the crowd whisked him toward the car.

Anneliese chuckled at Gemma's side. "He's happy because his job makes him rich and muscular. He's already had Dad draw up a renovation plan for an old house on the property. It's crazy!"

Gemma tilted her head. "Why?"

"What girl in her right mind would want to live in a house redesigned by Josiah?"

A faint smile rested on Gemma's lips. "I can think of worse things."

Anneliese shrugged with her hands and Gemma studied her profile. There was still a tinge of the fateful, earnest longing behind her cool eyes. But Josiah had told Mr. Martin and said Travis was out of the picture, and she trusted them. Still, she worried. Couldn't Anneliese still be in touch with him somehow? Or was it giving him up that had prompted the emptiness behind her irises?

Gemma watched as Josiah helped Anneliese into the car and felt more at ease. He could see it, too, and he was watching out for her.

After three weeks, Gemma had succeeded at wearing herself ragged yet again and was ready for another brief break. Bradley hardly showed at work anymore, and when he did, Mr. Franklin was always after him for doing something wrong. Farris cutting his second and third tooth had cost Gemma most of her sanity, especially since she had had no choice but to drag her frustrated, drooly baby around department stores in search of a dress to wear to the wedding. And yet strangers still stopped her to tell her how cute he was.

Now Gemma had it all settled and was looking forward to her trip. Despite the church plans that were formed and the extra tasks assigned at work, she was going to leave for the wedding and spend the weekend with the Martins. It wouldn't be much, but hopefully just enough to recharge her so she could storm once again into the battlefront of daily life.

Gemma almost felt guilty for asking for time off yet again, with all her unexpected absences. But Hollie and Mr. Franklin both assured her that it was the least they could do to spare her every once in a while for all the hard work she put in. Gemma kept reminding herself that, unlike school, it wouldn't stop at the end of May. She would work year-round and that would help keep her productive. Gemma had quickly come to realize that even though having a small child always kept her busy, having a purpose also kept her fulfilled, even if it did wear her out.

By the time Friday came, Gemma was enjoying her first day off work and settling last minute details. She had dropped Weasley at the Jameses' and was finishing up some clothes at the laundromat.

"Why is it that you never have any clean clothes?" she asked Farris, whom she'd stuck in a laundry basket of his things.

He smiled and waved his container of rice puffs at her before focusing on grabbing a handful and cramming them all in his mouth.

"One at a time, little buddy!" Gemma drew his slimy palm away from his face and fished the excess snack out of his mouth.

His teeth caught her finger and she jerked it out. "Ouch! Don't bite Mommy."

Farris lifted his chin and laughed, clapping his hands.

"Oh, you think you're so smart," she teased, pulling the last load out of the dryer. "There, all done." She stuffed it into a second basket and carried it all out to the car, Farris still on top. "Let's go home and pack, mister."

Gemma had decided to drive in as soon as she was ready on Friday so she could relax and enjoy the wedding without the pressure of a timetable. She laid Farris down for his afternoon nap so she could finish packing and shower. As she towel dried her hair, her phone rang. She smiled when she saw who was calling.

"Hello?"

"Hey, it's me," Josiah said. "Mom was wondering what time you would be in tonight."

"I'm almost ready to leave, but Farris is still napping. Once he wakes up, I'll head your way."

"OK. Well, your room is ready and we have plenty of food on hand, so make yourself at home when you get here."

"Have you seen January yet? Is she ready?" She sprayed some cleaner on a rag and began to wipe the fogged mirror.

"Yeah, she's spending the night in the girls' room tonight. Last chance as only their sister and all that stuff. She's pretty jittery, though, and I haven't seen her drop her smile yet."

Gemma smiled and set the rag aside. "Aw, I'm so happy for her. I guess you decided you approved of Patrick or this wouldn't be happening, huh?"

"Jan never listens to anything I say. But he did pass my tests, so he's good."

Gemma chuckled. "You're going to have to get accustomed to letting your sisters go. Someday when you're desperately in love with someone, you'll see the whole picture a little better."

"Hey, no matter who I fall in love with, I will never surrender my role as a protective brother. But I figure if *I* can find a girl without a brother on the scene, that will help my case."

Gemma rolled her eyes. "You're ridiculous." It played through her mind that she had no brother and she grew extremely grateful that their conversation was over the phone to hide her blush.

"I'm smart," Josiah said. "I'll let you get back to packing. See you tonight."

"OK, bye."

"What's this I hear about being in love?" Mr. Martin asked from the barn's doorway.

Josiah stuffed his phone back in his pocket. "Oh, that was just Gemma."

"That's precisely why I want to know, son."

Heat crept into his face and he continued his work in silence.

By eight o'clock that evening Gemma had arrived at the Martins'. Farris had been awake for the entire drive, but stayed content for most of the time. He was getting better about sticking his thumb in his mouth when something upset him instead of crying for his mother until she figured out what was wrong.

Still, Gemma was tired of driving on two-way country roads at dusk where there was no give except into oncoming traffic. The endless fields and occasional farmhouses that she passed reminded her of where she was going, and that helped refocus her.

Gemma crawled down the rutted driveway, trying her best to avoid the paths the water had cut where she could. They must have been getting more spring rain than she had. She passed the oak tree and pulled into the barren patch of dirt that served as the parking spaces and smiled as a terrified cottontail crossed the path of her headlights. Living in the city, she hadn't realized how much she had missed the wildlife. Only chickadees and butterflies visited, if she was lucky.

She thought she might have arrived unnoticed as she climbed out of the car and opened the door so she could unfasten Farris from his seat. Outside it was dark with a breeze carrying the distant sound of excited chatter emanating from the warmly lit house.

"Are you ready to get out and stretch, Farris?"

She heard footsteps scuff the dirt beside her and she jumped. But with her head still in the car, and her hair in the grasps of her baby, she couldn't get a look at who—or what—it was.

"Hello. Need some help?" Josiah asked.

Her heart stopped racing quite so fast and she let out her unconsciously held breath. "Hi! The suitcases are in the trunk." She tugged her shoulder-length hair out of Farris's drooly fingers and tucked the damp strand behind her ear before lifting him out of his seat.

She slid the diaper bag on her shoulder and slammed the car door. Straightening, her eyes adjusted to the lack of light and she could see Josiah's dark form wrestling the bags out of the trunk.

"Thanks."

"Sure." He closed the trunk and led the way toward the front door.

Squeals erupted as Gemma passed into the living room.

"Gemma's here!"

She was swarmed by all the small children as Josiah tried to lift the luggage over their heads and proceed to her bedroom.

Gemma surrendered Farris to Emmaline's capable hands so she could give hugs to everybody.

"How are you guys?" she asked, even though she knew the answers would come in a flood and she'd be unable to understand any of them.

"How long are you staying, Gemma?" Mariah asked.

"Just a couple days."

"Aww, we want you to stay for months and months!" Mariah spread her arms wide.

"Yeah, until you have another baby!" Lisabeth said.

January walked up, shaking her head. "They're crazy," she said, reaching over the brood to give Gemma a hug. "How are you?"

"I'm good. Thanks for inviting me."

January grinned. "Of course, girl! Thanks for coming."

Gemma set the diaper bag down and followed January into the kitchen. Mariah and Lisabeth each took one of Gemma's hands and Gail just stood in front of her and stared up at her face.

Mrs. Martin pulled a cake out of the oven and set it down on the stovetop among several others before she turned to give Gemma a hug. "I'm so glad you're here, Gemma."

"Thank you, so am I. Are the cakes for tomorrow?"

"Yes," January said. "We're having a picnic table with a variety. Mom agreed to make some and Patrick's mom is making the chocolate."

"To bed, kiddos," Mrs. Martin said. "You got to wait up and see Gemma."

There was no complaining, but they all hung their heads and gave Gemma and January somber hugs goodnight.

Gemma turned back to January once the children were on their way upstairs. "That sounds lovely. Josiah said you were getting nervous."

January scoffed. "What does Josiah know?"

"Hey, I resent that," Josiah said, taking a seat on a barstool.

"I am *not* nervous. I'm excited and filled with anticipation," January said pointedly, taking a sip of coffee.

"We'll see tomorrow, won't we," he said with a smirk.

For several dreadful minutes, Josiah wondered if his predictions might come true. After a full morning of icing cakes and fixing hair, the entire family managed to make it to the little, white church with an hour to spare. But moments before the ceremony was due to start, January was in a flurry, tweaking last minute details. Her hair was in a mass of curls and Anneliese had done her makeup, but she was still running around in yoga pants and sneakers.

"Jan, what are you doing?" he said when she almost plowed him over in the hallway.

"Oh, Josiah, there you are. Tell Patrick I love him and I'll see him in a few, yeah?" She gave her brother a quick kiss on the cheek and darted off.

Josiah rubbed his face and returned to the office where all the men had helped each other pass inspection. Patrick was fumbling with his tie when Josiah reentered, sweat gathering on his brow.

"Here." Josiah took the knotted mess and began to untangle it. "I just saw Jan."

Patrick's face lit up a little. "Really? How was she?"

Josiah stepped back and surveyed his work before making eye contact. "She said she loves you."

The tension in Patrick's face dissipated and he clapped his hand on Josiah's shoulder. "Thank you."

Josiah was glad not to see January still flitting around when they lined up and proceeded down the side aisle to wait for the women at the front of the sanctuary. He glanced around and noted many familiar faces among the first few rows where family sat. Most prominent was Gemma with her light blonde hair and Farris on her shoulder in a plaid shirt, khaki shorts, and bowtie. Josiah was glad to see Gemma had been seated with the family.

Several rows back sat Lydia with her parents. She looked stunning, he couldn't deny it. But it made a strange mix of doubt and guilt settle in his gut, instead of excitement or anticipation. She caught his eye and her face turned up in a smile. No, he was not looking forward to what he had decided to tell her later this afternoon.

Elias Jefferson, an usher, seated Mrs. Martin as the last of the family. Then the preacher Josiah had known his whole life made his way to center stage and the pianist switched her tune to something lighter.

First Emmaline, then Anneliese, and then Ginger walked down the aisle. They held simple white bouquets and wore iridescent silver-colored dresses. Josiah smiled and was struck by how pretty each of his sisters were. Next came Mariah and Lisabeth, throwing petals from baskets. Josiah grinned as Mariah made it a race to see who could empty their basket the fastest and Gail came—very slowly— behind them, studying the rings tied to the Bible he carried.

Despite what he had told himself, his breath caught when January stepped through the door, beaming on her father's arm. Gemma was right—this was going to take a lot of getting used to.

Within minutes, the couple placed the rings on each other's fingers and shared their first kiss. Anytime Josiah felt bitter about what was going on, he only had to glance over the shoulder of the groom in front of him and catch the look of intense admiration on his sister's face. That was enough to satisfy him for a long time to come.

No one remained at the church long, and everyone proceeded to the Martins' house in a long string of cars. Mrs. Martin, Lydia, and Gemma must have slipped away early, because by the time Josiah was climbing out of the car and reminding little sisters not to get their dresses muddy, they stood poised at the tables, ready to serve. The spread of roasted chicken, cakes, and punch was enough to make anyone's mouth water. But especially someone who had been stuffed in a suit all day.

Josiah relinquished his suit coat, since many of the groomsmen were doing the same, and went to scout out the food tables.

Much dessert and dancing later, he finally got a chance to hug his sister. "Congratulations," he whispered in her ear under the glow of twinkle lights at dusk.

"Thanks, little bro."

Patrick extended his hand. "Thanks for everything, man."

"Take good care of her," Josiah said.

"I will—I want to. Do you have any idea what that's like?"

Josiah glanced past Patrick to where Gemma and Lydia stood chatting. "Yes, actually. Yes, I do."

He bid Patrick farewell, said hello to his sister Belinda because he felt obliged, and made his way to Gemma and Lydia.

"I went the whole afternoon without a dance with either of you," he said, sighing dramatically.

Lydia smiled. "Alas, I'm afraid I'm due back home. I'll see if someone can take me. Mom and Dad went early since they weren't feeling well."

"I can do it," he said, remembering the promise he'd made to himself.

Her eyes lit up. "Really? You wouldn't mind? You might miss your sister's departure."

"She'll be back," he said with a shrug.

Gemma and Lydia laughed. "All right, then. Thank you."

He cut a path through the crowd for Lydia and pulled the car keys out of his pocket.

It wasn't very far to the Longs' house, so he wanted to be sure and say what he needed to, even if it meant pulling over on the side of the road to explain himself. But Lydia began talking first and he followed along as the sweat grew on his palms.

As they reached the outskirts of town, they came to a stoplight, and she paused her chatter. "Are you all right?"

He put his foot to the gas as the light turned green.

"Lydia, I—"

The sound of screeching tires, blaring horn, and scraping metal drowned his next words into oblivion.

Chapter 31

Gemma settled Farris in his playpen and stayed with him a few minutes to make sure he'd settled in before slipping back outside. After a long day, he was ready for bed earlier than usual. Gemma would have been glad to lie down and go to sleep herself, but she wanted to wave goodbye to the bride and groom.

As she entered the breezy evening air, she watched with amusement as January stood on top of a cleared picnic table and threw her bouquet. A girl she didn't recognize caught it and met much applause.

The Martin girls broke away from the crowd and regrouped with their circles of friends. Gemma's heart plummeted when she saw Anneliese slip beside the house. A voice wafted to her ears and her heart leaped to her throat. *Who on earth let him come?* Josiah would kill him . . . but Josiah had left to take Lydia home. He had told Mr. Martin, right?

Gemma kicked herself for believing Travis was truly out of her life and Anneliese's. But she couldn't very well butt into their conversation and demand he leave. She wasn't the type to make a scene. *And that's my weakness,* she realized. That was why Travis felt so comfortable showing up and toying with Anneliese right in front of her. He knew she wouldn't betray him publicly, the one thing he feared. Even if Mr. Martin knew, it looked like that would be news to Travis.

She crossed to a table for a glass of punch as January and Patrick made ready for their departure. Gemma watched Anneliese and Travis out of the corner of her eye and wondered if they were arguing about something. Curiosity would get the better of her in the end, she knew, but for now she would enjoy lighting a sparkler in the growing dark of the evening.

Gemma stood in line and let Mr. Martin light the coated end of her sparkler with his. She spied Anneliese line up across from her, so she breathed more easily. As soon as the double line of people, a good ten feet apart, had their row of sparklers crackling and spitting sparks, January and Patrick grabbed hands and ran down the aisle that was formed. They climbed into their car and drove away amongst a cry of cheers and applause, tin cans that had been fastened to the bumper forming their own applause behind them.

Gemma turned and placed her sparkler wand head down in the bucket of water Mr. Martin manned. She let her gaze wander, searching for Travis and Anneliese, but she did not find them. She straightened and looked again. A sense of concern flared inside her as she hurried to the corner of the house. It was growing too dark outside for her to make anything out at a distance, but she caught the shadows of retreating figures unmistakably in the light the house cast.

A sense of dread filled Gemma. *What is that girl thinking?* She looked around for someone who could help her, but Mr. Martin was the only other one who knew. *Not him, please. Anyone but him.* But Josiah was gone; she had no other choice.

She approached him quickly, giving herself no time to lose her resolve. "May I speak with you for a moment, please?"

He gave her a sideways look, but took pause at the gravity of her tone. He motioned for Mariah to come and take his place at the water bucket, giving her brief instruction.

"What's the matter?" Mr. Martin's voice was low and husky.

"It's Anneliese. I've just seen her headed toward the tree line with a large bag." She paused, searching his face for any sign of recognition. "She was with Travis Long."

His eyes dilated. "Don't leave yet, you're going to have to come with me." He brushed past guests, charging into the barn.

Gemma made her way to the corner of the house, fear gnawing at her insides. She just wanted to be through with this. He would need her, though; she was the only one who knew the entire truth. Upon reflection, she specifically remembered Josiah saying he had left her out of his revelation to his father. And now she had no choice but to tell it all. When he came back, rifle slung over his arm and flashlight in hand, he signaled her to meet him behind the house. She glanced behind her, but no one seemed to be paying them any attention under the cover of darkness.

After several paces toward the tree line, Mr. Martin spoke. "Gemma . . . how do you know all this?"

She swallowed. "It's amazing the things you learn when you can't sleep at night."

"Josiah said Travis had left and we both spoke to Anneliese." He sighed and his face held fatigue. "I hope you're wrong about this," he said as they started down the hill in a jog.

"Me, too. Save your flashlight until we can't see anymore. We can't afford to let them know we're coming too soon."

He spared her a glance. "You sound like you've done this before."

"Maybe."

They slowed as they neared the edge of the forest. The sounds of laughter and merriment had faded like a distant memory, encased in the light around the house on top of the hill. All that could be heard as they approached in the gathering darkness was the crunch of grass under their feet.

Then, "Did you hear that?"

Gemma jumped and looked at Mr. Martin. She was certain it had been Anneliese's voice.

"No, let's just keep going," Travis said.

The noise of trampled brush reached their ears as Gemma and Mr. Martin remained motionless.

"Travis, I don't know about this. I feel awful," Anneliese said. Already her voice sounded much more distant.

"Don't. You're with me, aren't you? I'll keep you safe."

A shudder danced down Gemma's spine at the very idea.

"I believe that's my job." Mr. Martin marched forward and flicked on his enormous flashlight, the beam bathing the forest in light.

Anneliese stifled a scream and fell back, shielding her eyes. Travis's hand went to her arm and he stared back at the flashlight the best he could.

"Not anymore it's not. She's decided to come with me."

Mr. Martin continued walking forward until he was inches away from Travis and his daughter. He re-secured his gun in the crook of his arm. "She'll do no such thing. Unhand my daughter."

Anneliese stood trembling, glancing from Travis to her father in the eerie white light. Her bag sat next to her on the ground. To Gemma's surprise, Travis released her arm.

Anneliese took a step toward her father. "Dad, I—"

"Silence!" he roared, raising his gun to Travis's chest.

Anneliese covered her mouth as sobs shook her slender frame.

Gemma rushed forward then, not wanting Mr. Martin to do anything rash, despite what it could mean for her safety. Then she realized she had never seen him load the shotgun.

Anneliese lowered her hands from her face as her bleary eyes met Gemma's. "You! I knew you were involved somehow!"

Gemma swallowed the pity she felt for the girl at the moment. "I'm sorry, I had to help you."

"What business is it of yours?" Anneliese said through her slur of tears.

"Anneliese, trust me, you don't know everything about him." Gemma looked at Travis, who had gone a shade paler.

"I know enough," Anneliese said. "More than you."

Gemma shook her head and Travis clenched his fists, ignoring the gun barrel resting on his sternum.

"Tell us what you know, Gemma," Mr. Martin said. "I want to hear everything this time."

Gemma swallowed and looked at Anneliese's tear-stained face. "Travis blackmailed me for money to repay old debts. I paid him so he'd stay away from you. That's why I took that money." Here she looked at Mr. Martin, whose stance softened ever so slightly. "You see, I met him at my high school in Texas." She looked straight at Travis's cold, calculating eyes and absorbed the fear she saw written there. "He's the father of my child."

Anneliese collapsed into a shocked heap. At the same time, Travis jerked the gun away from his chest and lunged at Gemma with a spew of profanity. She felt the force of his anger collide with her, her body smashing against a tree trunk. The wind was thrown from her lungs and she struggled to breathe as Mr. Martin tugged Travis off of her with one hand and threw him to the ground. He pinned him there with the gun.

"If you so much as move to touch either of these women again, I will personally escort you to the police station for assault. Now stand up!"

Travis did as he was commanded, his body rigid with loathing.

"Walk toward the house. And when you reach it just keep walking. Don't say a word to anyone. If I ever see you back here again, you should not expect mercy from me, young man, do you hear me?" He prompted Travis with the barrel of his gun and he nodded. "Go."

Gemma sank to the ground next to Anneliese and wiped the blood off the warm, throbbing spot on her nose.

Anneliese lifted hollow eyes to her face, hands still clutching her bag, but said nothing.

Between the two of them, Gemma and Mr. Martin managed to get a quaking Anneliese back to the house and in through the back door, unnoticed.

Gemma took her up to her bed, helping Anneliese undress and climb into a lightweight nightgown. Anneliese lay there hollow-eyed, staring into nothing, covers clutched to her chest. Gemma unpacked her bag, filled with clothing, food, money, and her letters.

Once Gemma had put the last thing in its place, Anneliese caught her gaze. "Why didn't you tell me?"

Gemma sighed. "Because I knew how much it would hurt you."

Anneliese dropped her gaze and her eyes filled with tears again. "Thank you."

Gemma nodded and gave her hand a squeeze before slipping back downstairs.

When she had checked on Farris and tried to recollect herself, she went back outside. Most of the crowd had diminished, but a few families still lingered. The Jeffersons were the only ones Gemma remembered talking to before.

Isaiah came up, a playful grin on his face. "You didn't catch the bouquet."

She shook her head, recalling their bet about how young she would marry. "I guess you owe me."

"Not yet," he said. "I'm holding out all the way until your twentieth birthday. When is it?"

"About eight months," Gemma said. "You might as well give up. I'll never be married by then." She registered a phone ringing in the background.

Isaiah shrugged. "Too bad we didn't agree on just a proposal, or I'd ask you just to save my money."

Gemma chuckled. "That's very flattering, but I believe I have a few years on you."

Mrs. Martin cried out and all the guests who remained turned to her in alarm.

"Joy, whatever's the matter?" Mrs. Jefferson asked.

Mrs. Martin stared at her cell phone in disbelief. She drew her eyes back to her friends and forced her tongue to work. "It was the hospital. They said Josiah had been in a—a car accident."

Gemma's heart nearly stopped beating as she waited for what came next.

"Lydia was with him." Mrs. Martin faced everyone else, terror written on her gentle face. "She died at the scene."

Gemma's hand flew to her mouth and tears pricked her eyes. She felt remorse for the twinge of relief she felt that it hadn't been Josiah . . . yet.

Everyone just stood there, too stunned to think or act.

"We have to go to the hospital," Mr. Martin said, putting his hand on Mariah's shoulder. "Anneliese isn't feeling well. Emmaline, can you stay behind as well?"

Emmaline nodded and took charge of the three youngest, shooing them inside.

Gemma followed her and helped reassure them that Josiah was fine. But her mind kept racing. What if he wasn't fine? What if he was critically injured and dying even now? She had to go with them to the hospital, but she couldn't—Farris needed her here.

She paused at the door to her bedroom and turned back to Emmaline. "Em, could I leave Farris? I mean, I want to go with them. Can I leave him here with you? I have plenty of milk in the freezer."

Emmaline nodded. "Please go with them. He'll want you there."

Gemma nodded without taking time to process what she meant. She slipped into her bedroom and changed into something comfortable with as much speed and silence as she could manage.

She leaned over the playpen wall and kissed Farris before she left. *It's going to be a long night.*

Chapter 32

Gemma, Mr. and Mrs. Martin, Ginger, and Elias all rode together to the hospital. Gemma's heart beat double-time for the entire drive. She couldn't quiet her mind or concentrate on any of the feeble attempts at conversation. The whole family stood like statues in anticipation as a doctor took them aside in a hospital hallway to tell them Josiah's condition.

"I've conducted some tests already and there's no need to worry. He'll live." Everyone visibly relaxed. "I was told a semi t-boned them on the passenger side, so he's lucky he escaped with nothing more than a dislocated shoulder and minor concussion. He's a little battered, but he'll be fine. No internal bleeding, which is always the big concern."

"Do you know anything about what happened to Lydia—the girl in the accident?" Mrs. Martin asked quietly.

"No," the doctor said. His features glinted dark in the fluorescent lighting. "I heard there was another passenger, but . . ."

"We were told she died," Ginger said, her chin quivering.

"I see," the doctor said, his deep-set eyes conveying true sorrow among his shiny olive features. "I was unaware of that. That considered, Josiah is very fortunate indeed. I still have to relocate his shoulder and then we'll see if he's ready for visitors. Please, have a seat in the waiting room."

The group trickled back down the hall and did as they were told. They sat in silence, the only ones in this particular waiting area, lost in their own thoughts.

"I can't believe Lydia's gone," Ginger said after a long moment of stillness.

Everyone else nodded as if by default. Gemma soothed her mind and wondered how Farris was doing. Then she chastised herself—she couldn't worry about everyone at the same time! The Indian doctor had said Josiah would be all right. He just had to get his shoulder put back in its socket.

Gemma shook her head, thinking of how painful that must be. Especially when still enveloped in the immediate trauma from being slammed by another car. It was so easy to be in a car wreck; there were so many variables. Every time someone went somewhere it was a risk—an accident waiting to happen. Then why was it always so surprising when it did happen?

Gemma remembered what Josiah had said about wanting to scale things back with Lydia. Had he ever gotten the chance to say anything to her? Or did she die thinking he was still just as interested in her as she was in him? Gemma's heart ached when she replayed the time Josiah told her about his greatest fear. He had always been afraid of death—causing death.

He's never going to forgive himself.

Gemma smiled faintly. She had been in the early stages of labor with Farris when he had told her that. She glanced around at the sterile, fluorescent atmosphere and wrapped her arms tighter around herself. She was very glad she hadn't given birth in a hospital. They made her feel so unsettled, as if she were in death's house. Someone might make a mistake and she would be taken.

After several more minutes ticked by on the clock, a nurse came to find them. She glanced at her clipboard. "I have a Josiah Martin ready for company?" She took in the crowd that got to their feet. "You'll have to be brief; he's in pain. Try not to distress him."

Gemma tried not to hold it against the nurse that all she did was state the obvious as they followed her down the hall. But what did she mean by "distress him"?

"Here we are. Just a few minutes." The nurse swung the wooden door open and waited for everyone to pass before closing the door again.

Gemma expected there to be a look of pain written on his face, so her mouth almost fell open when he met everyone with a grin.

"You didn't all have to come up here. I'm fine, really. Can't believe they're keeping me overnight."

Mrs. Martin gave her son a kiss and as severe a look as she could manage. "You follow the doctor's orders, you hear?" Her voice was low and quiet, heavy with sadness despite the good condition of her son.

Josiah seemed alarmed by her sullenness. "Yes, ma'am."

He doesn't know kept playing over and over in Gemma's head like a broken record. *He doesn't know about Lydia.*

Ginger also gave her brother a kiss and Elias and Mr. Martin patted his good arm.

"You'll be right in no time. I'll cook you something special as a reward for surviving hospital food," Ginger said.

Josiah smiled and watched her and Elias slip out of the room.

"We'll leave you to rest, son," Mr. Martin said. "We'll stay to see the Longs, so we'll be here for a while yet, I imagine. Let us know if you need anything."

Josiah nodded. "How is Lydia?"

Mrs. Martin blinked several times and Mr. Martin fell silent. At this response, Josiah looked to Gemma, fear flooding his olive eyes.

Gemma tried to hold his gaze, but couldn't. She let her eyes fall to the drops of blood on his white shirt and whispered, "She didn't make it." She glanced up in time to see Josiah's face wiped of all expression.

"Oh, Josiah, we thought you'd know," Mrs. Martin said.

Josiah shook his head as though it weighed ten times its normal weight. "They . . . they didn't . . . tell me." His head came up and his eyes jumped from face to face. "I was knocked out at the scene. I didn't know! Why didn't they tell me?" His voice was almost a shout.

Gemma tried to swallow around the lump in her throat and thanked God none of them were handling this situation alone.

Mrs. Martin rushed forward and put her hand on his arm. "I'm sure they were thinking of you."

"Me? What about her family? I have to see them! I *killed* her!" His palm slapped his forehead as a look of pain crossed his face.

Mrs. Martin held his head and shushed him in her firm but gentle manner. It was all Gemma could do to stand there and watch him suffer.

"This is not your fault, Josiah," Mr. Martin said. "Do not blame yourself for something outside your control."

Josiah nodded and shrugged his mother off, leaning back against his pile of pillows. "I know." His voice sounded calmer now, but thick with emotion. "But is that what you're going to tell the Longs? That their daughter was preordained to die?" He removed his hands from his head and met his father's sad eyes.

"I'm not going to say anything, son," Mr. Martin said. His voice sounded defeated and he turned to leave the room, holding out his hand for his wife to follow him.

That's what death does, Gemma thought. *It tries to defeat people until all that's left isn't truly living. Just like guilt.* "Don't let it defeat you, Josiah," she choked out before following the Martins out of his room.

If Gemma thought comforting her aunt during her uncle's funeral was difficult, nothing could have prepared her for the hopeless feeling that came when watching parents grieve over the loss of their child.

For the first few minutes, as Mrs. Long sobbed into Mrs. Martin's shoulder, Gemma wondered why they had even bothered to come to the hospital. Lydia was dead, not dying. But Mrs. Long disappeared at one point and Gemma assumed she had gone to see Josiah.

When Mr. Long blew his nose for the umpteenth time, he sighed. "I suppose I'll try and find the morgue. I need to know what we do next."

Mr. Martin put his hand on his friend's shoulder. "I'll go with you."

Ginger and Elias had gone to find the bathrooms, leaving only Mrs. Martin and Gemma to comfort Mrs. Long. Gemma felt very awkward and unhelpful, so she was almost relieved when the same nurse as before said Josiah had asked for her.

She stood, attempting to brush the wrinkles out of her crumpled dress, and followed the nurse down the bright hallway that made her feel so exposed. Every dazzling light and sparkling silver tray seemed to peer into her.

She escaped the synthetic hallway by slipping into Josiah's room. She was relieved to see more color in his face, even as he stared out the window into the dark. "I heard you asked for me," she said.

A distant smile formed on his lips when he faced her, but faded just as quickly. "I saw Mrs. Long. She doesn't blame me."

"None of us blame you, Josiah. They said the semi was at fault—he ran a stoplight."

She moved to the chair beside his bed and took a seat.

"I was going to tell her." Josiah turned to look at Gemma for the first time since she'd entered the room. She swallowed the emotion that choked her when his bloodshot eyes met hers.

"I was going to explain everything to her," he continued. "Tell her that I liked her, but I didn't feel the same way she did. I really was."

"It's OK." Gemma put her hand on his. "You don't have to explain it to me. It's just as well that she never knew."

Josiah opened his mouth to say something else, but then closed it again. He relaxed against his mountain of pillows. "You're right, it can wait. Sorry." He looked back out the window for a minute before resting his eyes on her face again. "Will you still be here tomorrow?"

"Yes."

He closed his eyes and squeezed her hand. "I'll tell you tomorrow then."

Gemma almost wished he'd change his mind back; even if he was in no condition to be talking, he had piqued her curiosity now.

She sat there a moment longer, contemplating what else she could say that might be comforting. "Do you want me to read to you?" She remembered how nice it had been when he had read to her while she was in the hospital.

"Sure," he said, not opening his eyes. "Don't be offended if I go to sleep on you. I've got an awful headache."

Gemma smiled and pulled her Bible app up on her phone. Psalm 121 was open and it seemed appropriate with its opening, "I will lift up my eyes to the hills—From whence comes my help? My help comes from the Lord, Who made heaven and earth." She hadn't completed a single chapter before Josiah's chest rose and fell with steady regularity. Gemma was about ready to doze off herself, so she let herself out of the room and notified the nurse that he was sleeping.

Her heart got another unhealthy jolt when she rejoined the others in the waiting room, only to find that Travis had arrived. She froze in the doorway and her eyes darted to Mr. Martin, who had returned from his expedition to the morgue with Mr. Long. He showed no sign of anything being amiss, so she took her cue from him and tried to maintain her facade of calm as she took her seat next to him.

She was shocked to see tears on Travis's face when he removed his head from his hands. But then she remembered that Lydia was his sister. Perhaps he could feel some remorse at her sudden death. Before Gemma could stop herself, she placed her hand on his arm. To her surprise, he let her keep it there as he wiped at his face.

"I wouldn't have heard if I'd left town as I'd planned." He said it so quietly Gemma almost didn't hear him. He shook his head and sniffed. "Why do good people die?" This was loud enough for the others to hear. "I should have died instead. It should have been me."

Mrs. Long's eyes filled with tears again. "Oh, Travis, please don't say that." Ginger patted her hand.

"It's true," he said, sitting up straighter. "You're all thinking it. Why did God let her die if she was so good?"

He waited for an answer that wasn't coming.

"I think . . ." Gemma said. "I think some people shine so bright they burn out faster than the rest of us. Lydia was one of those people. She was so wonderful that she finished what God had for her before we expected."

"What kind of God does that to people?"

Mr. Martin caught Gemma's eye across the coffee table and offered a fragile smile. "The kind of God who loves us enough to know what's best. In this case, I think He was sparing Lydia the future."

Travis frowned. "What do you mean? How do *you* know what her future would have held?"

"When Stuart and I talked with the doctor in the morgue," Mr. Long said, "he had just finished looking at the results of a scan performed on Lydia's body. They wanted to know what had killed her since any visible injuries had not been fatal. They found a tumor forming on her brain that would have become excruciating within a matter of weeks. It would most likely have been inoperable. It's doubtful she would have survived the year."

Everyone stared at him in disbelief, except for Mr. Martin, who confirmed his story.

After this eye-opening piece of news, the conversation drifted to memories and storytelling. As it neared midnight, the talk began to lessen and finally Travis stood. "I should get back. I have to catch a plane soon so I can report back for duty."

"Do you have to go?" his mother asked.

"I'll stay in touch. I'm sorry."

It was one of the first times Gemma had ever heard him utter that phrase, and the only time she believed he meant it.

Something compelled her to follow him as he took the hallway to the elevator.

"Travis," she said before he could escape.

He turned.

"Look, I know we've both had a pretty hard time of it, but I just wanted you to know that everything's all right."

"If you mean you've forgiven me and you're moving on with your life, then good for you. That's what I was working on this evening when you interrupted."

"That wasn't moving on, it was repeating your mistake."

He averted his eyes and sighed. "Why do you keep doing this?"

"What?"

"Talking like everything's going to be OK—as if you had nothing to do with the mess we're in."

"I did have something to do with it," Gemma said, "but I've put it behind me. Things can get better for you if you'll do the same."

He shook his head. "There's none of that finding religion stuff for me. I fell out of religion, you fell into it. That's just the way it goes."

"It doesn't have to be."

Travis punched the elevator button. "Why do you keep trying to be nice to me?"

"Because it was people being nice to *me* that made the difference in my life. Because I truly have forgiven you for everything."

"And just how did you manage that, I'd like to know?"

She smiled. "Simple. God forgave you first."

The elevator dinged and a nurse walked out.

Travis got in and waited, arms crossed. "If it puts your mind at ease, know I'm never coming back. And congratulations, you've become just as insufferable as the rest of them."

The elevator doors gritted shut.

Chapter 33

Gemma pulled the navy chiffon dress over her head and added a headband to her kinky hair. The whole house was getting ready, donning dark colors, but without the usual frivolity.

Josiah had been permitted to come home Tuesday morning and had spent the last forty-eight hours on bed rest for his concussion. However, when Mrs. Martin suggested that he could stay home from the funeral if he wanted, he had managed to shower and dress himself, even with his healing shoulder.

Gemma lifted Farris from the floor of her old room and joined the others for breakfast. Josiah sat in his regular place, arm in a sling, struggling to shovel oatmeal in his mouth with his left hand.

His face lit up when Gemma took her seat—or at least she thought it did.

"Feeling any better today?" Gemma asked.

"My head hurts less and I can walk straight. Stupid shoulder is still throbbing from forcing it in my shirt sleeve."

She fed Farris a bite of cooled oatmeal and wondered what she should say. All the little children hastily finishing their breakfast had caught the mood and watched their older brother with wide, solemn eyes. Gemma hoped they knew how blessed they were to still have him and that what happened to Lydia wasn't his fault. But of course Mr. and Mrs. Martin would have reiterated that by now.

Mr. Martin accepted a bowl of oatmeal from his wife with a kiss and glanced at Josiah's sullen face. "Sure you want to go, son?"

Josiah nodded. "It's the least I can do."

Gemma inwardly cringed. *He still feels that he owes the Longs something.* No doubt she would, too, if she were in his position. Thank God she had never had the opportunity.

All the way to the church in the Martins' van, Gemma watched Josiah's profile—sometimes listless, other times scrunched in pain— and prayed for him. Even riding in a car again had to bring back unwanted memories. *Dear God, bring him peace.*

When they stepped through the doors of the church, Gemma was struck by the sea of black and white. It was so different than her uncle's funeral; he had been a man stuck on a self-destructive path with few friends on whom he could count. But Lydia . . . she had touched the lives of everyone she'd ever known, as was plain to see by the multitude of people come to pay their respects.

Something similar must have struck Josiah, because his left hand balled into a fist as they moved toward the sanctuary.

Gemma was surprised to see the satin-lined casket open at the base of the stage steps. Had that really been a good idea? She had been killed in a car accident after all. But Gemma recalled the discussion at the hospital: her visible injuries did not appear fatal. Horrible as it was, Lydia had been pinned such that it would have been impossible for her to bleed out before medical assistance arrived. However, when the mortician had conducted the same scan that revealed her developing tumor, they had found several vertebrae near her neck that were fractured to say the least.

Gemma tried to push away the grim details of the situation as people filed into the pews for the funeral.

"Is that Lydia up there?" Mariah whispered, nodding toward the casket.

"Yes," Gemma said, giving her a side squeeze.

"Can I go see her, please?"

"Not yet. We'll do that later." Actually, Gemma wasn't sure it was a good idea for any of the small children to look at Lydia's dead body. *And Josiah definitely shouldn't.* No one needed to avoid a breakdown more, except perhaps poor Mrs. Long.

Gemma looked around, a twinge of remorse biting her. *Travis really did go back. He couldn't even stay for the funeral.*

The pastor mounted the stairs to the stage and invited everyone to join him in rejoicing over the life Lydia led. As friends and family shared memories, gave tributes, and sang songs, Gemma noted how much more hopeful the entire affair was than Uncle Wilfred's funeral. Of course, a pastor had been there to conduct the service, but it had been somber and depressing, as she imagined most funerals were. While there were tears here, everyone could take comfort in knowing Lydia had been a lovely person and had joined her Savior in heaven.

Gemma's mouth dropped open when she saw Josiah's name at the end of the program. A prayer stayed on her lips as he rose from the pew and faced everyone from the front of the church. *God, get him through this.* Even greater was her surprise when he not only remained upbeat but was able to evoke a laugh from the congregation. Still, emotion edged even his cheerful expressions.

"To wrap this up, Lydia was always an inspiration to me. God didn't give her a long life on earth and yet she managed to accomplish more than many aged people. I won't ever fully know why God spared me on Saturday and took her . . . but I intend to follow her example and do everything I can with the time He gives me."

Gemma tried to convey encouragement when his eyes met hers briefly before dismounting the stage.

As he came back to his seat, Mariah scooched into his spot, sacrificing her sacred position next to Gemma for him.

Josiah gave his sister a small smile as everyone stood for the closing hymn, *God Be with You Till We Meet Again.*

As the first verse concluded, Gemma's arm bumped Josiah's and his fingers found hers. A thrill shot through her and for once she didn't care what people thought. It was their problem if they had extra emotional energy to invest in rumors. Still, she didn't dare look at his face for fear she'd break down. Emotion threatened her voice as she sang and she didn't have the willpower to hold back tears for much longer. It had been an exhausting few days.

Mrs. Martin turned to her husband as the song concluded. "Would you like all of us to see Lydia?"

He threw a glance to where the people were already proceeding by her. "Yes, I think that would be good." Mr. Martin led the way down the side aisle and all of the Martins and Gemma fell into the line that had formed.

Now Gemma understood why the casket had been left open. None of these people had had a chance to say goodbye. This was their chance.

Gemma's heart beat faster as they stood just a few turns away from the casket and she wished Josiah would take her hand again. Did she really want to see Lydia without the light behind her eyes and the color in her cheeks? Did Josiah?

She almost wished he had sat next to her for the first part of the service, because changing spots at the end had placed him in front of her in line. How could she avoid reading the emotion that was bound to be present on his face?

Mr. Martin held Gail and Lisabeth up so they could see in. "See, her spirit's with God now."

"Was it her spirit that made her pretty?" Lisabeth asked in hushed tones.

Mr. Martin set her back down and stroked her golden hair. "Yes, I think it was."

Gemma lost herself in Farris's face, his cheek smushed against her shoulder. How difficult to lose someone so young! Yet everyone here seemed to be bearing it bravely. She stared at the weave in Josiah's suit coat as he paused at the casket. *God, don't let him feel guilty.* The rest of the family had continued ahead, shaking hands with the Longs. Josiah could have all the time he needed.

Finally, he took a step forward and Gemma ventured a glance at Lydia's face. She wasn't sure if it was her gasp that held him back or his own need to stare a little longer at her placid porcelain face.

His watery eyes met hers. "She's beautiful."

Gemma forced a swallow and blinked back the tears that assailed her eyelids anew. "Even in death." She took in Lydia's face— unnaturally still and void of expression. Her strawberry hair fanned out around her face, hinting of the color that used to lie there. The wonder was that despite the trauma that had occurred to bring death to her slender body, her face was unblemished except for some heavily makeuped bruises and cuts that were only noticeable due to the colors they lent her complexion.

Farris started and cried out, rubbing his forehead back and forth on Gemma's shoulder. Her concentration was broken and she moved to let others behind her bid farewell. Josiah had also pressed forward and gave Mrs. Long a one-armed hug.

Once the Martins had shared their condolences with everyone, they all piled into the van to travel home.

"I didn't know you were going to speak, Josiah," Mrs. Martin said.

He forced a smile. "I felt it was my place."

"Would it help you relax more if you laid down in the last bench? I think not seeing every car that passes us might be good for you."

He nodded and let his mother help him remove his suit coat, careful of his shoulder that was supposed to remain motionless for another week, as everyone else climbed in and claimed their preferred seats.

Gemma felt for Josiah with every bounce of the vehicle and stop they came to. Could anyone ever fully recover from something so traumatic, or would PTSD always lurk under his surface? He must have braved the ride fairly well because, once home, he politely deflected his mother's pleas for him to lay down for a while and instead engaged himself in board games with his younger siblings, providing a welcome distraction from their schoolwork.

Gemma watched him lose a game of checkers to Gail as she fed Farris some banana and wondered if he was putting on a happy face, or if he was truly healing.

Mr. Martin entered the kitchen and drew a glass from a cabinet. "I'm glad you were able to stay for the funeral, Gemma."

She dug a slimy piece of fruit from Farris's fist and placed it on the end of the rubbery spoon. "So am I. As unusual as things have been around here, this is still somewhat of a vacation for me."

"You're welcome back anytime."

A smile spread over her face. How long it had taken him to reach that conclusion! "Thank you. That means a lot to me."

He chuckled and swirled the water in his glass. "I know it took you just as long to warm up to me as it did me to you. I didn't always treat you as I should have and I want you to know I'm sorry for that. I was so caught up in trying to prove the . . . validity of my concerns to my family that I completely disregarded your kind and helpful personality and disrespected your feelings." He cleared his throat and met her eyes. "Will you . . . forgive me for that?"

Gemma blinked, trying to collect her thoughts. Nothing that Mr. Martin had ever done to her mattered anymore, but she was grateful that he felt the need to explain himself. It made her feel much less persecuted, even if it had all happened several months ago. Shifting her weight on her barstool, she floundered for a reply. "I . . . yes. You were putting your family first. I know what that's like now." She wiped Farris's face with his bib as he tried to repossess his spoon.

Relaxing some, Mr. Martin set his glass down and rubbed his wrist. "Thank you." He looked past her and Gemma turned to see Gail giggling at another victory over his brother.

Josiah must have felt their eyes on him because he turned from his position on the sofa and smiled at them. Gemma was relieved that it reached his eyes. It was genuine.

"Poor boy has a long road ahead of him," Mr. Martin said. "Somehow you always seem to bring joy and make things just a little bit easier for him."

Heat rushed to Gemma's face. Even if he really thought so, what on earth would make him confess it, especially to her? *Perhaps that's what Josiah wanted to talk to me about.* She chided herself for entertaining such a thought. Didn't he know he deserved . . . better?

"I'm glad," she said. She *was* glad, she just didn't know what else to say.

"So am I," Mr. Martin said. He gave her shoulder a squeeze before slipping out of the kitchen.

Gemma watched him go, puzzled.

After the bedtime Bible reading when all the little kids had been shooed to bed, the older kids kept the tradition of the day up and found another game to play.

"Don't you want to play cards with us, Gemma?" Ginger asked.

"Thanks, but I have to get Farris to sleep first."

"Hm, he doesn't look very sleepy to me," Josiah said.

Gemma had to admit to herself that he was right. But she grew more and more desperate for some time without a teething child on her hip. It was already half an hour past his usual bedtime. Perhaps she shouldn't have napped him so late in the afternoon.

"Here, let me hold him and you can play with the girls."

"You . . . only have one working arm."

361

Josiah cocked his head. "I got it. Come 'ere, kid."

Gemma relented, plopping the chunky six-month-old on Josiah's left knee. She took a seat next to Josiah's feet, leaning against the seat of the couch. "I don't know very many card games, so you'll have to teach me."

Ginger looked at Anneliese and Emmaline. "Spoons or rummy?"

"Spoons is better when we have more people and I can teach rummy," Emmaline said.

"OK." Ginger dealt each of the girls ten cards while Emmaline explained the objective.

"Same number or same suit . . . in a row," Gemma said. "I think I got it."

After two rounds, Anneliese suggested they start the scoring over so Gemma would have a better chance, since she knew what she was doing now.

Halfway through the next round, Gemma deliberated on whether she should take Emmaline's discard or not. Just as she reached for it, Josiah cleared his throat loudly.

All the girls' eyes went to his face.

Josiah shrugged his left shoulder and bounced Farris. "What?"

Gemma smiled inwardly. Would he help her win? There was no doubt he could see her cards. She drew from the card stack instead and rejoiced to see that it was a better fit.

Several turns later, Gemma again couldn't decide. If she played it carefully, she could win the round. She resisted looking up at Josiah for help, but wished he'd give her another hint. He didn't, so she drew and chewed her lip. How on earth was she going to use that card?

When Emmaline discarded again, Josiah leaned down and whispered in Gemma's ear, "Take her discard and switch your sixes."

"Are you helping her?" Anneliese accused.

"Josiah, you can't play favorites!" Emmaline said.

He lifted his chin. "I will neither deny nor admit anything."

362

Ginger grinned. "It's fine, she's new." Still, her eyebrows shot up when Gemma won the round, moving into first place.

"One more and then I have to put Farris to bed," Gemma said, reclaiming a tendril of her hair from Farris's clutches.

Josiah subtly nudged her shoulder once with his knee, causing her to stick to her original plan. Within a matter of minutes, Gemma was close to winning again. When she hit a dilemma of what to discard, she held up her options for Josiah to see.

"Guys, that is so cheating," Emmaline said.

"I can only make educated guesses, Em. Half of a card game is luck and tonight it's in Gemma's favor."

Her grumbling was appeased when Gemma's carefully advised discard played into Ginger's hand and she won the round.

Josiah grinned. "What can I say?"

Gemma slid her cards across the coffee table to Ginger and stood, her legs sweaty and tingling from being tucked up for so long. "You can say goodnight to Farris before he has a meltdown."

"Night, dude." He wiped his drool-covered hand on his jeans when Gemma scooped Farris up to take him to their room.

Thankfully, after changing clothes and getting a clean diaper, Farris was more than happy to be fed and fall asleep.

Josiah was fumbling to play cards one-handed when Gemma quietly shut the door behind her. "How am I supposed to play a game that requires speed if I can't even add to my cards?"

His sisters grinned at one another. "Exactly."

"Want me to help you?" Gemma asked.

"No!" Emmaline scooted her a pile of cards. "But you can play with us. Pick up the cards Josiah puts down one at a time and then discard one to Ginger. You want to get four of a kind. Once someone gets it, everyone grabs a spoon."

Anneliese spread the spoons evenly on the coffee table. "Ready? Go!"

Gemma was grateful she relied on Josiah's speed, or lack thereof, because she wasn't all that fast herself. She was watching carefully for another queen when she realized there was only one spoon left and reached for it.

Josiah was just as quick, dropping his cards and clutching the other end. It didn't take but a second for him to pull it from her hand.

"Josiah!" She made a mad grab for it, her face flying dangerously close to his. "I had it first, give it back."

"You can't steal spoons, nitwit." He brandished it like a sword against her attack.

"Watch me!" She bounced a little higher and snatched it from him, regaining her self-control. "Thank you. You're out." She smoothed her hair and smiled at the girls.

Josiah shook his head and chuckled, holding her gaze for a moment. "Whatever makes you happy."

Chapter 34

On Sunday—over a week since January's wedding and the accident—Josiah spent almost the entire afternoon in the office upstairs. Gemma knew only because she noticed his absence and asked where he was. She had hoped to see more of him on her last day with the Martins. However, he surprised her early in the evening with an invitation to see the land he had purchased from the Jeffersons for commercial farming.

"And what is it you're planning to farm again?" Gemma asked from behind the wheel. She had insisted she drive, despite his protests. Since they were the only two going, there was no other option.

"I'm going to stick with corn. Quality wheat has become higher demand with all the allergies these days, so I'd love to provide a good source, but it would be a lot of work for starting out."

"How big is your first crop going to be?"

"I've got irrigation systems in place for sixty acres. We started planting right after I got back from our trip to see you and David's baby."

She spared him a glance. "Wow, that's a lot. Who is 'we'?"

"I'm going in with Elias this first year. Between the two of us, we had money saved to cover planting enough crops to hopefully hit the 20,000 dollar profit minimum."

"Why is there a profit minimum?"

Josiah clenched the arm rest and closed his eyes as they came up to a four-way stop where another car sat. Once they had passed safely through the intersection, he relaxed.

He's traumatized.

"Um, a profit minimum is just what the company that's helping us finance requires. If we do well, we can stay on with them and continue to expand. You see, by planting sixty acres . . . with an eighty percent rate of maturity and at least 120 bushels per acre, we'll make close to, um, twenty-five thousand dollars at four dollars and fifty cents a bushel. And all of that's on the low end. We could charge more."

Gemma couldn't keep up with the mental math and drive at the same time, so she just pretended she had followed. "That's awesome. What changes if you can get on with the company?"

"They continue to finance us and we can put our annual profits toward expanding, so there's an increase each year."

"It all sounds very expensive to me."

A look of triumph lit his face. "Well, you have to keep in mind that I've already been doing a thirty-acre crop for six years now, besides working for the Jeffersons on the side."

Gemma's eyes widened. "That's really amazing." Still, she couldn't help but wonder why he was telling her all of this. Of course it was interesting, but it felt rather odd to be discussing the exact income her friend would be making. *Unless* . . . Her heart skipped a beat at the notion.

"Just turn left up here."

Gemma did and they drove down a dirt road so long that it made the Martins' seem short. She smiled when they came upon an ancient farmhouse after having already passed the Jeffersons'.

"Park near the house."

Gemma pulled them under the shade of a gigantic, sprawling oak and hopped out of the car. The expanse of open land dotted with prairie grass and wildflowers made her feel freer. She turned her attention to the farmhouse with its peeling paint, boarded windows, and splintering wood. It had two lovely gable windows on the second story and a front porch with a wooden swing that sat rather than hung. It would be delightful once fixed up.

"You're going to renovate the house?"

"I suppose—cheaper than building or buying, I hope. It's a decent size, but quaint and dusty. Come on, I'll show you."

Gemma got the full tour of both stories. Many of the things Josiah considered to be faults she found very charming, like the wood paneling in what had been the parlor and the entire wall of teeny pine cabinets in the kitchen.

There was one bedroom downstairs among the divided living spaces and kitchen, and three rooms upstairs with an attic.

"This house is incredible," Gemma said, trying the pump handle in the kitchen at the end of their tour.

"I'm glad you like it. It needs a lot of work, but it's got character."

"For sure. It's endearing." Gemma ran her hand over the wood paneling on the wall.

"Here, come see the back porch. It's screened and everything."

She followed him out the back door. They decided to try the swing this porch held since the seat wasn't chipping and the chain wasn't rusted.

"Isn't it beautiful? I couldn't be happier if I died in this swing."

Gemma chuckled. "Please don't. You can't go dying at the beginning of the project."

"Not now, I mean in seventy years or so."

"Well, we have a lot to do before then."

She caught Josiah smiling at her and she wasn't sure why. His smile slowly spread to her face, but her mind remained blank. "What?"

"You said 'we.'"

Her eyes drifted as she struggled to understand. Then the full meaning of what she had supposedly said hit her and her smile was replaced with a steady flush. "What? No, I didn't."

His smile only grew, his green eyes daring her to continue disagreeing with him. He had cornered her. "Yes, you did."

She smacked him. "Stop it! I did not."

Josiah laughed, the corners of his eyes crinkling. "You did, too, but it doesn't matter. In fact, it's quite perfect. Come here."

He took her hand, sending a thrill up her arm and through the rest of her body. He led her back through the kitchen, past the stairs, and out the front door. They stopped under the huge tree where she had parked.

Gemma willed her heart to slow down so she could concentrate on what it was Josiah was going to say.

"I never told Lydia I wasn't going to marry her, because marrying her made perfect sense."

"You didn't have a reason not to," Gemma said.

"Exactly. Well, I found a reason a few months back and I've been thinking it over ever since."

Gemma waited and spent the time retraining herself how to swallow.

"I've spent the entire week praying and all morning talking to Dad and I've come to a conclusion. I'm not ever going to get married . . ."

In the pause, suddenly Gemma knew how to breathe again. "That's very—"

He stepped closer and put his finger on her lips.

"You didn't let me finish."

Gemma held his gaze and didn't move.

"I'm not ever going to get married *unless* . . . you agree to be my wife."

The little bit of air that was going stagnant in Gemma's lungs came out in a single puff as her hands flew to her face. Had he actually just proposed?

Josiah waited only a few seconds before saying, "So is that a yes or a no?"

Her hands came away from her face, revealing a wide smile. "You're . . . proposing?"

He met her smile. "Yes. But I'll have to do it more formally later, because I don't have a ring yet."

Her expression dropped. "What about Farris?"

"What about him? He'll be ours, of course! You don't mind about the ring?"

Gemma buried her face in his shirt as relief, gratitude, and wonder flooded her. "I'm going to marry you! You honestly think I care about a ring right now?"

He put his arm around her and kissed her hair. "Well, I was really hoping not, but you never know."

She inhaled and exhaled deeply, taking in the woodsy smell. Was this really happening? "You should probably focus on your crop, and I have to move before we can get married."

"We'll get married as soon as the house is ready. How's that?"

"Perfect," Gemma sighed. She drew back and looked up at him. "And you're sure about this? Do you really know enough about me? You want Farris?"

He frowned. "Of course I'm sure! Farris adores me. And I know enough about you to see what a loving, selfless, and headstrong woman you are." His left hand lightly touched her hair. "Even more so as a mother. You have taught me more in your imperfect state than a million perfect people could have. Besides, isn't that what marriage is for—getting to know everything about one another?"

Gemma fought the emotion that had stolen her voice and nodded.

They looked into each other's eyes for a long moment before Josiah stepped back. "We'd better go before I kiss you, or then we'll really be in trouble."

Gemma laughed nervously and climbed into the driver's seat. It was ironic when she thought about it. She had stumbled upon that barn last fall in hopes of finding a place to rest. She could not have fathomed then what she had now discovered—a young man who loved her not for who she had been, but for who she was becoming through Christ.

Acknowledgments

First, thank you to my family for dealing with the insanity that is now my life, always encouraging me to write, and being supportive of my endeavors. Listening and making suggestions often forced me to be specific about what I wanted this novel to be. Particularly, my mother for driving me to conferences and marketing my novel, my sister for endless suggestions and taking time to read pieces of my novel at all different stages, and my uncle for the assistance you provided with the crippling details of cover design.

To my alpha readers: Gloria Haines, whose eye for what a scene lacked saved me more than I care to say; Ivy Rose, whose medical expertise, company, and excitement were priceless; Jamie Foley, whose experience with motherhood and the writing industry brought multifaceted assistance; Katie Grace, whose enthusiasm, suggestions, and fangirling with me at all hours of the night kept me smiling as I wrote; Madison Guy, whose lifelong friendship and continued interest astounds me. Your invaluable input through the early draft is what kept me motivated to keep writing. Thank you so much for your patience and kind handling of the total first drafts that I threw at you. I'm so blessed to count you all as friends and to be able to return the favor! Your investment in my story means everything.

To my beta readers: Anika, Becky, Chloe, Eliza, Faith, Grace Anne, Hann, Hannah, Jesseca, Jonathan, Maddy, Megan, Noor, Ray, Rebekah, and Victoria. Thank you all so much for the time and effort you put into my book. All of you are so unique and different and that is exactly what made you all so beneficial as beta readers. Every one of you had something new and thought-provoking to offer, forcing me to make my novel even better than I had hoped it to be. Thanks for putting up with the crazy deadline I threw at you! The revisions I made after digesting all of your feedback made the greatest difference in my manuscript's quality.

A special thank you to Evan Oliver for the priceless time you sacrificed to give me feedback on the first few chapters of my book. Having the encouragement and instructive criticism from a more seasoned writer was extremely beneficial and helped my writing to unify and take on the form of the more developed chapters in a manner I feared wasn't possible.

A huge shout out again to the awesome Jamie Foley, my very first writing contact and author friend. Besides the fun lunchtime meetings and goodies in the mail, your encouragement and advice is rooted in wanting the best for my book and believing in me. You'll never know how much that means to me! Your wisdom in marketing and publishing indie has been invaluable. Who knew that your suggesting I cut the epilogue would make this novel the first in a series?

Thank you to my amazing editor, Kelsey Bryant, for being an excellent communicator, flexible, and a joy to work with. Your keen eye added quality to my manuscript and your kind and instructive feedback, coupled with resources from one editor to another, went a step beyond my expectations. Your emphasis on not just improving my manuscript, but educating me so that I can avoid such mistakes next time, was greatly appreciated.

Thanks to the Perry Elisabeth Design team for the awesome formatting for both my Kindle and Paperback publications. You really helped my book come alive on the page and were a pleasure to work with. Thank you also for being flexible about the dates I engaged your services!

Also, to my lovely cover designer, Mandy Cave. I so enjoyed getting to meet you in person and discuss the details of the work cut out for us. Your sharing my vision, being excited and gracious, and tackling this project alongside me truly made the cover design process much smoother and more pleasurable than I thought possible. You have an amazing talent and I'm thrilled to be able to display it on my novel!

Blog readers, you have helped me form a community that encourages and uplifts me and makes me laugh. Without you, I never would have thought to share my work as I went to build anticipation or to do a blog tour. Thank you all so much for wanting to be a part of what I do. You never fail to make me smile!

Lastly, I thank my Lord and Savior for His patience with me as well (because writing your first novel is very distracting). But I blame Him for the crazy dream that inspired this mess to begin with. Without His guidance and the gift He blessed me with, this novel would still be merely a dream.

About the Author

Abigayle has been a writer for as long as she can remember, but did not begin seriously pursuing becoming an author until 2015. Since then, she has started a blog and numerous social media accounts, graduated high school as a homeschooler, and participated in the infamous NaNoWriMo. Other than writing, she is also pursuing work as a freelance editor. Writing is her ministry and reading is her pastime. Abigayle lives in Central Texas with her six younger siblings and parents.

Abigayle blogs at http://www.theleft-handedtypist.blogspot.com.

Watch for other titles in the *Martin Generations Series* coming soon

Made in the USA
San Bernardino, CA
03 February 2017